I0564938

ISBN-13: 978-0615913834
ISBN-10: 0615913830

For books contact:
A. Bryant Betsill
552 Old Greenville Road
Fayetteville, GA 30215

Look for *Broken Union*, available in paperback or Kindle at
Amazon.com.

Look for *White Canopy Only,* available in paperback or
Kindle at Amazon.com.

The Letters of Paul

a novel

By A. Bryant Betsill

I do have a sister named Cathy,
and she is very trustworthy.
She'll find my mistakes,
whatever it takes,
and they have been quite noteworthy.

Thank you very much my dearest sister for your painful attention to detail. ☺

Chapter 1

"Estate Sale," the white hand-lettered signboard announced that Friday on the side of U.S. Highway 78. It should have said, "Stop here - lose the next thirty days of your life - destroy thousands of dollars worth of property - and change the course of western civilization and philosophy."

"Do you want to stop?" Harley asked out of politeness for he was stopping regardless of Jackie's reply.

"You need to ask?" Jackie answered.

Harland, or Harley to his friends and family, was a six foot tall mid-build man sixty two years old with salt and pepper hair covering most of his head. His mustache covered his lips like a veranda roof. His mouth was always in a natural smile as if there was no crossness in him. He had deep dark chocolate brown eyes that held no clue as to his wit and charm. His arms and neck were tan only to the boundary of the short sleeve shirts he wore. His fingernails were cut on his own whim with his shop scissors. He had a slight paunch retained by a black leather belt. He stood as tall and as erect as the columns of the Parthenon. Harley's laugh was loud, deep, and could fill a football stadium.

He twisted the wheel of their Holland Model 3800 Silver Bow Motor Coach, directing the RV to a gravel drive leading to a clapboard farmhouse. The structure, coated in pastel green pine pollen, had at one time in its life, been painted white. This white lead paint under the pollen had faded to the pale yellow of age. It's peeling paint chips threatened to turn loose in the next breeze like dandelion seed and scatter across the backyard.

As Harley drove into the compound, he spotted a shaded area which would accommodate the height of the motor-home.

Jacqueline, or Jackie to her friends, pointed to the space in the deep shade of the enormous oak and ordered Harley to do the obvious, "Park over there out of the sun," she commanded.

"Yes, dear," he recited flatly. These were his two most frequently used words of their thirty six years of wedded bliss.

Jackie had the natural good looks coming from generations of women with good bone structure, proper eye spacing, and a great jaw line. Harley often thought the photo of Jackie's grandmother was a page taken right out of the Montgomery - Ward Catalog. Grandmother Hall struck a very attractive pose sitting on the fender of a 1938 Ford for some long forgotten photographer. Jackie was just as stunning as her mother. In point of fact, Harley thought, although he married the pick of the family, all Jackie's cousins, including the men, were very good looking people.

Jackie's primary feature that caught Harley's eye was her legs. Perfect in their proportions, he saw those twin columns from behind before seeing her face and pronounced to his friends that he wanted to marry the owner of those fabulous limbs. But then she turned around laughing with her friends and Harley's heart was captured forever.

Her countenance seemed to radiate light anytime she smiled. Still after the decades of marriage, her frame, even on that fateful day in September, was the same size as her wedding dress. Slender, standing a few inches below Harley, she was often mistakenly identified by strangers as being a sister to her own daughter.

If the DJ at the pub played "Brown Eyed Girl" by Van Morrison, Harley would grab Jackie's hand and pull her to the dance floor where he would sing along, for she too had dark brown eyes and the natural color of her hair was russet.

As they stepped out of the Sliver Bow they could hear the squeal of a spring coming under tension as a screen door opened. From far into the shadows of the front porch eve and roof they heard a woman's voice, a voice in the higher reaches of alto, possibly near soprano, calling out "Hello, you people here for the estate sale?" Due to the pitch, her volume was not an issue. From the depths of the shade there stepped a woman of a seventyish plus years of age. Her faded yellowing hair, at one time a natural blond, was in the high permanent curls that was the fashion of the early 1950's.

"It's Marie Antoinette," Harley muttered to Jackie. "That hair must be supported by some internal framework."

"Stop it!" she strongly rebuked him as she gave him her most withering stare.

Before either could answer the woman's question, she continued. "You people are the first two here. I only put the sign out last night. I was about to put out signs at the crossroads but ya'll can come on up and look around. The Times – Herald hasn't even hit the streets for people to see the ad. I've got some coffee on the stove you're welcomed to, or if you don't want coffee, I've got some really good well water in the sink. I also have some sweet tea in the frigidaire."

"Yes", replied Jackie to the first question when she thought the woman had stopped talking long enough to come up for air. "Are you ready for buyers?"

Once the woman had drawn in a full measure of atmosphere, she said, "Been ready for months now. My Aunt Barbara died and left me the place. It's been in the probate court since then. I just haven't had the time or willingness to sell her worldly goods."

There was a short-lived pause as thoughts formed and dialogue continued, "I don't really need all this, you know. I have a home in Tallahatchie, Alabama ... that's over near Wionia Lake, just south of the Madison and Chaptuckney county lines … Lived there since 1968. I just want to keep a few of Aunt Barbara's things and sell off the rest of the furnishings and the house. You don't need a good home do ya'll?

At this point, the woman paused in her discourse to take stock and realized that introductions were in order.

"My name is Eudora Bristow, 'Boo' to my friends, where you folks from?" It was not so much a question but more of a probe into the origins and names of these strangers.

"I'm Jackie Macklin and this is my husband, Harley. May we come in, please?"

"Why sure thing, honey, I'll be glad to show you around." She waved Jackie and Harley to join her on the porch as mermaids once summoned ancient sailors to their doom. Jackie was committed to go since she had entreated permission to enter. She took to the steps with hesitation and looking over her shoulder, motioned to Harley to follow. He shrugged it off. Harley chose not to fall victim under the spell and have to listen to the constant chatter of Eudora. "Nice lady," he thought, "just don't know if I could take the non-stop talk show."

"Anything for sale in the garage?" he called out as Jackie walked to the screen door. Harley had seen the 1951 Sears and Roebuck Model 347, E-Z Pull push lawn mower under a shed roof still attached to the outbuilding.

"Help yourself, honey. We haven't put a sale tag on everything yet, but it's all got to be sold," replied Eudora as she followed Jackie into the house. Eudora released her hold on the screen door and it hit its home rest with two slaps of a bouncing slam.

A small orange tag with a price of $50 hanging from the handle of the mower was fluttering in the breeze like a bright leaf in fall. Harley's hands pushed the mower handles and the machine failed to move for lack of lubricant. With just a little more effort the mower wheels did let go their grip and the lawn cutter lunged forward a few inches and stopped. With expectations running high he gave a bit of a stronger shove attempting to release the axles from the oxide grip of the wheels. Under weak protest, the wheels moved one quarter of their diameter and held fast. Harley abandoned his efforts for there were outbuildings to explore.

He had hoped to find a shed full of tools as he had done at many estate sales. He had seen and purchased a variety of tools for a variety of trades. Not necessarily things he needed, but the things that fascinated him. Like the pair of Pittler edge hooks, single and double edged, or the number 2 coller-meter butt gauge, the things no handyman could work without. Yard sales, camping and of all things, cave exploring were the hobbies Harley enjoyed and most of his purchases reflected those interests.

He tugged once on the handle of the shed door in vain hope it would readily give way. He pulled once more with an effort that threatened to pull out the screws holding the handle. The hinges loudly gave up the fight at being forced to move without oil. Harley leaned into the garage door to open it allowing a bit more illumination to the otherwise gloomy interior.

The darkness was shot through with tiny shafts of sunlight coming in between the nail holes of the tin roof. Light was leaking in from numerous holes along the degrading edges of metal enclosing the structure. A pale brown film of dust covered both flat and vertical surfaces.

"Looks like the place hasn't seen a lick of work in decades," Harley thought. He stepped into the dark space. With the light now behind him and with laser beams of sunlight streaming in, he was able to determine this out-building was not the tool shed of a skilled handyman.

There was a collection of lumber pieces on indefinite hold leaning into a corner waiting for that day far into the future when they would be needed for some un-foreseen repairs. Boring beetles and wood mites had eaten away all the soft parts of the shed's lumber rendering it half its normal weight. Termite spit was probably holding the fibers together. There was a cheap hammer being held against the fundamental pegboard found in every amateur handyman's garage. A pair of screwdrivers, a tape measure with rusting blade and a pair of garden snips beyond all hope of ever opening again kept the unused hammer silent company. There was an incomplete set of rust pitted wrenches in a pegboard holder. Missing tools left faded spots against the board to mark their passing.

Of the collection of junk hanging on the board, the most curious to Harley was a complete collection of chisels from 1/4 inch to 1 inch blades, all more eroded than the surface of Mars. He ran a finger across the blades just to check on their edges and, low and behold, along some points, they gave evidence that they were never used. These were the cheap foreign made tools found in the two for a dollar bin in a hardware store.

The shop's counter continued to support various laundry detergent jugs holding sinister looking liquids and some old batteries with their corrosion eating away at both the case and the shelf. A few nuts, bolts, and nails were in jars with brown lids sitting on the counter top. Rusting cans with fading labels announced their contents to be "Fix-A-Flat", brake fluid, charcoal lighter fluid, and Wonder-Clean one step car wash and wax. Always present in every tool shed in the country, sat a crumbling paper box of Miracle Grow Plant Food. All containers gave the appearance that if lifted they would turn loose their bottoms.

"Maybe the place was cleaned out years ago," thought Harley. "Or maybe Aunt Barbara was not that handy with tools."

Harley noticed a single pair of footprints in the dust. His eyes, now accustomed to the darkness, were able to distinguish the incoming steps going to a metal cabinet, from the set leading out. On the floor in front of the cabinet were several marks and scrubs in the dust. He went over, pulled on the handle, and it gave way easier than did the shop door.

Harley found only a box covered in canvas and held in place with cotton twine. This was the old fashioned kind of canvas. Not the plastic or nylon of modern canvas and tarps. This material was the wax impregnated linen with a folded stitched hem used by sailors of old.

"Heavy duty stuff this is," he thought pulling the box from out of the dark corner.

Setting it on the counter, he paused to consider the ethics of his next step. The ethics in his mind were that Eudora gave him permission to browse. Furthermore, if, his conscious told him, he should deliver the box to her, then, she would want it opened. Therefore, he would open it out here, you know, just in case there was something in it that might upset the old woman like a snake or spiders.

He pulled out the Swiss Army model 26a pocketknife given to him by his father on his graduating with a Bachelor of Science degree in Construction. It was his "tool kit in a pocket" as he called it. The sharp blade parted the string and he un-wrapped the canvas. Harley could see a very typical, relatively new white cardboard file box. Curiosity begged further investigation if, for no other reason, than to let Ms. Eudora know what he had found.

"What was so important that it was hidden in this shop?" he thought. "No harm in looking," he said to no one.

He lifted the lid and in the faint light saw three dark brown, leather handmade books. On top of these books were two parchment documents with words arraigned in two columns. The letters were of a familiar shape but in a language he had not seen before. He gently laid the covering pages to one side. Then he carefully lifted the first book and saw the spine of the book was stitched together. Again, the words were arraigned in two columns on the pages with the lettering very close together.

"Curious," was his next thought.

"Any idea where this box came from?" Harley asked Eudora. He sat it down on the coffee table in a room painted in the soft pastel butter yellow hue that matched some of the floral check upholstery of a big soft comfortable chair.

"Why no, darling, I haven't ever seen that box before. Why what is in it?"

Harley gently lifted the two loose pages from the box. "I can't tell, Honey do you know what this is?" he said handing it to Jackie.

Jackie was sitting on a Canapé sofa. It was a fine example of the mid-19th century Louis XV style, upholstered with a reproduction of an 18th century Aubusson tapestry in the theme of Aesop's fables. Eudora, leaning forward, was sitting in one of the two matching chairs. Antiques, camping and travel were Jackie's hobbies and she felt qualified to identify the pages. She took the frail and fragile documents from Harley and began to read silently.

"This is in Latin," she said, after a brief study. "It is basically a packing list or bill of goods for shipping."

Harley set sail for the other big comfortable chair.

Jackie could read, speak and write the ancient language of Latin. Her father, Doctor John Hall, first doctor in Milton County, South Carolina, had sent her to The Margaux

Academy. At this private girl's finishing school, she was instructed in the basics of English, Mathematics, History, how to properly pour coffee for a future husband, and she learned Latin. After graduation, her parents sent her to the Longley School of Medicine where she graduated Jacqueline Philomena Macklin M.D. in 1970. She worked in public health a few years then announced one day she "didn't like a lot of sick people" and went to work for the Center for Disease Control and Prevention in Atlanta. There she did outstanding work eventually advancing to head the Department of Travelers Health and to the discovery of Pantanal - Linhas fever. When she returns home, she and her father will sit around the dining room table and talk in Latin just to annoy her mother and Harley. He did not mind their having a private chat or even a laugh or two; it was the pointing and laughing in his general direction that bothered him.

"'Vis ligusticum apium VI modius' ... that is 6 bushels, *vis,* of *Ligurian celer,"* she read out loud. "I think that is a type of celery. *Vis Liquamen' Garum XXIV sextarois* or 24 - 3 liter jars of fish sauce. *Vis Ruta graveolens XV modius* or 16 bushel bags of rue leaves."

She looked up at Eudora. "Ah", she said in an animated voice, "this one I know, *Ruta graveolens,* it is an evergreen shrub. We have one under the window at our dining room. The leaves are bitter in large quantities, but small amounts of rue leaves can be added to cream cheese, salads and egg dishes giving it a pleasant musky flavor," she instructed. "People once used it like garlic to ward off witches and evil spirits. Some say the crushed leaves can be an effective insect repellent. Allergic reactions to the rue have been reported to us," she said referring to the doctors at the CDC. "Most are limited to a skin rash from handling the plant. Especially on hot days, just brushing against rue can cause water blisters and blotchy skin, like poison ivy." She paused to let the full measure of her superb learning flash and awe her audience.

Harley spoke up, "I thought leaving the cheese in the fridge gave it a musty smell."

"*Vis Ferula galbaniflua XXXIII mina*," Jackie read on though irritated by Harley's jest, "or thirty three pounds of frankincense. I think it is an herb from Iran. It is still used as incense. It's mentioned in Greek mythology as the plant that helped Prometheus to carry the stolen fire from the Sun to the Earth. It is also called the Devils Dung." Her voice was rising a bit in wonder at the way this list was running.

"So why would I want to burn that?" Harley asked.

Again, ignoring Harley, she continued to interpret, *"Vis Sal salis DLXIX mina* or 569 pounds of salt mullet," she read. "*Mellis XLV sextarius* or 45 – 3 sextarius jars of honey, and I don't know how much that is but I would guess it's about a liter ... *Vis stemma XCIV mina* or 94 pounds of garlic ... *Vis coriandrum sativum LXXXVI mina* or 86 pounds of cilantro ... *Vis siligoinis CXX pera C talentum mina* or 120 – 100 pound bags of wheat ... and *Visgold IV mina I unica* or four or five pounds of gold," she concluded quite proud of herself but was dumbfounded. However she was not as surprised as Eudora. She had sat silently by until Jackie finished the short list.

"What is it?" Eudora asked, "sounds to me like a recipe list."

"Gold?" asked Harley greedily. "Is it a treasure map?"

"No," Jackie's stated, "No, it's a bill of goods for a merchant by the name of *Gaeticulus Calisto Sceundus Paulius*. It is received, *vis*, or, of *Laurentius Honoratus* ... scribe to Shipmaster *Pavlos Akakios. Dies Martis xii Maius DCLXXXVIII A.U.C'.* or 12 May 688 A.U.C."

Carefully examining the second page she read out loud, "'this sacred Codex is this day presented to his most Holy Eminence The Cardinal Legate Gregorios Asbestas, Patriarch of the monastery of San Roco in the Archdiocese of Syracusana.'"

Puzzled for a moment she continued to read "Syracusana .. this twenty fourth day of April, in the year of our most Holy Lord God Almighty, *1056 anno domini.*"

"Well we don't know anyone from wherever this Latin comes from," Eudora said flatly.

"Who is this Calisto Paulius, is he famous?" Harley greedily asked, for he was hoping that this would be a known character from antiquity and the book possibly lead to a fortune.

"Latin was spoken and written during the Roman Empire, but this could not be that old," said Jackie, "and why and how did it get in your garage?"

"What would you want for the box?" Harley asked.

"Roman Empire?" inquired Eudora.

"It was also spoken and used in the Catholic Church for centuries," Jackie stated. "It could be an old shipping manifest between monasteries. I would need a few months to go through it all," she was guessing.

"I don't want any Catholic shipping lists or recipes." Eudora said with distain and declared, "we have always been good Lutherans!"

Eudora paused, shrugged and looking at Harley asked "How about $50.00?"

"Sold!" said Harley with no idea what kind of Pandora's Box full of troubles he just bought. But, he was damn proud of the bargain he thought he had made.

Jackie started to say, "Well Ms. Bristow," but was briskly cut off.

"Oh honey, just call me Boo, all my friends do, besides it has been so nice to have you and your husband stop by." She only stopped for a shallow breath this time, "It's been so good to meet you, do you have to run off?"

Jackie seized the opportunity created by "Boo's" question to continue her own train of thought, "We did not want to take up all your time." She did not stop but plowed on, "but there are other people here now." The screen door spring alerted all who were near, that the door had been opened.

"It's just Carrie. She is the woman that is helping me appraise the furniture for pricing. She's a professional estate appraiser."

"Well Mrs., ah Boo is it?" asked Jackie her voice rising a bit, "How did you get to be called Boo if I am not prying?"

Eudora told her of her two older sisters who would jump from around the corners of the house and yell Boo at their sibling. Seeing the fun they had in the little girl's fright they began to call her Boo and rather than constantly protest, she adopted the name.

"I noticed your price for the books," Jackie said pointing to the hand lettered placard on the bookshelf. "How did you come about a single price of $2.00 each?" Jackie's stance was that the price per book might be a bit low. "I mean the prices on the furniture are a little low but some of these books could bring a lot more in the right market."

Boo, once again was without comment.

"Your Aunt Barbara had a good eye for furniture. This is a very fine example of a William and Mary style, chinoiserie fall-front secretary bookcase, probably early 19th century."

Jackie caught the surprised look in Boo's eyes as Boo looked at Carrie the expert appraiser and asked, "Did you know this?"

Carrie now came over and looking with incredulity asked, "What do you know about these things? I have been in the antiques business for 18 years now. I even went to Washington, D.C. and spent the day in a class learning antiques."

Harley, returned the manifests to the box, took a step back and sat down to observe the cat fight.

Jackie, ever the polite one, refrained from a verbal battle with a stranger, said "I bought a reproduction of the exact same chinoiserie," as she pointed to the secretary desk, "a few years ago and I paid $950.00 for it then." This, Harley knew, was a bald face lie but he knew better than to intrude to contradict Jackie. He pretended to examine the first book in the box.

Jackie sailed on under full steam now that she was leading the conversation. "That was only a reproduction of this desk. I am sure that you could get at least that much, maybe more." Carrie's eyes now widen a bit for she was on commission plus a fee, and, while increasing the price could mean fewer buyers, it would give her wiggle room for negotiations.

"Boo, maybe we should mark this a little higher," suggested Carrie. Boo nodded in agreement and reached for a pen and a new tag. Jackie walked to the bookcase.

Jackie not only wanted to see Boo get a fair price for the estate, but was curious about the titles of the books. "Boo," she said, "These books, did you know some of these are first editions?"

"No," Boo said with surprised and looked at Carrie, "Did you?"

Carrie shook her head.

"Well this one," said Jackie holding up what was once the second highest selling book in the world, "This is a first edition Gone With The Wind, inscribed by Margaret Mitchell to William Eckland with the original jacket in excellent condition." She paused to search her memory then said, "This could easily be worth $10,000 at the right auction."

Boo and Carrie took steps in the direction of the bookcase.

Jackie pulled out William Klein's <u>Life is Good and Good For You in New York,</u> "This one is also inscribed to a 'good friend William Eckland'. Any idea who that is?"

Boo's face froze in regretful thought and then said, "You mean Uncle Willy?" She revealed the name was that of her Uncle William, the first and only husband of her Aunt Barbara. They separated about 10 years ago. He was William Taylor Eckland, Professor of Antiquity and History at Gilbert University, Atlanta, Ga. He and Barbara had an amiable agreement to separate.

"But then, he couldn't leave his teaching job at Gilbert and she could no longer take living in Atlanta," she said. "But then, it was her idea for him to retire and live on what was left of the farm here. But then, they continued to see each other and the family during the holidays, and during the summer months when school was not in session, and when he was not out of the country. He died last March, Aunt Barbara never knew of his passing. But then, she had suffered a stroke in May last year and never recovered," Boo said regretfully. "But then she passed on in April this year. She had left all her possessions to Uncle Willy if he survived her or to me if he died first. But he left everything to her when he died. So then, the probate court gave me her estate and his is still tied up in the courts."

Jackie and Carrie expressed their condolences. But Boo said, while regretting Aunt Barbara's passing "she was better off".

"Here is a picture of Uncle Willy and Aunt Barbara," she said getting up from the couch. She reached for a silver leaf frame sitting on the Italian Louis XV period "cartonnier". It was a studio photo probably shot thirty years ago, but had been kept in a prominent place at the front of the tabletop.

She handed it to Jackie. She saw the happy couple standing on some distant beach.

"And here is a later photograph of Uncle Willy and two men I don't recognize," said Boo handing Harley a gold leaf framed photo of three men. "Uncle Willy is the one in the middle," she said as she put her index finger on the photo.

Harley was looking at three men, all around the same age. He passed the photo on to Jackie and she studied the print carefully noting some of the details. The three were poised in front of a French Provincial Desk of a late 19th century style. To the left were stacks of file boxes not unlike the one now in Harley's possession. There was an Empire period, gilt bronze patina bouillote lamp on the table to the group's left. Dr. Eckland was the only one that sported a beard white with age.

Harley had been sitting by the whole time holding his breath afraid that Jackie or Carrie would point out his bargain and start demanding a rebate. He went to return the box top to its position and a paper, losing its static grip from inside the cover, fluttered to the floor. Jackie beat Harley to the sheet and held it to her eyes. The letterhead read, "The Office of Prof. William Eckland, B.A., Ph.D., Gilbert State University." There were only a few notes on the paper written in pencil.

"File is named Apocrypha," Jackie read. Below that was, "call Henry Lancard tomorrow." The name Professor Nicholas Szalasznyj was scrawled at an angle as if the author held the paper firmly under the wrist of the same hand holding the pen.

Sitting back on the couch, Harley looked at Jackie and said, "Huh?"

The screaming screen door announced the arrival of a buyer. "I'll see who that is," said Carrie and she moved into the front hallway.

Voices could be heard echoing from around the corner. Jackie and Boo saw a couple of women, lead by Carrie go towards the dining room.

"Boo, any idea who this Henry Lancard might be?" Jackie was very good at soliciting medical histories from people from her years at the CDC.

"No," she replied.

"Maybe a friend or co-worker?"

"No, I don't know the name. When Uncle Willy heard of Aunt Barbara's stroke he came as soon as he could. First he went to the hospital then to visit her in the Summit nursing home."

Boo was often there when he came by and said each time he left he was silently crying. Boo was also shedding a tear or two thinking about it. Boo went on to explain not long after Barbara was moved into the Summit, he brought friends of theirs from Atlanta to visit. They were a nice couple, about the same age of Aunt Barbara and Uncle Willy. Her name was Caudelle, but Boo could not recall the couple's last name. They had been long time friends of the two ever since Barbara and William first moved to Atlanta. They came back a few more times during the year. However, she was sure it was not Henry Lancard.

"Do you know that Uncle Willy would go by Aunt Barbara's house every time he visited her to check on things? He would. He put those timers, you know those things that make lights go on and off at different times during the night, on her lights. First time I seen it happen when I drove by it scared me something fierce. I thought Aunt Barbara's ghost was home," she chuckled lightly at her story. "Why he even paid the taxes on the property and paid the light and the gas and the water bills each month. I never asked him when I'd see him, but I got the feeling that he thought Aunt Barbara would one day just wake up and go home."

Jackie, being at a loss of words, patted Boo's knee.

"I know you must miss them both," Jackie said. "The important thing is that he kept his faith and hope that she would improve ... and that Aunt Barbara still had friends that cared about her. Did they come to Barbara's funeral?"

"Indeed they did, along with several other friends from Atlanta," said Boo.

"Do you still have the visitors or guest condolences book? Maybe some cards or notes?" asked Jackie respectfully.

"Why I kept the book and several cards, and some of the notes off the flower arrangements," said Boo remorsefully. "There were a lot of flowers, several from Atlanta. Maybe Caudelle sent one or signed the book. Then we could find out who they are."

"If you could do that and get that name to me it could help us find out how the box got in the tool shed and return it to the rightful owner," Jackie offered. Harley had visions of his $50.00 and any future re-sale value flying out the window, but said nothing. He knew better.

"Do you remember Dr. Eckland's cause of death?" Jackie asked.

Boo said she had Uncle Willy's death certificate sent by the medical examiner. All it said was "choking - possibility from smoke inhalation or pull-something ederma".

"Pulmonary Edema?"

"Yes! That's it. Never could understand all that medical stuff," said a relieved Boo.

This gave Jackie some consternation; it was a bit vague of a C.O.D. or cause of death. "Which was it?" she worried to herself, "S.I. or P.E.?" She felt that there was no need to alarm Boo with this, in any case.

They swapped phone numbers and hugs. Jackie also gave her $80.00 for the first edition of Life is Good and Good For You in New York. Jackie insisted that it was probably worth a lot more, possibly twice that amount being autographed by the author, and asked "wouldn't you want to hold it as keepsake, it being inscribed to Uncle Willy?"

Boo insisted that Jackie have it like a family member. Harley issued a check for the total due plus his offer of $50.00 for the box in case it turned out to be nothing much. Carrie began pulling books off the shelf looking for first editions with inscriptions.

Harley directed the wheels of the Silver Bow onto the highway and continued their homeward journey stopping only for red lights and antique stores. They were on the return leg of a camping trip that included a trip to Phoenix, Arizona, to see the grand children. Jackie's grand-mothering instinct had kicked in a fortnight ago. She just could not wait until Thanksgiving to see little Christopher and his older sister, Sandra. These were the children of their only child, Elizabeth. They had packed the Silver Bow with a two weeks supply of Chinese noodles and three weeks supply of clothes. Jackie said she hated to go on vacation and have to do laundry. She could stay home and do that. Harley tossed in four pair of pants, twenty four tee shirts, a few dress shirts and the usual one half dozen boxers calling it enough.

"You can get two to three days of wear out of the jeans," he would tease Jackie, "if you can stand the smell and the jeans being a bit stiff." Even then, Harley usually ran out of fresh clothes and had to put on yesterdays or last week's socks to get home. He also went to Sears for clean clothing.

Jackie sat riding shotgun. She was studying another page from the box. "The lettering is very smooth and regular, very old style Latin," she said.

"How old?" Harley inquired.

"It's very neat and legible. The hand was very steady and constant. These books appear to be journal entries. There are dates in Roman numerals. *Dies Lunae xvi Martius DCLXXXVIII A.U.C*

"Where do you want to eat?" Harley asked ever mindful of both the time of day and his desire for sustenance. Jackie ignored his question for she was now engrossed in the origin and author of these documents.

"*Dies*, means day, xvi equals 16, and *Martius* would be March," she said.

"Where do you want to eat?" They were passing a sign indicating they were entering the "incorporated" town of Cloverdale, Alabama. He did not want to wait until they got to Anniston.

"There is a very good seafood place in Anniston, remember?" said Jackie.

"You mean Papa Jo-Joe's Seafood?" Harley asked. Harley never forgot a restaurant's name good or bad. He could not remember the year they got married, or her sister's husband's mother's maiden name, but he could remember where he first ate Salmon Alexander, or toasted scrambled eggs.

"So it would be March six hundred, ninety three A.U.C. following the numerals," Jackie fumed.

"Huh?" Harley said in disbelief, "That can't possibly mean what I think it means. So is Papa Jo-Joe's OK then?"

"Yes, whatever," said Jackie getting irritated with Harley's stomach. "What is A.U.C.?" she demanded.

"It means from the founding of Rome. The first day Rome was started, according to Julius Caesar. There is a Latin phrase for it. I'm surprised you don't know it." He didn't dare look in Jackie's direction for he knew he was getting her withering glare. It is the one she fired at him when he was showing his superior knowledge in his usual smartass way. It was not often that he dared this, but he was driving and felt he would be secure from her scathing willowing stare while at the wheel. "I think it went something like, Ab, Uri, Condo?

That can't be right." He turned onto Black Warrior Parkway heading south.

"Yes, thats it! *Ab urbe condita* or *Anno urbis conditae* from the founding of the City!" she exclaimed trumping his short term victory. "Journal entry March sixteen, six hundred ninety three years since the founding of Rome."

"Huh?" he said and announced, "Here we are." as the Silver Bow rolled into the gravel and sand parking lot. "Papa Jo-Joe's Seafood and hey it's all you can eat catfish Friday."

Jackie rolled her eyes.

Chapter 2

The inside walls of Papa Jo-Joe's sported gloss white wainscot paneling running five feet up the wall, above that was it painted a pale sea green. The décor was the mandatory sea theme with plastic sea creatures fastened to the wall. There were starfish with their pointed arms under a light dusting of lint. Plastic and mounted fish of various and sundry species swam in their fixed locations.

Black and white photos decorated the walls at the corner cash register. Framed trophy photos of the powerful and famous that had once eaten at Jo-Joe's, held faces instantly recognizable from the front pages of all the world's newspapers. All the past Presidents, want to be President, almost President were prominently featured. Men and women were seen arm-and-arm with Joe and his wife Jo. "A" list celebrities and those on the "B" list were also recognizable.

Joe was in a few photos taken around a baby grand piano. There was a picture of five men around Joe, their favorite piano player, in some unknown club, having a good time. Of the five men in the photo, only Joe wore a tuxedo. The rest were in suits of various materials and patterns. All were smiling at the camera. Some were holding cocktail glasses half filled with a magic elixir. Three held smoking cigarettes between fingers.

When asked who the five men were, Jo tersely replied, "Mob … Dixie Mafia." Jo went on to name and point out each man. Along with the identifications, she included their current residence. One was a guest of the Federal Prison System in Atlanta, one, whereabouts unknown, and the other two now in a wormwood subdivision, having been interred under suspicious circumstances. At that Jo would go no further into her husband's past.

Harley requested the booth space in the corner of the room away from the hallway to the restrooms. Years of experience dining in strange and mysterious eateries along the highways, by-ways, pikes, and toll roads of this vast and hungry land, had taught Harley to never sit by the bathroom door. It takes away from the ambiance to watch patrons making the mad dash for the throne room desperately carrying smaller children. Parent and child both would have urgent expressions on their faces. And what can be said for the vapors drifting down the hallways should the prevailing wind shift direction. No, he would rather wait or dine at a smoked fill bar than to sit by the bathroom door.

Harley was inspired by some strange muse and started composing a limerick on a small wire bound notepad, waiting for the "all you can eat seafood platter". Jackie stirred the artificial sweetener into her iced tea.

"You know we could try to find that Henry Lancard. And I think Nicholas Szalasznyj could be a teacher at Gilbert State. Maybe both of them work at the school."

Harley stopped the doodling and looked at Jackie. She was always the one to want to get things done before they could be.

"Jackie," he quietly replied, "there is no use to worry about this now, besides we cannot start any research on the road. It will wait until we get home."

She folded the sheet of paper with the letterhead and put it in her purse. "We have the cell phone and a good signal in town. What about the laptop maybe we could plug-in to their internet?

Harley argued that the letterhead only listed the Professor's name, Gilbert State University, and his department; there was no phone number and extension. There would be a directory assistance charge for the school's number.

"And do you think Jo-Joe's has internet access?" He asked. "There are never any classes on Friday night."

Jackie frowned. She did not like being thwarted in her campaign.

"You're right," she conceded, "it will be Monday before we can find anybody at the school we can talk to about the books."

Harley said something about approaching this quest for answers with caution and some personal interviewing. He was very aware of Jackie's instinctive ability to discern truth from fiction by observing the very slight, tiny facial tick's people make when fabricating lies. Sometimes it might be a double flick of the *levator palpebrae superioris* muscles of the upper eyelids combined with a twitch in the *superior oblique* muscle in the orbit of the eyes. Left eye motion of a right handed person usually indicates the right side of the patient's brain was concocting a story. It was just an innate skill she used for personal gain. Harley quickly learned that he could tell a believable lie if he hid his face when answering Jackie's questions. They did lay down one rule about misleading statements. No fair asking what each other was up to after the Thanksgiving holiday until the

Christmas presents were opened. This was the only respite he could look forward to each year. Otherwise, he would have to hide behind a newspaper or wait until her eyes were diverted before answering problematic questions.

"What are you studying now?" he asked.

She had worked on the words recorded long ago as they traveled to Papa Jo-Joe's. She read from those notes the following translation:

Dies Lunae xvi Martius DCLXXXVIII A.U.C. or, 16 March 688 AUC

Today I am in Antioch and what a time to arrive in the middle of a Bacchanalia. Claudio has taken me with him to talk with the administrator of his estates in the hills. I have been looking forward to arriving in this city since we left home. I first saw the city from the mountains as we came down from home on the Via Antioch. It was much larger than Tarsus. I saw it again as we went over the hills above the city and descended into the Orontes gorge and the Beilan Pass. We have had such experiences as we traveled here. I spent last night in the tabernal of Quintessa in the hills above town. Claudio and I drank deeply from the fountain of Bacchus and of Liber so much so that we slept late into the morning. I was taken into the gardens of Quintessa by her servant, Kordula, where she did show me how much she knew of the pleasure of the flesh. There under the watchful gaze of our goddess Luna, I saw in the night, the lights of Antioch. Truly this town must never sleep. Claudio says this is the eastern capital of the Roman Empire.

Our carpentun driver tried to drop the wagon wheels into every hole in the road. It did bounce enough over the stones of the road as it was. Again I am with pain in the head from the vino but all is quiet in our villa and I did get some rest. I will go and explore this wonderful city tomorrow when Claudio meets with Marius over the quotas for the shipments of wool from our sheep and goats. Claudio and I will go out tonight to the theater of Agrippa in the hills. We expect to view the play of one Phoebus, a writer of dreams.

We passed under the arch before going into the city at the Amanic Gates. There were the twin towers overlooking the road. I was astonished at the walls of the city that ran up into the hills from the gate. The tax man at the gate demanded Claudio pay a tax of fifteen shekels. Claudio knew that the tax man was intent on keeping ten shekels for himself and the city tariff was five shekels. He was quite surprised when Claudio announced himself and the tax man knew him to be of much importance to the city. Members of his own family worked in the fields for Claudio, and he asked only for 6 shekels of which Claudio paid 4 to teach the man a lesson in honesty or else to be more cautious when asking a rich stranger for the tax.

The public baths are reputed to be the finest in all of the empire. None other than Mark Anthony did seek the soothing waters here on his way back to Rome from Egypt. I have great hope that we go there in the morning. But tonight Claudio will

*show me this city that never sleeps. There are oil
lamps mounted on posts alone the streets to light
the way at night. These were the lights I and
Kordula saw from the tabernae. We go tonight to
continue the celebrations of Liberalia, and to
Liber & to Libera. Mother has insisted that I visit
her kinsmen, Elias, in the Jewish quarter of town
but tonight we celebrate with Antioch and
Bacchus.*

"Ah yes," Harley said grinning, "Bacchus, god of the vine,
the wine, and having a good time."

Jackie repeated the words and names she did not
recognize to Harley and he wrote them on his note pad.
"*Carpentum*," she began to quote, "*Orontes* gorge and the
Beilan Pass, *Tabernae of Quintessea, Anitoch,* the
Amanic Gates, Liberalia, and to *Liber & to Libera.*"

He did not recognize *Belian* Pass and *Orontes* gorge,
but he knew the name of the ancient city of *Anitoch*.

"The Amanic Gates were located in the wall protecting
Antioch," said Harley all the while writing. The town is in
Northern Syria." as he recalled his Bible schooling, "It was
once a place known for all kinds of gambling, drinking,
whoring around, a real Las Vegas of its day. Liberalia, Liber
and Libera was it?"

"Yes, more Roman gods," she supposed.

Between the limited and ancient knowledge, they were
able to piece together the remaining list of gods as being
responsible for the celebrations of freedom from evil,
burdens, care and folly. All were a part of the general
celebrations to the god Mars, the God of War. Harley's
observation was that the roll call of deities was a cover-all-
bases sort of celebration.

"What about the date of 688 A.U.C. on the manifest?" she asked perplexed.

"Dating is tougher to do," replied Harley, "The A.U.C. is a date set by pure speculation by the emperor the day he started his reign. It is figured in part by guessing when Rome started and, if he wanted to cut out the last eight years of the former ruler, and, if his wife didn't like the year she was born in, all of which would affect the date he fixes as the Founding of Rome. Then there is the A.L.U."

"*A libertate constituta,*" she picked up. "Since the founding of the Republic, right?"

"Right, and then mix it with all those scribes, priest, alchemist, kings, queens, that have tried to start calendars based on the flight path of houseflies." Here goes the smartass thought Jackie as Harley continued to instruct.

"Adjusting for their personal preferences and what-not, then A.U.C. doesn't mean much. You need the name of a consul or governor or emperor to date the document in the Gregorian Calendar."

"Then the *A libertate constituta* is a better date than the *Ab urbe condita,* which is useless?" she asked.

"Unless," he affirmed, "you have a notable person's name somewhere in the document. That would provide a cross reference to the dating from A.U.C. and from the latest archeology dates. These books," Harley proposed, "you think are some sort of journal entry?"

"From a quick glance, and references to people and places, it could well be. What do you think they are?" she returned.

"I have seen these kind of books once before. It was in the museum at G.W.H. in the antiquities section. There were two books bound like these, both parchment stitched on the edges with a hard thick leather cover. They were the Codex Argenteus, part of a traveling exhibit of eleventh century artifacts. My God," Harley exclaimed, "we have found a box of codices."

"Codices?" she asked.

"Plural for Codex. We need to see someone at the college and get these codices verified," Harley said.

Jackie decided that she would contact Carly Spruill a member of the book club at the library. She recalled that Carly was married to someone that had something to do with Gilbert State University.

"Who is she? Have I met her before?" questioned Harley.

"No. She is always showing up and soliciting the club members for some alumni, athletic program, and sorority something or other in violation of the book club rules," Jackie lamented.

"Then she sounds like the one for introductions into the Gilbert State faculty," Harley noted.

"I'll see if I can find a home phone number and call her tomorrow," Jackie said formulating a plan of action. Harley pointed out that according to the calendar, tomorrow would be Saturday.

"But do you think her husband would want to examine the codices on the weekend?"

"OK," she pouted, "I guess I will have to wait."

Harley put the finishing touches on his interpretive literary composition and asked if Jackie wanted to hear what he had written. She consented with trepidation for Harley was notorious for coming up with some ribald limericks.

While stopping to eat on the highway,
never sit by the bathroom hallway.
To watch on each face,
the intestinal race,
to release the belt and flyway.

"Here you go, Honey" said the waitress dropping the all you can eat seafood platter on the table in front of Harley. Her timing was perfect and a cloud of steam obstructed Jackie's glaring censure.

Chapter 3

9:01 a.m. Monday morning found Jacqueline Macklin, M.D. waiting outside the Cherokee County Public Library, Harpursville, Ga.

"They're late" Jackie impatiently thought. Her mind was racing having had the weekend to translate a few more pages of the documents. She needed to see the head librarian for the book club members list and hoped that Carly Spruill's name, and more importantly, that her home phone number was listed. It had not been found in any other resource available to Jackie. A library volunteer approached the doors, twisted the latch and access was granted to all that entered. Jackie immediately went to find the book club list and her target was there. She pressed the numbers on her cell phone and hit the enter button.

Carly remembered Jackie. She said that she was married to Dr. James Spruill a Gilbert State University professor. Carly emphasized that he was *The Archeologist,* Dr. James Spruill, as if Jackie was supposed to know of him or his work. Seems he had been on the local morning news show every time he returned from some field trip with his students. He was always carrying a handful of ancient trinkets, pottery shards, or a religious figurine from some long gone civilization.

Carly gave Jackie James's direct office phone number and she dialed it in. His secretary, Patti Longnecker, gave Jackie an appointment to meet him that afternoon. Jackie did not say what the meeting would be about, other than she had some old documents and wanted an expert opinion on their value or source.

As soon as she got home Jackie shouted down the hall to Harley, "We're meeting James Spruill this afternoon."

"Who?" asked a dazed Harley as he continued to gaze into the mystical glow of his personal home computer monitor. He could totally "zone out" under the flickering images and the unlimited storehouse of knowledge that this marvelous crystal screen could tap. Mega thousands of hits would surface on searches for his hobbies. Jackie uncovered a new species living in her own home. She classified him as being in the family - *hominoid* genus: *neanderthalensis*; species: *pamaeolus*; genus: *subbalteatus*; species: *musculus*. The short version is a male Neanderthal hallucinogenic mushrooming rat.

"Dr. James Spruill at Gilbert State," declared Jackie entering Harley's office.

"Ah, yes," he acknowledged, "I thought that was who we might see." Harley had spent his morning studying the Gilbert State University web site for the listings of faculty and department heads. The Faculty page was in need of updating as Dr. William Eckland was listed as the Director of the Archeology Discipline in the school's Department of Anthropology. His phone call to the registrar's office confirmed the death of Dr. Eckland as well as the appointment of Dr. Spruill as the director pro-tem.

"He is the second man in that photo Boo showed us, you know the one of Eckland and the two men?" Harley called out as Jackie went fuming out of his office door.

He was having some apprehension about Jackie's headlong wide open pursuit to solve the mystery of the Codex. He was trying to keep an eye on his investment of $50.00. If, of course, the box was indeed stolen from the school then he would be the first to return it. There might be a reward which he could then munificently refuse to accept for being such a good citizen. If it were not stolen, then the ownership of the box needed to be established, possibly in the courts. If the value was great then he felt that Boo would be entitled to some of the proceeds of the sale, if, of course, it was established that she was the rightful heir to the property. She said there were no offspring of Aunt Barbara and Uncle Willy's union. That only left siblings to lay claim to their brother's property. If the value were great enough they would fight for their share.

Harley was considering all the angles. Even prior ownership before Dr. Eckland hid the documents. They could have come from somebody's collection, thought Harley. Who were the two people listed on the letterhead? Henry Lancard, the name on paper to call, and Nicholas Szalasznyj.

"Let's not stir the pot too much," he cautioned Jackie. But she would have none of it, for hers was a pursuit of truth.

Harley loved to visit Gilbert University. He had a deep appreciation of the care and craftsmanship of the good old ways of erecting buildings. Only the chapel was original to the initial construction on the school grounds. The school, founded in 1843, was to provide a proper education for all good southern gentlemen. The founding fathers, all good old time Scotch Presbyterians of good old southern families, used their cotton money to establish the school. The moneyed merchants and banker Jews in Atlanta contributed an equal share toward the establishment.

The location chosen was considered neutral ground, being half way between the budding community of Atlanta and the rural farming community that was known as Buckhorn.

The school nearly closed during "The War" as most of the male student body enlisted in Union or Confederate armies. The few remaining boys, about the age of fourteen years, were denied enlistment because they were considered underage. Near the end of the rebellion, age did not stop drafting the young men into the Confederate Army of Tennessee, commanded by Gen. John Bell Hood for the defense of Atlanta.

The chapel was the second building erected on campus with the central school structure being the first. But the church was the third public building in the Buckhorn community, the first being a public house or The Buckhorn Tavern.

Dr. Spruill's office was located in a campus administration building known as Old Central. His was an office Harley always wanted. Harley worked for decades in a space that would be considered an example of the typical 1950's office with high ceilings and florescent lamps humming the minutes of each day. Harley was grateful when B & W Construction gave him his own office so he could replace the harsh glare of the mercury filled tubes with more natural incandescent light bulb fixtures. Dr. Spruill's office did not have ceiling light fixtures at all. His lighting came from lamps placed around the office and were operated by the light switch at the door. There were dark panels on the walls. Harley identified them as having an oak grain in the paneling and the trim around them. Southern Yellow Pine had already disappeared by the time this room was constructed. Industrial grade gray and maroon vinyl tile flooring covered the floor. This tribute to economy was partially hidden with two area rugs of some unknown manufacturer. The office wall was littered with diplomas, certifications, proclamations, newspaper articles under glass, and photos of the good doctor at various digs holding up the trinkets, and pottery shards that one day he would show on local TV. This was the office of a man destined for mediocrity, thought Harley.

"Jackie would know who made the carpets," Harley thought as he and Jackie took the good doctor's hand in greeting.

Jackie identified the furnishings as 1950's executive office desk, credenza, reception or visitors chairs, and bookcases. There was one college display case with the flip up glass front. These things could fetch $500 to $1000 easy Jackie thought. Spruill's desk chair was a typical example of late twenty-first century Big Box Warehouse style executive chair, probably manufactured in Central China. Carlisle area rugs were under the visitor's chairs and under the desk.

Dr. Spruill was not at all the typical stereotype archeologist Harley had imagined. He wore jeans instead of tweed trousers, a nice dress shirt without a brown corduroy coat or a tie, and wore sports shoes, instead of cardboard shiners. Just under six foot tall, thought Harley. He probably tilted the scales at an average healthy weight for his height.

There were introductions, references given, titles stated and general chit chat about the weather and who they knew in common, which it really turned out only to be Carly.

"What can I do for you?" James finally asked.

Harley started to speak but was cut off by Jackie when she said that they had come into the possession of some old parchment papers and would he have a look at them and appraise their possible value?

"You have them with you?" he asked.

Jackie presented the manifest she had first seen in Aunt Barbara's home. Dr. Spruill pulled out a magnifying glass from the top desk drawer and studied the print. "This appears to be written in a later type of uncial script," he said. "Possibility developed from Roman cursive Latin in the later period."

He paused to study the document again. "See the broad single stroke letters?" He said looking at Jackie, but did not show her the page. "They use the simple round letter form as opposed to the angular, multiple stroke letters. The oldest examples of uncial lettering are the <u>De Bellis Macedonicis</u> manuscript in the British Library... The word separation is characteristic of the later. The style is possibly from the third or fourth century but most likely fifth or sixth." He paused to amaze and astonish his audience. "And you say you have more of these?"

Jackie carefully pulled out the next page she wanted him to see. It was the second one she had interpreted on the way to Papa Jo-Joe's Seafood House. She thought she would be safe in revealing this single document for the city of Antioch was an ancient city and there would be several historical references.

Jackie watched Dr. Spruill's face for tell-tale signs of what he was thinking. Dr. Spruill did not look up but continued studying the document. He began making notes on a pad.

Caludio, he wrote, *gardens of Quintessa, Orontes gorge, Beilan Pass* and *Antioch*. Jackie realized that he might find more clues as to the identity of the author than she realized. A combination of the names could give away the origins of the document.

Upon finishing his study, he sat back in his chair and looking at Jackie, again asked if she had more pages like these. She was playing a careful poker hand. Harley on the other hand was letting the excitement of the moment, combined with the possibility of profit get the better of his reserve of information. He spoke up first with "Yeah, I found a box at an estate sale ..." his voice trailed off as he felt a sharp jab against his ankle.

"In Alabama, and they were in a box of odds and ends," Jackie interjected. The nudge to his leg came from out of the sight line of the archeologist. She had observed something she could not quite place in his eyes. She felt or knew that it was not a good something. It looked more sinister than curious.

Dr. Spruill asked Harley and Jackie's permission to keep the manifest and the sixteenth of March document for identification, verification and further study by his colleagues in the Anthropology Department. "We will, of course, return the documents at anytime you feel you need them."

His tone was soothing and complacent and Harley was agreeable to leaving the pages with Dr. Spruill. He went on to say that the initial investigation would be free of charge.

"If the documents are shown to be authentic," James continued, "the university's verification would prove to be of value at auction and the school would ask for some compensation ... say ten percent?"

"Fair enough," said Harley. Jackie was still a bit more reserved and gave a more guarded response.

"We can have these back whenever we ask?" She wanted to be sure on that point. "And we want a receipt for the documents." She was trying to be more practical than Harley. Dr. Spruill, would have offered to have one typed up but Patti had left for the day. He offered a handwritten note instead. Jackie, ever the one to be polite, accepted the offer and they left the office.

"Did you see the name plate is still on Professor Eckland's door?" Harley asked Jackie as they walked to the elevator. She turned and looked at the door for a moment and said, "Yes."

"It is gray from smoke." This was Harley's area of expertise having re-built many an office after fires.

The other nameplates in the hallway are white with black letters carved in the plastic. Dr. Eckland's had a coating of gray ash on his. Harley ran his fingers across the door and picked up soot from the surface.

"So?" said Jackie, "Boo said he died of smoke inhalation. That would be consistent with a fire."

"But the door is not new, it's still in place and useable." They stepped in the elevator and the stainless steel doors slid closed. As they started down Harley made his case. "The soot on the nameplate and a door un-scorched means the smoke was in the hallway. The fire lasted only long enough to soot the outside of the door, but not burn the door on the inside. The hallway is newly painted. The vinyl floor tiles have not been replaced around the door." His conclusion was, "the smoke going outside Dr. Eckland's door … was low in duration … low in heat and destruction … and the smoke marks low on the door indicated it was stared on or reached the floor quickly." Harley paused considering what he had said. "Fire on a floor usually means arson."

"Arson? Why would Dr. Eckland want to set fire to his own office?"

"Arson is done almost all the time to cover other crimes …and what was that kick all about when Spruill asked if we had more parchment?" he asked being irritated.

The doors parted and they stepped into the lobby. Harley was not smug in making his point, for someone had died in this fire. He had seen it many times before in cleaning up other fire damaged buildings.

"I thought I saw something in his face when he looked at the March 16th document," Jackie related. "And you were going to blab about the Codex. What is the other crime?" asked Jackie.

On that note, Harley could only throw out conjecture and speculation. He knew that theft is at the top of the motive list for arsonist.

"Thieves would try to hide what had been stolen by setting fires," said Harley, "homeowners and business owners would do likewise. If the place burned to the ground, they could recover the insurance settlement and sell what they had removed beforehand. Sometimes stuff moves so fast that what they reported lost in the fire went through the pawn shop door the day before. Sometimes it is an act of revenge."

"But this fire could have been an accident," she admonished, "and why would Dr. Eckland want to set fire to his own office?" Jackie asked again when they got to his truck. Once inside Harley became silent his brow furrowed almost to a scowl.

"What is it?" Jackie asked him, as he inserted the ignition key.

"There is one other motive," Harley responded darkly as the key turned starting the engine.

"What?"

"Murder."

Chapter 4

"*Carpentum*" is a horse drawn cart with a cover for those able to afford one," announced Harley. That night using the few notes from Jackie's notepad, Harley had been immersed in his theology textbooks seeking answers. He also discovered that the Orontes gorge and the Beilan Pass Valley were in the general area of Antioch. "Seems our boy was travailing through these areas," Harley informed Jackie.

"Tabernae" Jackie said, "is simply a tavern. The *Tabernae of Quintessea* would have been the name of one such public house."

"But being that it was a tavern in a town full of taverns there was not much chance of ever finding any reference in literature. That could have been a tourist attraction" said Harley.

Armed with her note pad, Jackie sat down at her elegant early 20th century oak roll top desk from the Rome Furniture Company model 62 and began to unravel the markings on the documents they did keep.

Harley launched his own studies into unraveling the ancient Roman calendar, trying to match the *Anno urbis conditae, A.U.C.* to the modern Gregorian Calendar. It was proving to be a bit of a daunting task, even with an engineer's understanding of math. Jackie found him in his study with pad, pencil and calculator, opening internet calendar web sites one after the other. He was highly exasperated.

"It isn't easy," he said looking up from his notes. "First thing is a lot of Roman calendar information was systemically destroyed by the early church starting around 400 a.d. Second, these people used the calendar mostly to forecast feast days, festival days, sacrificial days, days to go shopping, almost every day in a year had a purpose except for work! There is A Day of Fasting after the Entry of the Reed - Then there was a day of Blood - One day for the Entry of the Tree and the Festival of Joy - There were the Bacchanalia Festivals – Saturnalia - Halcyon Days - A Roman New Year's Day and the Festival of Mars. The last being the one referred to in that 16 March 688 journal entry. There were calendars to forecast planting, harvesting, building and starting wars." He paused to hear Jackie's opinion, but she gave none at that time.

"I wouldn't want to be the building superintendent," he said dryly. "I have no idea how they'd scheduled contractors.

The Roman calendar was a tough nut to crack. His other obstacles were the Romans seemed to have 10 months and 106 days. They just did not count 61 days in mid-winter. Romulus, alleged to be the first ruler of Rome, is supposed to have introduced his calendar A.U.C. around 700 B.C. Then along comes Emperor Pompilius to add January and February probably to include the sixty one leftover days and make the calendar 355 days long.

"But this", Harley explained, "did not a solar calendar make. Pompilius realized the mistake as well and said' what the heck let's bring in a new month called Numa every other year, and if that doesn't cover the shortage then add Mercedinus after Febuary 23 or 24. For conquerors whose feats of engineering were the foundation of my education, their calendar was really lame. I would hate to be the bookkeeper come payday," Harley said continuing to complain.

Jackie observed "these guys should have studied the Pagans Stonehenge Calendar. They got it down to the minute."

He ignored the jibe and continued, "Nevertheless, some forty six years before Christ, Julius Caesar stood up in the Senate that day and said that it had been 639 years since Romulus founded Rome. It should have been 638 but Julius was afraid of even number years. Meaning, stay with me now, this puts the Birth of Christ in 663 A.U.C. and our boy wrote the journal entry, if accurate, would be read as 16 March 26 a.d. He could have been around when Jesus died."

"Being that he lived in Antioch," Harley realized, "he probably heard Peter and Paul preach. This Codex could be nearly two thousand years old. Come December 31 we should say Happy 2,762 *Anno urbis conditae* instead of 2009."

"Very good," Jackie chimed in," I am so proud of you. There is a problem with his having written the journal 26 a.d.

in Antioch, as nearly all writing from that time and that region was in Greek."

Harley stopped his victory dance. He knew she was right.

Chapter 5

"Good morning!" said Harley as he entered the kitchen, "do I smell pancakes?"

"Morning," replied Jackie, "Yes, why don't you take your meds and watch CNN for a few minutes while I finish up?"

"Yes, Dear," he said as he headed towards the den with newspaper under his arm.

"I finished a journal entry last night," She called out once he sat down on the sofa.

Harley sighed quietly and got up. He hated to shout a conversation between the walls, so he walked back into the kitchen. Leaning against the counter top he asked, "What did he have to say in this new one?"

"This one is good," was her tease. "This one is the first entry of his journal."

"How can you tell?"

"Because he says it is. I'll get it after breakfast. Now sit down, the eggs are getting cold."

"He says it is the first entry?"
"Yes. His mother gave him a new parchment journal along with pen and ink for his Bar Mitzvah."

"Bar Mitzvah, so he is a Jew?" asked Harley. "I thought he was a Roman citizen."

"So did I," Jackie said, "but he says his mother was raising him a Jew. His father wanted him to follow the goddess Minerva and the god Mercury."

"Dual worship," said Harley, "somewhat common in households then and now."

"I'll get out my notes after we eat. Your eggs are getting cold."

Once the table had been cleared, Jackie brought in the journal page and her note pad. She had nearly consumed the entire yellow legal pad in the last few days. Once she had a hot topic, she could write some notes. This was proving to be one of her most challenging assignments since retirement.

"Here is my translation of the journal entry for Friday May 12 685," she said as she read her notes.

Dies Veneris xii Maius DCLXXXV

"Today I become a man, according to that which is the custom of my mother. It is she that has suggested that I begin this journal to record my thoughts and the events of my life. My father is Calisto of Tarsus where we live in an amplitudo domus. Mother is named Odera. My sister is Aurelia.

Mother took me to the synagogue this morning. Rabbi Kleopatros gave me a special blessing making me a member of mother's temple. I am a son of the commandment in the tribe of Levi the descendents of Moses. Mother expects me to follow the commandments of her god. Father believes that the god Mercury will watch over his business. He believes the goddess Minerva will watch over the leather craft. He says that Bacchus will watch over our vineyards by the lake of Rhegma. Mother insists that I be brought up to make up my own mind one day. I have studied the Greek books of the sons of Abraham since childhood with our slave, Achaicus in the hallway of our home. He is from Achaia on the northern coast of Peloponnesus. I will be allowed to read from the Torah on Sabbath. I have had to memorize the words and lessons of the great philosopher Chrysippus of Soli. He was born here like me. Father say Chrysippus gave his donkey wine until it became intoxicated, then Chrysippus died of laughter. I have been practicing writing my words and letters. I have been using a stylus and scratching letters on a wooden board covered with wax. This is the first time I have written on parchment. It feels good to know that I can keep my words with me."

Harley spoke up reciting the opening line of, "'Today I become a man,' that has not changed in thousands of years. You are right. It is his Bar Mitzvah. Father is Calisto, mother Odera, and they live in Tarsus ... In an *'amplitudo domus?'*"

"Yes," said Jackie.

"I recognize that word *domus* as house? But what is *amplitudo?*"

"Grand house, or as a direct translation would be like amplified house. My house is bigger than your house," she said teasingly. "Does the name 'Rabbi Kleopatros' help date the journal?"

"Not unless he was a Rabbi of some notoriety. If he was a famous Rabbi, then his name might appear in histories or other diaries. But, I am not familiar with the name," answered Harley. "Curious that his name is Greek, Kelopatros?"

"Not really, if that is the only name the little guy knew him by. It was a common Greek name. There may not be a direct Greek to Latin translation. "The lake of Rhegma?" she asked, "does that ring any bells?"

"Lake region above Tarsus in the hills overlooking the city. The place is still there. They must have been well off ... Merchant class or publican."

"What about the philosopher Chrysippus of Soli? Did he exist? Does that help the dating?" asked Jackie.

"Chrysippus was one of those minor Greek philosophers. He came up with a philosophy. The short version is, 'if evil means brings about a good ending then it is OK' … or something like that. But he says Chrysippus was born there, probably before our author was born …Chrysippus was born a few hundred years before Christ."

"So he could been a b.c. child?"

"Not by much," was Harley's guess. "Yea we have a 700 year range."

"Any truth to his story about the donkey?" she asked. "Chrysippus got the donkey drunk and then he laugh so hard watching it that he died? Is that possible?"

"Don't know, but that story has been around a while," he answered.

"He could have had a coronary or a stroke." was her diagnosis.

"What he needed to do was to write down the name of his emperor. Tiberius, Nero, Caesar, someone that was notable in history. Then we have the day of his Bar Mitzvah."

"Drunk donkey," she noted, "sort of had two asses in the street that day?"

It was Harley's turn to roll his eyes.

Chapter 6

Dr. Spruill studied the trusting couple as they stopped at the burned door. He did not have privilege to Harley's comment as he wiped his finger across the soot coated nameplate. But he did have access to the conversations in the elevator. As soon as he could reach his desk, he picked up the phone and dialed four digits needed to place a call within the university phone system.

"Does the closed circuit television in the elevators have voice recording as well?" he asked. After the answer came back from his confederate he asked, "Then could you e-mail me all recordings you have for the elevator down the hallway from my office?" There was a pause as the other party asked for the time frame. "Just the last 15 minutes or less. I am looking for an older couple. They will stand out as visitors."

He waited for the accomplice to acknowledge his request then said, "Good, I will look for it in a few minutes then we need to get together and talk."

Spruill flipped through his file cards for a phone number. Even though he was well versed in the art of using the P.C. he held on to some of the old ways. His finger paused over the edge of one card. He pulled back the ones before it to keep his target in sight.

He got up and went to his file cabinet. Taking the keys from his pocket he unlocked and opened the bottom drawer. His fingers flipped over the tabs on each folder until he found what he was looking for. Pulling it out he opened it on the desk beside the Macklin's documents.

Spruill turned in his chair and faced the monitor. Fingers quickly entered his password opening up his in-house e-mail account. There were thirty four new messages. This time he did not scan the list for spam, but went directly to the last entry. There was the message with a video file attached.

It took only a few minutes to download the five meg. file. It ran for five minutes. It showed the janitor getting on and off without comment, and a couple of girls talking about Professor Elliot's dry class on Shelley, Browning, and Bryon. When Harley and Jackie entered the car, he turned up the volume and heard Harley's observations about the nameplate, the office door, and floor tiles. He leaned forward, took the mouse and put the pointer directly over the position bar. He left clicked and held the button. With this, he drags the position indicator back to where he wanted to replay the video.

"Arson is done almost all the time to cover other crimes," he heard Harley say. "And what was that kick all about when Spruill asked if we had more parchment?" Spruill did this twice then let the recording run its course. He paid particular attention to Harley's comment "what was that kick all about when Spruill asked if we had more parchment? ... When Spruill asked if we had more parchment?"

"More?" thought Spruill. His fingers now punched numbers into an outside line and when the party answered informed the other person, "I think I found the Codex."

Chapter 7

The next day Harley went into Harpursville for supplies and hardware to replenish and repair the Silver Bow. Jackie sat down with the Latin dictionary and began to translate more of the parchment. Harley came in to check on her during the day, but otherwise stayed out of her hair by hiding in his shop. He did come in about 7:00 as the September sun descended in the late afternoon.

"What's for supper?" asked Harley as he washed his hands in the kitchen sink.

"Whatever you feel like cooking," came the reply from her retreat. Either could assemble meals worthy for themselves or for a party. Harley's courses would have a more outdoor grill kind of simplicity, while Jackie's tended to be healthier. Under normal household operating conditions, she would have been the master chef. Jackie, entrenched in her warm and fuzzy rug filled cocoon, was staying there until she finished the current translation. The kitchen chores now fell by the side and it was every man for himself.

"*Lasanum*," he proudly proclaimed for he was learning some Latin himself.

"Don't do Lasagna tonight. I do not feel like cleaning up that much mess. Get out a frozen pizza tonight," she commanded.

That suited Harley, for he would not have to cook or clean up.

"I have a new one ready!" she called down the hall. "Just finishing it."

Dies Martis xxv December or Tuesday, 25 December

Today I am a Corax, having been initiated into Sol Invictus. I am not to discuss any of the rites of initiation with anyone not even my friend Novatus. Father did not let him come to study with Achaicus. Father took me into the hills and covered my eyes with a cloth so I did not see. He took me into a cave he called the "mithraea". There were twenty five followers of Mithras waiting for us. I know some of the men as those who do business with my father. I cannot say who they are. There was a patrician from Malta of whom I will say no more. In the middle of the cave was the statue of Mithras killing the bull. Along the walls were benches carved into the walls. Father says that Mithras is the son of Phanes. When we came out Apollo was descending in the west. Luna followed us as we walked home in her light. We did not speak much of what we had done.

Father says that I must not tell Mother about Mithras. To do so would mean death or disaster to the family.

The followers had sculpted the constellations of Taurus, of Canis, of Hydra, of Corvus, and of Scorpio in the ceiling of the mithraeum. They were in the shape of the sky where Mithras did slay the bull. The high priest told me of how Mithras would slay the bull when his sun passed through Taurus. This would be the re-birth of Mithras and the return of the sun. But of late Mithras, had moved the universe so that the sun no longer travels through Taurus as it returns to our earth by way of the bull, but by the way of the Lamb. Such is the power of Mithras.

Achaicus, in his lessons, has often said that Aries the Ram, is the constellation of the Hebrews. The Sun God traveling through Aries would foretell the time when his Messiah will return to Israel. He warns there have been many false prophets.

I now know why Father likes to go into these hills on the day of the Sun. It is the day for the worship of Mithras. Mother does not like this and believes I should worship her god on Saturn's day.

Father and I shared some bread and some wine, which are to represent the blood and body of Mithras. I am in possession of the secret words that will be required of me as I passed under each constellation. Father explained these words would give me passage to live forever in the stars. The high priest says it is there that the true being dwells, without color or shape, that cannot be touched by reason alone, the soul's pilot cannot *behold it, and all true knowledge is knowledge thereof.*

Once the door on the oven closed, Jackie called for Harley to join her. She wanted to pick his brain for any information about the newest names, titles and other subjects she had unearthed in her digging for the truth. She was stuck on understanding what she was seeing in the last few lines of the Latin text. Her understanding of the Latin was not the problem, it was the way the English translated words related to each other.

"*Sol Invictus,*" he said recognizing the term. "It was a cult of the Sun God, *Sol* for sun. *Invictus* for holy. Mithras, was another sun god," he had read extensively on the cult of *Sol Invictus* but he knew little about the cult of Mithrais. He did tell Jackie, this was what religion scholars considered to be a mystic cult of Eastern origins. 'Gods living on earth like men.' was a common saying among ancient pagans.

"Do you read this as an initiation entry?" she asked.

"Yes. Once our boy hit puberty around twelve or thirteen, his father had a party, in a cave, with his friends. Sounds like my kind of party. Maybe had some of the Roman herb or Greek Ouzo!"

Ignoring his comments Jackie asked, "But did you see that this ceremony was conducted on a Tuesday, 25 December, a day revered by several religions?"

Now, Harley had something to work with. "After dinner I will consult the star charts and find the years that Christmas was on a Tuesday. It would narrow down the dating a bit." Harley noticed that she had written out a passage from the Latin text." What's that?"

Nos partis nonnullus panis quod nonnullus vinum quod es ut reddo cruor quod somes Mithras.

"It begins simple enough," said Jackie. "*Nos partis nonullus panis quod nonnullus vinum*'. That would be, 'we shared some bread and some wine." She paused to ponder the next words. "*'Quod es ut'* meaning 'which are to' then *reddo*"

Harley stopped her line of thinking when he said "*Reddo?*"

"Yes," she answered. "There are several ways to interpret '*reddo'* as in 'to repeat', or 'represent or restore."

"And the *cruor* part?" asked Harley.

"*Cruor* has several meanings too." She stopped and studied the order of the words again. "'*Cruor*' means 'murder, gore, or blood'. '*Quod*' means 'that' and *Somes* means 'body." She had listed the English words under the Latin quotation. Harley studied the sequence as well. He was the first to see the association and the probable intent of the author.

"*Reddo cruor quod somes Mithras,*" he quoted "represents the blood and the body of Mithras." The passage would mean they shared bread and wine to represent the blood and body of Mithras."

Just then the oven timer went off. "Dinner is ready," said Harley on his way out of the room.

Chapter 8

A cold front from Canada had moved across the plateau on which Atlanta was built. The warm moist air smothering the city like a wool blanket was now changing into a fog. Visibility was limited to as far as headlights could penetrate. Anyone standing around the parking lot of the Saint Gabriel

Cathedral in Atlanta would have seen Dr. Spruill walking up to the back door. Anyone watching would have seen two other figures entering with him as a fourth man opened the door from the inside.

One of those men entering had on a dark suit, white shirt, thin black tie and a pair of patent leather shoes. The shoes looked as if they were made of cardboard and painted a glossy black. His suit fit the clothes hanger better than it did him.

The other figure wore a smartly fitting gray uniform shirt and black trousers with blue strips running the length of the legs. He was wearing leather work shoes and a belt with the tools of his trade hanging in various holsters. On his left hip rode one black steel and polymer 9mm Glock pistol.

The man opening the door was wearing a white collar that could be seen standing out in high contrast to both the night and the black shirt he wore.

They moved quickly and quietly talking among themselves. Their topics were about the fog, the local sports teams, and politics. Once inside a small conference room with the door closed, the man in the white collar began to speak.

"Let us begin with a prayer."

His Eminence, Dr. Wilton E. Fellwater, lead the three men in reverent prayer. "Be seated, gentlemen... Now James," he said looking at Spruill, "What was that phone call all about? You said you had the Codex?"

"None of what we say here can be discussed with anyone, not even with each other, outside these walls... understand?" Spruill said looking at all three men. All nodded in agreement. "I said that I think I found the Codex Syracuse." He was emphasizing his earlier message to his Eminence. "I think I know who has it."

H. R. Bagnilla, the man in the ill fitting suit, seemed surprised at this announcement. The man in the security guard uniform Curtis Paraskvas was not.

"We have a lead," said the guard. "We have a video of a couple that paid James," he remembered his position and paused to correct himself, "I mean Dr. Spruill, a visit on Monday."

They turned back to look at Spruill. He had opened his notebook p.c. and powered up the machine. He turned the monitor screen around so the group could see for themselves the evidence.

"Mr. Harley Macklin and Dr. Jackie Macklin came by to see me on Monday," said Spruill. "They wanted me to have a look at these two pages for authentication."

With that, he pushed the contents of a manila folder to the center of the table. Dr. Fallwater reached for it first and lifted the edge spilling two pieces of ancient parchment. Bagnilla fingered one and pulled it to him. Dr. Fallwater gently, lovingly picked up the other. His was the 16 March document.

Pointing at the page held by the priest Spruill said, "That one has several references already recorded in the Codex Alexandria. *Carpentum, Orontes gorge* and the *Beilan Pass, Tabernae of Quintessea, Anitoch, the Amanic Gates, Liberalia, and Liber and Libera.*" He finished his list and looked at his Eminence.

"Yes, yes," he said in reverent tones." It matches the Codex Alexandria in all respects. Are these the documents you saw in Dr. Eckland's office?"

"No," Spruill replied, "Eckland showed me a different entry about Antioch and festivals. I made a few notes on what I could remember, but don't forget I cannot read Latin … not like your grace can."

"Let's see that video," ordered Bagnilla.

Spruill hit the enter key and the screen powered up. He had edited the video down to the portion of the Macklins in the elevator.

"Listen to what they are saying," he said turning up the volume so all would hear Harley's observations.

"The smoke that got outside Dr. Eckland's door ... was low in duration ... low in heat and destruction ... and the smoke marks low on the door indicated it was started on or reached the floor quickly ..... "Fire on a floor usually means arson."

"Arson? Why would Dr. Eckland want to set fire to his own office?" Jackie had asked.

"Arson is done almost all the time to cover other crimes .... and what was that kick all about when Spruill asked if we had more parchment?"

The video ended as the two stepped off the elevator. Spruill left clicked and held the cursor over the replay bar. Moving it back a few pixels he released it to hear Harley say again, "the time to cover other crimes. And what was that kick all about when Spruill asked if we had more parchment?"

Three of the group looked nervously at each other but said nothing.

"Other crimes?" asked His Eminence, "What other crimes is he referring to?"

Bagnilla and Curtis looked at Spruill. "Listen to what he is saying about more parchments, his being kicked. While I was asking if they had more documents he was about to say something when I thought I saw him jump as if kicked. She is hiding something about having the other documents." He hoped His Grace would forget about the "other crimes" comment.

Bagnilla spoke up to ask, "You think she was covering up they have more of the Codex?"

"Yes," Spruill affirmed, "watching his reaction when I asked for more … yes." Each was turning thoughts over in their heads. The only sound was the squeak of office chairs turning on spindles. Then His Grace spoke up.

"Can we ask these people if they have more documents?" as if he had not been following Spruill's comments on the video.

"I don't think they will give that information up easily."

"Could we approach them about a possible purchase of the Codex?" asked Fallwater.

Bagnilla spoke up to say, this might tip their hand as to the real value of what they were holding. "We would need to keep it a low offer."

"They will be asking for the return of these two pages once we've had time to analyze them," said Spruill. "I could denounce these pages as fakes and ask if they would consider 'donating' these for teaching purposes."

"When did you say that you would have them analyzed?" asked Curtis.

"I did not give them a date. But I would expect them to call by next week or so."

"Ask for the documents as a donation," said Fallwater, "if that fails, make a small offer to buy them."

"What about the rest of the Codex?" Spruill asked for His Grace kept forgetting that these were but two pages of a possible four hundred fifty six page Codex.

"Oh, yes," was his only response as he sought an answer.

Then the silence returned.

Bagnilla broke this with his suggestion, "we need to find out more about these two, who are they, where have they been, she said something about Alabama. How would they have come into contact with Eckland. Did he pass these along to them? Is that where he hid the box? I don't think they would come walking into my office with suspicions about..."

his voice trailed off as he considered what he had let slip, "about why Eckland gave the Codex to them, only to have a few pages returned."

"Good point," said Curtis. "Sort of return to the scene of the crime?"

Spruill shot him 'shut up' idiot glance. He got the point.

"Then they do not know what they have. They just sort of found it?" asked Bagnilla.

"Looks like it. I have no idea what Eckland did with the box before he … died … and no idea how these people found it."

"Maybe he hid it at their home? Do they live next door?" asked Curtis.

"We searched Eckland's remember? Carly told me the woman is a friend from her book club. That is how they found me."

"What I am hearing is Eckland hid the box. He died. They found the box not knowing what they had, called Carly, she referred them to you. Right?" asked Bagnilla.

"Sounds logical," Spruill agreed. "Where the box went and how they found it is not the issue here. The issue is do they have the entire Codex and where is it now?"

"We could ask them?" said His Grace.

Spruill was getting frustrated with Fallwater. The old man could not hold a thought in a five gallon bucket. Looking at Bagnilla he inquired, "Can you find out more about these people? I will ask Carly if she knows anymore about the woman, Jackie."

"I'll see what I can find out," Bagnilla confirmed.

"Then Curtis and I will keep investigating what they might know about the Codex."

"How will I do that?" Curtis asked.

"Watch for their return and keep track of any video that is taken while they are at the school. See if they talk anymore about the Codex."

"Can we not buy the Codex from these people?" asked Fallwater again.

"I think that will be all." said Spruill.

Chapter 9

Jackie's next translation gave the couple pause to consider and remember their own family. She wrote it down as follows:

Dies Veneris xii Aprilis
Friday, 12 April

My former powers fail me for words, my lute and my lyre is silent with my grief. To fill this empty space is a great and terrible pain. The characters of my marking are such an insufferable labor. I cannot bear the thoughts of what has happened. We have cremated Father in the previous month. Father had been stricken with the Cough of Perinthus for several days. We went to the temple of Salus on the day of her festival and asked the goddess for health. We left five heqalims of silver and three loaves of Mothers bread on her alter. The priestess told Father to put powder of roses in his balneum. We did this for thirteen days. Then Apollo gave us his sign of the impending woes; for in the east the clouds

*were black in the rising sun and the edges red
with blood.*

*That very day, Libitina came unto him and
carried his spirit up to the stars. I know I will one
day be with him for he gave me the secret words
that will allow me to pass the constellation of
Taurus. When his ashes were collected my Mother,
Aurelia and I carried his remains to the
pomerium. The stone masons interred father in the
eastern wall of the city. I will go there every day
to venerate his memory. I do not know why the
gods did not favor our sacrifices. I went daily to
the temples of Hygeia, and to the temple of
Asclepius, Novatus, Achaicus, Aurelia and
Afranius. All my friends and Aurelia went with me
to implore Asclepius to send his sons the Machaon
and Podalirius to administer to Father. But they
desired that he be with them in the heavens. Oh
Orcus, why must you rend my heart so? Oh
blessed Father, watch over me. Guide my feet in
the path of your choosing for thou has gone before
me to prepare a place for me on Mount Olympus.*

"That is really sad," Harley said as he was reading this
latest translation. "Poor man lost his father."

"His father died the month before," Jackie acknowledged.
"It was written by an author with some education. His prose
is very elegant in his description of his suffering and grief.
The *Cough of Perinthus* could have been several
diseases, the Flu, Pertussis, Whooping Cough or Diphtheria,"
was Jackie's diagnosis and speculation. "Having a thirteen to
fourteen day gestation it could have been anything in the
lungs ... The rose pedals in his bath water, the *balneum,* the
fragrance probably gave him some relief."

"*Libitina*," said Harley, "was the same as saying the Grim Reaper".

"*Hygeia*," observed Jackie, "is the root word for hygiene."

"*Asclepius, Novatus, Achaicus, Aurelia* and *Afranius*; *Asclepius* and his sons the *Machaon* and *Podalirius*," said Harley as he read out loud the list of gods. "This is about all of the gods of healing. All his sacrifices of cash and homemade breads did not help," noted Harley. "This son was rooted in the beliefs of his culture. He named all the proper gods, basically in the proper order of influence and rank. Trying to cover all his bases, he persuaded his friends and family, and 'Aurelia', to prayers, as well. He had a good religious upbringing for his day," Harley told Jackie.

"Do you recognize the term *pomerium*?" asked Jackie.

"A building feature of city walls," he said. "It was a space between the walls of the city Romans considered a holy place. To put the ashes of his father in the wall was to provide spiritual protection to all inside."

They broke from the study for a while and went into the den. Harley picked up the remote and sent the signal to power up the television. Once the familiar glow of the pixels was seen, Harley punched the channel numbers for CNN. Jackie sat down and together they watched the nightly news.

"Usual stuff," moaned Harley as he began to flip through the channels.

"I can't stand this channel hopping," complained Jackie. "I'll just read." She picked up her latest copy of the A.M.A. Journal and began to flip through it.

Harley could not resist the irony of the moment and said that she was page hopping just like he was channel hopping. She stopped her search, rolled the magazine into an offensive weapon and gave him a whack on his arm.

"Ow!" he complained from the sting.

"Oh stop being such a baby," she said. "Are there any messages from Spruill?"

"Nothing on the machine. I called his office a couple of times. Patti keeps saying that he is in class and will call back."

"Why don't you go over there tomorrow?" Jackie asked.

"You going with me?"

"No, promised mom I would visit her, unless you want to come too."

"I'll go see Spruill," he said.

"Do not let on about how many more pages we have until we know what his interest is in them."

"Yes, Dear," and he hit the channel button again.

"And don't let him know where we found them. I would not want anyone to bother Boo," ordered Jackie.

"Yes Dear," and he hit the channel button again.

"Are you listening to me?"

"Yes, Dear," he said in his dead flat tone as he hit the button again.

"You are ignoring me?" not so much a question but more an observation.

"Only after you asked if I wanted to visit your mother."

Smack! was the sound of a rolled magazine hitting the arm of a smartass husband.

"Ow!"

Chapter 10

As Harley was on his way to see Spruill, he noticed the door to the burned out office was opened. He stuck his head in for a quick look around. The office was stripped of furniture and ceiling tiles. The vinyl tile flooring was clean in the middle but for a twisting burn mark. One end of the scar pointed towards the wall outlet. The other end pointed toward the center of the room before it faded away. All four walls had white squares and rectangles about the size of diploma and certificate frames. He thought those of smaller shapes could have been photos of something memorable. There were larger spaces from floor to head high that did not have edges as defined as the wall mounted ones. The patterns were the areas behind the cabinets that bore witness to the awful events of the night of the fire. "Furniture," thought Harley.

"Hi, Patti, is he in?" Harley nodded in the direction of Spruill's office door. She said he was and she would announce him.

The men exchange pleasantries as they shook hands. "What brings you by today?" asked Spruill as he closed the door cutting off any more of the conversation from those not licensed to hear.

"Any word on our document?" Harley asked getting right into the meat of the meeting.

It had been nearly two weeks since Dr. Spruill first saw the papers. Patti had delivered Harley's phone messages and not knowing the nature of their business, urged her boss to return the calls. He was not expecting Harley today, but was expecting the question. Spruill answered the question with one of his own. "How many more pages like those two did you buy?"

"We only bought the two. Why?" Harley replied hedging his answers.

"I want to hold on to the first ones you brought in for further study and analysis. We want to run some test to accurately date the documents."

Harley wanted to know what kind of test.

"Hyper-spectral imaging, sometimes referred to as spectral imaging, or S.I. We put a very tiny piece in an electron microscope and measure the catho-do-luminescence in the spectrum. It should give us an accurate reading on the type of ink used as well as the age of the parchment."

Well it certainly sounded impressive, intensive, and expensive but before Harley could ask, Spruill spoke up, "We will do it free of charge. We would like to do all of your documents at once. So we do not waste time re-calibrating the equipment. You do understand?"

Harley caught Spruill's saying "all of the documents", instead of doing the two. He realized Spruill was on a fishing trip.

"You have all our pages, both of them," said Harley.

"You never did say where you found these two," Spruill said pressing on.

"No, we never did. Did we?" There was a pause as each waited for the others next move. Spruill's next move was to sit back in his chair. Harley's next move was to advance his own agenda.

"You mean you will do this spectral imaging for free even if the documents are not as old as you think?"

Spruill was thrown a little off by this tactical question and gave up the quick response of "yes."

"Will you use the scanning transmission electron microscope or the electron probe micro-analyzer?" Harley had done his homework and now was doing some probing of his own. Spruill, quick to reestablish his authority in his field said that it would be the EPM with EDS mapping. "Trump?" he thought as he finished.

"When will this be over and we get the results? We want to sell them as quickly as possible and recoup our investment," said Harley.

Spruill speculated that the test would be done next week and the results would be analyzed the one after that.

"So you have a buyer?" asked Spruill.

"No. Depending on the school's analysis we will either keep the pages, contact Christie's Auction House in New York, or we'll be putting them on eBay," replied Harley.

"And if they prove to be fake?"

"We'll have to see first, won't we?"

"Question might be how fake?" replied Spruill, "Are they really good fakes? Fakes of whose journal? When was the fake made? Knowing who and when and why gives different values to the pages," explained Spruill. "All those things affect the value of things of antiquity. "Could you go back to the store and find more? This could prove to be quite a find and very valuable."

Harley measured his next response for he suspected the good doc was still probing to find if there were more and how close they might be.

"We would need to find some time to get back and see if we can find anymore pages." He was trying to be vague about distance and quantity.

Spruill realized this verbal waltz could go on indefinitely until one tripped himself up or tripped up the other. Harley quickly understood that this man might be holding something back. He had a bit of experience in contract negotiations and knew when to stop and rethink. The two gave it one more shot, just in case.

"So, there might be more, it's just a matter of returning to this," Spruill paused ever so briefly as to give a more sly inclination to the word, "store?"

Harley let Spruill's leading question answer for itself and replied, "That's right. Right now it would be inconvenient for us to go back."

"Then it is not near here?" Spruill went for the direct frontal attack and gave away his intentions.

"Dr. Spruill," emitted the intercom breaking the battle. "It's your wife on line one."

"Thanks." He reached for the receiver and with his finger on the button said, "Would you excuse me?"

"I'll show myself out," said Harley reaching for the door knob.

Harley said goodbye to Patti and headed toward the elevator.

There were noises of scraping and banging coming from inside the burned out office. Harley stopped again and looked inside. "Howdy," said Harley to the man on his knees.

The workman stopped prying up floor tiles, turned, returned the greeting and added, "can I help you?"

"Name's Harley Macklin, how are you doing?"

"Matt, Matt Turncock," said the young man laying down his hammer and rising to his feet. He shook Harley's extended hand. Harley stopped and looked around the walls, floor and ceiling. He paused for Matt to observe what he was doing. "So, this was Uncle Willy's," he paused, sighed as if in grief and continued with "his old office?"

"Uncle Willy?"

"William, Eckland. I'm an old friend of the family." Not an entirely false statement he thought.

"Oh yes. This was his. No one wanted to move in after it happened so we cleaned it up and shut the door. Now there seems to be some rush or something to get it fixed up. I have a work order to finish the remodeling."

Harley paused before continuing the conversation. His mind was racing to find the real reason for the rush work. "Someone moving in?"

"No one that I can get a name for to order a new nameplate," said Matt.

Then Harley noticed that the nameplate was indeed missing.

"Did you know Professor Eckland very well?" ask Harley.

"Better than most of these old cranks," Matt replied, "He always had a good morning or hello for me and everyone else. He would remember my birthday and give me some small something he had picked up on one of his trips. Not much, a paper weight, or a real fountain pen. You know the ones that you have to load with ink."

"Yea, I ruined many a paper in school using those things," Harley added with a chuckle.

"Yea, he was a great guy," Matt's dejected eyes looked towards the floor, "hated to see him go."

"Do you have time for a break, get some coffee or something?" asked Harley. "I'd like to hear some more about Uncle Willy."

"Yea, sure. I can take a lunch break," said Matt as he laid down his putty knife. "There's a cafeteria across campus," said Matt when they exited the building. He pointed in the direction of the Student Life Building off in the distance. "We could take my work truck."

"Is there a coffee shop nearby?" asked Harley.

"Just outside the West Gate."

Harley did not want to chance someone from the school eaves-dropping on the conversation.

Matt ordered his coffee straight up with sugar. Harley had hot chocolate with some peppermint flavor added. They sat down at a corner table.

"So what happened?" asked Harley. "How did the fire start?"

"Fire investigator said it looked like the power cord to the space heater shorted out or something and caught the rug on fire.

"So, Uncle Willy died of burns?" asked Harley knowing full well such was not the case.

"Coroner said it was smoke inhalation."

"But the office didn't look like it was destroyed by fire."

"No it wasn't," said Matt. "I got in there later that night. The office wasn't burned at all, just full of smoke damage and some water. Fire department did that."

"Nothing burned? I mean other than this electric heater?"

"Nothing burned but the rug where the electric cord shorted out," said Matt expecting Harley to not believe him. "All the plastic stuff was melted but nothing burned."

"Then the heat was low enough not to burn the furniture, but produced enough smoke to kill a grown man?" Harley mused aloud as his thoughts turned over in his head.

"Strange isn't it?" asked Matt. "Never understood why."

"Not strange at all. Ever put a candle in an upside down jar," said Harley.

Matt nodded, for it was a common middle school science class demonstration proving the presence of carbon dioxide.

"The candle burns until the smoke reaches the flame, then it goes out, same thing with this fire." Harley stopped so Matt could absorb the implications of this statement.

"So a closed room will smother the fire inside?" asked Matt.

"If the room is tight enough, yes. Who reported the fire?" asked Harley.

"Dr. Spruill."

Just then a figure was seen walking past the window where the two were sitting. He saw Matt and the two waved. The man continued on his way.

"Security guard from the college," said Matt. "His name is Curtis, from Egypt."

"Is he assigned to one building?"

"Yes the one I'm today."

"I have more documents translated." announced Jackie from her office as soon as she heard Harley closing the back door.

"Hello to you to dear," Harley said with just a tiny hint of smugness. Too much smugness and his dinner would be served on the patio … cold ... and alone.

"What did you find out at Spruill's office?"

He went down the hallway and into her office. She was sitting behind her desk cluttered with the yellow pads of notes, her reading glasses perched on her nose.

"Somehow Spruill knows something about us. He seemed certain that we have more documents. Kept trying to get me to say how many and where. How is your mom? Still like vintage wine … sour?"

She contracted her *corrugator*, *procerus*, and *orbicularis oculi* muscles, pulling her eyebrows down and in to alert Harley she thought his jab at mom was unfair and unwelcomed. She pushed her glasses up Passavant's Ridge closer to her eyes. Otolaryngologists call it scowling. Harley calls it "The Look, part II".

"What do you have?" he asked passively.

Dies Iovis xiv Novembris DCLXXXVIII or, Thursday 14 November 687 A.U.C.

Bacchus has made me but a fool if I were not one already for embracing the god. Mother has married Claudio Socorro Patroclus who I met at the mithriam the day I became a corvus. He has promised to buy citizenship papers for me. Claudio sought my consent to marry my mother. He and mother did show their desire holding hands in front of the public baths. Mother will keep our home, but she will live with Claudio in his villa. Aurelia and I will live here with Achaicus and the other slaves to attend to us.

The priest made the offering of the cake to the God Jupiter. Mother and Claudio ate of the cake and the celebration began. There were several breads, salad and olives. There was cheese Asiago, pressato, parmigiano, provolone, and fontina. Almonds and dates were served. There was meat and chicken, fish and vegetables. Jars of honey into which we dipped our grapes.

We escorted mother to the home of Claudio. Being taken with age he could not carry Mother over the threshold but he did escort her into the house. We did not stay to see Mother light the fire.

Novatus, Septimus, Cassius, Aristocles, had drank deeply from the vessels of Bacchus. The goddess Ate was directing our path to the god Caerus.

We went to the stables of Didotus and did lead a cow from his stables. We, the fellowship of five, directed the bovine up a flight of stairs onto the roof of the stable. We expect the wrath of Didotus who is of much age and has but little hair. We did not steal his cow, for the cow is still at his stable. Didotus will have to make a feast of the animal on the roof and we will all dance with the god Bacchus again.

Burrus did not go with us in our merriment. I last saw he and Aurelia walk into the garden. I think Burrus and Aurelia will next go to the priest.

Claudio has said that the time has come for me to join him in service to the Republic. He will send letter to the commander of the III Gallica

Cohors Milliaria asking that I be made a Princepales or a Immunes.

I would that the healing goddess Akeso would hurry to my side and bring relief to the vapors that are in my head.

We fellowship of five give thanks to the goddess Demeter for her blessing of grain and for her son Semele who matched her gift by giving us wine. For filled with the good gift we forget our grief, gain our sleep and end the troubles of the day. There is no other medicine for misery.

"Did you say he stole a cow?" Harley asked.

"Yes and why did they lead it onto the roof?"

"Cows will go up stairs, but they won't go down," Harley said with a chuckle realizing what the author had done. "The Fellowship of the Five did not steal the cow. The cow is still on the property of what's his name?"

"Didotus," she supplied.

"Didotus, and he still had ownership of the cow. The cow can still be milked. But the cow is not coming down. That's funny," said a grinning Harley.

"So what do they do to get the cow down?" asked Jackie skeptically.

"Nothing you can do. You either have to feed and milk the animal until she dies or..." at that he shrugged.

"Or what," Jackie asked in a foreboding voice.

Harley made the slashing motion across his throat with his finger and winced. "Barbeque and brew!" This time it was a little jig of a dance around where he stood. Jackie was constricting those *orbicularis* muscles again.

"Claudio Socorro Patroclus his step dad? Does that ring any bells?" she asked, "Can we get a name on this guy now?"

Jackie's investigative ire was being rankled by Harley's lack of sincerity in the discovery of the author.

"Now that name Burrus," he said upon stopping his jig, "he is a person of interest as they would say in those days."

"Why, who is he?" Jackie asked.

"Itchy has his Scratchy, Laurel had his Hardy, Caesar had his Brutus, and Nero had his Burrus," was Harley's answer. "That puts the guy around 50 to 60 or so a.d. on the Gregorian Calendar. Then with that, I can work out the A.U.C. calendar our little guy's watch was running on. What was the date?" Harley asked his own memory.

"687," Jackie provided.

"He bar mitzvah at age 13 in 685 so that makes him 15 or 16 years old and stealing cows!" exclaimed Harley.

"Then you can date the author with the reference to Burrus?" the investigator Jackie asked.

"Not with Burrus alone. I would need a second name or even a first or last name. Burrus is like Tommy or Joe, it's that common in Roman literature."

"So we still have a 700 year range for the author?"

"I'll look up the history of that *III Gallica Cohors Milliaria*, maybe Burrus was an officer in that unit. If he was an officer in 55 a.d. and if Burrus can be tied to Nero the emperor, then, we have a match!"

"Good, do that and I'll start supper," she said.

Harley went to his office but not to research *III Gallica Cohors Milliaria*. His goddess Muse had come to visit.

Jackie could hear him from down the hall.
"There once was an old farmer from Tarsus,
And five boys influence by Bacchus.
Whose brown cow was led,
To the top of its shed,
And   now   we   will   have   a   smoked   carcass."

"HARLEY!" she cried with frustration.

Chapter 11

Church bells were still announcing the end of Dr. Fallwaters' service when Bagnilla approached Dr. Spruill on the church steps. "I have some information for you," he said.

Spruill glanced over at Carly who was talking with members of her morning Bible study group. They were making arrangements for some outing later in the week.

"I thought we agreed not to discuss this outside of the room?" admonished Spruill.

They paused a moment looking at each other waiting for one to speak. Spruill motioned with a nod towards a tree shaded section of lawn. They could see anyone approaching from the vantage point.

"Harley's full name is Harland Randolph Macklin," said Bagnilla, "born December 15, 1944 in Cleland County, Ga. Attended Cleland County High School graduating about the middle of the class. Went on to graduate at Leidhold University in Macon, Ga. B.S. Building Construction. I found it interesting that he took theology classes in the Gerald – Wilcox Howell School of Divinity every quarter."

"Theology classes?" this perked Spruill's attention.

"He was hired right out of school by Belfort & Williams Construction in Atlanta. Retired two years ago."

"B.W.C.? Don't they do a lot of government construction, schools and such," Spruill asked. "Seems we had them do the Thomas – Vinson wing addition a few years ago?"

"Yes they do government contracts, but Macklin worked in the intermediate level office park division, probably had nothing to do with the school contract."

"Still we can't rule him out. What about his wife?" asked Spruill. "Just a minute," he said lifting his hand and waving at Carly. She waved back and headed off to another cluster of women.

"Jacqueline or Jackie Philomena Macklin M.D." Bagnilla began. "Born 1945 in Milton County, town of Stratford in South Carolina. Seems her father, Dr. John Hall, was the first practicing doctor in the county. She went to something called the Margaux Academy. It's a private girl's finishing school, been there since before The War."

"War?"

"Civil War," explained Bagnilla, "Did her undergrad at Leidhold with a B.S. in Biomedical Science. She graduated top of her class and went to the Longley School of Medicine on a partial scholastic scholarship. After graduating top of her class, she went to work for the Bibb County Medical Center for three years, then went to the CDC in Atlanta. She worked several different departments eventually advancing to head the Department of Travelers Health … discovered something called Pantanal - Linhas fever."

"That's all?" asked Spruill, "Where did they meet?"

"Met and married while attending Leidhold and Longley. They are living in Harpursville. Did Eckland know them? Did they have any reason to visit him in his office?"

"What other family did Eckland have apart from his ex-wife?" asked Bagnilla.

"Barbara had a niece," replied Spruill. "Bestow is the last name, I think. She lives in Alabama."

"Do they know Gowen, Szalasznyj, or Gill? Any common interest, hobbies, season ticket holders or something?"

"Gill was closest to William," Spruill answered. "But if Gill had any knowledge about the Codex I think he would have approached me with it."

"Nothing connects the Macklins to anyone at the college except Eckland, he's dead, and they have all seen the Codex," decided Bagnilla.

"Yes, one owned the whole thing and the other owns at least two pages. Probably more," observed Spruill.

"I'm thinking they hold the entire Codex," Bagnilla said.

"It's interesting that Harley has a background in theology. Anything we ought to know about there? Does he have some education or experience in ancient documents?"

"No." said Bagnilla. "They go camping - they own a R.V. and he is a spelunker."

"What does she do?" asked Spruill.

"Well," started Bagnilla, "she was a doctor until she retired, about all she did was work, shop for antiques and go camping as well. Nothing connects them with Eckland."

Spruill and Bagnilla were stumped for answers.

"Curtis reported Macklin and Matt Turncock, one of the school's maintenance men, left Eckland's office together. They went to the Nut Hut on the corner. He didn't come back for 30 minutes."

"Any idea what they talked about?" asked Bagnilla.

"I asked Matt when he returned. He said they talked about Uncle Willy's death. Harley kept asking how Eckland died."

"What does Macklin know?"

"Nothing much according to Matt," said Spruill, "Matt told Harley Dr. Eckland's death was an accident. Odd thing was Matt said Macklin kept referring to William as 'Uncle Willy'."

"Who is Uncle Willy?" Bagnilla was lost on this point.

"That's what Harley kept calling Eckland, 'Uncle Willie'," noted Spruill, "but they are not related that I know of."

"That is odd," said Bagnilla.

"You said Dr. Macklin collects antiques?"

"Why yes," Bagnilla realized, "Maybe that is the connection. She may have met him or attended one of those community seminars he held."

"Could be the connection," said Spruill.

"I could search her credit card statement for the past couple of months and see where she has been shopping."

They quietly continued the discussion about the next step. From time to time one would look up and around to see if anyone was getting too near. Finally the two agreed that they needed to keep Harley and Matt from sharing notes. Spruill would get Matt fired the next day. He would have Curtis keep an eye out for the Macklins.

"You can do that?" asked Bagnilla.

"When you are the Department Head," said Spruill with a wink.

"What's next?" Bagnilla asked. "Want us to start a deeper investigation?"

"See what you can find out. Can you do that without anyone finding out?"

"I'll do a person of interest, make it a semi-Homeland Security thing," offered Bagnilla.

"You can do that?" asked Spruill.

"That and much more than you know."

"You're scary, you know that?"

"My job to be" said Bagnilla.

Carly came over to say hello and let James know that they were going out to lunch today.

"Call me after you get back from your ... trip," James said to Bagnilla.

He just nodded and with a wave walked toward his car.

Chapter 12

"The next entry is one you'll like, it describes a party," Jackie said as she placed the plate of fried eggs at the breakfast table.

"Party?" said Harley and he got up off the couch to investigate. Going into the kitchen he asked, "What party?"

"A regular *Sulum diligo Saturni noctis*," Jackie recited. "He is suffering in more ways than one."

"What is one of the ways? And what is that '*Saturni noctis*'?" asked Harley as he sat down, "Saturday night?"

"After breakfast," she instructed, "and it's '*Sulum diligo Saturni noctis*' ... everybody loves Saturday night."

With that they sat down to eat.

Dies Domminica xxii Martius Sunday, 22 March 688 A.U.C.   Cepi ut refugium of meus cella

I have taken to the refuge of my room. Much has occurred over the past days. Claudio and I went to the hippodrome and saw the chariot races. We dressed in our finest silk. Claudio wore his tunica angusticlavia and I wore my best tunica. Abudantia, was with Claudio for he did do well in choosing the Spaniard when placing his bets. He has an eye for a good team of horses and driver. His team must have been heated by the steeds of the Virgin. I choose the team that had pearls threaded into their manes. I thought them quite colorful.

A chariot of the blue team spilled over at the turn and dislodged the driver into the path of the Spaniard. He was trampled to death under the hooves of the horses. But the Spaniard did not quit and he did win that race.

That night Abudantia left Claudio and he did not do so well at the game of the three balls and did lose much money at the table. She came to me instead and I did quite well at Duoecim scripta. I have perfected the use of the throws to my advantage and am hard pressed to lose. Claudio, at a loss in the three balls, did have his feelings laid bare. Recriminations were uttered and the air resounded with Discordia's brawl. It was everyone for himself and the angry Diviniteis held sway in the taverne. Nicolaus called for new table sand. Those able to stand and those able to see did return to the dice and balls.

I was led to the apartments above by the harlot, Felicia. The goddess Carnea did open her door and lead us in. There she had placed the wine upon a table by the bed. A candle shown in the darken room. She had seen me playing at the tables and had laid in wait like Empanda to draw me into her web and show me the pleasures of the goddess Voluptas. She was of thin build, with light and fair hair falling like golden rivulets around her countenance. But, low I did not want her that night but to lie upon the couch and in each othres arms tell each the story of our lives.

She had been sold into this life by a step-mother. She came from the city of Damascus. Felicia listened as I told her of what I had learned of the one true God of the Jews. She too had heard of this God and of the Redeemer that was to come. We talked and drank late into the night. She fell asleep. By the light of Diana's shield I looked on her face and my arms went powerless.

I, who was that evening so savage, was now as suppliant and at peace. So too was the contentment in her features. She opened her eyes, smiled, and with the tenderness of her heart did give me her best kisses that I would snatch three thunderbolts from Jove for more. Those kisses were far better than I gave and was embarrassed that I could return her none better.

We were awakened by the crow of the cock and the noise of the house in the new day. I begged her to come with me to the house of Claudio in the hills. To leave Egestes and this taverne to live away from Mefitas. But Suadela failed in her efforts to move Felicia to this treason for fear that her mistress would have her flogged in the market.

I left with slow steps and heavy feet. My path went not home but to the door of Elisha. We talked of the events of the night past and in his counsel did proclaim that he thought I was in love with the harlot. To this misery I did fear Cupid would lead some other to be a victim of her charms. I would entreat Claudio to purchase her freedom and bring her to our farm.

We met at the baths. Claudio was now the owner of feet that were slow and unsteady. Securitas and Strenua had abandoned him. His body bore many bruises and scars inflicted of Mars during the previous night's battles over the tables. Once the soothing touch of the god Aesculapius had healed his wounds we went to seek out an artist for a new mosaic for our home in Tarsus.

Mother wants the triclinia to be re-built to include a hypocaust and Claudio wants a mosaic for the floor. We were invited by friends to view several they have. I favored the dancing skeleton with the two pitchers of wine. This, I pointed out, would be most suitable to install on the floor of the triclinia, for if served too much wine at dinner you would join the servant. Claudio was much amused by this. He wanted the depiction of the Battle of Issus. I had studied this with Achrius. We agreed that Mother would not approve of this and would have it installed in his own officium. We both agreed on a boar hunt with hound and with a rabbit in the field.

We prepare for the feast of the Natalis Solis Invicti. The god Attis returns tonight and tomorrow we attend the day of blood resurrection ceremony of Mithris. Claudio says he will ask that I be allowed to partake of the rites to become Scorpio. For Apollo has passed the constellation of Aries, the days of re-birth are upon us.

"Wow!" exclaimed Harley, "one hell of a party animal. Drinking, fighting, gambling, whoring around."

"Just a minute," said Jackie," I want to say in Felicia's defense, she and he did not mess around."

"Ha! Just like you to take her side. She was in the business." He knew he would get the look but did not expect the slap of her open hand against his sleeve, just a little slap.

"Just like you to take his side. But he only," she searched for the passage," 'wanted to lie in each others arms.' She was not in the mood either." On this Jackie was firmly convinced of her feelings and would not be moved.

"I know the phrase '*tunica angusticlavia*' a sort of royal or publican tunic, and of course our young man was wearing his best."

"Probably made of silk, do you agree?" she asked.

"The best was of silk. Expensive too. These guys were filthy rich and did not mind getting filthy with it," said Harley.

"Well, I made a list of the gods and goddess that he refers to. I remember some of them but Roman Mythology was not taught in the Margaux Academy for Young Girls. Studying Roman Mythology, beyond the main group of Olympus, was not a part of the curriculum … such things were considered pagan."

"Stuck up girl's school," said Harley, "let me see the list."

"Here," snapped Jackie, "Why are you being so difficult this morning?"

"This is cutting into my Sunday Morning news. Give me a little bit and I'll pull out the old school books and find you your gods."

She returned to her kitchen chores and Harley disappeared into his study. She was pleased to hear him shuffling the books in his library. There was the thud of heavy text books dropping on the desk. She went about her usual Sunday morning chores before sitting down with the latest J.M.A. and finding the Infectious Disease Reports.

After an hour she stuck her head in his doorway and asked how it was going. He answered that some of these gods especially the goddess were hard to find in the indexes. He was going on-line as a short cut to seek out the rest. He was making notes as fast and furious as she had done in her interruptions. "Want anything?" she asked.

"Some root beer would keep me going."

Another hour had passed before he emerged from the man cave. "Got em'!" he exclaimed.

Jackie had fallen asleep on the couch with the J.M.A. across her lap.

"What did you say?" she asked.

"I found them all, and this guy was deep in his knowledge of his gods. No aspect of his life was without some god or goddess to appease. You couldn't turn a corner until you threw a sacrifice around it."

"If you don't stop being a smartass I'll throw you around a corner?" she threaten.

"Let's start at the top of the page," Harley said as he put down his tablet next to the names she had written out:

"*Abudantia* Goddess of luck, abundance and prosperity … she was helping Claudio at the track." said Harley. "Once *Abudantia* left Claudio and went to sit on the shoulder of our author, then *Discordia,* Goddess of discord and strife came through the door and the angry *Diviniteis'* came with her. Then it was Mars that cried 'havoc and let loose the dogs of war'!"

"To quote the Bard?" asked Jackie referring to William Shakespeare's Julius Caesar.

Harley ignored the remark and continued, "The goddess *Carnea*, now is obscure because of the brawl, but a perfect reference. She was the goddess of love and get this," he paused for effect, "the goddess of door handles." *Empandas* was spider woman ... *Voluptas* a goddess of love ... For *Securitas* and *Strenua* to leave his side is funny."

"How so?" "They were there to keep you healthy, sober, and upright!" he chuckled. "Then there is Attis, a kind of night goddess. There you have it, and you missed some."

"What missed some?" she asked.

"Egestes, Goddess of poverty ... *Mefitas,* Goddess of poisonous vapors from the earth ... and *Suadela,* Goddess of persuasion especially in matters of love."

"Does the Battle of Issus help date the author?" Jackie demanded trying to get Harley back on course to discovery.

"Not really," he said, "The battle was where King Darius got his butt kicked about 400 b.c. so that doesn't help. Took place near Iskenderum, Turkey, just a town near Tarsus and their home."

"The *Natalis Solis Invicti* and *Mitheris* appears again," she said.

"Yea this guy is really into advancing in the cult," noted Harley.

"When did *Apollo*, pass through Aries?"

"The axis of the earth did not shift until around 100 a.d. causing Apollo to cut through Aries for the spring equinox!" Harley grew animated." We are getting close. He would not have seen the sun passing through Aries every spring until sometimes after 100 b.c."

"Great," said Jackie, "I knew you could do it. What about *Aesculapius*?"

"*Aesculapius* isn't Roman but the Greek god of healing."

"So this guy was educated in the classic as well as the contemporary gods," Jackie observed.

"Yes, a regular high priest of the Holy Roman Deities."

And here came That Look.

Chapter 13

Harley entered the stairwell in the administration building and began to climb. He took the stairs to stay away from the all seeing closed circuit camera eye that was in the elevator. He put on his B. & W. Construction hardhat with the company logo on the front plate. Opening the stairwell door, he checked the hallway for Spruill or anyone else. He headed for the late Dr. William Eckland's office. The door was open and construction noises radiated from within; hammers, cordless screwdrivers, and the sound of a metal step ladder being closed. He stuck his head in the door expecting to find Matt.

"Can I help you?" It was the new supervisor of the re-modeling crew. "Cedric" was the name stitched in blue on the field of a white patch above the right shirt pocket.

"Just looking around," said Harley then he asked, "where's Matt?"

"Mr. Turncock is no longer an employee of this university," was somewhat of a curt answer to a friendly question. Cedric said. "He does not work here anymore."

"Can you tell me how to get in touch with him? I was to meet him here today. My company was supposed to bid on a job in this building."

"Sir, he no longer works here," this time the answer had a more forceful delivery.

Harley thought for a moment of how to get the information he wanted. He was also wondering why Matt, an eight year employee, having medical insurance, would up and leave a good position.

"Did he take that job with Morrison Construction?" he asked trying to sound like a friend of Matt's.

"I don't ..." he paused, "I can't say why ..." Cedric carefully considered what he was about to say, then answered "I can't say."

He looked over Harley's shoulder directly at the closed circuit camera ball clinging to the ceiling tile in the hallway, "why he ..." as he shifted his eyes, "was fired." Cedric could frame a wall but could not frame an answer. He nodded his head in the camera's direction and returned to work.

Harley stood in the doorway a moment longer and turning around, saw that dark tinted all seeing eye of the security camera and felt it staring right through him. He knew that it would not have heard a word of the conversation, but whoever was watching might pickup on the body language.

"I'll be at the Nut Hut for the next hour, in case he should stop by. Can you let him know Harley Macklin came by to say hello?"

Cedric turned and nodded as if to say yes then went back to work.

Business was slow when the Nut Hut door opened. Matt walked up to Harley's table not quite knowing what to do next. It was Harley that broke the icy mood. He went to his feet, put on his big grin, and extended his hand. "Hello Matt. Good to see you got the message."

Harley said it with such enthusiasm that Matt was thrown off his path of righteous indignation. He was working out what to say to the man he believed had something to do with his being fired.

"Fired?" said Harley in astonishment to Matt's announcement. "Why would they fire you?"

"Something about staff reduction, budget cutbacks ... Orlantha, she's in charge of personnel, couldn't look me in the eye and give me a straight answer. All she kept saying, it was out of her hands ... above her head," said Matt sadly.

"It's a right to work state," Harley said knowing all too well there was no protection against firing afforded to the blue collar workers in Georgia except by union contracts and the Federal Medical Disability rules. No excuse need be given.

"Eight years, no complaints, good record, always on time. Then out of the blue comes this. I thought it might have something to do with you."

"Why do you say that?"

He explained no sooner had he returned to Eckland's office after his lunch break, than Spruill came in and began asking questions about Harley. Where did they go? What did they talk about?

"I told Spruill that you were asking questions about "Uncle Willy's death. And I told Spruill that I told you that it was him that reported the fire to campus security rather than call the fire department directly."

"He seemed irritated at my talking so much about him and Dr. Eckland to you."

"I certainly did not intend to get you fired, Matt. You believe that don't you?" said Harley

"I don't know what to think," Matt said in frustration. "We need the income and insurance."

"Cedric called you, didn't he? Does he need to worry about being fired too?"

"No, he went into the janitor closet, about the only place they didn't put cameras and microphones, and called me from in there."

"Smart man," said Harley, "I didn't know if he understood that I might be able to help you."

"Help me, how?"

"I can help you alright. I am retired from B. and W. - Belfort & Williams Construction. You've heard of them?"

"Built the Thomas – Vinson wing addition?"

"Yes, I didn't have anything to do with that project but I know the man that did. Jerry has some pull with the Board of Regents, I'll give him a call. Can't promise anything, but it could get you reinstated, maybe with back pay."

"Great!" Matt's attitude toward Harley improved greatly.

"And," Harley added feeling full of himself, "if he can't do anything then I can probably get you on at B&W."

They moved their meeting from the Nut Hut to a Waffle House two miles down the road. No one paid them any attention as the two had the Bert's Blue Plate Special, the famous Chili Cheeseburger with a side of Chili Cheese Hash-browns. The meal is the one doctors warn people not to eat. "There is enough cholesterol fat to choke all of Harpursville", Harley advised Matt.

"Spruill was working late the night Eckland died?" inquired Harley.

"That's what he told the investigators. I was called in to help get the hallway cleaned up and ready to open for school on Monday."

"So it happened on a Friday night?"

"Yep," said Matt partly choking on the mouthful of cheeseburger. "Friday night," he repeated when he stopped for air. "I got called in about 1:00 a.m. and they said the fire occurred around 10:00. Funny thing is the place is usually as quiet as a graveyard on a Friday night. No classes."

"No reason for the two of them to be there at 10:00 at night?" Harley was not asking a question as much as making an observation.

Matt realized that Harley might just share in his suspicion that all was not up and up in Dr. Eckland's death, and said as much.

"These guys often stay late during the week, grading papers and such, but never on a Friday night. Dr. Eckland is usually the first one in and the last one out. Dr. Spruill is the opposite," said Matt.

"Why do you suppose the Professor was using a heater?" asked Harley. "What time of year was it?"

"March 26," answered Matt. "You said before that the fire could burn itself out?"

"If the room is tight enough, where fresh air cannot enter fast enough to sustain combustion," answered Harley. "Question now comes why a grown man could not escape a burning extension cord?"

"Coroner's report says Dr. Eckland probably did see the fire. He started for the door but tripped and knocked himself out on his glass desk top."

"Glass desk top?" asked Harley, "Why would the coroner say that?"

"Dr. Eckland's desk had one of those glass tops. Coroner said Dr. Eckland may have gotten up in a panic, tripped, fell and hit his head and was knocked unconscious. Then the smoke got him."

Damn tempered glass thought Harley, but this hitting his head did not sit right with him. It was possible to die of inhalation but the smoke rarely gets thick enough to kill someone on the floor. The cold fresh air runs into the fire to replace the hot rising air. Harley knew from firsthand experience, that you can breathe in a room full of fire and smoke if you keep your nose on the carpet.

"Did you see Uncle Willy's body?" asked Harley.

"No," said Matt, "they had taken his body away before I arrived to secure the room."

"So you did not see where he hit, what part of his skull he hit?"

"No."

"Was the glass top intact?" Harley continued with the examination, "was it broken?"

"I didn't really notice. I was busy cleaning up the boxes and stuff damaged in the fire. But when we moved the furniture out next week, the top was gone. "

"Gone?"

"Yeah. I don't know who would have taken the table top," said Matt.

"So, Spruill and William were there on Friday night. Anyone else see the two together?"

"If anybody did it would have probably been," Matt stopped and considered who might have seen the pair. "Security! Security would have any video tapes of the two."

"They might have video of when the fire started too," said Harley.

"They could have but with it happening over six months ago," Matt's voice trailed off when he considered that the video might not exist.

"The investigator would have asked for it, right?" again said Harley as an observation.

"Yea, the fire investigator asked if there was a tape that night, I remember."

"And was there?"

"Yes, Curtis went to get it."

"Curtis?"

"Curtis in security, he was on that night."

Matt looked nervously about the restaurant for a face he might recognize, and finding none returned to his Blue Plate Special. It was getting cold.

Chapter 14

"*Dominus Dommo Deus tego texi tecium quod patrocinor nos pro nostrum concillo est iustus. Nomen of Sanctus Abbas - Sanctus Filius - Sanctus Phasmatis-ahmen,*" pronounced his eminence. "May the Lord God protect and defend us for our cause is just. In the name of the Holy Father, Holy Son, and Holy Ghost, Amen."

"Now James, what can you tell us about these people?" asked the reverend Fellwater, "the Macklin's, is it?"

It was Wednesday evening and all was quiet once again as the temple's back door had opened admitting three men from the parking lot.

"Again, I must remind all of you to keep what we say here within these walls," Spruill instructed the gathering. His was a dark and foreboding mood.

"Before we hear from H.R." he said nodding to Bagnilla, I have something to tell you. "Macklin is on the path to discovering who may have had something to do with Dr. Eckland's death."

No one moved at this announcement. Their eyes shifted nervously around at each other, except for His Grace. He sat looking somewhat perplexed at the reaction to this news.

"What makes you say that?' asked Bagnilla as he exchanged looks with Spruill and nodded towards the priest, "I mean what would we have to do with an accident?"

"Curtis says Macklin has been talking to Matt Turncock, a former maintenance man in my building," said Spruill. "They met after Harley came to me asking about the documents he left. Curtis saw the two together, I called Matt for a brief chat. He said Macklin was interested in Eckland's death. They met again two days ago."

"So? How did Harley find Matt? I thought you got him fired?" H.R. asked.

"I did, but Curtis you tell them."

Curtis pulled a black leather bound notebook from his right shirt pocket, flipped it opened and turned to the page with his entry and began to read; "On September 23rd at approximately 2:48 p.m., I saw one Harley Macklin enter the building by the emergency stairwell," reported Curtis. "We can't lock the stair doors during office hours. Seems the professors like to take the stairs for exercise," he explained. "Nevertheless, Harley was seen entering Dr. Eckland's old office and spoke briefly with Cedric saying he was looking for Matt. Mr. Cedric Alexander informed Mr. Macklin of Mr. Turncock's dismissal. He also informed him that he took Matt's place. Mr. Alexander said he only spoke to Mr. Macklin because Mr. Macklin represented himself as a sub-contractor to the school. He told Mr. Alexander that he was there to bid on some re-modeling."

Curtis paused for any questioning, but there being none continued. "At approximately 3:00 p.m. I saw the aforementioned Mr. Macklin leaving the emergency stairwell. I followed Mr. Macklin to the Nut Hut Coffee Shop, whereupon approximately thirty minutes later Matt Turncock, ex Gilbert University maintenance technician, did enter the Nut Hut Coffee Shop. Seven minutes later the two left for a Waffle House located at the corner of Grady and Mills Avenue. They were there long enough to eat Bert's Daily Blue Plate Special."

"Thank you Curtis for that detailed report," said Spruill.

"Did they see you?" asked Bagnilla.

"I don't think so," answered Curtis.

"James you said you thought..." said Bagnilla with his voice trailing off.

"Well, I just thought with him having another meeting with Matt ..." Spruill stopped and asked Curtis, "how long did the two meet?"

"Little more than an hour."

"Having the Blue Plate Special, one could normally be in and out in say 30 – 40 minutes?" Bagnilla said. Everyone, save His Holy Eminence, had eaten at a Waffle House at some point in their lives. Bagnilla practically lived in one.

"So they were there too long for just lunch," said Spruill.

Curtis replied that they sat there as the waitress poured and re-poured their cups several times.

It was Bagnilla's turn. He was carrying a manila folder, heavy, thick, spilling over with the pages inside. He withdrew four stapled collated copies of his report on the background of Harley and Jackie. His report included the original background information about the couple he had given Spruill on Sunday.

"Spelunking?" Ask Dr. Fellwater.

"It is the exploration of caves, your Grace," explained Spruill.

"Do these people have the Codex?" asked his eminence.

"I believe they may have Eckland's entire collection or at least know someone who does."

"Did you offer to purchase the documents?" Dr. Fallwater was focused on obtaining the Codex through legal means.

"Mr. Macklin and I talked again. He was quite unwilling to divulge how much of the Codex was in his possession," said Spruill.

"But you think he has the documents?"

"Very much, Your Grace."

The question before the group was how did these two with no apparent connection to Dr. Eckland, come into possession of the Codex. The discussion included possible shared contacts which led nowhere. No church, social, club or other contacts were ever made between Dr. Eckland, his friends and the Macklins or their friends or family. Finally Spruill spoke up to ask Bagnilla if he had any clue where the pair could have been on the night of Dr. Eckland's death?

Bagnilla did not know the answer but would pursue the proposal that maybe they had some sort of accidental meeting with the Doctor as he was in the act of hiding the Codex just before he died.

"But why did they wait until now to come looking for the school's authentication?" said Curtis. "Why didn't they just put the box on eBay or something?"

"We were the closest and only university in Atlanta qualified to test and authenticate such important documents," noted Spruill. "I am beginning to believe that they are near the collection, and that they know Dr. Eckland once owned them."

Meanwhile, Bagnilla was pouring over his dossier. "I have something," he announced.

Chapter 15

"You just don't call up the police and accuse someone of murder," cautioned Jackie as she stirred the pan of chicken Marcellus.

"Why not?" asked Harley. His mind had been stirring thoughts since his meeting with Matt. Why did an appliance with an unblemished record of safety have its extension cord overheat and catch fire? Why was the heater running when the building heat was on? Why would the doctor not know how to get out of his office? Why didn't it surprise him that Spruill was involved? Why were they both working so late on a Friday night?"

"Could have been having some sort of meeting," Jackie tendered when Harley mentioned the last thought out loud. "Wash up and sit down, it's almost ready."

"Why can't I call someone at the police department and ask them to re-open the case?"

"Well, for one thing, their own coroner has ruled it an accidental death from smoke inhalation."

"The professor should not have died of smoke inhalation," said Harley.

"That would be contrary to the autopsy and fire investigator's reports," Jackie explained. "They would have had to agree on the C.O.D. before issuing a Death Certificate. Trust me Harley Macklin, I was in the business for 30 years. That's how it's done. He was old - he was in a fire - he hit his head. End of story. Now sit down, supper is ready."

"He was old, but that does not mean he was in poor health. He was in a fire of a suspicious nature. How hard did he hit his head?"

"Hard enough to knock himself out."

"Can you do that?" asked Harley.

"Oh, yes, happens all the time, it's called a concussion." Her tone had now begun to rise just a bit. Her authority and expertise was being called into question by her own spouse.

Harley sat slowly stirring the remainders of his basil and olive oil coated capellini. He had not been paying much attention to his nightly news programs. War and taxes held no interest tonight.

"What is it?" Jackie asked observing his mood.

"The autopsy report," he slowly asked. "Would an autopsy have been routine in the case of accidental death, right?"

"Not if the severity of the accident was enough to cause death, and you look at the person's age and health and circumstances, in this case a fire," Jackie explained. She was the one that processed the numbers, causes, natures, diseases that cause death in the population. She knew how the system worked.

"Look Harley, Dr. Eckland was what seventy, eighty when he died? He was found on the floor of his burned out office. You could look on the bright side and say at least he could not have suffered for long." She hated herself for saying it the moment it got out. "Start brain before engaging mouth," she thought.

"If he was so lucky then why is he dead?" was Harley's retort.

"Can we look at the just the facts?" asked Harley. "They go like this." At this he began to make his case before the judge. "Electric space heaters have been sitting around offices, homes, garages, for years heating away with no problems. These things don't just catch fire unless they have been damaged ... or tampered with. Dr. Eckland should not have needed heat that night as the building heating system was running. Smoke from a fire will draw fresh air from under the door, from cracks around windows, from the air conditioning ducts all going to a fire that should have started on the carpet. The fresh air, being colder and heavier than the rising hot air, should have kept a live person still breathing ... alive on the floor. Your case," said Harley ending his points.

"I don't have access to all the facts in the case," was her retort. She could only go on what the investigators on site the night the death occurred for her rebuttal. "The coroner, the fire marshal, the police all said it was accidental."

"How do you know what is in the autopsy report? All Boo has is the Death Certificate, right?"

"Yes, and I don't know what is in the autopsy report," she replied, "but I can sure find out."

"How will you do that, ask for one? I thought that kind of stuff was kept secret until the person had been dead for 30 years? Like the presidents."

She answered with a sly tone of inference about how she might be retired but her friends still worked at the CDC and some at the Health Department downtown. "I have my ways. Three phone calls usually puts you in touch with anyone."

"Not if it is the insurance company," Harley sharply said. I can get the fire investigators report. I'll be right back." he said as he headed out the back door.

The house phone rang. Jackie look puzzled at the caller id as it was from Harley's cell phone. She answered and it was him calling her from the workshop.

"How lazy can you be?" she asked.

"If this doesn't show you," he answered. "You will want to come to the shop."

They had built a combination workshop - green house in the back yard. She could do some gardening while he did his puttering around. Entering the side door, she saw Harley standing by the electric outlet on his workbench. He held an extension cord plug in his hand ready to stick it into the outlet. The other end of the orange extension cord ran to power a space heater Jackie had been using to keep her small green house warm during winter nights. He had taken the heater's electric cord, split the cord in the middle, laid bare the two parallel wires, which would cause a short circuit and spark. He then laid the split cord on a carpet sample where he had placed a few drops of mineral spirits - the stuff cigarette lighters use to burn.

"What are you doing to my heater?" she exclaimed.

"Watch this."

He then pushed the plug into the outlet. Immediately, a spark rose from the center of the carpet where the extension cord crossed the carpet. Flames began to erupt almost as fast. Then the carpet began to smolder as the fire continued to emit a foul toxic odor.

"God!" exclaimed Jackie as fumes touched her nose. "That stinks. Did you blow up my heater?" she was as hot as the fire before her.

"That is how you can do it and make it appear to be an accident."

"Do what?" asked Jackie as she reached for the button that would start the garage door opener. The fumes were reaching toxic levels. Harley had just squatted to his knees and continued to watch his handiwork.

"Make an extension cord appear to be defective and catch the carpet on fire." He was fairly beaming at his successful science experiment. "You can't just squirt lighter fluid on a floor and set fire to it. Fire burn pattern will be suspicious, starting an arson investigation. You need a plausible point of ignition. When in doubt, they blame the electrical system! Shove some file boxes against the cord and bang, there is your fire."

"OK so you have proved it can be done. Uncle Willy still hit his head on the way out of the room. That was ruled an accident."

"You have seen how bad the stuff smells, the burning nylon carpet stinks." Harley said "He could not have stayed in the room for long. The moment the fire started it should have run him out of the room, if he was still alive."

They paused and watched the fire die down as the carpet was fire rated for office buildings and would not sustain the flame once the lighter fluid burned off. With this revelation, Harley said in subdued tones, "An investigation would have revealed the use of accelerants in starting the fire. Blame the electrical system indeed."

"We need that coroner's report," said Jackie.

Chapter 16

Phone rang in the Bristow home around 7:00 p.m. Wednesday night. Eudora put down the crochet dollies she was making for the church yard sale. She took off her crochet reading glasses and, laying them to one side, put on her reading glasses. She also had a cooking pair, and a cleaning pair.

"Hello, Bristow residence," she said when she finally picked up the receiver.

"Mrs. Bristow?"

"Yes."

"Boo this is Jackie, Jackie Macklin," she paused to see if Boo remembered her.

"Who?"

"Jackie Macklin from Harpursville, near Atlanta. We, my husband Harley and I, stopped by Aunt Barbara's house," she did not have time to finish, Boo cut her off.

"Well yes it is! Dr. Jackie, how are you doing? Didn't expect to hear from you so soon. You know I have a flair up of bursitis in my elbow, can you tell me what I need to take for it? I have some B/C powders here but I can get daddy to go get me something else. Or, I have Tylenol, Ascriptin, Bayer, Bufferin, Ecotrin, Advil, Motrin, and Aleve. And I got something Dr. Samuels gave me last time it flared up. I also got some Vioxx, some Anaprox and something called Celebrex and one called Lodine."

Good God thought Jackie. She knew Harley's parents owned a pharmacist's nightmare of drugs that were out of date, out of use and over prescribed - medications that should have been thrown away years ago. She had not "treated" patients since completing her residency and was not about to "treat" one via telephone. In any case Boo had stopped at that question in vain hope that the good doctor would have a cure.

"Well," Jackie said not knowing how to proceed, "Boo, I just wanted to call and see if you had had time to find those names we asked about?" With that she dodged the medical question by tossing out a curve ball.

"Honey, I came straight home and pulled out the book of remembrances for Aunt Barbara's funeral and found those people's names right off. Let me see if I can remember what I did with them."

Jackie heard sounds of papers being shuffled and drawers being opened as Boo must be searching for her notes.

"Honey? You still there?"

"Yes Boo take your time. How have ya'll been?" Jackie winced at this forgetting that this might clue Boo into re-asking about how to treat her bursitis. Luckily, Boo either did not hear her or was distracted by the hunt.

"We are getting along just … wait, here it is. Jackie heard a drawer being closed.

"Caudelle and Gill DeLauzun of Deep Springs, Georgia. Never heard of Deep Springs. Have you?"

"It is a community in North Atlanta, not far from Kennesaw State University. I don't suppose they left a phone number?" This in a book of remembrances would be asking for too much good luck.

"No honey, do you need me to try to find one for them?"

"No. Thank you, Boo. I will find the name in the Atlanta phonebook. DeLauzun can't be that common a name. Maybe he works at the college?"

"It could be."

"Boo, would you mind mailing me that book? I would really like to see who else might have signed that book at the funeral. It could help us trace the owner of Uncle Willy's box of documents." It was Chrysippus's decree, for sure and Jackie had no problem telling such small lies in the course of pulling information from people, as long it was for their own good.

"Sure thing Honey. What is your address?"

Jackie took a little time relaying the information across the phone lines between Harpursville and Tallahatchie, Alabama. She ended with an offer to pay the postage. Boo would have none of it if it meant returning Uncle Willy's box to the rightful owner.

"Boo one more thing before I go."

"Anything you want honey."

"Boo did you say the coroner mailed you a death certificate for Uncle Willy?"

"Yes, Aunt Barbara being his only known next of kin, it was sent to her. So I got it in her mail."

"Boo, would you mind very much sending that paper or a copy of it along with the box?"

"Why? Whatever for?" The tone in Boo's voice was not one of indignation, more of a curiosity.

Jackie realized that she might have overplayed her hand at this request. She wanted to see for herself the report. Also, she did not want to unduly raise Boo's suspicions and get her upset at the possibility that her Uncle Willy was a victim of foul play. Boo might ask for a new autopsy when one was not needed.

"Just a copy will do, in case we need it to show anyone that Uncle Willy is dead," Jackie winced at this white lie as well.

"I will send it all along tomorrow. Now what medicine did you say I should be taking for my bursitis, the B-C powder or the Tylenol, Honey?"

Chapter 17

H.R's announcement now had the attention of all in the room. He had been studying the illegally obtained credit card statements of Harley and Jackie Macklin going back to 2008.

"They recently returned from Phoenix, Arizona, through Hamburg, Arkansas to Anniston, Alabama to their home in Harpursville," Bagnilla said.

"How do you know that?" asked Curtis.

"They stopped at the Bayou Crossett State Park in Arkansas the night of September 11th. They stopped at the Studs and Spuds on Highway 82 in Hamburg, Arkansas, where they purchased $148.32 in regular gasoline, that's around 42 gallons of gas."

"Forty two gallons?" Spruill asked to confirm the volume.

"They own a motor-coach ... an RV," said Bagnilla as he continued. "They also purchased groceries to the tune of $23.89 for a total of $172.21 charged on 12, September, 2009 at 9:36 a.m. The next charge was at Columbus, Mississippi some place called the Witwell's Antiques Mall, again on U.S. Highway 82 for an unspecified item in the amount of $42.89. They stayed at Oak Mountain State Park near Birmingham, Alabama the night of September 12. They had breakfast at Fast Eddie's Restaurant in Hoover, Alabama. There was a stop at the Kwick Mart on Gardner Road in Pell City, Alabama later that morning. There was a purchase made at the Old Mill Mall in Oxford. They had dinner at Jo-Joe's Seafood in Anniston, Alabama on the Black Warrior Parkway. One meal was the AUCE Platter, all you can eat platter I suppose, the other was Grilled Chicken with garden salad. They had one Zinfandel wine, one Corona."

"I thought Columbus, was in Alabama. Isn't that near Columbus, Georgia?" asked Spruill.

"Phenix City is in Alabama, across the river from Columbus, Georgia," said Curtis. "They stopped in Columbus, Mississippi."

Spruill quickly googled a map search for Pell City, Alabama. There along U.S. 78 and Interstate 20, sat a small insignificant Alabama town between the Anniston, Alabama, and Pell City. Spruill's eyes went wide. He recognized the town immediately - Lincoln, Alabama.

"Their route ran right past Barbara's house." No one spoke at this revelation. "William's wife, or his ex-wife ... her home was in Lincoln," Spruill said incredulously.

"You don't suppose he hid the Codex there?" asked Bagnilla once they caught Spruill's message.

"What do you think?" Spruill asked. "It's about two, maybe two and a half hours from here. That would be a five hour round trip."

At this Curtis spoke up to inform the group that Dr. Eckland did not get in his office until late that fateful afternoon. "He is usually the first one in the door every morning."

"Couldn't you check Eckland's credit card statements, see if he charged anything along the way the morning before ... " Spruill asked.

"Very well could. I'll do that tomorrow morning when I get in the office," answered Bagnilla.

The discussion then went into the next phase, the recovery of the Codex. His Eminence continued to ask about a possible purchase. The rest were discussing other means to obtain the box.

"Run a complete background check on Eckland as you did on the Macklins. Shake the tree, see what falls out. His estate had to go somewhere, or to someone. He may have left his property to the Macklin's," said Spruill.

"Who was his beneficiary from the schools life insurance?" asked Bagnilla

"I'll find out." said Spruill.

Chapter 18

"Dr. DeLauzun?" asked a startled Harley as he put down the peppermint hot chocolate he had been sipping. What startled him was the man was one of the three in the photograph he and Jackie had seen at Aunt Barbara's. The good doctor agreed to meet Harley earlier that day. Harley suggested the Nut Hut and asked how he could identify him? Gill said he was six feet tall, brown hair, and wearing a red flat golfer style cap. It would not be hard to spot a red dot on a six foot man. Harley had been trying to compose a limerick based on the red hat and Gill, but was finding that the muse was not with him.

"You can call me Gill," said the good doctor, "and you are Harley?"

"Harley Macklin," he said as he stood to take Gill's hand, "and allow me to introduce my wife, Dr. Jackie Macklin. Good of you to see us."

"You said you were friends of William's? How did you know him?"

Jackie was the first to speak. She felt she could better ease into the transgression they had committed.

"I will have to admit that we never met Dr. Eckland, and for that I must apologize. I got your name from Eudora Bristow ... Boo Bristow. She is why I am here."

"Boo?" Gill was a bit surprised. "Is everything OK, and who are you?"

Jackie explained that during their travels they had gone through Pell City and Lincoln, Alabama where they stopped at Boo's estate sale.

"Once she got to talking there was no stopping her," Jackie said, "Boo has told us about Dr. Eckland's sudden accidental death."

"That's Boo, talks on and on. How's she doing?"

"Boo is doing well," Jackie said. "I spoke to her recently that's how I got your name."

"Your phone number I got from the school's webpage," said Harley.

"Then why didn't you make an appointment with my secretary?" Gill's voice was getting a little edgy. "I get this call from you about William's estate, then, you won't come to my office. I can't come to yours. What is this all about? Why all the cloak and dagger?"

"As I said I am here on behalf of a matter that relates to Boo," said Jackie.

At this point Gill was losing patience with the couple's vagueness. Harley and Jackie decided earlier, that, until Gill mentioned the Codex, they would not bring it up either. Harley wanted to wait and see. He was wondering if anyone else had seen the big white file box.

"I know that you and Dr. Eckland were close. You went to Aunt Barbara's funeral and saw her in the nursing home. You and Caudelle were close to the Eckland's," said Jackie ending the statement.

Gill was still guarded but said they were close to the truth.

"I know that his death came as a shock," Jackie said "but did you think the way he died, the smoke inhalation, the fire and all, wasn't that in some way a bit odd?"

"Odd? How do you mean, odd?"

Harley broke into the conversation and began to lay out the points he made to Jackie about the events surrounding the night of the fire. Why did an otherwise healthy man, on a night with the school's heat running, need to run his own electric heater? Why was he unable to find his way out of his own office? Why was he there so late?

"I had the same questions," Gill admitted, "but the coroner said William hit his head in a hurry to get out of the office. I did have some suspicions about why William would be running a heater. He liked the office on the cold side. Students would complain to me about how cold it was sitting in his office for conferences. His running the heater on that night was odd. You never saw his office?"

Taking Gill's question as rhetorical, they merely sat with blank expressions.

"The way he had boxes of papers and files laying about, no wonder he could trip trying to get out. I have tripped trying to get in," at that he gave a little chuckle. "I never understood the fire. Why was there enough smoke to kill William, but not enough fire to consume his office and all the furniture?"

Once again, Harley the fire inspector explained how fire behaves in a closed space. Gill understood immediately.

"What do you remember about that day?" Jackie asked. "Was there anyone who had ill feelings against Dr. Eckland?"

"No one that I can name," Gill answered. "It was a Friday. I came in for half a day that morning; I had some papers to grade. I looked in on William when I got there, wanted to see if he was up to going to a concert Saturday evening. Atlanta Symphony was to perform Beethoven's Ninth. It was his favorite. I have season tickets. Queer thing was he was not in his office that morning. I did check on him when I left just after noon but he still wasn't in.

"Did he have any other health conditions, or problems say with his heart?" Dr. Macklin wanted to know.

"Nothing I was aware of. We were entering charity runs and races. We did the Peachtree last July and wanted to sign up for 2010."

"Did he have any prescription medication - was he taking any cough medicines?"

"No. Like I said he was in good health. He had a check up and his shots before he went to Syracuse in August, just before the semester started."

"You need inoculations to go to Syracuse, New York?" asked a skeptical Harley.

"Sicily," explained Gill, "Syracuse, Sicily, on the east coast of the island," said Gill.

"Sicily?" asked Jackie. "If he was going out of the country, he would have to have had his Hepatitis A and B, tetanus – diphtheria booster and rabies vaccination. Typhoid and polio vaccines would not have been a bad idea. Those should not have caused him any problems. He might have come into contact with tick borne encephalitis. Not common in Italy but we were having some cases reported. Do you know how he got to Syracuse? What route?"

"Flew to Paris, then to Rome," replied Gill. "From there he caught a commuter flight to Palermo. He said he drove the Autostrada del Sole to San Giovanni. From there he took the ferry to Syracuse."

"He could have contracted Malaria that would account for feeling chilled and possibly fainting ... May have caught cholera."

"But he wasn;t sick when I last saw him," replied Gill, "he only looked tired."

"The Typhoid vaccination might have caused some arrhythmia, possibly a heart problem. But that would have happened on the way, not after he returned."

They sat for a moment with their thoughts when Gill spoke up to emphasize, "I don't think he was sick, only tired, like he had not slept well. He never said anything about a fever or anything," said Gill. "What do we do now?" he asked and, after taking a long pause, ventured the question, "do we go to the police and tell them we think William's death ... wasn't an accident?"

"You cannot go around just accusing anyone of murder," said Harley before Jackie could gather her words.

Jackie gave him an incredulous glance. "We are just asking around. Once we feel like we have enough probable cause we will go to the district attorney and ask him to reopen the case. Thank you for your time, Gill, We will let you know if we find anything."

Chapter 19

"Well, we know where the Codex came from," Jackie said once they were in Harley's truck. "Syracuse, Italy."

"And we know who once owned it, that Saint Louis Cardinal Greg Asbestos fellow," added Harley.

"But that was in 1056. I doubt he is still the legal owner," Jackie reminded him. "Should we see if the monastery is still there? Maybe Eckland did steal the box."

"We agreed that 'Uncle Willy' wasn't a thief."

"Well yeah, but ..." she said.

"Well but maybe they gave the Codex to the professor to study and authenticate. Maybe they were afraid that someone would steal it and sell it. Maybe he bought it at some other estate sale."

"Now you are being silly," Jackie said.

"Once we figure out what is in these journals, then maybe we will know why Uncle Willy was murdered for them. Right now these are just the musing of some long dead Roman womanizer."

The rest of the ride home was filled with possible scenarios and theories about how Uncle Willy came to possess the Codex. At one point Harley forwarded the idea that Uncle Willy wasn't the culprit that hid the box in the shed, it was a total stranger that knew the house was empty.

"Harley, I have another journal entry translated, do you want to see it?"

Harley put down his New York Times Sunday Magazine and went to her office. She was sitting at her desk watching the Black Capped Nuthatch pecking at the bird feeder outside her window. Most of the feeder birds had gone to warmer climates, but not the chirping Nuthatch.

"What is our boy up to now?" asked Harley.

"Some of these pages are letters from his mother wishing him well. Some are from his sister. But here is another entry about his stay in Antioch." With that she gave him her legal pad which bore her notes.

Harley began to read:

Dies Iovis xxix Martius Thursday 29 March

Bacchus has let loose his hold upon on my brain, my limbs have found their strength and their vigor in Strenua. Fabulinus has restored my tongue. Juventas has restored me after two days of the celebrations of Bacchus and Liber Pater. I have done all that I could to appease and honor Bona Dea, Consus, Conditor, and Faustitas with sacrifices of the fruits, and of the grains, and of the honey and of the olives of our farm and with the temple priestess. I carried my family argie in the processional following the phallus of Liber through the town. There I tossed it on the pyre built to send sacrifices and the prayers with the

*argie to Mount Olympus. My prayer is that Numa
be pleased with my argie and the celebration.*

*Achaicus has lead me to the Prosopeion of
Charonion. Achaicus says it has been here when
he was a boy. He says his father told him it was
the great and wise seer, Leios who said the
Charonion would protect the city. His uncle said
it was ordered by the ancient King Antiochus of
the Seleucids. The most favored goddess Demeter
sits on his right shoulder with her calathus filled
with her bounty of grains and fruit. I laid a
wreath of braided ears of corn on her head in
hopes that she will bless our crops.*

*We went to house of my Uncle Elias. He told me
a story of the time he put a frog in mother's milk.
He had captured a frog and brought it home.
When grand-mother called to him, he did not want
her to find him holding a frog in the home as it
would bring the bad luck. He dropped the animal
into the closest pitcher at hand. Unfortunately for
his sister, it was the pitcher the maidservant had
just brought from the cow. The maidservant
poured my mother a cup of milk. He did not
acknowledge the existence of the frog. Whereupon
she put the cup to her lips and begin to drink until
the deceased frog touched her lips. She spied the
carcass and with a scream that could be heard on
Mount Olympus, she did fling the cup across the
room smashing the container on the wall. The
dead frog fell upon the floor. My grand-mother
demanded to know who brought the frog into the
house. "Praise be to the Most Holy God," Elias
said he cried out," for He has sent his prophet*

Moses with the plague of frogs because of the sins of Antioch." Grand-mother was not amused.

I talked more with Uncle Elias. He is a priest in the tabernacle of Antioch and is held in high regard in his community. He instructed me in the ways and beliefs of my mother's people, of the divine deliverance at the hand of his prophet Moses when pursued by Pharaoh's army. He spoke of the many and great battles that the prophet Joshua won against the Philistines. He instructed me in the beliefs of my mother's people and of the never ending and never fading watchfulness of the one true God of whom Elias would not speak His name. He said that the one True God would one day restore the kingdom of His house and His will would be the only law of the land. Elias believed that day was at hand.

Elias said that men of wisdom and learning from ancient eastern lands did pass through here before I was born. They tarried with Elisha only a night for they were in a hurry to leave the land of Palestine. They feared they would be captured by the king Herod and forced to reveal the location of the baby foretold to them by the stars, and who would be the savior that Elias had been praying for.

Only when the breath of Nox crept through the doorway did we realize that Luna was upon us. Uncle Elias said that it would be a hazard to take the roads back into town for there were many robbers and thieves lying in wait upon the roadside. But I was not afraid and asked safe passage of Nemestrinus and for Luna to light the road to Antioch. It was the beginning of the celebration of Quinquatrus but I arrived too late to participate in the procession to the temple of Minerva. I am at home and writing to help me remember all that has been spoken to me about the un-named God. I have heard so many different tongues, and seen so many different men, and passed so many temples that I know not to which god I must sacrifice. I believe that every tongue and every race has a representative in this town that never seems to sleep.

Harley stood looking again at the pages. "King Herod, is this right?"

"Yes, of course it is right. Do you know about this King Herod?" Jackie asked. "Does it give us a date?" She was getting excited at the possibility having found a person from history to give them the author's approximate age.

"Yes!" said Harley nearly shouting. "Herod . . . Herod the Great! The Bible claims he ordered the killing of the one year old males at the time of Christ."

"That King Herod?" asked Jackie. "But it reads that these wise men passed through Antioch, stayed with Elias for a night, before Jesus was born. Before our author was born."

"Yes, but while in the life time of Elias, his uncle, brother to his mother, which means the boy was alive very near the ministry of Christ." Harley was nearly shouting. "Did you check that part about the wise men passing through Antioch?"

"You mean the part about 'men of wisdom and learning from ancient eastern lands did pass through here before I was born'? Yes I saw that and went over it again. '*Sapiens quod antiquus ex Orientales*'. *Sapiens* meaning man, *quod* meaning wise, *antiquus* meaning ancient, *ex* of the east was referred to as the Orient or *Orientales*."

"Jackie, did you translate this correctly?" His finger was on a section that stood out to her as well, 'the baby foretold to them by the stars?'"

"*Infantia predico sibimet per astrum,* "she said." Infant predicted to them per or by a star."

"And what about this?" His finger shifted only slightly along the line. "*Quod exsisto - nuntius - ut – Elias – fueram - precor – pro.*

"And - would be - the savior – that - Elias - had been - praying – for," Jackie quoted.

They took a long pause. Harley put down the notepad.

"Was this man alive at the time of Christ?" asked Jackie.

"The man could have very well been," said Harley.

"But the documents could not have been written at that time," Jackie said. "He may well have been Roman. He was well educated. His step-father was well off and seems to have been a Roman citizen. His mother was a Jew. They would have spoke mostly in the Aramaic Greek. He was born in Tarsus, went to Antioch for a while. He would have written in Greek. Latin was not in common use until 300 a.d. Our man did not write these letters."

"But, what if someone else translated them from Greek to Latin?" asked Harley.

Jackie mulled this thought over for a moment. "Yes, that makes sense. The original author, the one that went to Antioch and got wasted, he would have written his journal in Greek. Someone in maybe the third or fourth century translated the journal into these Latin documents."

"Then the Codex made its way to Syracuse and then to Cardinal Gregory Asbestos in 1056," said Harley, "then on to Dr. Eckland last summer."

"Gregorios Asbestas," she said to correct him. "You mean these pages could be 1,600 years old?"

"If not fakes . . . yes."

"What is this *Prosopeion of Charonion*?" Jackie asked.

"It's an ancient carving of a face overlooking the city of Antioch. No one knows who did it or why, until now. It's near the tomb of Saint Peter but has no connection to it. Something of a tourist attraction back then," said Harley.

"We need to figured out why the good doctor was hiding these books in his tool shed," Jackie noted.

"And, from whom," said Harley. "I did like that story about how his uncle put the frog in his mother's milk.

"Why?" she asked with misgiving.

Harley smiled and began to recite,

"A boy once brought home to his folk,
  a frog he did hide in his cloak.
  Then placed it in a pitcher,
  from which drank his sister,
    and blamed Moses for the practical joke."

"Oh, God," said Jackie and pushed him out the door.

Chapter 20

"Mr. H.R. Bagnilla is here to see you," said Patti into her speaker phone.

"Send him in," said Spruill.

Once again the door to Spruill's office closed behind Bagnilla and things that others should not hear were blocked from leaving the room.

"What do you have?" asked Spruill.

Bagnilla opened a folder and withdrew pages of credit card transactions. This time, they were for Dr. Eckland.

"Eckland was in Anniston the night of February 28, 2008," he said putting his finger on the top page."

Spruill studied the statement. The entry jumping out at him was one for a gas station on Highway 74. Eckland stopped at Jo-Joe's Seafood on the Black Warrior Highway, same place that the Macklins stopped at in September. Spruill looked as if a bomb had gone off in front of him.

"That son of a bitch," said Spruill. "I'll bet he hid the Codex at Barbara's house. Anniston, Alabama is about a half an hour to Lincoln."

"You mean his ex-wife Barbara?" asked Bagnilla.

"Ex legally not in reality," explained Spruill. "They got together several times a year, always around Thanksgiving or Christmas. It was her family's farm."

"Why would he hide the box there?"

"He knew we would search his home, watch his friends and search his office," said Spruill. "He thought with them being divorced we wouldn't look there. Her having a stroke and being hospitalized he could go to her home as he pleased. I think she died after … he did. I tried to talk some sense into him … begged him to give it to the university for study or let me buy it. But he wouldn't have any of it."

"The Macklin's likely happened upon it by accident then?"

"Someone must have been selling Barbara's estate when the Macklins bought the Codex," Spruill agreed.

"Do you think they knew what they were buying?" ventured Bagnilla.

"If they did, then why did they bring it to me for authentication? There must have been something or someone that led them to come to see me. They found it accidentally."

"Well they are asking around about you now not before. Something or someone has warned them about you. That's why they are hiding the Codex!" said Bagnilla."We have got to get that Codex and fast before they discover what it is and what it means. How do you want to proceed? Like we did with Eckland?"

"I can't do that again," said Spruill.

"Why not? You did it before," said Bagnilla.

"That was an accident," Spruill said strongly defending himself.

Chapter 21

"Package for you," said Harley as he came in with the day's mail. "Looks like it came from Boo."

"I'm in my office," Jackie told him, "Would you bring it in here, please? I saw Waldon over in Public Health and asked him to get me the M.E.'s autopsy report on Eckland." She had been studying it between translating the Codex, gardening and doing some of the general housework.

"What's in it?" asked Harley.

"I haven't had time to go over all of it, but there are some things that raise more doubt. I finished another page in the Codex. This one has some more names in it that I think you might find interesting. She pulled her yellow pad from under Boo's envelope and began to read to Harley.

Dies Lunae xviii Maius or 18 May or May 18,

Three days have passed since we were delivered by the grace of the God of Achaicus. The One True God, creator of all the earth and everything upon it. It was but four days ago that we set our sail to take advantage of the fair west wind given us by Favonius. We saw favoring skies and seas. Once upon the deep of Neptune he did send Tempestas to drown us and all our crew. The gods no longer favored us. I and Claudio began to burn frankincense upon the alter of our Actaean ship. We entreated the gods in our behalf. The seas grew angrier. The captain called for all crew to toss the cargo overboard that we might lighten the ship and be saved. Together, Claudio, I and Achaicus tossed our cargo to the waves. 35 amphorae's of wine, the crated Ferula galbaniflua just arrived from Persia. Jars of Judean Honey, even the new monopodium of Egyptian Cedar I bought for mother, all went to Mercury with no avail. We cried out to Salacia that we three were unprotected in number. My father, myself and my servant were without strength. We were begging for refuge and sanctuary in the City of Mrya harbor. Four times did we call out to Triton, Oceanid, Albion, Benthesicyme, Charybdis and Rhodes worshiping them with our prayers at the altar on the puppis. We gave all our frankincense to Tethys. Yet there was no harbor for our anchor.

Four times did we give offerings into Amphitrite seas. I cried out to Thanatos and Hypnos asking shall the birds stand upon my unburied bones on the shores? Will there be no hand to close my eyes? Will my mournful soul go into foreign heavens? And will no friendly hand anoint my body laid out? I cried out to Phrxus, bring his golden sheep and woolly fleece to bear me over the stormy seas. But there was no shore.

As the waves broke over our bows and all appeared lost, Achaicus stood upon the deck and with arms upraised did cry out to the One True God, "Eli, Eli, where is thy aid and comfort! Eli,

Eli, there is none like you O, Lord; you are great and your name is great in your might! Only the fool does not fear your wrath and power! For among all the nations this is your due and in all their kingdoms there is none like you. Yet you, O Lord, are in the midst of us and will leave us not. Calm your waters that we may pass in peace." And at once the waters grew calm and the wind died down and we could see the shores of Myra and a safe harbor.

I am astonished and humbled by the power of the One True God of Achaicus. I asked him to teach me more of the power and of the compassion of this God of my Mother, and of Elisha. He says he is a poor teacher of such matters but that I should entreat the Pharisee in the Temple of the One True God when I return to Tarsus.

I have gone to see the Seder Elijah Rabbah in the temple here. He shows me how to bless the wine before asking a blessing for the day. He teaches me what is forbidden. That a man may tie up flesh and cheese in the same cloth provided that they do not touch one another. He has instructed me in the teachings of the great Rabban Gamaliel who says: Two passing guests may eat at the same table, the one flesh and the other cheese, without scruple.

This is the path I will take willingly with mother and with Aurelia. We will all go to follow the One True God in love and in peace.

The gods of Olympus have failed me when I was in greatest need. They did not give heed to all my prayer and supplications before my father died. I did all that was required of me, and yet Thetis was absent beyond the prescribed time. These false gods have led I, their creation, away from my true Father. Mother will be pleased that I will renounce my false beliefs. I fear that Claudio will not embrace The One True God as I have and will shun me. Then might I be cast out of his home and from his good favor. I will go to Jerusalem where mother has kinsmen and learn from the Great Gamaliel himself. Blessed is the One True God.

"Are you sure?" asked an astonished Harley, "The Great Gamaliel, is that what it says?"

"Is this a significant name? One that will tell us the date of the journal entry? And what about the Seder Elijah Rabbah? Do you know anything about him?"

"Gamaliel is a well known name in the New Testament," said Harley. "He's the one that had Jesus Christ executed... just a minute," and with that he took off down the hallway to his office. He gathered books from the shelves. Harley pulled down the New Testament study guides, *Introduction to the New Testament, Understanding the New Testament,* and a few others textbooks on the New Testament life and times.

"According to this," Harley said walking into Jackie's office holding a textbook, "there were two Gamaliels the first one and the second one."

"First one and second one," Jackie asked, "like senior and junior?"

"Gamaliel the first," began Harley, "was a leading Rabbi at the end of 100 b.c. Gamaliel the Great was the grandson of Gamaliel the first. But more important to our establishing the author of the Codex is the date of Gamaliel the Great, so called, for he was the leader of the Sanhedrin. The Gamaliel that defended Jesus before the Sanhedrin and later his disciples was, the teacher to Saint Paul."

"But our author is a Roman citizen. You said so yourself, that he was well versed in the Gods of Olympus, his father an established merchant."

"But his mother took him to his bar mitzvah. Read it again. The part about his mother would be pleased."

She re-read the notes picking out the important phrases. *filiolus Olympus deficio mihi*, Gods Olympus failed me. *Matris mos commodo quo EGO mos abdico meus reproba fides,* mother – will – pleased – that – I – will – renounce – my – false – beliefs."

"He has converted to Judaism," Harley deduced as he sat down beside Jackie.

"Do you know the name Seder Elijah Rabbi?" Jackie asked again. "Does he help us fine our date?"

Harley dug into the index and footnotes of his books for a few minutes. "Got a reference," he nearly shouted. "Seder Elijah Rabbi, an early first or second century rabbi. He composed a compilation of rabbinical wisdom. First Rabbinical reference to the Messiah's claims of both Jesus and Athronges ben Emmaus."

Jackie took hold of her pencil and began to write. Gamaliel 1st - and the Great, Seder Elijah Rabbi – Elias. She was starting a list of the names found in the Codex hoping that Harley could find a common date where all could have been alive in the life of the author. She also wrote 'born a Roman in Tarsus, lived in Antioch, converted to Judaism'. The investigator was composing her suspect list.

"Don't forget the shift of the earth axis around 100 a.d. remember?" said Haley as he watched her write. She put that down also.

"What about Athronges ben Emmaus? When was he alive?" she inquired.

"130 – 136 a.d. or sometimes around there."

"That throws the whole thing off, doesn't it?" observed Jackie, "You said these other men were around 100 b.c. – 100 a.d. right?"

"Ben Emmaus doesn't change a thing," said Harley. "Hey, look here." He pointed to the paragraph of Athronges ben Emmaus in a textbook on the New Testament. Athronges ben Emmaus, rebel leader of Jews around 100 b.c. Claimed to be the Messiah. Ruled the region until Gratus captured and crucified him and his followers."

"That 100 b.c. throws off our dating the Codex," Jackie stated. "When you have Gamaliel the First in 100 b.c. and the Rabbi Elijah writing about Athronges from 100 b.c., there you have it. The Codex is first century b.c. wouldn't you say?"

"Not necessarily," argued Harley as he looked up from his textbooks. "Rabbi Elijah only wrote about Athronges, I never said the two were contemporaries. The good Rabbi could have been writing in the second or even third century. Gamaliel the Great, as we call him today, would have been alive between 40 – 60 a.d. It's not impossible to suspect that Gamaliel and Rabbi Elijah could have been contemporaries along with Jesus. What, or who was that manifest made out to?" asked Harley.

Jackie dug up her initial note pad." *Gaeticulus Calisto Sceundus Paulius,*" she began. "Recieved By *Laurentius Honoratus* scribe to Ship master *Pavlos Akakios',*" she said as her eyes came to rest on the first page of notes. Then she transferred the name to her new list. Harley looked at the spellings for Jackie had left him behind in the pronunciation.

"Jackie," said Harley, "how do Romans know what to call each other, I mean we have a first name, a middle name and our Christian name. Did they do the same?"

"I didn't study ancient Rome and Roman lexicons," she said, "but I think the first name is what you would call a person every day. What his mother or sister would call him. The second name is his father's name and I think the third was the ancestors or clan's name. But having four names, I'm not sure which name his family would call him. I saw a page in the Codex, one sent to him by his mother. She addressed it to her Little Bull, Why?"

"Bull?"

"Yes, *Paulo Taurus*." Jackie told him. "It could be *Paulius*, the little Taurus."

"Are you sure you got that right?" asked Harley in a guarded tone.

"Yes, I'm sure it is *Gaeticulus Calisto Sceundus Paulius,* and his mother called him Little Bull."

"*Paulius*? You are using the Latin spelling?"

"Yes, right from her own words."

"Then he could be Paul … Saint Paul," said Harley in reverence. "You need to start digging for more names,"

There was a long pause as Jackie and Harley took in what he just said.

"And that's why Spruill wants to get his hands on this Codex," an astonished Jackie muttered, "it is priceless."

Chapter 22

Harley fumbled with the pocket knife in the right front pocket of his *Extra* cut blue jeans. With a thumbnail under the blade point he flipped the 5.5 c.m. blade into the open position. The sharp edge ran along the fold in the top of the heavy padded envelope he had retrieved from the mail box. He placed the envelope on Jackie's desk. The long awaited book of remembrances had finally arrived. There too was a copy of the death certificate for Professor William Taylor Eckland. Born August 7th 1934, died October 26th 2008. Cause of death according to the coroner was smoke inhalation after striking his head on the desk top rendering him unconscious.

"Well that is according to the coroner, not the M.E." said Jackie in disgust. "Only the Medical Examiner would have completed an autopsy. That document, along with the fire marshal's report, would render a complete picture of what happened to Dr. Eckland." Expecting this, Jackie had taken some pre-emptive measures on her own accord.

"What did you do?" asked an incredulous Harley.

"Just ran into some old friends," said Jackie coyly.

"And where did you run into these old friends?"

"While strolling the grounds of the CDC," said Jackie. She might have been retired but her co-workers, all of whom respected her, did not seek the greener pastures. "Bennet Bishop thought I still worked there ....asked me if I had gotten his memo on Infectious Diseases of India, the travelers update. I told him 'no', and would he please send a copy to my office and I kept walking."

"Is he the one that everybody convinced there was such a thing as Red Snipe Fever?"

"Let's see who else might be interested in this," Jackie ignored Harley's reference to the hazing the office staff gives new hires, and opened the book of remembrances. She flipped to the page with the names of Caudelle and Gill DeLauzun. Next was Dr. James Spruill.

"Why doesn't that surprise me," said Harley.

Other than Spruill who lived in Atlanta and the DeLausuns that lived in Deep Springs, most hailed from around Sparta, Tallahatchie, and Anniston.

"Why would Spruill be there?" asked Harley out loud to no one or maybe to Jackie for she responded that he might have been there with Gill and Caudelle. "Just felt like he owed it to his former co-worker or something, who really knows."

"Maybe he was looking around for the Codex?" Harley considered. "Maybe he spoke to Boo while he was there. He came alone, did you catch that? What did you find in the M.E.'s report?"

"'Cause of death; pulmonary edema from inhalation of toxic gases and possible concussion," said Jackie as she finished studying the C.O.D. box of the form. "But read this," she said handing the report to Harley.

There he saw the notations about the condition of the cadaver. There was a description of Dr. Eckland's height, weight, and apparent age, evidenced by the graying hair and beard. He was wearing a short sleeve white Arrow shirt, blue wool trousers, a Timex digital watch, black socks, brown leather tennis shoes. Found in his pockets were 78 cents in change, a wallet containing three one dollar bills, two twenties, and a fifty dollar bill. The other pockets had carried car and what could have been house keys. But the note that had caught Jackie's eyes and Harley's as well was the entry, "Contusion and discoloration in the shape of a triangle with the trailing point proximal towards the right ear, as the result of a blow to the upper right quadrant of the victim's forehead. This appears to have been caused when the victim struck the corner of his desk or table. Contusion was *pro mortalitas*"

"*pro mortalitas*?" asked Harley.

"Just before he died."

"But triangle shaped?" asked Harley. "Could he have hit himself on his desk corner to knock himself out?"

"Anything is possible," said Jackie. "Depends on how high a fall you took, general health, several things would be considered. Although, Eckland did not have far to run, or far to fall."

"And which way was he running when he tried to get out of the room?" asked a puzzled Harley.

"Remember that picture Boo showed us of her Uncle Willy, with Spruill and the unknown man?"

"Vaguely," responded Harley.

"I remember the desk, it was a French Provincial Desk, late 19th century style. There were file boxes stacked to the left of the group."

"What are you getting at?" inquired Harley.

"The files were stacked to Eckland's left?" she asked the rhetorical question.

"Yes."

"Then Dr. Eckland would be sitting behind the desk, that night, right?" She was now getting more excited in her statements.

"Yes" agreed Harley but he was falling behind Jackie in her goal shot.

"He would have been walking to his right to get away from the fire." she was now rounding third and could see the home plate.

"Yes," he conceded.

"Then if he tripped on his way to the door, it would have been his left temple that would have struck the desk not his right!" Home run!

"I see it!" exclaimed Harley. "If he was at his desk, then yes, it would have been his left side of the head that he hit, unless he was returning for something or did a 180 turn when he fell."

"Even if he did turn he would have a bruise *pro mortalitus* on the back of the head probably right side," said Jackie.

Harley never the one to take statements at face value wanted to duplicate the cause of the bruise. He motioned

Jackie to get up from her chair. He sat down and said, "Ok, I am Eckland. I have boxes stacked to my left," he said as he pointed to his left. "Are you sure about the boxes?"

"Yes," said Jackie.

"Then I'll wake up,"

"Wake up?" asked Jackie, "Why wake up?"

"If he was awake, he would have smelled and seen the smoke before the carpet caught fire, right?"

"Yes, go ahead Mr. Poirot," said the mystery detective."

"He stands up," said Harley as he moves to the right of her desk. He does a bow to the right and stops his left forehead at the desk's edge.

"The autopsy should have read, 'Bruise on left temple, wouldn't you say?" queried Harley.

"And not have a trailing point towards the right ear," announced Jackie as she read from the report. "If he had turned the point of the desk . . . here turn around."

She took Harley by the shoulder and spun him 180 degrees. "Now mimic a fall back towards the desk edge." He did as he was told. "Then the back of his head would have impacted the desk edge first with possible tearing of the right ear. When you fell to the front your whole forehead should have a bruise or at least the left temple region."

Try as they might, they could not position themselves any other way to mimic the bruise described by the autopsy report.

"I need to call Boo again," said Jackie.

"For what?" asked Harley.

"I want that photo of Uncle Willy, Spruill and Gill. If memory serves me, there was a lamp on the desk."

"I don't remember a lamp," said Harley.

"Yes, there was," said Jackie. "It was an Empire Period bronze lamp. The lampshade was around the shaft of the lamp, not on top like most. There was at least a foot of the lamp above the shade, the fennel was a ring shape. The lamp sat just behind the mystery man to his right. I saw a little over half of the lamp but I am sure I saw one."

"What does a bronze period lamp have to do with ..." but he was cut off by an excited Jackie.

"What it is ...is a lamp that is heavy enough to be a blunt instrument. In addition, the base is square. Four triangle shaped points."

"We need to call Boo," said Harley.

As he flipped through the notepad, he was inspired to compose another Harley'ism.

> There once was a teacher named Spruill,
> Who taught at a mighty fine school.
> With the bronze table lamp,
> Eckland's head he did stamp.
> How could Spruill have been so cruel?

Jackie could but roll her eyes.

Chapter 23

There had been a break from the last three days of cold rainy weather, when a dark Ford Crown Victoria slowly pulled to the front of the Macklin's home. The car stopped at the bottom of the driveway.

Bagnilla admired the country cottage style home with the stone sides over a stacked stone foundation. He took a moment to exit the car to gaze upon the purple Lantana's still in bloom. Jackie took great pride in her Lantana's ability to attract butterflies even into late summer of September and early fall. He checked his appearance and patted the Browning 45 automatic pistol under his jacket. It was an

American made gun, heavier than the Glock favored by most law enforcement agencies, but the extra weight could be an advantage in a hand to hand fight. He walked around the front of the car with his fingers trailing along the hood as if to check for dents or to feel the warmth of the quiet engine.

He could see the motor home the couple owned. Parked along side of the Holland Silver Bow was Harley's 2006 Ford F-250 dark blue pickup. Jackie's bright red 2008 Saturn VUE was parked aside the Silver Bow. Mounting the steps to the front door, Bagnilla grasped the white wooden hand rail and climbed to the porch deck. Once there he paused, removed his dark tinted sunglasses, and holding them away from his face, did a smudge check. Once this was completed he replaced the shades and stood with his hands on his hips, again taking in the surroundings. "Nice Lantana's," he thought.

Harley was watching Bagnilla's little dance from inside the front living room. Unknown visitors are rare to the Macklin's since their child Elizabeth moved away. Harley did not like the looks of this visitor.

"What the ..." thought Harley, "this man is selling something we don't need." He had watched the man in the ill-fitting black suit exit his car. Harley also watched the whole thing with the sunglasses and wondered why the man needed to continue to wear the tinted lenses with the sky still overcast.

"There is a strange man at the front door," Harley said entering Jackie's office.

That the stranger had not used the side door automatically made him a suspect. All their friends know to use the back door to the kitchen. No real Southerner lock their back doors.

She was sitting at her desk once again, her pad filling with notes. The Codex was opened to about mid-way of the volume. Fine lines of Latin script ran over the face of each page, and leathery musk was the odor filling the room.

"What do you mean?" she asked. "Strange as in 'we don't know him', or as … in he has a horn growing out of the middle of his forehead?"

"I mean strange as in I have never seen him before. And he could have a horn growing out the back of his head. He's not turned around for me to see."

"He's at the front door, so he has to be a stranger," was Jackie's optimistic observation. "Maybe he's lost?"

"He was patting his gun in his shoulder holster," Harley said.

"Gun?" Jackie was now a bit startled and apprehensive. "You saw a gun?"

"No, I did not see a gun."

"Then how do you know he has one?"

"He has a bulge in his monkey suit," said Harley.

"Monkey suit?" asked Jackie. "The man works for the zoo?"

By now Harley knew he had entered into a smart ass contest without being fully qualified and was mismatched at the beginning. He was losing his semi-pro standing and patience. "I don't know who he works for … just his suit would probably fit a gorilla better than it does him."

Jackie was about to continue her contest but Harley realized he was falling behind in points. "Who do you think he is?"

"By the looks of his car, his suit, his patient leather shoes, and the gun in a sling, my first guess is he is a cop of some sort . . . maybe a detective."

"Detective?" said Jackie. "I want to see for myself." She got up from her leather upholstered swivel executive chair, and headed for the doorway. Harley put his arm across the path to block her exit.

"Don't go out just yet, wait till he knocks. Then go through the kitchen into the living room and listen in at the front window. Don't let him know you are here yet."

"Why?"

"Let's see what he wants first before we go all in."

"You think this has something to do with Dr. Eckland?" Jackie fearfully asked.

"Could be," Harley speculated. The man might be a local detective looking into a closed case, or a private insurance investigator. Either way I want you to be out of sight just in case the man is up to no good."

There were four knocks, quick rapid sounds of knuckles hitting the wood trim surrounding the frame.

"Four raps," thought Harley. It indicated that this was not a friendly knock. At least friends opened the storm door and rapped twice on the door's stain glass window. Four quick raps meant the man was in a serious bent to get his business done and wanted the occupants to respond as fast as possible. Harley delayed leaving Jackie's office.

"Why don't you answer the door?"

"Let him wait on us," said Harley.

"Why?"

"It's a mind game," Harley responded. "We use it in contract negotiations. Let the other side get the feeling that they don't rate our immediate attention. Make them wait on us."

"You're one for playing mind games," she said with a slight smirk. "You're in the stadium but forgot your equipment. Why don't I answer the door?"

"If something happens, then I would . . ." He was cut off by another machine gun fast knocking.

"You're sweet," said Jackie, "but what if something happens to you? What makes you think that I wouldn't come to your rescue?"

"Because you will be hiding behind curtain number three in the living room with your finger on 911 speed dial."

The stranger rapped again, this time enough to rattle the window in the door. Harley stepped into the hallway and over his shoulder told Jackie to wait until he was outside to sneak into the living room. Knowing the stranger's elevated anxiety level would have him peering into the door window, he would see Harley's distorted shadow through the leaded glass. Harley walked as slow as he could to get the anxiety level in the stranger even higher. Harley could see two hands cupped to the opaque window to shield the owner's eyes from the glaring light bouncing off the window.

With slow clumsy hands Harley reached for the thumb latch to make the turn that would draw in the deadbolt from the frame. Then he fumbled with the door lock, rattling the knob until the inner workings released and its bolt could retract.

"Can I help you?" asked Harley as he pulled the door until the full length of the security chain was taut.

"Can I come in?" Bagnilla asked in a short brisk voice.

"No ... I'd rather you didn't until you tell me who you are and what you want."

"Sir, would you step out here then, please?" Bagnilla was not asking but telling Harley what he wanted him to do. With Harley having gotten Bagnilla's goat, H.R's voice now carried a greater threat level.

"What's the matter?" Harley asked drawing out his already southern drawl. This usually gave the opponent across the negotiation table the impression that Harley just might not be the sharpest nail in the box. Harley could turn it on and off as he needed it.

"Sir, I am Special Agent H. R. Bagnilla," the agent said. He gave Harley just a beat to adsorb this thunderbolt when he continued, "with the FBI."

"Who?" asked Harley, again to keep Bagnilla's anxiety level elevated. "You are who?"

Bagnilla had to repeat himself, which he hated to do. This time he withdrew his badge and I.D. card from his left front coat pocket. He opened the holder to quickly display the documents for Harley's inspection. Then he returned the folder to his pocket.

"Could I see that again," Harley said putting three long a's in the word "again". "I don't have my reading glasses."

"I'm hitting an all time high with this dim idiot," Bagnilla thought. "Any slower and I'll be here all night."

He gave the case to Harley, who withdrew the little black folder inside the door.

"FBI Special Agent Horatio Russell Bagnilla," Harley read loud enough for Jackie to hear. The photo on the card looked as if the man had been dead for some days. He held it for a moment and returned it. He glanced at Jackie who had taken her station at the window with the cordless phone in hand. Her finger lingered on the speed dial button. He nodded to her and released the security chain.

"Horatio? God of good eyesight?" Harley's words trailed upwards as if it were a question.

"Sir, I am Special Agent Bagnilla," he repeated with a robot's monotone. "How are you today?"

"I'm fine," Harley responded. "Just getting up from my nap ... walking, talking, and sucking air. How are you?"

"Sir, are you Harland Randolph Macklin, born 1944 in Cleland County, Ga?" This was not a question, but more a statement of fact.

"Yes, but its Harley, or all my friends call me Harley. What is this about?"

"Sir, is your wife Dr. Jacqueline Philomena Macklin formerly of the CDC in Atlanta . . . is she home?" Bagnilla thought he could elicit more information from the pair. One might spill something the other wanted hidden. Harley didn't want to answer this question just yet, not until he could get the bearings on Bagnilla's heading.

"What's this all about?" Harley would stick to his target as his contract negotiation experience taught him to never give up all your information at the beginning.

"Sir, do you know Dr. Eckland?"

Since Harley would not summon Jackie, Bagnilla would continue his interrogation to see how much honesty he could elicit from Harley.

Harley had the where-with all to know no one asks a question in these circumstances without already knowing the answer. He did not want to answer falsely if this was a real investigation into Dr. Eckland's death, but he wanted to be economical with his answers. Something was missing or *off* in the man's presentation or manner or something. Harley now wanted to have Jackie with him. She would know dead on if the man was on the up and up.

"Just a moment, please. I think I heard Jackie in the kitchen. I'll go get her."

"May I come in, sir?" Bagnilla asked reaching for the door handle.

Harley paused not wanting to seem rude, "Wait here, I'll be right back," he answered closing the front door.

Harley went in and walked straight back to the kitchen. From the corner of his eye, he could see Jackie heading in the same direction. This was what negotiators would call a respite to reconnoiter the situation and size up the opposition.

"What do you think he wants?" they said asking each other the same question. Harley gave his opinion that this was an investigation into Eckland's death.

Jackie disagreed, for a murder investigation would begin at the local level. "Usually people are called to come in to the police department, be asked a few questions and then sent home. The Bureau doesn't send field agents to people's homes." She stopped, frozen in mid thought, "If," she strongly stated, "if this is a simple murder investigation."

"What else would it be?"

"Harley, we never sent investigators into the field alone, for their protection and that of the patients. We had Bureau trainers conduct interviewing techniques and personal safety classes all the time. He should not be here alone."

They heard the one hinge on the storm door squeaking. The metal frame carried the squeak through the whole network of frame and door casing. Trying to find the offending piece of hardware that it may be lubricated was difficult. But, they enjoyed having a built- in door opening alarm.

Bagnilla heard the squealer as well and stopped in his effort to gain entrance to the home. Knowing his action was probably heard throughout the home he called out, "Mr. and Mrs. Eckland?"

"Watch him and put the phone on the hall table just in case," instructed Harley. Then he took her hand and led her down the hall to the front door. He opened that squeaky screen door and gave Jackie time to put down the phone. "She was in the nursery," he explained. "Now, what is this about?"

"May I come in - please?" Bagnilla asked. The day was not so warm that people would need refuge in the air conditioned interior. This was a day for sitting on the front porch. Neither wanted an out of place stranger carrying a gun to enter the home. His presence was disturbing enough.

"Nice day isn't it?" Harley observed. "Why not sit out here?"

He pointed to the twin rocking chairs on the front porch. They were white painted Red Oak Wheatly Rockers from Mentone, Georgia. Bagnilla paused and saw he had little choice. He did not have a search warrant and no valid reasons to be here but for his own agenda. He sat down in the first rocker as Jackie and Harley walked past to take the front porch swing. They sat side by side with Jackie lightly resting her hand on his knee.

Bagnilla made his introduction to Jackie. This time she held the identification documents until she had thoroughly examined the documents. She had seen other such I.D.s but it was usually at a glance. "Nice to meet you Special Agent Bagnilla," said Jackie returning the wallet. "What is this all about?"

"Do you know Dr. William Eckland?"

Harley was quick to respond, "We never met the man before he died," then quickly added, "I know who he was."

Jackie sat silent.

"I am here looking into a possible theft of something that might have been in his possession at one time," said Bagnilla.

"And what would that have been?" asked Harley.

"A book ... a very old book. It could quite possibly be from the fourth century. It would look like it was handmade. It is a leather cover and parchment pages. It is called a Codex."

"Codex?" Jackie asked with a little girl innocence.

"That's right," Bagnilla confirmed. "Refers to a book that is made by hand in the past. It's copied from another book or Codex, mostly by priest ... possibly made around the 5th century. I am looking for the one Dr. Eckland might have had before his death?"

Jackie took note of the singular reference Bagnilla made. He said I, not we, as if to say this was a personal expedition.

"Why are you asking us?" asked Jackie.

"You delivered two pages similar to what would be found in a Codex to Gilbert University. Dr. Spruill notified me about the page."

"Yes, we delivered the two pages," said Harley.

"Why?" asked Bagnilla.

"We hoped he could tell us what we had," answered Jackie. "Did he tell you?"

Bagnilla was now under interrogation from someone better practiced in the art. "Dr. Spruill only said that it could have been from a Codex that Dr. Eckland had taken from the school." Bagnilla paused and clumsily added, "for personal study." Again he paused but added, "at home."

He could not fool Dr. Macklin. She was in the game now and playing all out. "Personal study?" she asked, "Why would he not study the two pages in his office?"

Before Bagnilla could respond, Jackie continued her attack. "Why would he not want to keep the pages under lock and key in the school? Would this not be something the whole archeology department would be involved in studying?" She was now leading the conversation.

Bagnilla could only fumble his response. "I don't know," was his lame answer. "We think it was his intention to keep the Codex, possibly to sell it."

This accusation that Dr. Eckland stole the Codex came as a surprise to the couple. Jackie instantly gave slight pressure to her fingertips resting on Harley's knee to indicate to him to reserve comment. But it was not needed. Harley remembered to never give up information until asked.

They sat silently side by side looking with blank expressions at Bagnilla. He stopped his gentle motion in the Wheatly Rocker and tilted forward. "Where did you say you obtained the pages?"

"We never did say," Harley confirmed remembering the conversation with Spruill and his attempt to discover the location of the place of purchase.

"Well, will you tell me, please?" begged Bagnilla.

"Why?" asked Harley. Jackie was pressing harder with her finger and hopped that Bagnilla did not see the flexing of her *palmar interossi* of the index and middle fingers.

"I want to see if your source has any more documents, possibly the entire Codex. It would help in my investigation into the theft." He had tripped up revealing his intentions.

Harley heeded Jackie's clue in her finger movement and said nothing. She spoke up first.

"There seemed to be only the two pages," she said with as much innocence as would possibly be believed.

Bagnilla would not be moved from his path to locate where the Macklin's obtained the documents.

"So you told Dr. Spruill you bought the pages?"

"We bought the pages," Jackie said defensibly.

"Where?"

"From the seller."

"Where does this seller live?"

"They do not live where we bought the two pages," Jackie answered.

"You said you went to the seller's home and bought the papers," said Bagnilla.

"No," replied Jackie in a measured tone. "What I said was 'I bought the pages from the seller. A house is a structure and a home is where a family lives. This is our home, she said pointing to hers. If it was empty then it would be a house."

"So where does this seller live?" His tone was one of frustration at this circular conversation. "Where is her home?"

Bagnilla tripped again thought Jackie. He knew that the seller was possibly Eudora and not Ed. She wanted him off the porch.

"I do not remember if they said where they lived. Do you remember, Harley?" she asked while pressing his leg again.

"I don't remember their name or address, if they ever said," he responded.

"They?" asked Bagnilla. "So it was two people?"

"They can be used in a singular reference," said Jackie. "I never said it was two people."

"Who was it then?" Bagnilla's voice was beginning to rise in frustration. The couple knew they had the upper hand and played it now.

It was Dr. Harland of the CDC that spoke with the full authority of her former position.

"Mr. Bagnilla, are we suspects in this theft?"

"This is just an investigation, a friendly chat," Bagnilla said. "Just wanting to see if you were on the level." He began to back pedal.

"Well," said Jackie, "I do not appreciate the implication that we came about the document in any sort of unlawful manner, and I will not divulge any more information until I see a warrant for said information."

"Who are you protecting?" demanded Bagnilla "You could be impeding an investigation into theft of school property."

"And I could be protecting an innocent person in this matter."

"That is for me to say," argued Bagnilla with his voice rising.

"Whoa," said Harley. "Jackie wants to see a warrant. We do not give out information about friends or family without good cause. And you're saying this is an investigation into a possible thief of school property is just that, your words."

"Why didn't Spruill say anything when we brought the pages in?" asked Jackie. "Why didn't he call us himself? We would have gone to the school and talked with him."

The conversation had come to a void and would go no further. Realizing this, Bagnilla took a different route.

"Do either of you read Latin . . . Dr. Macklin?" he said looking at Jackie.

"I know medical Latin."

"Medical Latin?"

"Yes, most all medical terms are Latin."

"Yes, of course. But do you read Latin, say in a book like the Codex?"

"Some."

"But not a lot?"

"Am I the one under investigation?" she asked.

"No, just wanted to," and he stopped, "see if you knew what you were buying?"

"I took the pages to Spruill for evaluation. I buy antiques," she responded. "I liked the look of the old paper. I had thought I might have them framed."

"And then what?"

"Then hang it over the downstairs toilet." It was her ironic gag, with paper having once been priceless, and the parchments seemed priceless.

Bagnilla almost gagged at this suggestion. He also realize he would get nowhere with these two and gave in. He stood up to leave.

"Well, I have enough information." It was next to nothing he had gained. It was a waste of his time and theirs.

"Good day." With that he turned to go back to the Crown Victoria.

"Mr. Bagnilla?" Jackie called out as he walked down the driveway. "You asked if I knew some Latin."

"Yes." He replied hopping she would reveal that she knew what was written in the Codex.

"Bagnilla, that is of an Italian origin right?" she asked in a leading manner.

"Yes it is," he said puzzled. "My grandfather was Italian."

"Bagnilla from the Latin root word *balnea* or *balemum*."

"I never looked it up," he said. "So you know some Latin? What does it mean?"

"The Balemun ... it was the common name Romans gave to the man that was the public bath attendant," she said as sweetly as she could, "You come back now, you hear?"

Chapter 24

"Who the *hell* does he think he is?" Jackie was beside herself. "Coming up here and accusing us of conspiracy to steal the Codex. Why if I wasn't... if he wasn't ... and if he wasn't carrying a gun." With that she stopped her tirade. Bagnilla was armed and things could have taken a more drastic turn. If he was up to no good then what would have stopped him from forcing his way into their home.

"Balemun," repeated Harley, "does that really means bath house attendant?"

"I'm going to make some phone calls," she said flatly. "Yes it does."

"Great one, Jackie." He gave the match to her and once again knew he was standing next to true greatness. "Who are you going to call?"

"I don't know," she was still livid. "But I am going to call someone at the office and see if I am right about agents always going out in pairs."

"Let's go inside," Harley suggested. He picked up the cordless phone from the hall table. They walked down the hall to her office.

"This Codex must have something in it we have not found," Jackie said. "He was trying to see if we had any idea what was in it. That's why he asked if I could read Latin."

"Like I said the other evening, this could be the personal journal of Saint Paul. That alone would make it priceless. And ... it could open the door into Paul's psyche. Have you found any more names we would know?"

"I thought we did not have enough testimony to accurately date the journal," said Jackie the investigator.

"No, but we are getting awfully damn close," Harley responded. "I mean dropping the names of men who were contemporaries of Jesus, Athronges ben Emmaus, The Rabbi Elijah and Gamaliel the Great or the second one, puts him traveling in a famous circle of bible celebrities. Then he was from Tarsus, raised in Antioch, it is looking like we have Paul's personal journal or someone who lived around there. And then his name is in the manifest entry and that note from his mom."

"But he would have written Aramaic Greek," said Jackie, "This is fourth century Latin."

"But Horatio said the Codex he was looking for was possibly fourth century."

"But you don't believe Uncle Willy was trying to steal the Codex?" asked Jackie.

"Not for a second. It would make no sense for him to try to steal something from the school only to turn around and sell it. The moment it came on the market they would be all over it."

"But wait a minute, if it were stolen, why didn't Spruill tell us this to begin with?" Jackie asked.

"Maybe it wasn't stolen?"

"Not until Bagnilla said it was stolen," was Harley's observation. "Then, what is Spruill hiding or doing?"

"But," she started again.

"But what?" said Harley cutting her off.

"Well, they know each other ... Bagnilla was asking us things from our conversation with Spruill."

"Or the claim that the Codex was stolen is genuine and he interviewed Spruill," injected Harley.

"And, he might know Boo," said a fearful Jackie.

"How did you come to that?"

"He asked, 'where does this seller live? Where is *her* home?' That is exactly what he said."

"He knows it was a 'she' that sold us the pages," said Harley.

"We might need to warn Boo," she said.

"About what? He didn't make any threats or anything about Boo," said Harley. "But you said you were going to call her for a photo?"

"I'll call her later, after dinner. I was working on another journal entry. I had finished it when Bagnilla arrived," announced Jackie. "Our author has taken to Judaism."

Harley returned the phone to the charger base as she picked up her yellow pad. Jackie sat down at her desk and turned on the lamp. The sunlight was fading now and she began to read the translation of the journal entry dated Friday, 26 June, 688 A.U.C. if Harley's calculations were correct, then that would have been 26 a.d.

Dies Veneris xxvi Junius DCLXXXVIII

I have returned to the town of Antioch with Achaicus. We went to the home of Elias. I spoke at greater length with the learned sage about the teachings of the prophet Moses and of Abraham and of Isaiah. Elias said it is the fundamental belief that all men have within themselves the command of their own actions to do good or to do evil. The doing of these good deeds he called mitzvah. Elias says that I need not consult the priest of Antevorte. He teaches that all men are constantly faced with the choices and are not directed by Parcae, Nona, Morta and Decima.

His is the one Lord God Jehovah and has given to his people the Law through their prophet Moses on a mountain called Sinai in the region of Egypt. Elias teaches that all Jews love their God and follow his laws. They want to be like Him, creator, divine spirit, and loving father. How one acts in this life will determine how one will be remembered. Elias teaches me the foundations of his faith and of the Law given in ten commandments.

He teaches me that we will experience heaven on earth once all men treat other men as brothers. The Jews seek a return to the garden in which God spoke with two that he first created - ones called Adam and Eve. It is wonderful, simple, loving faith.

I confronted him with the reality that the Roman Empire are the lawgivers of this land and that the gods favored Nero. Elias explained that while this was true, it was the will of God and was his punishment for the sins of his people. He said that one day, he will bear witness to the advent of the Redeemer. And on that day all nations would see the light and follow the guidance of the Torah. He believes this Redeemer will lead all men to give up war and strife and embrace each other as brothers. The Redeemer will rule from a hilltop in Judea called Zion. As I had already been ordained into the Judaism since the days of my youth, I could participate in the rituals and services that very day. Sopater helped me to wash and prepare for Shabbat.

"He has converted to Judaism," Harley agreed. "Taken to the ritual washing before the Sabbath."

"Sabbath?"

"Starts Friday evening at sundown. See the date?" said Harley as he put his finger on the date Jackie had written at the top of her translation. "He begins with ritualistic hand washing before breaking bread on the Sabbath."

Jackie prepared her evening meal of baked chicken coated in bread crumbs, garlic mashed potatoes, black eyed peas cooked with a piece of ham, and oven baked rolls. All washed down with liberal amounts of sweet peppermint tea. She had taken time earlier in the day to make Harley's favorite dessert, Lemon Meringue Pie. She used the real condensed milk filling not taking short cuts with pre-made fillings, all of this over a crushed graham cracker crust. Harley appreciated her *passion pour maisonnée* in all she did for him.

"So what are you calling Boo for this time," asked Harley?

"I want that photo of Uncle Willy and Gill. The one she showed us at Aunt Barbara's house."

"Are you going to warn her about Bagnilla?"

"We don't know what he is up to, yet," answered Jackie. "I will try to see if he has called her. I'm calling Boo, before it gets too late, you get to clean up."

"Boo lives in the Central Time Zone," he responded trying to get out of kitchen duty. "You could call her later. She is an hour behind us."

"I don't care if she lives in the Twilight Zone. I am calling her now." She flipped the dish towel to Harley and disappeared through the hallway door.

"Yes, Dear," he mumbled and in this moment the water nymph Muse came to him.

Jackie could make a great chicken,
For her, he was love stricken.
But when dinner was done
And clean up time had come
Twas a chore that he really disliken.

Chapter 25

"Well, what did they say," Dr. Spruill asked Bagnilla on his return from his interview with Jackie and Harley. Spruill closed the door to the outside world as Bagnilla began to replay the conversation.

"I think they have the Codex," said Bagnilla. "I think it is time to call them in and demand they give it up before something happens to them."

"We cannot have another confrontation like we did before," advised Spruill.

Bagnilla nodded in agreement but added, "We've had no repercussions have we?"

"We?" asked Spruill incredulously. "I had nightmares for weeks. Even now I get uneasy every time I pass Eckland's door. Now with the Macklin's showing up?" He left the questioning statement hanging without support, expecting it to fly on its own.

"Get over it. What's done is done and we both know we would do it again if we have to," Bagnilla said with his disposition, never that good in daylight, now headed into the darker side of existence. "We have to do all that we can to protect our church."

"That does not include murder," Spruill responded. "Our Lord would not approve...." his voice trailed off.

"What about Curtis? How's he holding up?"

"He's fine. He could face deportation if he says anything," said Spruill.

"Well, we certainly do not want to tell 'His Grace'," instructed Bagnilla.

"If not for your intervention with the coroner's report, we might all be facing ...well you know. What are we going to do?" asked Spruill.

"First thing, let's bring the Macklins in and tell them we know they have the Codex. Then we'll make them an offer like Fellwater wanted to do," was Bagnilla's advise.

"And if they don't accept it?"

"Eckland didn't accept our offer," answered a threatening Bagnilla.

Spruill stopped at what Bagnilla implied. His frown reflected his dislike to the course Bagnilla was proposing. He was becoming frightened of his own colleague and co-conspirator.

"How about the threat of something happening, do you think that would do it?"

"Threat?" exclaimed Bagnilla. "I don't threaten ... I do!"

"Whoa now," cautioned Spruill. "What if they go to the police?"

"As an FBI agent, I overrule a police investigation," he said, "and a dead witness can't testify."

Spruill paused at this man's determination to find the missing Codex.

"What are you talking about, dead? You don't mean murder again?"

"That is exactly what I'm talking about and you and that stupid rent-a-cop, Curtis, are going to help."

"What are you suggesting, we bash their heads in with the lamp again?" asked Spruill.

"Bring them in to talk," instructed Bagnilla. "Have them meet you at the Old Central building, late at night when no one is on campus. Curtis can be scheduled to be on the front desk. Use one of the top floor conference rooms."

"Won't they be suspicious meeting late?"

"Tell them you have a full schedule and a night class," said Bagnilla. "Good God man, think for yourself."

"What do I talk to them about?"

"Make them a final offer. Go up to $1,000.00 for both pages."

"$1,000.00," exclaimed Spruill, "Fellwater will pay whatever they want."

"Any more and they will know how desperate we are to get the rest. Now don't go over $1,000.00 for the pair."

"What if they take the offer?"

"Offer them $10,000.00 for the rest of the Codex."

"What if they should refuse to take any money?"

"Then Curtis and I will take it from there."

"How?" Spruill fearfully asked.

"Accidents happen," he said. "Even in college elevators."

"Can you do that?"

"When you have watched how stupid people get caught, you learn how not to get caught," Bagnilla revealed. "Only one of the elevators will be running that night. I suggest you take the stairs when you leave."

"H.R., don't you think this is going too far?" pleaded Spruill.

"No. If I had had a chance to speak with Eckland before you killed him, then I could have gotten the Codex back then."

"It was an accident. That old fool would not listen to reason,"

"Well you had your chance. Now it's mine," H.R. stated. You bring them in, understand?"

"And where will you be?"

"Listening in … we're going to get that book one way or another."

"We can't find the Codex with them … dead. How are we going to find it then?" asked a worried Spruill.

"I can arrange search warrants and they serve up dead or alive. Now make that call."

Chapter 26

"Yes, I will tell him."

Harley had come in from his shop to find Jackie on the phone.

"I think that will work," she paused to listen. Then she said "OK, we'll see you then."

"Who was that?" asked Harley.

"Spruill."

"What does he want?"

Jackie went back to her cooking. Dinner tonight would be penne pasta with a tomato based sauce. Cubes of chicken were sitting on a plate on the counter waiting their turn to join the rest of the ingredients in her cauldron. The fragrance filled the home. Garlic bread sat on top of the toaster oven, waiting to become garlic toast. "Wash up and open that bottle of Calon Segur."

"That's a Bordeaux," noted Harley. "We're having chicken."

"I want red," demanded Jackie.

He pulled the corkscrew from the drawer and twisted the metal curls into the cork. It pulled easy enough under his arm.

The cork, inserted in 2003 according to the label, left the portal with a slight pop.

She extended a familiar bit of stemware. "You can pour me a glass, *sommelier*," she said in a regal French tone of voice.

"As you wish," he said and dribbled the sweet nectar into the stemware. The container was one of a pair he had engraved with the letter *J* on one and *H* on the other. They were presented to her as a wedding anniversary gift during the week they spent in the Great Smokey Mountains of North Carolina. She took a sip, and sat the glass on the ceramic tile countertop.

"Now, what does Spruill want?"

"He wants to meet us at the university on Sunday afternoon," she said as she dropped the chicken into the pot.

"Why? And why Sunday?" asked Harley.

"He has information for us about the pages we left." she said. "There is a symposium for college presidents and admission officers at the university. He'll be attending and we will see him afterwards … seventh floor conference room of the administration building about six or six thirty."

"What information?" he asked probing for Spruill's intention.

"Information about where the pages came from. He was saying about how they might be a part of some stolen historical art collection," she said cynically.

"He's definitely working with the bath room attendant," Harley said.

"Spruill mentioned a reward or possibly the school making us an offer to buy the pages."

"Yeah?" said Harley. "A reward for returning something that wasn't stolen in the first place, and he said the school wants to buy them?"

"Yes," she said as she put the bread in the toaster oven. She placed the timer knob to the six minute mark and turned to Harley.

"They want to buy stolen property?" he asked."Doesn't make sense."

"We'll go talk to him anyway. I want to see what he is up to. Now sit down and eat your salad."

Another fine dinner was once more put away by Harley. They had talked of the weather and how the cooler temperatures would make for beautiful fall foliage this year. They had polite argument whether the trees needed rain first or frost first to make the brightest color season. Each defended their position by recalling past autumns. They reached no concurrence over what stimulus the trees need for the best results, only that the length of the day would trigger any change at all.

"I'll have another, please," Jackie requested as Harley poured himself a second helping.

"You were saying that you finished the next page?" he reminded her.

"Yes. An army entry, I think. Talks about being injured, going on patrol." She was quite animated about the entry. "Here," she said pulling her notepad off the top of the microwave.

"Dies Lunae xvii Maius."

"Monday, ten," said Harley as he did some conversion himself, "five and two, Monday, seventeen, May, what year?"

"689 and he doesn't say A.U.C or A.L.U."

"He's getting sloppy," said Harley.

"He is getting frugal with his ink," she responded. "Do you want me to finish this or not?"

"Will it get me out of doing the dishes?"

She made her face again, "No." and began to read him the journal entry of 17 May.

Terentius Rufus goes about the village seeking information on where we might find the bandits. For days the word in the camp has been of the likelihood of an attack on the market. There was writing on the wall of a house along the street. The message said that a deliverer was near. These criminals that call themselves believers of the Lord God Almighty, wait forever for their deliverer who has forsaken them. Why can't they acknowledge their sins and pray God's forgiveness? Caius took a bucket of water and washed away the blasphemy.

The surgeon does not think my leg has been broken by my fall. I should have been more watchful of my lance. It is the desire of Claudio that I continue this training to become a cataphracts in tenth Fretensis. I find the archery to be most favorable and enjoyable. My prayer to the Most Highest El Shaddai has been to speed Neptune, Venus and the goddess Angita riding atop Taurus to heal my wounds.

I will mend my broken lorica squamata tomorrow when Novatus and I will go into Jerusalem. I need to find the leather to make repairs. It is my prayer that Gamaliel will allow me to sit at his feet and be trained in the deeper mysteries of the Most Highest El Shaddai. He has not given me his favor as I am marked as a solder and to be suspected of being a spy. I watch and listen as best I can to the teachings of Gamaliel.

Achaicus will bring me what he has taught the other men.

Aurelia sends word of marriage to Afranius Burrus. My old friend is a good man and will take care of Aurelia. I would that I could have attended the wedding. It does bother me that they married so quickly. Burrus was always a cautious man. Mother was not pleased at the union. She thinks they have rushed into the marriage without proper forethought. When they go to Jerusalem I shall be happy to see them when I go into the city.

Terentius Rufus has orders for us to march to Ctesiphon and arrest King Artabanus. We had another strike against our troops in the southern region of Galilee. The Jewish brigands Anilai and Asinai from the land of Tiberius are understood to be behind this action. Lucius Vitellius has sent word that we are to keep vigilance against these cowards attack. After the death of King Herod the rebels have grown more daring in their raids. Now they will strike the cohorts from the hills. When we attack they flee into the hills and woods. Some in the legion believe this is the start of another revolt. Our governor has sent petitions to the Senate asking that another legion be formed and quartered in Galliee. We all fear that Third Gallica is too far north to reach us should the people began an uprising.

Claudio has found opportunity to gain some income as we serve our two years. By virtue of his position and with the knowledge of business, he has become a praefectus castorum and quaestor to the legion. Authority is given him to dispense our weekly viaticum. Our most gracious governor has ordered 82 denarii be paid to those that would join us in our fight to keep the peace. Claudio does not pass the full measure on to the others, but holds the extra viaticum unto himself. As his princepales, I will keep his counsel and we will share in the profits.

Achaicus comes. Shema begins. May His great Name be blessed forever and ever.

"Ok," said Harley, "Sounds like he is backsliding into the old paganism with that reference to Neptune and Venus. I did not catch that, what was it, *cataphracts*?"

"It says, 'training as a *cataphracts*' probably a soldier. He was using a bow and arrow and a lance."

"Yea, that knocked him off his high horse," Harley said with a chuckle. "I have not heard of the Tenth Fretensis, probably a legion name. I could look it up."

"See where it was stationed," Jackie suggested.

"Jerusalem. You said so. Don't think our boy could have studied with Gamaliel the first or the second one," Harley said.

"Why not?"

"'I am marked as a solider'," Harley reminded her. "Means he was tattooed and that violates Jewish Law. I think it is probably in Leviticus, most of the Laws are. Gamaliel would not allow the infidel anywhere near the temple."

"Could be more metaphorical, a figure of speech," she said. "As if he were 'marked' for being a soldier."

"Still if he were a known soldier, marked or un-marked, a Roman soldier or citizen would have a big problem getting anywhere near Gamaliel."

They bent over the note pad and studied the translation each pointing to terms and words they did not understand.

The author spoke of his broken *lorica squamata* and Harley found it in the Tactical Guide to the Roman Army; defined as a leather vest with plate metal sewn on it. The first armored plated vest. Jackie's original notes had in the margin defined *viaticum* as prize money, but in the context she felt it was better suited to be called a weekly paycheck. Also in the marginal notes she had translated '*a praefectus castorum and quaestor*' as a 'prancing beaver judge.' Harley came close to falling off the chair when she read that one. Once he regained control over the *faus pax*, his Tactical Guide defined the two terms in Army lingo as a Major's position and bookkeeper to the unit. In that position and with his step-son as his second, they could defraud the emperor and the keep a portion of the troop's weekly pay.

"That's terrible!"cried Jackie.

"Well goes to show that a soldier's pay has never been that good. Besides, when in Jerusalem...." began Harley, but stopped at Jackie's glare.

"Dishes!" she demanded and headed down the hall with the remnants of Calon Segur swirling in her head.

Chapter 27

Dr. Spruill sat back in the conference room chair looking nervous, exhausted, and very anxious having failed to convince the Macklins to sell the documents. Nor was he pleased that his efforts did not hold enough sway to cause Jackie and Harley to give up the location of the rest of the Codex. Having all offers rejected, he appealed to the couple's sense of civic duty and return what he continually described as stolen documents. The meeting did not last long. Spruill revealed the documents did date back to the second or third century a.d.

He was desperately trying to get the Macklins to cave in and give up the full Codex knowing their fate should he fail. The thought had occurred several times in the negotiations to reveal their impending doom should they elect to keep silent. Bagnilla threatening to expose his culpability in the failed attempt to persuade Eckland to give up the Codex, kept him from his better nature.

They returned to the elevator. Once the doors slid open they entered the chamber and the doors, as silent as a tomb, returned to their place. Before Harley could turn around to see what she was doing, Jackie leaned past him and pressed the button that should deliver them to the lobby. The brake released the cable and the car started down the vertical metal path. It had dropped only a few feet when they felt the increased pull of gravity as when the car comes to a floor, only it had not traveled enough to have reached even the sixth floor hallway.

"What's wrong?" Jackie asked looking at her personal maintenance man.

"Elevator stopped," he deduced.

"I know that, I mean why did it stop?"

"Why didn't you ask that?"

"It started then stopped. We haven't reached the next floor. The door isn't opening," she was getting impatient with Harley's laconic attitude.

"Well," he gave a studied response, "could be something such as a point switch, or contact switch opened or closed too soon. Some safety device has activated too soon or not soon enough. Elevators have many electrical contact points all have to mesh for it to work safely."

"Computer glitch?" she asked even though she did not understand how an elevator operated, she did understand the inner workings of computers.

"Elevators don't use computers, mechanical safety switches have been in place for over a century. If it ain't broke don't fix it," said Harley. "It will reset and start again in a minute."

A noise was heard by the pair in the car. The echo in the vacant space of the shaft prevented Harley from determining what it was, and where it was. In any case, it was not a sound that he was expecting to hear in the early night, in an empty building. If an elevator was slow in arriving, people pound on the hall doors in vain hope of somehow making the car arrive earlier. This was not that kind of sound. This was more of a metal door slamming a metal door frame.

"What was that?" Jackie asked.

"Quite, please, I'm trying to listen." He placed his index finger to his mouth for emphasis.

She started to speak but gave heed to his warning, paused, and in a whispered voice wanted to ask what he thought he was listening to, but the car went dark.

"Oh!" Jackie said in a very curt, quiet exclamation. "Now what?"

"I don't know, but I don't like this," said Harley in quiet tones.

"Why? What's the matter?"

"Elevators don't go dark unless the power goes out," he said.

"Then we're having a black out?" she nervously asked.

"But we stopped before the black out, not during," was his point. "And this isn't a black out."

"Oh!" she quietly exclaimed again. "How do you know it isn't a black out? Lights are on in the hallway," he worriedly explained. "We are four feet above the sixth floor stop."

His finger pointed at the vertical slot where the two doors of the car meet. There was a narrow stream of light penetrating the carriage from the floor below.

"Why?" she asked returning to her voice to its original volume.

Just then another noise could be heard. This time it was the sound of metal striking metal. It was followed by a hushed voice with a few words that neither could make out. They heard the metal sound again.

"What's that?" Jackie asked in the guarded tone she used before.

"Sounds like a wrench," responded Harley.

"Someone is working on the elevator? On a Sunday?"

"A lot of maintenance gets done weekends," said Harley. "But elevator maintenance is usually done when the car is at the bottom - in case something does go wrong – and during the week."

"Wrong?" asked a nervous Jackie.

He motioned with his finger for her to give heed to the noises being generated. Now it was clear to him that the source was from above.

"Should we do something?" asked Jackie. "Push some button or call someone?"

"Ever look inside those phone boxes?" he said nodding to the one in the console.

She pulled the knob to open the cover. Inside was a dark space, a single wire dangled from the top of the cabinet.

"The one in our building," she said, "has a phone in it."

"You mean the C.D.C did, but it's not a school. Vandals pull the phones out all the time," he said, "can't keep replacing it."

"Well, what now? How about this button?" She pointed to one that had the word 'Call' in red embossed lettering over a bell symbol.

"Press it," Harley said. "Let's see what happens."

Given the recent experience with the phone box she asked "Why?"

"If it is routine maintenance, then it should signal the technician that someone is in the elevator. But our getting in and starting the elevator should have told him someone was here."

She pressed the button - waited - and hearing nothing, she pressed it again. There was no noise of any bell going off. Harley had a concerned frown on his face.

"What?" she said reading his emotion.

"Should have heard the emergency bell going off," he replied. The only sounds they were hearing now was the constant clanking of a wrench being applied to a bolt, somewhere in the mechanics of the shaft.

"We are getting out of here," he said and reached for the key chain in his pocket.

"How?"

"I'm going to open the doors," he answered.

"NO!" she said in a hushed exclamation again. "What if it falls? What about we start yelling and kicking the door? Won't someone hear us?"

He gave pause to her reasoning and then said, "On your way in, did you see anyone besides the security guard that let us in?"

Having seen only one student upon entering, she knew he was right.

"Hello!" she cried out loudly. "We are in the elevator!"

Harley said nothing, waiting on Jackie's plea to bring aid to their situation.

The only indication that she was heard was the wrench noise abated for a few moments. The noise returned as if the mechanic was un-moved by Jackie's voice.

"Please," she mournfully appealed to the un-seen people at the top of the shaft. "Will you help us get out of the elevator?"

Harley's hand fished out the key chain. He felt the objects one by one until his fingertips touched the square edges of a tiny flashlight secured to his key ring. Holding it between thumb and index finger, he pressed the button on the light. A soft blue glow emitted from the LED bulb. It was not a lot of light, but enough light. He gave her the key ring and she pressed the light into use. He put his hands on each side of the vertical crack between the doors. Pressing his fingers into the narrow gap and the doors began to separate.

"What are you doing?" she demanded to know.

"Getting out of here." The wrench noise, steady in its work, continued unabated.

"Why? Are we going to fall? You said there were too many safeties on an elevator for it to fall."

"Yea, but it sounds like one of the safeties or something is being taken apart."

No longer could she resist and being in violent opposition to his opening the doors, Jackie kicked the side of the elevator car and yelled, "Hello! Anyone there?"

The pace of the wrench picked up.

"Hello." she said in a plaintive, pleading voice. "We are trapped here," should anyone within earshot of the cry for help did not know, she added, "in the elevator." The wrench that had stopped at the first cry did not stop this time.

"Now, can we get out of here?" Harley asked as he pulled the carriage doors apart.

"Are we going to fall?" asked Jackie.

"Not from opening the doors. There is a safety switch that stops the elevator the minute even a finger pries the doors apart. It can't start up until the doors are closed. Put the light here." With that, he pointed to the doors that sealed the shaft entrance from the hallway. His hands felt for the mechanical parts that made up the door lock. He found what he was feeling for, and with a press of a small lever, the door latch released its hold on the twin hallway doors. He inserted his fingers between the second pair of doors, and with the some exertion, the hall doors sprang open. They saw the carpet of the floor some four feet below the elevator.

"Jump" he said quietly looking at Jackie. The wrench paused in its travel back and forth, its owner now straining to hear the new sounds from below.

"Jump?" she verified. "Statistics show that people our age have a greater risk of hip and bone fracture from falls of this height."

"Do the statistics also show how many people are murdered by falling in an elevator?"

Jackie looked at Harley with an expression he had not seen in their thirty six years of marriage.

"Hold the door," he instructed and Jackie moved in to replace his position. He laid on the elevator floor, parallel to the opening, and, being experienced in moving in and out of all manner of caves and building spaces, he rolled the lower half of his body off onto the sixth floor hallway. His feet softly landed on the carpet. He held the door and with his head motioned for Jackie to follow his lead. She laid across the opening and with a more hesitant move, rolled off the elevator carpet onto the building floor. He released both the doors and they slammed shut.

The wrench sounds, once continuous, now quit. Voices began to be heard. There was a static noise of a radio then an electronic voice was heard saying "Roger". He grabbed Jackie's hand and she followed him to the sign glowing in the hallway - EXIT.

They hit the panic bar, releasing the latch holding the door in place. They ran down the stairs as fast as their legs could move. The automatic closure pulled the exit door into the frame with a loud bang. As they passed the door marking the fourth floor, they heard from above, another door being slammed by another closure.

Jackie looked up the stairwell to see who the second door allowed to pass.

"Go!" said Harley for her move caused her to hesitate in her steps. He gave her back a nudge and she resumed her hurried flight. Now three sets of feet were pounding the stair treads echoing up and down the stairwell.

"A voice shouted, "Stop! Or I'll shoot."

"Who is it?" shouted Jackie over the din in the stairwell.

"Sounds like Bagnilla," Harley yelled back.

A shot rang out, something metallic struck the hand rail and rattled down the steps in front of the couple.

"Go!" shouted Harley at his wife.

She could not jump the flights as Harley could. He was gripping the hand rails on each side of the steps and would throw his feet down the pathway, nearly jumping from landing to landing. As luck would have it, the owner of the handgun above them was more interested in stopping them with a good shot. Watching his own feet and looking for his opening, he had to move with greater caution.

The gunman was still nearly three flights up when Harley landed at the bottom. When she arrived he was looking at the panic hardware locking the exit door.

Someone on the outside of the exit door was un-locking the cylinder. They heard radio static coming from the other side as the pursuer from above spoke into his walkie-talkie.

"Now what?" asked Jackie as she could see the door begin to open by an unseen hand. The radio static popped from outside again. Harley pulled up his shoulder and lunged at the opening exit door. His put his full weight into the door face and slammed it into the body of Curtis knocking him to the pavement outside. Harley nearly tripped over the man's body sprawled out on the sidewalk.

"You killed him!" Jackie cried upon seeing the man with blood oozing about his head from the collision with the hard concrete surface. Dr. Macklin bent to examine Curtis. "He's not dead." Curtis gave up a moan when Harley knelt beside him and gave his limp body a shove toward the door.

"Don't move him!" Jackie cried. "Let me look at him, I'm a doctor!" She, of course, had not touched a patient since medical school thirty years ago. "What are you doing?"

"If he isn't moving, he can block the door!" Harley shouted. "Someone in there is coming out to shoot us."

Jackie put her weight into Curtis and together they pushed him against the closed exit door.

"Let's go!" Harley said grabbing her hand.

"We can't just leave him here," she cried.

"We can't be here when Bagnilla kicks the door open either," said Harley as he began dragging Jackie down the sidewalk.

Just then they heard the panic hardware release the exit door. Curtis moaned again but did not move from his appointed position. Bagnilla shoved again. The door still opened only enough for him to see the Macklin's flight across the parking lot.

They looked back to see Bagnilla shove the door enough to get his gun through the opening.

A silver Jeep Grand Cherokee sped around the corner of the building and pulled alongside the pair. Harley was nearly out of breath, but Jackie, who was accustomed to her daily jog only slowed in her pace. A window opened and from inside they heard a woman call out, "Get in!"

"Who are you?" asked Harley as he stopped running. He was panting heavily, bending at the waist in hope that this would somehow improve his ability to breath.

"It's me Mr. Macklin, Patti, Patti Longnecker."

"Patti?" he asked and he needed another breath, "What?"

"Hold it!" they heard Bagnilla shout, and on the next sound wave came the crash of a gunshot fired into the night air. Bagnilla had rounded the corner and was headed at them full tilt. "Halt or I'll shoot!"

They needed no further begging by Patti and jumped into the open back door.

"Hit it!" shouted Jackie once Harley landed on the seat.

There was another shout and shot from behind the car, but nothing hit the vehicle as they rounded the building corner.

"Put us out next to that GMC pickup," said Harley.

"No!" ordered Jackie, "He might catch us before we get away."

"I'll take you to the police," said Patti. "I heard the whole thing."

"The whole thing? You were listening in tonight?" asked Jackie.

"No, last week."

"This is Susan's, my best friend, it's her car," Patti said, "I didn't want to be seen driving my car. You know in case Dr. Spruill saw me. I didn't want him to know it was me that told."

"How did you know last week that something was going to happen?" asked Harley.

As the car sped away down Ponce-De-Leon Boulevard, Patti explained how the heating vent was located behind her desk, and how she could hear everything that went on in Spruill's office. Harley's deduction was that the school split an existing space giving Spruill an office and Patti a reception space. Rather than install separate return air ducts for the air conditioning, they put a single grill on each side of the wall to allow the air to flow. No one considered that sound waves would ride the air currents and save a life one day.

"I have heard nearly everything that goes on in there," she said.

"Why didn't you tell someone, call the police?" Jackie asked. "Where are we going?"

"Bagnilla is with the FBI. I have heard him say that he can tell Harpursville Police anything. He and the Fulton County D.A. play golf all the time. I couldn't call them and say you have a FBI agent about to kill some people that brought a couple of old parchments to the school, could I?"

"Wouldn't make sense to me," said Harley. "Turn left on Old Brison Road."

"Well, what's next?" asked Jackie.

"They intended to get you to the college tonight," Patti explained, "and if you didn't turn over this Codex book thing, then Bagnilla would search your home with a search warrant. He said dead or alive, he is going to find the book."

"Well, it was close to dead," said Harley, "Turn left on Zion Church Road."

"Take the next left," said Harley. "What the hell?"

They could see blue lights flashing in the darkness that surrounded their home. Several city and county police units were in the drive and parked along the street. An officer motioned the Jeep to move forward.

"What do I do?" asked Patti turning to Harley.

"Don't look back. Let's just drive on. You haven't done anything."

They proceeded as directed, passing the officer as he waved traffic on. He paid no heed to the passengers inside as Jackie watched people tramp the Lantanas out front. They assumed rightly that Bagnilla, using the false pretense of art theft and his position, had sent agents out to search the Macklin's home once Spruill failed. He falsely believed they would be away. It was his back-up fail proof plan. Even if the

Macklin's relented to Spruill's demand for the documents, he would have them anyway.

Chapter 28

The weather had cooled the Atlanta air into autumn temperatures. Brilliant nuclear orange Sassafras leaves, always the harbinger of fall, again announced the end of summer days. Her trees show only a hint of the color of the approaching autumn.

"Look at my flowers," said a despondent Jackie as Harley pulled into the driveway with his recovered pick-up truck.

They had spent the night with their rescuer discussing the possible paths they should take. The most obvious decision was to return home and survey any damage Bagnilla's agents wrought.

The consensus was reached that Patti had escaped identification by virtue of using Susan's car for the get-a-way. She volunteered to return to work and keep mindful of Spruill's activities. If it were not for the fear of the consequences, she would relish the role of spy.

"Look at the mess," said Harley, for he had seen boxes of articles and shelves of clothes piled on the front porch. There was another black car across the street. Harley considered making a universally recognized hand and finger gesture, but would not give them the pleasure. The screen door stood fixed in place by one of the rockers. The other was turned in its place to face the door, as if to bear witness to the coming and going of the agents.

Jackie went directly to her office and found all her translations note pads gone. Her desk drawers were in disarray, piled on the floor before the open file cabinet. She could see deep scratches in the mahogany top that were not there before. She had catalogued each and every one in her mind's inventory of her precious antiques. Nothing else had been taken, only the notes.

"Harley!" cried Jackie. "Bagnilla has the Codex!"

"Oh no," Harley replied flatly.

"I left it on my desk," she despondently said. "It's gone with all my notes too."

He stared intently at her until she caught his glare.

"What?" she wanted to know.

He only winked and nodded she should follow him outside.

It came to Jackie's mind that Harley might have had an original thought and took pains to hide the bargain books that now cost so much.

"When?" she demanded to know.

Leaning into her ear he whispered "While you were upstairs dressing."

As if he had given her directions, she whispered back instantly, "Where? And why are we whispering?"

"It's not in the house," said Harley. "And there is a black car out front with two men in it."

"What?" she asked.

"That car across the street," he said, "I haven't seen it before, have you?"

"No. You don't think?" and she stopped and took another look out the windows.

"Probably Bagnilla's men," he said.

"Do you think we are bugged?" whispered Jackie.

"Very likely, even if it is un-Constitutional," answered Harley quietly. He turned on the TV in the den and punched the button to increase the volume.

He removed the Wheatly Rocker standing guardian at the screen door. The squeaky hinge ceased it's crying once the door was pulled home by the closure. He nodded again that she should follow him to the garage.

Jackie paused at the trampled Lantanas outside the kitchen door, the purple buds now buried in the brown dirt. "They were about to die anyway," thought Jackie as her hand left the trailing stem.

Harley looked around as the hawk does hunting his prey. He felt the two men inside the car were watching him with binoculars. However, taking no chances, but depending on the shrubs in the front to screen their motions, Harley walked around the RV with Jackie in tow.

"I'm going to see if the Codex is where I left it. I want you to help distract their attention."

"How?" she inquired. "And where did you leave it?"

"I'm going to walk around the truck, kind of like I'm doing an inspection. You get in the driver's seat and flash the lights, turn on the turn signals, honk the horn things like that to draw attention to yourself up front. In the meantime I'll look and see if the box is still ours."

"Where?" she demanded to know.

"Just wait," he insisted. Jackie knew better than press Harley for information as to the whereabouts of the Codex. He loved his little dramas, so "humor him" she thought.

Since they didn't bother to lock the back door to the house, why bother with locking the door to the camper. The agents made a thorough search of the camper. They also searched the workshop.

He walked about the Silver Bow waving hands and shouting directions to Jackie to hit the brakes, turn on the lights, etc. as he pretended to inspect the Silver Bow's lighting system. There was little interest in this show and anyone watching might have returned to the sports page of the Atlanta Paper.

No one on the street could see Harley as he crouched and opened the hatch covering the septic tank drain and its associated control valves. There too, were the hose and fittings that took away the contents of that most repulsive human waste.

"What the ... "Jackie thought as she watched her husband pull a trash bag holding something shaped like a familiar white box from the septic storage space. He closed the hatch and motioned Jackie to join him inside the home.

Stooping like a quarterback hiding a football and keeping the bushes and automobiles between him and the agent's view, he carried the box inside. Should anyone have been bold enough last night to hazard playing with the nasty sewer tubing, they might have struck gold.

"How did you ..." Jackie started to ask but Harley put his finger to his lips indicating silence was needed.

"The best place to hide something is usually out in the open," he softly said. "That's why I didn't lock the hatch. Locking it would draw suspicion. Why would anyone lock the septic drain hatch? But, most important, why would anyone want to pull the septic drain hoses out?"

Jackie announced that she would make some breakfast. Harley announced that he would begin taking out the trash left by the raid. They spoke loudly that the surveillance team would know their bugs were still working.

They saw Harley fooling around with the RV and took note of the occurrences. Harley now made a performance the two agents could see as he left the kitchen door with heavily loaded plastic bags. The kind of white bags one would find in most kitchen trash cans. He carried these behind the Silver Bow where the same agents had been inspecting the trash for clues about the whereabouts of the Codex.

There were sounds of a toaster banging up slices of bread, a skillet being cleaned possibly of eggs, plates being distributed on a table top and chairs being skidded up to a table.

"What if we call Tommy Benicar?" they heard Jackie ask.

"Being a lawyer, he would only, and could only recommend, that we cooperate with a federal investigation and turn over any information that we might have," Harley said as if he were reading a script.

They heard the pair discus what they had been told by Spruill. They recounted the desperate escape from the elevator of death and saying the stairwell shooting was at the hand of Bagnilla. The agents took note of the improbable story of attempted murder by elevator and the harrowing escape attributing the tale as an attempt to incriminate their supervisor.

As the day progressed, noises from the covert listening devices fed the agents a constant buzz from a television. The channel was set to CNN 24 Hour News. There was some conversation from time to time from some of the other bugs, but so far nothing about the target of their search.

Harley continued to appear at the back door carrying white trash bags, headed for the receptacles on the other side of the Silver Bow. Jackie running the vacuum cleaner inside the home only added to the useless noise.

They were seen going to the front yard to survey the damaged flower bed. Harley walked to the mail box to withdraw envelopes and flyers left on Saturday. From there he glanced at the Ford but could not, in the brief moment and against the sun's glare, catch a good look at their faces. He was successful in establishing they were indeed being watched.

They had no illusions about their presence going undetected. It was part of the Bureau's tactics to intimidate suspects into some rash behavior that might lead to evidence.

Harley was accustomed to playing waiting games as well. Trash bags continued to be taken away. No phone calls from either the home phone or their cell phones were made going out. Some friends called in asking about Jackie's attendance at upcoming social events and general girl talk. She acknowledged the invitations and said she would attend. Harley shifted his F-150 pickup to park beside the shop. He moved Jackie's VUE to park beside the house. And the Silver Bow, was parked behind the house. The agent's day passed without any further incidents of note occurring.

The second shift of agents parked in front of the Taurus. The new agents were in a white Ford E-250 van. It was plain and without signage, but with dark tinted windows on all doors, reeked of suspicion. All the agents got out of their vehicles to discuss how boring the detail had been. Mention was made about the weather cooling off, and the replacements discussed running the motor to keep warm. All agreed that it was acceptable in the policy guidelines to do so, as long as the field agent in charge was informed. Proper phone calls were made and logbooks passed between vehicles. The Taurus pulled away but the van did not move into the former's position. The new parking spot further blocked Harley's movements.

A light frost was expected that evening and news of its impending arrival went out over all forms of media. There was no surprise that afternoon when Jackie and Harley could be seen bringing rolls of plastic sheeting out to cover the plants. Each carried a 5 gallon plastic pail. Jackie would take rocks from the bucket and place them at the edges of the sheeting to hold it in place. Harley appeared to be carefully watering the plants pouring the contents of a sprinkler bucket along the ground. Once all was covered they returned to the house. The door closed and lights upstairs were seen coming on.

"Did they see us?" asked Jackie.

"Couldn't help but to see us," said Harley.

It was about 9:00 p.m. when the agents were blinded by the headlights of the Saturn VUE suddenly coming on. The two agents pulled their night vision goggles off as the glare from the car lights washed out everything in their field of view. Then they could only see the front of the home and the car in the drive. They would see the silhouette of Harley as he crossed in front of the car.

"Get in and buckle up," said Harley as he helped Jackie climb into the Silver Bow. After much discussion the night before, they had come to the conclusion that whatever was in the Codex was worth someone dying for, worth someone killing for and worth someone willing to put their career on the line as well. Until they knew what they had and who to turn it over to, they decided to hide out. It was a given that all forms of communication, from the home phone to their cell phones, to even the email would be tapped, watched and listened to. They would hide out and Jackie would translate.

All day long they had been working in plain sight. Each carried bags one way from home to what the agents assumed was the trash or garage. Secreted in each of the white plastic bags was clothing, dry goods, can goods, groceries, pasta, rice, crackers, and two chicken breasts, the only fresh meat in the house. To this they added soda and bottle water. Everything they thought they could get on board and live for the next few days as they sorted out their next move. Neither would sit by and wait for Bagnilla, but would take charge and make him play catch up.

The house had shielded his movements around the back of their motorized home as he hitched the SportCraft 4 wheel drive ATV. His hope was to add confusion to the description of their get-a-way vehicle. Their home also shielded the wide path that led from the back yard into the woods. Tall pines lined each side of a wide path casting a dark shadow even in broad daylight. Harley often envisioned the trees as creating a green tunnel. The pathway was last used two decades ago as a logging road when timber was taken from the property. Before that, it was the way sharecroppers took taking their products to the Harpursville Markets.

Nearly a century ago, the path was built by the long gone Western Atlantic Railroad that was the backbone of the Marthasville station. It was a sixteen foot wide flat road bed with a solid unmoving foundation of gravel and coal ash from the numerous trains that rolled on its course over the decades. Other abandoned railroad lines around Atlanta like this one had been converted into suburban pathway parks. This abandoned roadbed ran into the War Woman Bike Trail which crossed Georgia Highway 92 from time to time. One of those intersecting points was four hundred yards from the back door of the Macklin's home and deep in the Georgia Pines. Had the agents been able to see Harley, they would have seen he had been clearing tree limbs along the gravel trail that would have impacted the Silver Bow.

Once the RV was hidden, Jackie sprayed painted over the bold lettering *Silver Bow* on the side of the truck with white paint. She swapped the VUE license plate with the Silver Bow plate. She also gathered her personal pharmacy of antibiotics, antihistamines, anti-inflammatories, and anti-pain medication she had accumulated over the years, just like Boo. Even expired medicine still has some use left in it she would say to justify keeping it. When they hit the road they would be as prepared as they could be.

Jackie watched Harley, from her vantage point deep in the cab of the Silver Bow, as he pulled a lighter from his coat pocket. He bent to the task of igniting a fluid on the driveway. The little trail of flammable vapors moved slowly across the yard. It was a blue flame with a small yellow tip. This one small flame began to grow, not up but sideways into a little wall of flame. It did not race across the lawn but went slowly, leisurely, almost an amiable saunter in the cool air. It was fueled by the slow burning kerosene Harley kept in the workshop.

Harley turned from the fire to the Silver Bow. Jackie continued to watch the flame crawl across her lawn, into her flower bed, and under the plastic drapes they had placed earlier that day. She, Harley, the agents across the road, and anyone within one mile of Old Brison road with hearing and eyesight, would be dazzled as those plastic drapes exploded into a ball of flame not unlike a nuclear bomb. The composition of flammable liquids Harley had sprinkled earlier and held in place by the plastic sheeting had ignited.

"Here we go," said Harley and he put the gear shift in the forward position. He headed for the War Woman Bike Trail. Jackie winced as she saw her trees catch fire.

"Isn't that gate locked?" asked Jackie about the metal obstruction in their path. It had sported a rusty chain and lock for years. She doubted that it would ever open but Harley had already separated the links. Now he slowed the RV and gently nudged the gate open with the front bumper. Three hundred yards down the old Western Atlantic Railway roadbed he stopped at the highway crossing. Looking to his left, he turned the Silver Bow to the right and disappeared down Georgia Highway 92. The jogging path cut twelve minutes off the usual driving time. Fifteen minutes later he was on the interstate headed for the infamous Spaghetti Junction and a choice of four different directions.

Chapter 30

The grandfather clock in the hallway had just struck the tenth hour of the evening when the front door bell began to ring the arrival of visitors.

"Who in the world could that be," thought Boo as she laid down another knitting project. She pushed the lever to drop the footrest of her recliner, gave shove against the padded armrest and rose to open the door. She turned on the porch light to see, to her happy surprise, the friendly faces of Jackie and Harley.

"Come on in, you dears, it must be freezing out there," she cried out once she opened the door.

The sun had been down less than three hours but the afternoon warmth had gone quickly into the night air. Still, fifty degrees was cold to most who are Southern born and raised. Boo had the heat on in the house, and would wear a coat if she went out. In the summer she and her friends would sit in the shade of her front porch at eighty degrees and discuss putting on a sweater.

"Thank you," said Jackie. "We hate to arrive unannounced but we could not call. I hope we did not come at a bad time."

"Surprise visits are the best," replied Boo. "I guess those things don't come with a phone," she said pointing to the Silver Bow. "No, this isn't a bad time. I was just sitting here with Johnny watching the TV. Nip Tuck is about to start. Do you watch that? It is the most scandalous show," she giggled as they entered the den. "Honey, this is that nice doctor Jackie Macklin from Atlanta, and her husband."

Harley could help but to note that Dr. Jackie's name was remembered while he was introduced only as her husband.

"This is John," she said.

"Hi, John, call me Jackie," she said as she took John's hand, "and this is Harley."

"Nice to meet you," John said. "Boo certainly thinks the world of you and your cures. Cleared her bursitis right up," he said referring to the last phone call.

"Glad to help," said Jackie.

"Have a seat," offered Boo. "Now what brings ya'll to Tallahatchie this time of year, or are you just passing through?"

They paused for a moment. One reason was of concern and one of warning. The matter called for some tact and a careful course. Jackie did not want to upset Boo beyond a reasonable measure,

"Boo," said Jackie, "Did you keep that lovely gold leaf frame picture of your Uncle Willy and the two men we saw at Aunt Barbara's?"

Boo looked surprised at this question and paused to consider what she had done with the item after the sale.

"Yes, I did keep that," she answered. She got up again and went to the end of the shelves that ran the length of one wall of the den. There she reached down and pulled to her the requested photo. Turning and walking to Jackie she asked if they had come all the way from Atlanta just for the frame. Jackie said that they were stopping by on their way west. She left it at that vague point.

Jackie took the photo and Harley looked at it with her. There were the three men, all smiling for the camera. There too was the desk with the glass top, and there also, was the Empire period, gilt bronze patina bouillote lamp on the table to the group's left. The shaft supported a dark green tole shade. It was a heavy looking lamp even to the eye of the camera. The glint of the camera's flash off the square base shone like a star. Above where the three arms joined the shaft, there was enough of metal conduit running to the fennel for a man to grab with both hands.

"Do you have this lamp?" asked Jackie and pointing it out to Boo.

"No, I guess that was in his office. I didn't ever see anything that came out of Uncle Willy's office except for some personal things, you know from his desk."

"What things?" Jackie slyly asked.

Jackie and Harley had moved onto the same Canapé sofa that they had sat on only a few weeks before.

"Ink pens, note pads. There was a picture of him and Aunt Barbara when they were young, maybe right after they got married. He had several post cards. I guess from the places he had been to. Did you want to see them? " Boo asked. "I don't think I kept much of that."

"No, that's OK," said Jackie. "You don't know what happened to the lamp?"

"Honey, I have no idea," Boo said.

Jackie returned to studying the photo to gain some time to consider her next question. She studied again the file boxes in Dr. Eckland's office resembling the one now resting in the Silver Bow outside. "Boo, did any of these file boxes come here?"

"No," she said and added, "Now that I think about it that friend of Aunt Barbara's, his name is Gill de something."

"Caudelle and Gill DeLauzun," Jackie reminded her.

"Yes, he called to ask what he should do with Uncle Willy's estate."

"And what did you tell him."

"I really did not want to fool with another estate sale. The will said if he was not survived by Aunt Barbara, then it all went to the university. I told DeLauzun to turn it all over to them. I trust that he did."

"Then Gill might know what happened to the lamp and the files," Harley contemplatively said to Jackie.

They continued their visit with general topics. Boo offered to make some coffee, which they initially declined given the late hour. The two women went into the kitchen to start the coffee maker. Jackie said that Harley would just as soon have a glass of sweet tea. John finished watching Nip / Tuck with Harley.

Jackie did not have to request the sweet tea to be brewed, for all good southern women sweeten their ice tea with real sugar and keep a jug of it on hand. Boo poured Harley a glass of her dark, rich, thick, 40 weight, soda powder, aged 3 days in the frigidaire sweet tea. It was her own version of a home-made brandy.

"Are you in any trouble?" asked Boo. "You don't seem yourself."

"We had some trouble yes."

"What kind?" she asked.

"My home was searched by the FBI," she did not mentioned the near fatal elevator ride, the desperate stairwell escape, and blowing up her flower garden.

"The FBI?" asked the startled Boo. "Why, whatever for?"

"We believe they were looking for that box of Latin books you sold Harley," replied Jackie. "An FBI agent came to our house and said the books were stolen property of the university."

"No," responded a surprised Boo. "Uncle Willy would never steal any books."

"Oh bull!" proclaimed John from his recliner.

"I know, I know," said Jackie. She reassured Boo that they had testimony from Gill that Dr. Eckland came into the books in a legal and lawful manner. This calmed Boo to know her family member was not a thief.

"So why did they say that?"

"I think this agent is cooked," was how Jackie put it to her. "I think he wants the books for himself... maybe to sell."

"Do you think they are that valuable?" Boo asked.

"I don't know. But we are going to find out," Jackie said stopping short of telling Boo what she had translated so far.

"Well Honey, the coffee is ready."

"Why did you ask to see the photo?" Boo asked after drinks were served.

"I didn't want to get you upset, but we are beginning to think that something might have happened to cause Uncle Willy to die." Jackie tried to put this news as delicately as she could.

"Whatever do you mean?" asked John turning off the television.

"We have come across some evidence that the fire might not have been an accident."

"You mean that someone may have murdered poor Uncle Willy?" Boo was both startled and upset at this news.

"We are not saying murdered, just that the fire might not have been an accident. That someone may have started the fire to cover up something else. His being there and dying of smoke inhalation might have been unintended ... an accident," she left it like that, hoping to calm Boo.

"Have you told anyone about this?" asked John.

"No, we are still trying to sort this all out before we go to the police."

They spent about an hour with the Bristows. Their conversations included warnings that the couple might expect a visit from the local FBI. Jackie advised them to tell anyone from any law enforcement agency the truth as far as they knew it.

"You don't have to tell them what you think we are up to," Jackie said, "as we did not tell you what we are going to do.

Just answer their questions honestly but try not to add anything extra. Be careful."

Boo cut her off. "Yes honey, we know, 'anything you say can be used against you in a court of law.' We watch COPS all the time, and my Lord, how people will shoot their mouth off and get into more trouble."

"Well," said Jackie, "they might come by, and don't be surprised if they say that we stole the books too."

Boo's response to this was to call the very notion an expletive eight letter word that involved the excrement of a large barnyard animal of the bovine species. As Harley was not expecting this sweet dear old Sunday School woman teacher to use such barroom language, he nearly blew sweet tea out his nose. Jackie sniggered herself.

Chapter 31

"We have something." said Special Agent Judson Harmon to a livid Bagnilla. "Credit card transaction just came in from a grocery store in Breman, Georgia at 9:27 p.m. last night. They bought meats, vegetables and bottled water."

"About god damn time someone found something," said Bagnilla nearly screaming with the frustration of having lost the whereabouts of the Macklins. "Where the hell is Breman?"

"A small town on the west Georgia border," said Harmon. "Looks like they are headed to their daughter's home in Arizona," he theorized based on his experience seeing most crooks on the run go to family for aid.

"I want to issue an all points bulletin," Bagnilla ordered, "to all agencies west of here to be on the lookout for that motor-home. It can't be that hard to miss. Be sure to include the license plate," he continued unaware of Jackie's deceptive switch.

The investigation was now being treated as an art theft crime. Bagnilla, was the agent in charge of the Southeastern Arts Crime Division of the Department of the Bureau, and had been instrumental in the recovery of the lost ceremonial sword belonging to Junior Lieutenant Alexander T. Hastings, Concord Rangers, 53rd Regiment, Georgia Infantry. In 1862, none other than the legendary Stonewall Jackson bestowed upon the junior lieutenant a gold gilt handle presentation sword. His decedent donated it to the Confederate Museum in Charleston, South Carolina where it was stolen fifty four years later during the commotion caused by Hurricane Hazel in 1954. He was now pursuing the Codex under the pretense that it too was a stolen artifact.

A call was made on Harley's cell phone and was picked up by the three towers along the Georgia state line where Interstate 20 crossed into Alabama. The call had been placed 9:37:16 to a number in Phoenix, Az. It was eighteen minutes and thirty eight seconds in duration. The number traced to Mr. and Mrs. Allen G. Condra. Then the cell phone towers reported nothing further as Harley had removed the battery there-by preventing communication between the phone and towers.

The Macklin's internet service provider was contacted and told to provide a history of use, but they were fighting the inquisition until a subpoena was produced. Bagnilla had not charged the Macklin's with the theft, only that they might be in possession of the stolen Codex. He was working on the evidence to prove their complicity in the theft and win a subpoena. Curtis was manipulating the video tape of the couple entering the stairwell long after school hours, entering a vacant lobby on a Sunday evening and passing Dr. Eckland's office door.

A report of a large white RV camper similar in description to the Silver Bow had been seen in the words of the witnesses, barreling down the War Woman Bike Trail. The incident occurred just minutes after the two agents stopped their pursuit at the Macklin's burning driveway. Seems a Cub Scout Pack was having a campout in the back yard of their den leader's home just off the bike trail. Campfire talk had taken a turn to the dark side with the cub master re-telling the story of the Ghost Train of the War Woman Rail Road.

With as creepy a voice as he could muster, the Cub Leader began the ghost story, "The train was supposed to have crashed in Confederate Creek with a load of wounded Civil War Troops returning from Gettysburg." The Cub Leader paused only for effect, "today, those of us who live along the old tracks will hear at midnight what sounds like a train and mysterious lights go flashing by." As he said this, the Old Silver Bow came racing by with Harley blowing the horn at a deer crossing the path. Cub Scouts were running up pine trees trying to escape the Ghost Train. The Cherokee County Sheriff Deputy was laughing his badge off as he took the Cub Leaders doubtable report of a speeding RV on the old railroad bed. The deputy was not laughing once he received the lookout bulletin for the Silver Bow.

The general details of the above incident made it to the Atlanta Headquarters. It gave a break to an otherwise somber investigation. But in Bagnilla's eye, there was no mistaking that these must be desperate people and they must be carrying the Codex. He checked the computer for any more transactions.

Throughout the day, Bagnilla returned to the credit card window on his p.c. That afternoon he saw a purchase for 48.3 gallons of gasoline at $3.7159 per gallon, totaling $179.65. The purchase had been completed at a station in Pell City,

Alabama. This transaction took place that morning at 11:46:19 a.m. local time.

The one detail the transaction would not reveal was the odd occurrence at the Quick Fill station just south of the Saint Clair and Chaptuckney county lines. A little old woman and an elderly man, possibly her husband by the way they behaved, pulled up to pump number 3 and inserted a credit card in the pump. They did this twice as they were confused trying to follow the screen's instructions. When the equipment authorized the card, they took turns at the pump filling up. She topped off her dark green, 1998 Oldsmobile Delta 88 Regency. He filled up his 1963 Chevy half ton pick-up truck and three, five gallon gas cans in the bed. They put the 48.3 gallon purchase on the card Jackie had given them that morning, which would be about a fill up for a RV motor home. The station was at exit number one fifty eight. "A" in Pell City, Alabama.

Jackie and Harley had parked the Silver Bow in "Boo's" back yard and spent the night. At 6:00 a.m., which is late for most farmers, they awoke to John knocking at the Silver Bow door. During the breakfast of farm fresh eggs and homemade biscuits, Jackie asked if they would not each mind having a free tank of gas. Only catch was they had to use her credit card and make the purchase late that morning in Pell City. They did not tell the couple that they would be approaching the Alabama – Tennessee border by then. Jackie felt if they were questioned as to the whereabouts of the Macklins, then no answer would be the honest answer.

Chapter 32

"The colors are lovely aren't they?" Jackie said from the plush comfort of the passenger's seat. She did not care if he answered for she was not asking Harley. It was that kind of statement one always makes when coming off the top of Sand Mountain in Alabama and looking up the Tennessee River Valley, across the Nick-a-Jack Lake, to see the mountainside glowing in the many colors of autumn. The bright light of the sun unobstructed by clouds amplified the depth of the visual sensation.

Earlier that morning, the Silver Bow had left Boo's taking the U.S. Highway 231 north and picked up Interstate 59 going northeast toward Chattanooga. At Fort Payne, Alabama, they left the freeway on U.S. Highway 72, and went northwest to Scottsboro. This path carried the Silver Bow over Sand, Fox and Tray Mountains. Past the whistle-stop towns of Rainsville, Cloudland, Thunder Falls, Blackankle, Fabius and Old Fabius; Minuscule towns that had zip codes and little else. The valleys of the North Alabama landscape, are broad and flat given to raising cattle, horses, corn and cotton. Field and pasture stop abruptly at the tree line that begins the sheer cliffs of these mountains. There is no ground for the tread of the tractor, the boots of the farmer or hooves of livestock, except for goats, as the foundations of these mountains rise at angles too steep for any agricultural use save that of weeds.

There are no peaks on these mountains. The tops are as flat and broad as the valleys on each side. Under it all, are the caves where Harley and his fellow cavers would spend hours and days wandering the passages in the halls of midnight sun.

The economy along U.S. Highway 72 corridor is fueled by three industries - chicken production, selling antiques and having yard sales. Here, the yard sale is a cottage industry.

For some, the yard sale is a home based career. There were a few amateurs holding yard sales here and there as Harley drove along. Buildings in every whistle-stop town left vacant by the depression and boil weevil plagues had been converted into antique stores or flea markets. Even the mom and pop convenience stores had a metric ton of rusting plough blades, railroad lanterns missing the globes, and pitted enameled pots hanging out for sale.

In Scottsboro, Alabama, in the Little River Valley, there lies a massive complex of steel buildings. Hundreds of acres of prime farmland are underneath steel roofing and inside the climate is controlled by York Air Conditioning. This was not an automobile manufacturing facility. This was not a mammoth chicken processing plant. Inside these immense rows of steel enclosures lies the Mecca of shopping centers in Alabama, and most of the Old South - *Unclaimed Baggage*.

This is a bargain hunter's dream land. The final resting place of unclaimed baggage once feared to be forever lost in transit from all modes of public transport. If you lost it, they have it. Jackie loved to explore antique stores and this bargain barn and found a conspirator in Molly Conner.

Mr. Jubal Conner and his wife Molly carved niches in their stand of Tulip Poplars for a few people to park their campers and stay a spell. The creek that ran across the farm originated with the water falling out of the opening of Poplar Ridge Cave. Generations ago galvanized steel pipe placed in the cave entrance, was connected to a pump and running on Mr. Roosevelt's rural electrification, supplied water to the farm and home. This crude water system expired when rust perforated the piping more times than could be patched. The Conners no longer drew the household water supply from the cave spring, but bored a well on the property.

Harley asked why they did not continue to pump water from the cave. "Damn cavers kept stirring up the mud," answered Jubal.

Molly would not let him ban cave explorers. The spelunkers knew how to grease the wheel and did so by naming formations and the dark rooms after her and her family. They would return her favor with photos of these geo wonders for her to keep.

The big man at the end of the drive turned his head as the Silver Bow rolled up to see who was coming. Jubal was the big man, big as in taller than most of his generation. He stood six feet, five inches tall. A carnival hawker might put his weight at three hundred evenly distributed pounds. His nose reflected his girth. It was an enlarged, bulbous, and red nose. Jackie's first impression and diagnosis was he had Rosacea. It did not seem painful to him. He never brought it up and she would not violate his privacy and tell him that the nose could be reduced with tetracycline, minocycline, erythromycin, or doxycycline.

Jubal was at the feed trough in the coral. He thumped the slop bucket against the bottom of the feed trough in order to dislodge any and every nibble of feed that he could. The Silver Bow came to a stop bordering the coral fence.

"What brings you to this neck of the woods?" asked Jubal as he upended the bucket and placed it on the fence post. "You and your friends going caving?"

"No sir. It's Jackie and I this time…just the two of us."

"Come to take in the color? Or is Jackie here for Antique Alley?"

"We are just traveling through, thought we would stop by, just stay the night." Harley said in a nonchalant way.

"Traveling through to where?" asked Jubal for he was all about economy of motion. He did not believe in just driving for the sake of driving. He did not move until he knew his starting and finishing points.

"Just here and there," Harley answered being purposely vague with his friend. Boo had become involved in their escapade, and he would resist including others.

"Left here and went there," joked Jubal. "You hungry? Let's see what Ma has on the lunch table."

Harley and Jackie sat on the bench at the kitchen table. Someone during the depression had made the furniture and out of necessity used grooved planks from old doors in its construction.

The group talked of family and current events in the national news. Jackie invited Molly to go with her to the antique stores. While Molly loved to get out and browse the bargain stores, Jackie loved the thrill of the hunt in genuine antiquing. Jubal had chores around the farm and Harley volunteered to assist.

"Aren't these lovely?" Molly asked pointing to a pair of vases. They were tall, slender, and very elegant. The rims, top and bottom, were of cobalt blue with graceful blue handles. Two golden cherubs held aloft a gold crown above the alabaster figure of The Dauphin.

"Aren't these lovely?" Molly asked again to Jackie who was quiet and disconnected this day.

"Jackie?"

"Yes," answered Jackie leaving her the thoughts of the recent days and focused on Molly's question. "Sorry, what did you say?"

"These are French?"

"Yes, 19th century Faience Vases," answered Jackie. "What do they list for?"

"$100.00," Molly said as she held aloft the vase to find the price stuck to the base.

"That's a good deal. Probably would sell for twice that maybe more in the right market."

"Really?" Molly said returning the porcelain to the shelf. "And what would I do with it if I bought it?"

Jackie did not answer. She had drifted up the aisle with her thoughts as well.

"Jackie?"

"Yes? You should buy it."

"Jackie? What is bothering you? You haven't heard a word I've said since we arrived."

"I don't want you to get involved," was Jackie's half hearted reply. She did want to talk with someone other than Harley to regain a perspective. She was sure in their decision but still felt the need to reaffirm the choice.

"Involved with what? You and Harley having some trouble?" Molly said moving closer to her friend.

"No, nothing like that," she answered understanding the implication. "We are on the run."

"Run?" Molly was aghast. "What are you running from?"

The two moved outside the building and found what used to be called a hardware store now converted into a cafe. In these abandoned farm communities, empty train depots are now antique malls and old general stores are converted into a gallery of trendy art photos.

They took a table in the corner of the wrought iron fence that corralled the patrons of the Café Carolina. The server of the day presented the specials of the day. Jackie ordered an espresso macchiato and tried to get her older friend to do the same. Molly would have none of it and asked for a coffee. She had to repeat the order when the server asked what kind of coffee. She was a straight up instant black coffee drinker. She did add a little cream and a little sugar when it arrived.

Talk turned to the events of the past. Without revealing how they came into possession of the Codex, Jackie explained how they had to flee their home. Now she felt that they were criminals running from the law.

Molly sat listening to Jackie's tale with little interruption breaking into her story only for clarification and order of events. Molly raised the possibility that the books might be stolen from somewhere else. She suggested Dr. Eckland had come into possession of stolen goods by honest means. "Kind of like buying farm tools at a flea market Saturday morning not knowing they were stolen Friday night," was Molly's illustration.

"I don't think this was the case," Jackie said. She felt that if someone had brought to Uncle Willy's attention that the Codex was stolen, he would have been willing to return the books. They continued to discuss the possibilities of motivations to hide the treasure, and those that drove an FBI agent to misuse his position to recover the books. Try as they could, they found no rationale for the beginning and no foreseeable favorable conclusion to Jackie's dilemma.

"This FBI agent?" Molly asked as they were turning into the drive of the house. "Who did you say he was?"

"I didn't," said Jackie. "I do not want to accuse someone falsely. He might have had honorable intentions."

"Still, I could tell Jubal to call someone," Molly offered with her voice fading.

"Call someone?"

"Yes dear, after all he spent twenty five years in the Secret Service. He has been retired for twenty years now but he still touches base now and then."

It was never their intention to impose at dinner. Jubal and Molly insisted the two save their rations and share the evening meal with them. Molly stuffed fresh quail with sourdough bread crumbs and sausage cured out with sea salt and fresh ground black pepper from Jubal's smokehouse. Jackie was allowed to peel the shallots that went into the stuffing. Molly would not suffer the intrusion much but did allow Jackie to make an Apple and Parsnip Soup using the fruits and herbs from just beyond the barnyard. The braised quail rested atop a wild mushroom hash made with chopped red potatoes Jubal had retrieved that afternoon from the garden. Harley had gathered from Poplar Ridge Cave, some porcini and chanterelle mushrooms. From the small wine cellar aboard the Silver Bow came a 2003 cabernet from Sebastiani Secolo vineyards. Afterwards, they all took coffee, black, on the patio.

The conversation during dinner quickly focused on the plight of the Macklins. They knew Jubal was in Dallas, Texas, November 22, 1963. He was not close enough to Dealey Plaza to have heard the noises coming from the open park that infamous day. He was packing up to return to Washington and resume his duties as a member of the team of Secret Service Agents assigned to travel in advance of the President. He had a hand in preparing the limousine, in removing the protective roof, in clearing the trunk, and checking under the hood. He continued to serve in the Treasury Department, once providing security for the former governor of Alabama, George Wallace. He was dismayed but not shocked to hear that one of "Hoover's Boys" had gone "off the farm". He agreed with Jackie that the front porch interrogation was not standard policy. He could not fathom what Bagnilla was up to, but would make some calls, as Molly suggested.

"I'll see if I can find Andrew Oaks. Last time we spoke he was on the trail of some counterfeit Franklins with a decidedly North Korean Accent. Seems old Ben was sneaking into the World Bank by way of a Chinese printing firm. I'll bet Andy could get us some intelligence."

Jubal gave points to Harley such as not using the cell phones as they would be traced and quickly if Bagnilla was tapping the recipient of their call.

"Go buy a hand full of those pay-as-you-go phones ... the ones without plans," was his advice. "Get a few for you and Jackie at different stores. That way you shouldn't draw suspicion should you be seen buying a dozen phones at one."

"Why buy several?" asked Jackie.

"Use them one or two times and throw them away. Get the minimum number of minutes. When the agent is monitoring phone calls he'll watch the caller id each time before picking up. He'll be looking for say ... Harley's id before he starts recording. You don't want to be wasting time listening to someone calling about the weather. When an agent sees his target's id, then he can start a trace. Make them work to find you. And take the batteries out as soon as you hang up."

"I do want to call someone," said Jackie. "I want to talk to Gill again. I want to know where that lamp is."

Harley nodded in agreement.

"Speaking of which," Jubal said, "can we see the book?"

Harley retrieved the white file box from the storage space under the couch in the motor home. He brought it to the glass top patio table. He removed the top and reached for the recent notes Jackie had made. These he laid to one side. Jubal picked up the top notepad and began to read. Molly gasped as Jackie gently pulled up the top book.

"Is that it?" Molly asked with the reverence due such an artifact.

"Yes…one of three," Jackie whispered.

"Three?"

"Yes, I think this is the first volume."

"Why? How do you know?" asked Jubal now returning from his study.

"He starts his journal with his bar mitzvah."

"Bar Mitzvah?" asked Jubal, "so he was Jewish?"

Jackie and Harley began to tell of all they had discovered, of the author's Jewish rite of passage, the initiation into the cult of Mithrias and the introduction into the debauchery of paganism.

"Then he had an epiphany … he committed to Judaism," Jackie told her audience.

"Really?" asked a surprised Jubal. "What made him do that?"

"Near drowning," Harley explained. "Happens all the time. When people see their god, or belief system failing them in their time of crisis they jump ship. No pun intended."

"I'm not so sure about that," stated a sneering Jackie.

Harley began his social history lesson. As he explained it, back then, superstitions not only abounded but they ruled every single aspect of daily life. People were afraid to walk through a doorway without saying some incantation of protection. They would not plant until all the signs were favorable and the offerings had been made. They were afraid of even numbers in things like calendars or business. Ancient people thought demons could hide under leaves of lettuce waiting to be swallowed and take possession of their victims. If you sneezed, someone would ask a blessing. If you were alone, you asked for yourself. Childbirth held the deepest fears. You thanked Diana for fertility, and asked her overall protection during the pregnancy.

"I remember from our obstetrics classes The *Parcae*," Jackie added.

"They were three Roman goddesses of destiny called *Nona, Decima* and *Morta*," Harley said. "Nona referred to what we call the eighth month of pregnancy, *Decima* referred to what we would call a nine month birth, and *Morta* referred to stillbirth. After your child was born, *Carmenta* was called upon to determine the child's fate. In short, you didn't take a," as he winced to indicate a bowel movement, "without asking some god's permission."

Jubal and Molly were intrigued at the revelation of both the daily life of a Roman and the deep convictions of the unknown author.

"So once he nearly drowns and his Hebrew slave Achaicus prayed, and the storm quieted, he was converted?" Jubal asked.

"Yes," Harley said. "He had his revelation, his moment on the mountain. He committed to the one faith that was proven to deliver the miracle when called for. And he joined the Roman army. You can find hundreds of books by hundreds of people, each with their own personal epiphanies. One common thread is there is some calamity or impending crisis, during which or just after surviving, they have their moment of truth. They convert from patterns of self-destructive behavior into new patterns of mostly non-self-destructive behavior."

"There are no atheists in foxholes," Jubal injected quoting the famous World War Two journalist Ernie Pile.

"Something like that," said Harley. "When in doubt, pray to them all and hope you appeal to the right one."

Jackie introduced her latest translations exposing more of the drudgery of army life under Terentius Rufus. There were more gripes and complaints about the quality, quantity and variety of the food supply. There was always grain from which they made their own breads. Olives and grapes were in abundant supply while in season. Some vegetables could be found from time to time. Most of the produce and all of the meat would come from merchants at the market. For the soldiers, this would mean daily trips to the town square and being exposed to the local culture and to attacks. They could count on being pelted by rocks from over a stone wall or from a roof top, from a hedge, or from someone hiding in the crowded market.

"Things haven't changed in two thousand years," said Harley when he heard her report.

She had discovered the author had an interest the deeper mysteries that is Judaism. "He writes that he had to stand afar off and strain to hear his mentor Gamaliel as the learned teacher would not waste his time on the Roman infidel," Jackie said.

"Yes," added Harley. "Only a few of the other students, followers and devotees would tolerate his Roman presence. Some of the more radical would express their feelings openly. Other than glares, growls and hisses, they would spit upon the ground in his path to soil his feet with the mud that they made... and these were the nice guys."

"He saw himself as being a teacher one day, "Jackie said, "in similar fashion as his idol. He goes on about the lessons of Gamaliel. Seems he spent all his days off at the man's feet or as close as the others would allow," said Jackie.

"Now who is making bad puns?" Harley asked. "Idol? If it is Paul," he added, "then this might coincide with the passages in Acts chapter 22."

"Acts 22?" asked Jubal as he put down the notepad.

"Paul announces himself to have been born in Tarsus early in chapter 22," Harley said. "He would have spoken Aramaic. He was raised in the Antioch. Since it is written that Paul was standing in the Jerusalem Temple before the Sanhedrin, it matches what our writer says about his experience." Harley had revisited his earlier education in Christian Religion, paying close attention to the book of Acts.

"Do you think this is the journal of Saint Paul?" Jubal asked now intent on learning more about their find.

"We can't say for sure, just yet," Jackie answered. "We have found some close references to Gamaliel, Antioch, and King Herod Agrippa."

"King Herod? Haven't I heard of him before?" asked Molly as she carefully laid the Codex she was holding on the table. "He isn't the one that killed all those babies is he?"

"Alleged, and I'm afraid no, it was his grandfather Herod the Great," Harley explained. "Our journalist wrote that his uncle had seen wise men passing through Antioch on their way out of Galilee. Since Antioch is north of there, they were from the East, then they had to have been on the lam," Harley gave a chuckle at this pun that no one else acknowledged.

"The writer did not know Herod?" asked Jubal.

"No, not personally. But his uncle met some Wise Men - they met Herod."

Molly let escape a slight gasp."Well, if this is the journal of Saint Paul, then it must be worth a fortune."

"We are not interested in the money," Jackie said taking the high ground. "We want to understand what we have and try to gain some understanding of what Eckland was going to do with it, and why Bagnilla wants to take it."

"Excuse me," injected Harley, "I paid for it. I will decide what happens to it and how much it sells for. I always wanted to go to Christies Auction Barn. Probably get two maybe three hundred dollars for the entire collection," he said teasingly.

Chapter 33

Next morning a pale dark sky in the east saw the Morning Star sitting atop Lookout Mountain. To the west the constellation Taurus was descending upon Mount Eagle, marking the passing of the vernal equinox. One of Harley's eyes opened at the sound of someone in the campground trying to "silently" chop firewood. It never failed. He could count on it as he could a digital alarm clock. At 6:00 a.m. sharp, someone would be up, aware that those all around were still in slumber, and try to start a campfire as quietly as possible. Harley would open his door and glare at the offender.

"Whops, sorry," they would say when they caught his glare. "I was trying to be quiet as I could. I hope I didn't wake you." They would apologize knowing they had broken the peace for all in the community.

"I'll bet Jubal is up," he thought and slipped silently out of the motor-home.

The air had become heavy with both chill and the moisture needed for the morning dew. Jubal noted the evening before that the morning would probably be thick with fog. The camping couple made plans to stay the next day as Jubal would contact Agent Oaks. Molly invited Jackie to join her later in the week canning some jams and jellies. Jackie had not done this since childhood when she watched and helped their maid make homemade preserves. Molly enjoyed the company, as long as they did not get in the way. Harley would work around the farm with Jubal.

Jackie and Molly wanted to experience the Cumberland Mall of East Ridge, Chattanooga, or so the billboards along I-24 urged shoppers to do. They spent a part of the day wandering the aisles and passages of various and sundry department stores and boutiques. Jackie went into every electronic store that sold cellular phones and left the mall with three pay-as-you go phones. Each time she paid cash and gave a different name and address. Molly asked for Jackie's old phone saying it could come in handy for misdirecting.

They stopped by an organic food store on the North Bank of the Tennessee River, a trendy upscale community of Chattanooga. They bought fresh smoked gouda and Molly was out of cayenne pepper. Jackie needed grappa for dessert. Even though it was expensive, there was no substitute, so she splurged on behalf of her friends. Their dinner plans that night would be twelve-spice pan seared beef tenderloin, with smoked gouda and a sweet sausage risotto. This was turning out to be a camping trip where Harley and Jackie might gain weight.

Jackie call Gill DeLauzun. He was asked about the table lamp. He remembered the item on Dr. Eckland's desk. He had admired it himself many times. "Looked antique," he said to Jackie from the other end of the phone call.

"Late 19th century," was Jackie's response." Any idea what might have happened to it and the rest of the furniture?"

"Well, to mention it," he said brooding, "James became director pro-tem, he would have dispensed with the furniture, files and whatever else was left in the room. He would have been the one to issue the work order to have the office re-painted."

"What would he have done with the furniture?" she pressed him for more information.

"Would probably have Matt, the maintenance tech for the building, haul everything away or store what needed to be stored. I think some of it might be in the basement," referring to the basement area of the Old Central.

"Matt? Matt Turncock?" she asked. "Do you have his phone number?"

"No, but I know who does ... Patti Longnecker. I'll put you through if you wish to speak with her."

The phone rang twice when Patti answered.

"Patti? This is Jackie Macklin. How are you?"

"Fine and you?" she asked.

"We are doing well enough," Jackie said haltingly, trying not to gush too much in appreciation for the heroic rescue. "Is this a good time to chat?"

"Yes, go ahead."

She wanted the news from Patti's end so she might learn what Spruill and Bagnilla were up to. Patti reported that the school was in the middle of the semester and Spruill was quite busy. She had not seen Bagnilla since the Sunday night when he was taking shots at them. Patti had put through several calls from the agent to her boss. Jackie asked for Matt's phone number.

"Sure, can I ask why?"

Jackie hesitated, not wanting to give Patti more information than was necessary. But she considered Patti might know the whereabouts of the lamp and said, "We want to find that lamp Dr. Eckland kept on his desk. We saw in an old photo Dr. Eckland had a bronze 19th century table lamp on his desk. It would be very heavy … had a small dark green tole lamp shade. Did you ever see it?" asked Jackie.

"How did you know about that?" Patti instinctively whispered. "Yes! I loved that lamp. Dr. Eckland would kid about leaving me the lamp when he died," her sentence ended in quiet remembrance. "Dr. Spruill had Matt clear out and clean up his office after the fire."

"What did they do with the lamp?"

"I didn't see it after the fire," said Patti.

"If Matt can get the lamp, tell him not to clean it and by all means try to handle it by each end," instructed Jackie. "We might want to dust it for fingerprints," was all she said.

"Got ya," Patti assured her. "Call me in a couple of days."

Temperatures were moderate enough that night to warrant having dinner on the patio. Jubal and Harley built a small fire on the brazier in the middle of the tiled terrace. Jackie and

Molly served the dinner they had shopped for. Talk was of the day's activity and bargains purchased, and of a most excellent beef tenderloin dinner. The phone call from Andrew Oaks came in during the Grapes in Grappa with Marscapone Cheese Sauce dessert. Jubal was hard pressed to leave his portion with Harley at the table. They could hear the device chirping, signaling that a call was coming in.

"I'd better see who that is in case it is Andy," said Jubal.

The three continued to finish their helping of Grappa Marscapone and discussed dividing Jubal's portion.

"I have good news and bad," he said on his return.

"Let's have it both at once," instructed Harley, "because I have the feeling that one turns on the other."

"Not this time, sorry to disappoint you. Good news is those "Hoover Boys" haven't a clue what happened once you left Pell City."

"And the bad?" asked Jackie as she finished off the remains of her glass of 2003 Mondavi Reserve Cabernet.

"They have upped your status. You have gone from being 'persons of interest' to actual felons … real live art thieves. You are now thought to be in possession of stolen art treasure and you are to be arrested by any law enforcement officer and turned over to that Agent Bagnilla."

"So we are accused of stealing the Codex?" Jackie said as she slumped on the table and propped herself by her elbows in a most un-lady like manner.

"That's the word from Andrew. He did not ask and I did not tell him why I wanted to know. We just understand each other that way. I was his senior partner when he joined the Service. I showed him around the Carter White House."

"So you can trust him not to..." Harley trailed off.

"No, he didn't press it further. You're safe for tonight. I would recommend that you sleep well and head out for where ever you are going tomorrow morning."

"Sounds like a plan," Harley announced.

"Oh look," Jackie pointed, "Is that the new moon or the old?"

Before anyone else could deliver an answer, Jubal spoke up to declare it to be "The Waning Gibbous Moon. Backwards C low in the west," he informed everyone. "Indicates approaching bad weather, and it's in the constellation Taurus, another bad sign. If you believe in that stuff."

Foreboding thoughts now flooded the hearts of Jackie and Harley. He nervously added, "not as much as our journalist."

Chapter 34

"I think I got a lead," announced Special Agent Jay Cooke when he joined Special Agent Harmon and Bagnilla in the agency's Thursday morning briefing. He went over the essential elements of a phone call he received from agent Francis Blair of the field office in Seattle, Washington the previous evening.

"Seems that Special Agent Blair had a phone call from, as she put it, 'an acquaintance, a Treasury Agent, named Andrew Oaks'," reported Agent Cooke. "Agent Oaks had called her asking if she had heard the name 'Macklin' around the office. When asked why, Agent Oaks told Agent Blair he had overheard the name while investigating a counterfeiting operation."

"Who is the agent that called you?"

"Francis Blair. She's been with us six years now. I know her to be a 'by the book' type person. She was passing along the information in her daily report. You want me to call her back?" Cooke said.

"Call her, see what she told the G-Man, and get his phone number."

"OK, but they're three hours behind Atlanta."

The office voice mail held eight incoming messages. One was from Bigfoot George, as the agents called George. He would have a few stiff drinks, see Bigfoot in his yard, and call the FBI to arrest him. Others were business calls from Washington. Then there was the one Bagnilla told Cooke to put through. Special Agent Blair picked up the receiver when she heard Cooke.

"It was really the evening before," she had to admit when she returned the call. "It was a mix of personal and business phone call. It's not against regulations," she told Agent Cooke referring to the prohibition on dating within the agency.

"No, of course not," Cooke assured her. "Can you tell me exactly what you told Agent Oaks?"

She spilled the beans. She had given him the updated status report filed electronically in the FBI's system. She also told Agent Oaks that the field agent's interview with Mrs. Eudora Bristow and her husband John, had revealed nothing. They had recovered the credit cards the couple used to send Bagnilla in the wrong direction. But Boo and Johnny, despite the pressure put on them, did not fold and repeatedly said they had no intelligence on the Macklin's whereabouts.

Treasury Agent Andrew Oaks picked up his phone as the receptionist announced he had a phone call from the Federal Bureau of Investigation, Atlanta Branch, Art Crimes Division, Special Agent Horatio Russell Bagnilla. Andrew listened to Bagnilla's insistence that the Macklins had stolen art treasures in their possession. Bagnilla lectured Agent Oaks on how he should know better than to interfere with the pursuit of the criminals. But Andrew did not take the rebuke well. He knew he could trust Jubal Conner, his mentor, not to put him in harm's way. However, he had to do right by his oath. He told Bagnilla he could not immediately provide Bagnilla with Jubal Conner's phone number, but he would check the incoming call log and retrieve the number.

"It may take an hour or so," Andrew explained, "our logistics agent isn't in yet."

"Well, get back to me as soon as you can," demanded Bagnilla and with that he hung up.

"Damn G-Men," said Bagnilla to Cooke.

"Damn Fed's," said Andrew Oaks turning to face the agent in charge of logistics for the Treasury office in Seattle. "You going anywhere?" The agent shook his head. "I might want you to look into something later today."

"Fine, I'll be here all day," the logistics agent said as he turned to his computer screen. "Let's get together before lunch."

"I can wait until after lunch" Andy said.

Agent Cooke thought two hours to be a reasonable amount of time to investigate and reverse track a phone number for an overbearing FBI agent.

Bagnilla had been lurking around his office so as not to miss the call. He left only to attend to a few necessary personal matters, and to pay the pizza delivery person at the front desk. After Agent Oaks sent Jubal's phone number, Bagnilla quickly traced the phone number.

"They are near Chattanooga," Bagnilla exclaimed to Cooke. "The phone number belongs to Jubal Conner of South Pittsburg, Tennessee. Call our office in Chattanooga and tell them I'm coming with an open warrant."

"Do you want their agents to meet you somewhere or are you going to their office first?"

"Cancel that," he ordered as he looked at the wall clock and calculated, "it will be midnight by the time I get there and get a team together to find these people. "No," he went on to say. "I'll get a hotel room and be there first thing in the morning. I'll just go in. No need to call ahead."

"I should let them know you are coming," insisted Cooke.

"I'll leave a message in the voice mail," assured Bagnilla. "Go home. You've been a big help," he said almost grinning. "In fact you probably provided the lead that will get us the arrest. I'll be sure you get the credit."

Agent Cooke clocked out and left Bagnilla to assemble his belongings. He would be driving to South Pittsburg, Tennessee thirty six miles to the west of Chattanooga, and on the border with northern Alabama. He had secured a good address for Jubal Conner and he would serve the warrant himself - alone. He would retrieve the Codex alone. He hoped to find everyone together and isolated in the Tennessee hills.

"Probably living up there in a trailer," he thought badly of the Conners. He was carrying enough ammunition for any contingency. He was also packing a rifle that had been confiscated, one he had reportedly destroyed.

"Good night. Have a good one," offered the cheery parking booth attendant as the dark Crown Victoria carried Special Agent Bagnilla away from the covered garage into the dark night.

"I intend to," he slyly replied under his breath. "I intend to."

Chapter 35

The cold damp air dropped into the valley during the night which forced someone to smash an axe head into a block of seasoned hickory at the first light of a new Thursday. This was noted by Harley to have taken place very near 6:00, again.

"God, why?" he prayed in vain and slipped into his deerskin moccasins. He opened the door and shuffled to the front of the Silver Bow in his cotton pajamas. Glaring across the lane at the young man with a small hatchet held aloft, he shook his head.

"Sorry," the young camper said sheepishly. He pointed the ax toward the small backpacker's tent and whispered "She wanted a campfire before breakfast. Sorry."

Harley returned to the Silver Bow galley and filled the electric kettle with water. "I like a campfire as much as the next guy," he thought, "but not at six bloody o'clock in the morning." He glanced out the front window and saw the zipper on the offenders tent close. Returning to the kettle he plugged it into the outlet. He shuffled and straightened the papers Jackie had left on the table top. He stopped as he read the passages she had jotted down on the pad.

"*Quare operor vates semper procedo terra Galilee.*" Under each Latin word was her initial understanding of the English translation. " Why – do – prophets - always – proceed – land – <u>Galilee</u>."

"Damn," he whispered.

She had underlined the region she recognized as being significant in their pursuit of the identity of their journalist author.

Harley sat down and flipped the note tablet back a page to where Jackie had started. There was the date; *Dies Solis xxvii Martius DCXCV A.U.C. 695*. He had gained enough Latin to know that this read as Day of the Sun, twenty seven, March, and by his conversion of A.U.C. it would be the year dated thirty three *Anno domini*.

"Damn," he muttered astonished. "Sunday, Thirty three a.d., in the land of Galilee." The limerick muse would have to be quelled.

He considered chopping some onions on the cutting board to wake her up, but, good judgment rendered that he could be in for marital strife should he interrupt her slumber. Upon pouring the hot water in a mug, he added a powder mix to create hot chocolate. To that brew he added peppermint flavoring and tossed in some small marshmallows. This was his second favorite camping beverage. He had no fresh root for his favorite, sassafras tea sweeten with Tupelo honey. He had seen the brilliant orange leaves of the little tree along Jubal's fence line while walking to the cave.

It was cold in the motor coach and he nudged the thermostat setting up a notch. As a consideration to their host not to put too great a load on their electrical grid, they would allow the Silver Bow's cab and kitchen to drop to 65 degrees as they kept a small electric heater in the bedroom. The heat pump began to vibrate and warm air rose from the ducts in the floor.

He took another sip of his chocolate as he sat down at the table. He continued studying her notes, fascinated at the details she uncovered.

"There has arrived yet another one of these prophets from the hills of Galilee. This one is also making claims that he is the son of the one true El Shaddai."

Harley knew *El Shaddai*, usually translated as God Almighty. It was one of the many names Hebrews used to avoid the name of the one True God. There were the names Jehovah, Yehoshua and Elohim. He saw a list of other contenders to the title Messiah. There was John who baptizes, the prophet Josiah, he who is unshaven, and Micaiah the "dirt eater," Micaiah, the one that eats dirt captured by Crynius, jailed forever, then executed.

He returned to *John, the one who Baptizes*. John the Baptist. John the one who lived in the desert and ate honey and locust. Harley never believed the locust to have been the insect but a tree with pea pods growing on the branches. As far as he knew, they were eatable and could be gathered much easier than grasshoppers.

"John the cousin of Jesus," Harley thought, "prophesied his coming, baptized him, and was martyred before he was. John was beheaded by King Herod years before Jesus arrived in Jerusalem in March 27 a.d." Harley recalled too there were many other saviors trying to capture the hearts and minds of the Hebrews and cleanse the Holy Land of foreign occupation. They sought to recreate the Kingdom of Israel as did the Maccabees three hundred years before. Josiah was captured and crucified.

There was a stirring noise from the back of the motor coach. Jackie was up now and walking into the galley greeted Harley with morning salutations.

"Got your hot chocolate?" she said as she looked for her bag of green tea.

"When did you do this?" he asked.

"Good morning to you, too," she said annoyed at his lack of protocol.

With his best tenor voice, he extended his vowels and sang out, "Good Morning! When did you do this?" he insisted.

"Why?" she answered coyly, for even she knew that this passage was important. "You went to sleep early. I think it was after you opened that bottle of Ramos Pinto Port. Remember? I could not fall asleep so I stayed up a little and worked on this."

"Why? He excitedly exclaimed, "Galilee … 33 a.d. … John the Baptist? I mean this is it! Jesus Christ! He saw Jesus!"

"Is that the new man he refers to?" she asked demurely. "I wasn't sure I was translating *Iesus* correctly," she said as she pronounced it with the double or long /e/ sound - E-sus.

"Where?" his excitement was overcoming him.

"Give me that," she lightly demanded and took the tablet from his hands. She pulled the Codex she was studying before her at the table. She started reading from her notes the journal page of March 27.

There has arrived yet another one of these prophets from the hills of Galilee. This one is also making claims that he is the son of the one true El Shaddai. Why do they always come out of the land of Galilee? First there was John who baptizes, then it was the prophet Josiah, he who was un-shaven, then Micaiah the dirt eater. This new man Iesus entered into town riding an ass, dragging the foal of the ass with him. All the while, his own followers cry out that this savior of Israel has come to deliver the people. They quote the Oracle of the prophet Zechariah, The king is coming. That he, the savior, has arrived on the foal of an ass as foretold. Rumors have preceded that he too has also performed miracles and restored sight to blind men. Again, these crowds of Jews and Gentiles with lesser instruction in the Law did encourage him with cries of "Hosanna" and calling him "Blessed". Again, they have torn the branches off the palms that line the road into Jerusalem, and toss them into the road.

This time he did not stop and preach rebellion against the high and ordained sons of Aaron and against our defenders, Rome. This would be messiah went directly into the portico of the temple and attacked my friends in the act of doing business with the pilgrims. Poor old Eleazar. This new prophet came in and rushed upon him from behind beating him with the rope that he had tied to the foal.

He kicked over Eleazar's tables. When his money spilled onto the ground, the crowd rushed upon it and stole it from him. I know that Eleazar's coins are not the counterfeits given in the trade of other lenders and he has lost much.

These who rebel against our Laws and our protectors are becoming more than a nuisance. They begin to threaten our very peace and traditions. Rome will not allow this civil disobedience to continue. Gaddi and Thassi and I rushed to seize him. His followers leading the mob blocked our path. He stood and cried out that this was a temple of prayer, but that it is now a house of thieves. The worshipers in the temple have to exchange the idolulators coinage in order to give to us their tithe and to purchase clean animals for the sacrifice. It is not our Law but the Law of the Most Highest El Shaddai.

This would be warrior king fled and escaped from our capture. He was not so brave when we rushed to arrest him. Rumors hold that he has hidden in Bethany. He cowers with the olive maidens. I think him not any prophet, messiah, or king, but a common criminal coming in the midst of a riot he and his followers created in order to steal from us. The mob quickly dispersed once their leader ran off.

Gaddi and I caught and arrested several of the thieves, and forced them to return the money.

The man we caught was one of the followers called Judas, a known conspirator with the Zealots that live in the desert east of here. Our spies have reported that many more of such men roam the hills around us crying out against us. They long for the days when Mattathias, the son of John, and the sons of the priest Joarib and the Hasideans did rule this land and restored the worship to the temple. Caiaphas told us of the prophet Athronges of Emmaus. He did rule that region until Gratus captured and crucified him.

They wait with Judas, a Galilean, in the city of Gamala. He sought to take with him the Pharisee Zadok. They conspired with zealous to draw the people to a revolt. This did not last for Publius Quirinius, did crucified these two radicals. They all wait in vain hope of a return to those days. But, Caligula, our protector and defender will keep the peace of our lands. Tomorrow I will go to Caiaphas and ask his blessing to track down these extremist militants and bring them to our justice. May the Most Highest El Shaddai keep me safe and in His care.

Harley could hardly breathe. Jackie asked if he was all right. He nodded that he was and stared at the Codex while she read her notes.

"I am," but he could not continue to describe the flood of emotions sweeping over him. Harley was ecstatic, humbled, elated, reverent all the feelings going up and down with the rise and fall of his chest.

"Did it mean anything, this riding in on the foal of an ass. What is that?" she asked puzzled.

"Refers to a prophecy in Isaiah, or Zechariah or one of those guys," he guessed. "The messiah was to come riding into town on the colt of a donkey. What that meant to them, I have no idea and I don't think anyone else has."

"He said, Zechariah, right here," and she pointed out the name to him in the Latin text.

"Looks like it to me," he said after a brief study.

"Tearing down the shrubbery and screaming and carrying on, sounds like a riot to me," she said as she got up to pour the hot water into the tea pot. "They all should have been arrested."

"I wonder who this man Eleazar was? He says poor old Eleazar was attacked, beaten and robbed."

"Yeah," she stated, "and right in church as he was minding his own business. What was the thing with the clean animals about? Is this the money changer story about Jesus?"

"Yes," Harley answered and went on to explain how, at this time, the Roman coinage bore the "graven image" of the current emperor, and in this case, Julio Claudian Caligula. In Harley's opinion no one wanted to see this man's face, but the Laws of Moses stated that engraved images were not allowed in the temple.

"Therefore," he said, "pilgrims to the temple had to have their coins changed, at fair market rates, into temple coins to pay the required tithe and purchase a clean animal for sacrifice."

"Sounds like a fair deal to me," Jackie concurred. "Why did Jesus have to beat this poor man and destroy his business? Why couldn't they talk this out?" she cried out in mock rage and shook her fist.

"Typical of all people," was Harley's observation. "Take from those who have and give to those who don't ... the basis for all wars and conflicts."

"I thought wars were about honor and glory," said Jackie.

"No," Harley returned dryly. "Honor is what they give the living - glory is what they give the dead. War is always about those who have not wanting what the other has. Land, money, food, access to ports, access to trade, I could go on and on. Religion is used for propaganda."

"So what did Eleazar have that Jesus and his followers wanted?" she asked puzzled.

"Power ... access to Pontius Pilot. The scribes and high priest were the ruling party, backed up by the Roman Governor. The rest had to fend for themselves," he mocked. "Did you say Mattathias?"

She read again the passage with the name Mattathias, son of John, and the sons of the priest Joarib and the Hasideans. "Who are these, some local mob?" she laughed at her joke. "And you know maccabee can be interpreted from Latin as hammer?"

"Mattathias Maccabee," he spoke reverently, "first book of Maccabee, second chapter, the man and his sons started the revolt that returned Palestine to Hebrew control for the first time in 300 years."

Neither spoke for a moment lost in their own thoughts of all that she had uncovered. Jackie did ask about the final name mentioned, "Caiaphas. He says he will go up to Caiaphas and ask his blessing to track down these extremist militants and bring them to justice."

Astounded at the wording, Harley asked if she had the phrases interpreted correctly. "You mean, *'investigo illa extremus bellicus*" she said, "track down extremist militants? Yes, I think I got that part dead on. You see the irony?"

"Yes. Caiaphas was the high priest at the time of Christ and was his accuser before Pilot."

"Damn," was all she could say now, that and, "I wonder if Molly has any breakfast ready."

Chapter 36

Harley had just started making himself another grilled ham and cheese sandwich using Jubal's smoked ham and Jackie's gouda cheese, when the phone rang. Molly picked up the cordless unit and looking at the caller id went into the adjacent room closing the door.

"You sure you don't want a pound of bacon to go on that sandwich?" Jackie mockingly asked. "What is that your third or fourth sandwich?"

"Second if you don't mind," replied Harley. "It's damn good ham."

Jackie was about to admonish Harley for his gluttony when the door was snatched open by Molly.

"You have got to go now," demanded a worried Molly.

"What is the matter?" Jackie asked of her friend. "Something wrong?"

"You have got to get out of here. They are coming to arrest you and possibly me and Jubal too," she breathlessly exclaimed.

"Why? When? How do you know this?" asked an astonished Jackie. Molly was not known for giving into female hysteria or doing Harley type theatrics. "What has happened?"

"I didn't trust the Bureau or the Treasury," as she referred to both branches of the Federal Government. "So I asked my friends in the Agency to keep track of their phone calls and watch for your names to come up. You have to leave and the sooner the better. I expected him to be here by now."

"Who?" Jackie nervously asked.

"That damn Fed Agent ... Bagnilla. He has been back tracing the phone calls Jubal made to Andrew. It took him a day and a half but he has found where you are."

"How?" asked Jackie.

"I have it that he left Atlanta around 9:15 last night," Molly informed them. "He was seen going up Peachtree Street in Atlanta in the direction of I-75 north."

They all knew Interstate 75 skirted Chattanooga on the East Ridge. There, I-75 joins with Interstate- 24 which leads to South Pittsburg, Tennessee and it takes about three hours to drive from Atlanta.

Harley glanced at the green numbers on the microwave and announced that it was 1:00. "Bagnilla is overdue if he were driving straight through."

"If he was driving straight through," Molly agreed. "But he left at nine last night. He most likely got a hotel room and is lining up a posse to serve any warrants. But from what you describe, I don't think that is his intention. I think he means to come here and arrest you guys by himself."

This sent some apprehension through the couple.

"How did you find this out?" Harley began.

"I don't want to and can't talk about how I know," Molly said as she led them across the yard to the Silver Bow.

"Molly," chided Jackie, "you said 'Agency' and you know how I am about such things? Which agency? How do you trace phone calls during the middle of the night?"

"OK," she confessed. "I am still in the C.I.A. But you can't tell a soul," she confided.

"C.I.A.?" asked the astonished Harley.

"I had a suspicion you were still in," Jackie said knowingly. "Every now and then when I call up here, Jubal would answer and claim you were not here. He would say he knew where you were but would not say where or how to contact you."

"OK, so I do a little bit of moonlighting for the Agency now and then. Right now you had better beat it."

"We better get moving, I'll take care of the outside," Harley advocated and headed to disconnect the Silver Bow's extension cord from the outlet and the water hose from the spigot.

The next half hour was spent in frantic haste as Molly helped Jackie secure the pots and pans, plates and glasses that were about the camper. All the while the two continued to talk. Harley caught parts of the conservations as he stored the picnic table cloth, and chairs and other camping gear.

"I heard you never really leave the Agency," Jackie said. "If that is true, I mean what kind of assignments do you get?" she said alluding to the fact that Molly was five years her senior.

"Do you remember seeing in the news a story about a group of British bird watchers being arrested in Greece at the Souda Air Base?"

"No, I don't," Jackie responded as she returned the couch cushions to cover the storage space underneath.

"I do," Harley chimed in. "Back in 1999? A group of retired English schoolteachers, a Bird watching club, booked a tour of Greece for some birding. The Greek Army arrested the old gals when they found them taking pictures of Canadian Geese around the air base... Right?"

"They were the Lesser White-fronted Goose from Norway," Molly retorted. "Endangered species," she went on to say. "We were arrested by the Greeks and thoroughly searched. They found most of my film and they confiscated my 5.6 lens and my Nikon. Never did get that back."

"Most of the film?" said Jackie quick to catch her clue.

"Most," Molly quietly answered with a sly grin. "We learned that the Greeks were allowing the Sauds to park their private jets there for maintenance. But Iranians were the ones getting on and off."

"OK," Jackie returned. "I never would have suspected that you were still going on assignments..."

"At my age?" said Molly as she continued Jackie's sentence. "As if you didn't work for the Agency too."

"I never worked for the C.I.A.," was Jackie's defense. "When we left the country we did so at the request of State Department," she said referring to the CDC's many programs to send American experts, doctors, technicians, and volunteers to governments around the world to help solve their problems.

"When the crown prince of this desert or president for life of that country, ran out of food or water, they called the State Department for an advisor to help train their people to fix their own problems. Teach a man to fish as it were," Jackie illustrated. Then it hit her as to what Molly was alluding to.

"Is that why we always had to fly through Dulles?" Jackie said referring to the International Airport in Washington, D.C.

With a sly grin on her face, Molly nodded her head. "And SFO on the west coast," she added referring to San Francisco International Airport.

"You mean those briefings and de-briefings by someone from the program ... while we were going in and out of the country?" she asked, "they were C.I.A?"

"Yes," Molly replied sheepishly. "I once copied your camera film while you were being interviewed about your progress and meetings in that Kenya Rift Valley Fever outbreak. That was the same day we went out later to have lunch at Hugo's, remember?"

"You mean while I was at the airport customs office?"

"Yes," she continued as if embarrassed at being caught. "I was in the next room, copying all of your group's film. We saw the terrorist Bunya Viridae standing next to your supervisor. He was arrested two weeks later... kept claiming to be the Deputy Minister of Agriculture. By the way, the digital cameras make downloading much faster."

Jackie could not help but to stand and stare at what she once considered her best friend. She considered Molly to still be and would continue to be, but to discover that your confidant, your comrade, your bosom buddy and her mind went on and on… was spying on you.

"What other times did you spy on me?" she lightheartedly demanded slapping Molly with a small pillow.

"Do you really want to know, besides we don't have time for all of it," she said locking down the cabinet doors.

"How did you know Bagnilla was coming?"

"With the new Homeland Security and all, we are all sharing more information. And then there is the consulate."

"Consulate?" asked Jackie.

"Yes, the Saudi Arabians have a consulate in the same office building as the Bureau in Atlanta."

"But the Agency only spies on them, right?" Harley added as he came through the galley bringing in the portable radio from the picnic table.

"Yes," Molly answered, "and Treasury has the duty to provide protection for visiting dignitaries and envoys. Bureau watches them inside our borders, we watch all of them outside. But we need to know when they're leaving. We can do that watching the parking lots when our agents at the gates time stamp their parking tickets," she said sheepishly grinning.

"Molly," Jackie began. "I don't know how to thank you."

"You know you don't need to," Molly replied. "I've got to take care of my shop mate. Now get going."

The pair embraced as Harley twisted the key and the Silver Bow's motor began to hum. He put it into the driving gear and eased out of the camping site.

Jubal had just come out the kitchen door. He waved to get Harley to stop.

"God," he thought, "I hate to just leave old buddy, but ..." he did stopped as Jubal came to the driver's window.

"I got a phone call from my fishing buddy, Carl in the Jackson County sheriff's office," said Jubal. "Bagnilla's on the way to see Archie ... the sheriff here in Marion County. You need another campground?" Jubal offered.

"How about Clear Creek?" Molly added coming alongside the window.

"We go there all the time," answered Harley. "They may be watching our usual campgrounds."

"Then try for a National Forest campground," advised Jubal. "They have no reservations and most don't have camp offices."

"We'll keep it in mind."

Jackie and Harley made their goodbyes again as the Silver Bow eased down the dirt lane.

Harley turned onto the tree lined country road running the length of the mountain. Through the dust trail behind him he could see Jubal's pickup truck following them.

"What's he doing?" declared Harley starring into the mirror hanging outside his window.

"Who?" asked Jackie.

"Jubal is following us."

Harley watched as the truck stopped in the middle of the one lane bridge that crosses Cave Spring Creek. Harley continued around the bend of the road and his rearward view was obscured by the dust. What he did not see was Molly in her Buick following Jubal. He pulled a thimble size tool from his pocket, inserted it in the tire air fill valve, and released the air from the tire.

"God speed," he prayed after his friends and got into the Buick.

"God speed," added Molly. "Now," she declared, "praise the Lord and pass the ammunition. Lets' go see what this Bagnilla is up to."

Chapter 37

A black Crown Victoria pulled up to stop at Hog Jowl Road and U.S. Highway 27. The thick heavy cloud of sandy brown dust that had been trailing the vehicle now rolled over it and onto the highway. When the tan dust settled a bit, the two front windows of the Crown Victoria went down with electric motors. Bagnilla looked at his map. His GPS had been fluctuating and changing in the deep cracks and crevices that are the landscape along the Tennessee – Alabama border. On a mountaintop the signal was clear and his position precise. Along the shear vertical rock faces that line each side of the roads up and down the mountains the GPS signals faded in and out.

Now he confirmed his location by visual and electronic means. "Damn it!" he exclaimed as he was now eight miles south of Bridgeport, looking at a sign advising travelers that another Dairy Queen was nine miles ahead in Stevenson, Alabama.

He floored the accelerator pedal and wheels, now flush with power, kicked dust, dirt and gravel back up Hog Jowl Road until the rubber tires began to burn on the warming asphalt. He picked up his cell phone that had been bouncing next to him and punched in the number for the FBI office in Chattanooga.

"Special Agent Gowen," the man answered. "How can I help you?"

"I'm Agent Bagnilla," he growled, "Atlanta office. I'm in pursuit of stolen art documents and have an open warrant with me. I need your help in locating the suspects." Bagnilla realized he probably would not surprise the Macklins or Conners at eight o'clock this morning and surrendered that plan to the three Fates.

"Yes sir," Gowen responded, "Your office called just now to see if you had checked in. I told them I hadn't heard from you. Is there a problem?" Gowen was wondering why Bagnilla had not followed protocol by reporting his presence and the case he was working yesterday.

"Problem is my GPS has been going in and out. One minute I'm on track, the next the screen is in search mode."

"Where are you?"

"U.S. 27 and Hog Jowl Road headed north."

"Where do you want to go?"

Bagnilla gave him The Conner's address. Agent Gowen did a map search using three different services and came up with three different locations.

"Seems this is not a good address or it's not in anyone's system. You'll have to consult a local map."

"Where do I find a local map?" a weary Bagnilla asked for he had been driving all night.

"Try the South Pittsburg Police, or I'll get you the Jackson County Sheriff's phone number," Gowen offered and added, "You need back up in any case."

"These are not drug dealers," said Bagnilla trying to discourage the intrusion. "I'm looking for a couple of senior citizens in a recreational motor-home."

"You shouldn't take any chances and it is agency policy. We can't be there for forty five minutes to an hour at the fastest."

"Can't wait. These two slipped a stake-out in Atlanta," he winced at the revelation.

"In a motor home?" Gowen asked incredulously.

Bagnilla could hear a snicker in Gowen's voice. "They trapped my agents in a wild fire and drove off on an unused road." That should justify the failure to follow such a lumbering vehicle.

Bagnilla found a sheriff's deputy at her desk. The young woman was quite impressed receiving a Special Agent of the FBI "We don't get many of you guys around here," she said as she authenticated his identification. "We usually are called to back-up the D.E.A. or Customs on a drug raid."

"You see a lot of that around here?" he said making small talk for the moment.

"Why yes. We are within range of aircraft coming out of Mexico or Cuba, and with the number of small private airstrips around here, flat mountain tops, and deep valleys, we stay quite busy." She called in her supervisor and made introductions.

"Carl Buckner," the deputy cheerfully said extending his hand. "Glad to meet you."

They huddled around a map as Bagnilla read the address he was given for the Conner's campground.

"Poplar Ridge Road?" asked Deputy Buckner. "We don't have a Poplar Ridge Road in this county. There's one in South Pittsburg," and he put his finger on the northern edge of his map. "Comes into Jackson County here and changes into Hog Jowl Road".

Bagnilla was on Highway 72 again this time seeking the Marion County Sheriff in South Pittsburg, Tennessee. Deputy Buckner had called ahead to assure them the man was en-route and to expect one highly irritated and frustrated Federal man, as he called Bagnilla.

"This one has been roaming all night and all over Sand and Fox mountains from what he tells me," added Carl.

"Thanks for the heads up Carl," returned the High Sheriff of Marion County, Archie Mergenthaler.

The tan and black Crown Victoria, with squealing tires, steered up to the front door of the courthouse. Sheriff Mergenthaler was standing on the white courthouse steps talking with an assistant district attorney about the proper use of the Whitlock Red Fox Caddis for catching largemouth bass. Archie, as he liked to be called, argued the season was right for the dry version and the D.A. argued for the wet version of the same lure.

Bagnilla, not waiting for acknowledgement of his presence by either party, cut in on the conversation loudly asking for the county sheriff. He was momentarily ignored as Archie and the deputy D.A. finished their discussion and agreed to meet early the next morning by the side of Lake Jackson and prove which Caddis Fly will lure the largemouth bass to the surface.

"That must be Jubal and Molly Conner's campground," said Archie acknowledging knowing about them and several similar couples that moved into the valley. They came for land driven to bargained prices when the iron industries closed as well as the open air mines.

While this made for a nice travelogue for some, Bagnilla was after different fish to fry.

Archie rounded up a sheriff's posse of three more deputies and headed up Poplar Creek Road. Bagnilla had missed the county signpost in the dark that morning. Now he was following Sheriff Mergenthaler's car in a cloud of dust. As they went around a curve the lead car came to a sliding stop. Bagnilla slid to a stop just inches short of the High Sheriff's car and got out.

"What is it?" he demanded to know.

"Someone's left a pick-up truck parked in the middle of the bridge," announced the High Sherriff but Archie did not admit to knowing it belonged to Jubal.

They walked up and investigated the obstruction Jubal had left that morning.

"We'll need a tow truck to move it," said Archie reaching to his left shoulder for the microphone hanging there.

"Pop a window and put the transmission in neutral, then we shove it into the creek," Bagnilla instructed.

"Can't move it … flat," Archie said pointing to the airless tire.

"How much further to the campground?" asked Bagnilla.

"About a mile, not more than mile and a half, why?"

"How long will it take for a tow truck to get here?"

"If South Pitts Wrecker has one available," Archie said pausing to calculate the distance, "about an hour at the most. I'm going to call dispatch and get the next available. It could be less."

"Can we come in from the other end of this road?" asked Bagnilla.

"Yep," said the Archie in his long Tennessee drawl, "but it would take over an hour on these roads. We would have to go back to the highway and then over the mountain."

"It will take us, what, thirty minutes to walk there?" Bagnilla suggested.

"Walk?" Archie dubiously asked.

"Walk. We do it all the time in Atlanta," Bagnilla flippantly said. He snatched his search warrant from the car and started up the road with the posse grudgingly trailing.

"We have company," Molly announced to Jubal. Molly had set up the telescope they used to observe the edges of the gibbous moon, to watch the road. She had been expecting the posse all afternoon. Other campers heading out were advised to turn left and go over Fox Mountain to avoid the bridge where Jubal left his truck. Molly told her campers the bridge had washed out. That it had not rained that week did not occur to those leaving, but they would do as they were advised.

"Yeah, he's with Archie all right," she yelled to Jubal over by the coral.

"Let me guess, Bagnilla, white tie and black shoes?" came the satire.

"Always," she quipped. "What's the plan?"

"We are going caving," he announced.

No one came to the front door when Bagnilla rapped quickly four times. Not receiving an answer, he twisted the door knob only to find it locked. He went to the back where Archie knock lightly on the back door. Receiving no response, Archie opened it and stuck his head inside and called "Hello, Sheriff's Office." Looking back at Bagnilla's surprised face, he informed him "kitchen doors are always opened around here."

"Nothing, no one home," Archie told Bagnilla.

They formed a plan to interrogate the remaining campers. Each officer went door to door or tent flap to flap asking about the Silver Bow. Some remembered seeing a 28 foot motor home leave that morning. No one noted that the truck's model name had been spray painted over. Nearly all reported seeing Molly with the owners loading up the Silver Bow. Two campers reported seeing it leave about an hour ago with Molly and Jubal following in their vehicles. Although Molly's Buick was in the yard, no one knew their whereabouts at that moment.

"We've been set-up," determined Bagnilla. "These hillbillies have set us up."

"Now hold on a minute," Archie said coolly. "You don't go around accusing people of interfering with your investigation just because you can't find them."

Bagnilla paused in his pacing. "How are you going to prove that?" He extended his arms in different directions and shrugged. "You tell me ... does this not look like they knew we were coming?"

"Well ... I am suspicious with the truck being in the middle of Poplar Creek Bridge," said Archie, 'but again, flat tires happens all the time around here."

"But in the middle of the bridge?" he asked again incredulously.

"We got here anyway. Maybe not as fast as you wish, but we got here. That is not interfering, just delaying."

"While these people... the Conners got away too?"

"To where?" Archie asked pointing to Molly's Buick in the drive. "They could be up in the hills for a stroll or something. Happens all the time out here."

Bagnilla realized that this conversation was headed nowhere. He reluctantly agreed to return to the bridge and retrieved his car. Once there Bagnilla said his goodbyes and speed off to meet with Special Agent Gowen.

"Why didn't you tell him Jubal was probably in the cave?" the deputy asked his boss.

"Damn Fed. Come up here acting like we are all a bunch of … and he has no respect for fly fishing. Let's go, I have to show the Michi how to use a Caddis Fly."

Bagnilla hit the interstate and headed east. On any normal Friday afternoon it would take about 45 minutes to reach the outskirts of Chattanooga. The highway was crowded with hundreds of automobiles and hundreds of lumbering motor homes, RV trailers, popup campers, pick-up trucks, and eighteen wheelers. The University of Tennessee at Knoxville was expected to kick-off on Saturday and Interstate 24 east bound was the road carrying fans of the Big Orange to their parking spaces in their respective parking lots. Motel and hotel rooms during the Big Game, would become as hard to find as an honest politician. Some of these fans would be spending the night in the many Federal, State, Local, and privately owned campgrounds. A number of fans would be driving motor homes. Four Winds – Bounders - Georgie Boys – Fleetwoods – Keystones and Hollands, all would be operating on all the highways and by-ways, as Bagnilla made his slow progress to the Chattanooga office.

Chapter 38

Harley did not need to get the Silver Bow up to highway speeds as he maneuvered onto Interstate 24.

"Would you look at that?" Jackie said astonished at the traffic on the highway. "What *is* going on?"

With a glance at the banners and flags flying from truck windows, Harley was able to forecast a football game would be played tomorrow.

"If Bagnilla is following us he'll have a tough time picking us out won't he?" Jackie worriedly asked. "If they realized I swapped the license plates … what then?"

The Silver Bow continued crawling along with the sludge of other R.V.'s, 18 wheelers, and general afternoon traffic. Harley, conscience of his slower moving vehicle, stayed to the right, allowing faster moving traffic to pass on his left. He watched the approaching line of cars with worried interest, all the time fearful Bagnilla was back there in his black Crown Victoria as the endless parade shuffled by. He read license plates as they passed. Most were local to Marion County, Tennessee. Some tags were from points west and south, Alabama, Mississippi, and one Dodge Grand Caravan flying orange flags from their windows passed by with Missouri plates.

"Harley," Jackie now cooed, "do you think we could stop at a motel tonight?"

"Why?"

"I would love a long hot bath," she answered lovingly. The Silver Bow was equipped with its own shower. It was a stall squeezed in between the slide out living room and the bedroom. The traditional British red phone box was larger. The shower head was similar to the kitchen sink spray nozzle. Jackie complained the flow rate was about one gallon per hour. Occasionally, when they were on the road for some length, they would splurge and take a room in a motel for the night and for the convenience.

"How much cash do you have left?" he asked.

"Not much, about $200.00. Can we get anymore without alerting Bagnilla?"

"I need to fill-up before we get much farther down the road. We will need nearly $150.00 to do that. I have that much in my pocket."

"Good," she said. "I could use a ceramic bowl for a minute."

"There's a gas station up ahead in Wildwood that always has lower priced gas and clean restrooms…at least the men's are clean. We'll stop there."

"If they can keep the men's clean, the woman's should be operating room clean," she replied.

There were two stations ahead, each with gas selling ten to fifteen cents lower than the stations he had passed on the way. Jackie got out and went in to the ladies room. Harley continued to watch the meter on the pump build up the charges. "$156.28" he muttered and pulling his wallet out of his pants pocket went inside to settle the account by emptying his wallet.

Moon Pies, 2 for $1.00 the sign said above a display of the infamous southern pastry. He picked up the manufactured vanilla flavored marshmallow plastic wrapped cookie and a couple of bananas.

"God," she said with disgust when she saw the junk food. "What are you doing with those things?"

"Moon Pies!" he exclaimed as they met up in the store. "Big as a Moon. I have survived many a caving trip on nothing more than two of these for breakfast, lunch and dinner."

"Yech." she returned. "they're pure sugar."

"Nope, they have flour, baking soda, and marshmallow cream, says so right on the wrapper."

"I stand corrected."

Jackie pick up an apple from a basket with a sign on it that said it was locally gown and two bottles of water. Harley went around the back of the ATV trailer to check the tie down straps. Hanging on the rear bumper of the Silver Bow and the trailer were license plates he had not seen before. They were Tennessee plates from Marion County.

"Honey," Harley called to Jackie. "Come back here would you?"

"What is it?" she asked from the edge of the door.

"We have a new tag on the Silver Bow," he answered, "from Marion County, Tennessee."

"Jubal, I'll bet," she said. "Molly was inside with me all the time."

"I never saw him until we started out."

"Must have done it while you were packing up inside."

"May have ... Why that... " he shook his head and headed for the side door.

"Those two have got more up that creek of theirs than we can imagine," Jackie said settling into her passenger seat.

"They have my vote for most surprising couple of the year."

They began to merge back into the crowd on the freeway. He was watching for an opening to pass a truck. Jackie opened his Moon Pie and gave him the pastry. They sat in silence for a mile when Harley saw in the mirrors a dark dusty brown car approaching in the left lane. An opening occurred in the line of traffic as an eighteen wheeler pull over into the right lane. The dirty brown car sped up in the fifty yard long space. As it pasted Harley's window, he could see that it was dust, similar to the layer covering the Silver Bow, that turned an otherwise black Ford Crown Victoria into a tan two tone vehicle. Even the windows were tinted brown. The entire car was of two shades of dust.

"Damn," Harley exclaimed watching car tags go by.

"Government tags on a car from Georgia.... Fulton County!"

The impact of this observation hit Jackie as hard as it did him. "You don't think?" she asked fearfully.

"I couldn't see the driver's face and I don't know if I want to."

"Where is he now?"

"Up there," Harley said pointing to the left. "That black dusty tan looking car."

"He was driving a black car when he came to our house," Jackie said.

"If he has spent the night driving around and over Sand Mountain, then I would expect his car to change color …. and he has Federal Government tags."

They continued to watch the suspect vehicle pull away from them. Harley had eased back on the gas to the derision of the truck driver behind him. The driver of the rig makes his income by the miles he clocks, so the faster he goes the more he makes in a day. When too much of a gap occurred in front of Harley he let the Silver Bow know it with a long blast of his air horn.

"Harley," she urged, "at least keep up with the truck in front of us."

"I was afraid of getting too close."

"I have an idea." as she got out of her chair. She went to the closet and pulled out his black John Deere ball cap. She grabbed her dark wrap-around shades and arraigned them all on Harley.

"There," she proudly said of her costuming, "I hope it works."

Bagnilla slowed to a stop behind a Pathfinder. He saw a white R.V. approaching on his right. He dropped his head enough to see some of the drivers face in the dusty outside mirror. The man, wearing a black ball cap with some sort of green patch on the front was also wearing what he thought looked like women's sunglasses. There was no passenger along, or at least none he could see. The traffic moved ahead a few yards and he accelerated to match.

"Whoa." Harley said breathlessly. "That was close. I'm sure he was checking me out. I saw his face in his outside mirror."

"Did he see you?" Jackie asked from her sitting position on the floor.

"I don't think he did or at least he isn't pulling us over."

The game of catch-up continued for a couple of slow miles. Cars began to fill in between the Silver Bow and the suspect vehicle. Finally, the car was too far ahead to be seen.

"The motel," he said as the thought returned. "Does it have to be fancy?"

She hated questions like this fearing that Harley, who can sleep on a muddy cave floor, would accept anything in a motel room. She tendered her answer with a reserved question, "Why?" But then she paused and qualified the response with, "does it have a bath?"

Harley did indeed know of a clean and decent place west of Chattanooga. Given the slow traffic and Bagnilla on the road as well, he thought it would serve them to head for a small quirky little motel along U.S. Highway 41, north of the interstate.

"We have to pass the Tennessee State Patrol office to get there," he warned her.

"Does it have a bath?"

"Yes, he does. Just don't expect anything like a Hilton or Comfort Inn."

"You are referring to Flipper's place?" she carefully advanced the question.

"Why yes, I am suggesting Flipper's place," he said with chagrin.

"As long as it has a bath and is clean, then I'll take anything."

The autumn sun, now at a low angle, was easing the shadow into the valley where this monument to funk was glowing with pink and purple neon lighting accents running along the eves of the building. The roof lines suggested that it was built to simulate a row of small Swiss mountain chateaus. The style also suggested that it was built in the 50's when untold numbers of eccentric, oddball, and strange themed motels sprang up during the decade when America discovered the highway and still had cheap gas to take to the roads. The paint appeared to be freshly applied, the parking lot was clean. The office did not reek of cigar and cheap booze. "It would do," she thought.

He backed the Silver Bow into a space at the far corner of the motel parking lot which was no easy task when pulling a small trailer.

"Hello Harley," exclaimed Flipper Wallace the man behind the counter as the couple entered the tiny lobby at the Cave Inn. "I wasn't sure that was your RV until I saw you trying to back in with a trailer."

"Honey, this it Flipper Wallace, he owns the place. "Flip", you remember my first wife Jackie?"

"Glad to see you again. You're driving the big rig," he observed. "There are no cave-in's this weekend."

She shook hands with the tall lanky man with wire thin red hair. He had a smile that could be used to light up a cave. She never understood the caver's world. They wanted it dark and did all they could to keep their hobby and adventures hidden. As Harley put it, "having seen natural wonders of untold beauty you cannot describe to the day walkers ... what walking, crawling and even sleeping in the underworld and returning alive means to your psyche ... To be continuously pronounced crazy by your co-workers and family alike ... well, you just don't bring your hobby into everyday conversation."

"Cave-in's?" she looked confused. "I thought this was the Cave Inn."

"This is the *Cave Inn*," Flipper explained pointing to the brochure on the counter. "But when all us cavers get together, it is called a cave-in. An antonym of *cave in* would be a *camp out*."

"I'm glad to meet you," she paused, "Flipper?" she said with a rising questioning tone. "My but that is an interesting nickname?"

Harley stepped up to say, "Flip loves wet caves, you know the ones full of water ... the Florida springs and such. The only time we see him is when he comes up for air, like a dolphin, so we call him, Flipper," and he sang a bar from the 60's TV show of the same name.

"My real name is Robert, but Harley probably didn't know that," he said with a chuckle.

She feigned a smile to indicate she understood, but, she wanted her hot bath.

"Cash OK?" Harley offered before he registered.

"For you, sure," Flip said, for it was not his policy. Having had so many cavers leave solid brown rings around his tubs from washing their mud caked clothing in the bathrooms, he usually wanted an open charge card to cover clean up. "Will room eighteen do?"

"Sure as long as it has a tub and hot water," said Harley.

"Just don't do your laundry in the room," Flipper teasingly ordered his friend.

"Laundry? They have a Laundromat?" asked Jackie.

"Yeah, made by American Seating," Harley said, referring to the name on the toilet tank.

"If you would fill this out," asked Flipper flipping a motel registration card across the counter to Harley. Jackie shared his gaze at the recording instrument and considered not leaving their information and a trail for others to follow. He saw Jackie's eyes widen and she pulled in her lower lip as her face now reflected her concern about registering. However, as they had told Flipper nothing, they would pretend nothing was wrong and Harley, catching Jackie's slight nod, put ink to paper.

True to Harley's preview, the room was spartan. It had a queen size bed being the largest room and bed that Flipper offered. A number of rooms were so small that a twin size mattress would fill up the space. All of Flipper's rooms would allow a night stand with a lamp and a clock. All had a closet rods but some had no closets. Few had showers, but most had tubs. The Cave Inn was nothing fancy, but was clean, efficient and affordable. Room eighteen did have space for a round table and two vintage orange chairs leftover from the 1960's. Jackie expected a bare light bulb to be dangling from a wire in the middle of the room and a single mattress on an iron bedsprings.

Upon entering the room Jackie hoisted her suitcase to the folding luggage rack. She gave Harley only a brief invitation to use the toilet before settling for in a long hot soaking bath.

Harley used Flipper's garden hose to rinse the dust from the Silver Bow. Returning from his chore, he found Jackie with her trusty pencil and pad at the reading light with one of the journals. She was jotting down the words, erasing, re-entering and charging on in her translations.

"Harley," she motioned him to join her. "Does the name *Aeneas* mean anything to you?"

He paused to consider and came up empty.

"Well he says that *'Aeneas has directed Caiaphas to give us leave to go into the shops and inns to demand the taxes and the tithes due.'*"

"*Caiaphas* was the high priest that had Stephen arrested by Paul," he explained. "Hey, his father-in-law was *Aeneas*, chief high priest at the time of the crucifixion. Did it really say that?"

"Yes," she went on," they were given orders or warrants to take the tithes due the temple."

"Shake down money,"

"Sounds that way," she agreed. "And here he complains about the "*rebellis*" or rebels continuing to miss-lead the faithful. ' *Pharisees es eruditio proditio obviam templum priest quod ut lentus nostrum auctorita*'," she read out loud to him. "Pharisees are teaching treason against the temple priest and to supplant our authority."

"He really hates those rebel teachers ... the Pharisee," Harley joked.

"Yes," she said ignoring his jibe. "He constantly stresses the lineage of priesthood as he puts it, from Moses on down."

"Problem was Moses was not the priest, his brother Aaron and his tribe, the Levis, were. But I am sure no one bothers about that minor detail."

"Well," she continued," looked like the temple was running out of money and he and his friends were assigned to collect the money owed."

"Shake down, like I said," he continued with a deep horrible gangster accent. "Pay up or we'll send Brutus over to break your legs."

She returned to her notes and motioned him over for the next reading.

"*Elionaeus,*" she looked up at him, "Mean anything to you?"

"No."

"He was recruited by the *Optiones Varius Marius* to spy for Pontius Pilate," Jackie said, " *Optiones,* that was the rank our author held in the army?"

"Yes," affirmed Harley, "sort of a junior officer under a centurion."

"He says they are commissioned to find the rebel leaders and turn them in to Pilate on a charge of treason against Caligula."

"Licensed bounty hunters, huh?" teased Harley.

He pointed to the beginning entry on the parchment. "Is that Tuesday the twenty ninth?"

"Very good, two days after the Sunday Jesus arrived," Jackie said.

"Look, is all this making sense to you?" she asked not understanding the New Testament.

"Well, it is, or it can," Harley answered a bit confused himself. "I mean Paul describes himself as growing up in Tarsus … knows just about every mayor or governor of every town in the region … and says that he studied with Gamaliel," he paused to consider the facts, "which means he had to have spent time in Jerusalem." He stopped and considered again the facts uncovered in the journal.. "Yes, it is making sense. And now this thing about collecting taxes. It seems to me that he has quit studying and become a temple cop."

"Why quit his study? Didn't they all study at the same place?"

"Well the Pharisee taught in the street. The priest ran the synagogue school. So if he is working as a cop, then he would not have time to study. Now if you find the name Stephen, then let me know."

"Why? Who is he?"

"Stephen was stoned to death before Paul. I think it was Acts chapter 2 where the people doing the stoning laid their coats at the feet of Paul. That would put him in charge of the execution."

It was Harley's turn in the shower as Jackie continued to translate. A hot shave was equally enjoyed. He returned to the bedroom and found she had fallen out on the bed for a nap. He lay down to join her for what they thought would be an hour or so.

Chapter 39

Special Agent Gowen had not seen such a sight as Special Agent Horatio Russell Bagnilla now presented trailing dust through the Chattanooga FBI office. He was covered in fine brown dust, from his brown hair to the once shinny black shoes he wore. The briefcase he carried matched the dust brown tan of his shoes. It was all Gowen could do to stifle his laughter especially as Bagnilla briefly related the quest for the Macklins.

Agent Gowen knew Archie Mergenthaler and those like him in the surrounding mountains. These men were locally elected into their own realm, much like the Sheriff of Nottingham. They were not abusive of the high trust, but felt they had free rein to interpret and enforce the law in their own eclectic way.

"Has my office called?" Bagnilla asked expecting any new information to be forward to Chattanooga.

"We have an update on the vehicle tags," Gowen said.

"Let's have it."

"Wouldn't you rather get cleaned up?" he said more worried about the dust cloud that trailed the agent.

Bagnilla was more focused on the capture of the two felons, but relented on the matter of personal appearance and office decorum. He returned to his car and withdrew clean clothes. These he exchanged in the bathroom, stuffing his old suit into the waste bin and washing his face and hands in the sink. Restored in appearance he returned to find doughnuts and coffee along with the new reports.

"They changed plates with her SUV," Gowen reported reading Cooke's report from Atlanta. "We have a tag number on a missing utility trailer."

"Utility trailer?" Bagnilla asked.

"They have registered one trailer ... a Westlake model 275 utility trailer. It's not at the home address. And missing too is a SportCraft, 1400 c.c. four wheel drive All Terrain Vehicle."

"I want photos of all these," Bagnilla said. "They can change tags all they want, but they cannot change shape or the paint color."

"We can get photo's from the manufacture. We have the VIN numbers on all these." Gowen said proudly.

"Any new credit card transactions?"

"Nothing since that one in Alabama," he replied.

"What is with all the traffic on the interstate this morning?"

"Tennessee Volunteers plays University of Georgia in Knoxville tomorrow."

"They might try to use this as cover to move," Bagnilla said. "Can we get copies of the photos to state and local police?"

"We can e-mail copies to the locals but they will not display them until they have roll call on each shift, and we're too late for the day shift. We could include Federal and State Truck Inspectors, you know at the weigh stations."

"Good idea," said Bagnilla. "The more the better. I'll need a desk until we locate the targets."

"Use this one," Gowen said pointing to an empty cubicle.

Bagnilla sat down and proceeded to pull up the manufactures web page for the Holland Silver Bow series motor coaches. He downloaded the photos of the Model 3800 and produced a color and black and white print. He also found the A.T.V. catalog on line and downloaded those photos as well. He put copies in his briefcase and sent copies to law enforcement agencies in three of the seven states tourist are told they can see from atop Lookout Mountain. Alabama authorities were also alerted.

He net was well made and well spread. But from where he sat, if he had telescopic eyes, he could have focused on the base of Signal Mountain, on the west bank of the Tennessee River, and seen the gaudy pink and purple neon glow of the Cave Inn with a Holland Silver Bow model 3800 in the back lot.

Agent Gowen stuck his head in the cubical to check on Bagnilla. He asked the agent if he was hungry as he had put off eating lunch. The pair walked down the street to Whitewater Bar and Grill. An ancient tavern, one of three original to the center of Chattanooga, had been re-purposed as a restaurant. There the two caught up on Agency business, then compared acquaintances, and discussed the assignments in their careers.

Talk drifted into hobbies, interest, and religion. Gowen and Bagnilla discovered they both attended Mass. They both believed in the inviolability of the Pope. They agreed with the current Vatican stand on birth control, celibacy in the priesthood, feminism, and the list of sexual taboos went on.

A quick bite at the Whitewater stretched into nearly an hour. Bagnilla noticed that the index finger on Gowen's right hand was pointed into his left palm. It was a hand position that no one would take notice of, but Bagnilla recognized this to be a sign to those initiated to receive the message.

"Do you agree with the experts that say the Christ was crucified with nails in the wrist?" asked Bagnilla venturing into a new topic during the pause.

"I never see the Wounds of Christ on the wrist, but in the Hands of Carpenter," answered Gowen.

"I too have felt the Suffering in my Hands."

Gowen now looked a Bagnilla's hands. He had his left index finger pointing into his right hand, returning the sign.

The tone and volume of the conversation reduced to only the realm of the table in the restaurant filling with the late diners.

"This box of parchments documents, it isn't a *Codex Argenteus* you are looking for, is it?" asked Gowen.

"No. I had to put something on the warrant," Bagnilla replied. "What these people have are several volumes of the *Codex Syracuse*."

"Syracuse?" Cowen excitedly asked. "You mean they have the actual codices?

"Three maybe four books ... I have recovered two pages."

"Three or four codices," Cowen asked excitedly, "that would be the most complete set ever."

"Yes it would," Bagnilla replied proudly of his discovery.

"Which books do you think they have?"

"From the notes recovered from the house, the first journal for sure. They gave our Brother James Spruill something we have never seen before."

"What was that?"

"A shipping manifest issued to Saint Paul. They also gave him a page of his journal entry for March 16, 693."

"First trip to Antioch," Gowen acknowledged. "Bacchanalia and a nights stay in the *tabernae* of Quintessa."

"Very good, not many of us have studied the Codex that much," said Bagnilla.

"Not many of us can withstand the heresy in the books."

"I know. I get angry with those that suggest we consider the documents to be authentic and begin a dialogue with the heretics."

"I know what you mean." Then Gowen asked with quite anger. "Do these people know what they have?"

"I don't think so, or at least not yet."

"Are you afraid they might find it out?"

"That doctor knows Latin. She would have to know at least Latin medical terms."

"At least that," Gowen agreed. "But is that enough to read the Codex?"

""I think her medical Latin would help some. It would give her a basis to start interruptions," Bagnilla said. "It would be slow going though. She couldn't possibly understand the Latin adjectives, conjugations and declensions. Sentence structure is hard for me to grasp at times," he explained.

"That is working for us. If they ever realize what they have," Gowen said his voice trailing off as the two began thoughts of what disaster might ensure to their faith should the pages be made public.

"Well, they don't understand it for now," Bagnilla said breaking the silence, "or we would have heard from her by now. How long have you been a member."

"Since I was an altar boy. You?"

"Same," he replied. "I praise the day I joined the Knights."

Gowen was the first to notice how much time had passed. They were walking back to the office when he pointed to the dust covered Crown Victoria sitting in the parking lot. He did not see the government tag on the car, and mentioned what a mess it was.

Bagnilla paused for a moment to study his car when he began to recall the events of that morning. His near miss at the campground, then the drive with the many R.V.'s on the way to see the game. He also realized that he had seen one motor coach similar in appearance to the photo of the Holland model in his briefcase. He remembered passing a motor home pulling a trailer with a SportCraft 1400 ATV on it. But what stimulated his recall was how similar the tan color of the dust on his car was to the dust on the Holland and SportCraft's cover.

"Damn," he exclaimed and he began to nearly run toward the office.

"What?" said Gowen matching his pace.

"They're headed this way. I think I passed them on the way here."

"Where?"

"I-24 headed this way."

"So they could be in the area?"

"They were on the interstate at the Tennessee State line."

"From Alabama?" Gowen asked confused.

"I think," Bagnilla replied just as puzzled, "I thought I left Alabama when I got to South Pittsburg."

"You were in Georgia," he said explaining, "I-24 dips into Georgia at Whiteside. You were going through a valley after crossing a lake, right?"

"Yes."

The elevator closed as it began to carry the pair back to the office floor.

"Then you were in Whiteside," Gowen said, "You passed the Tennessee Welcome Center?"

"Yes."

"There are two gas stations just past there. Cheaper fuel taxes. Everyone stops there to fuel up. I'll bet they have security cameras," exclaimed Gowen.

"Good idea. How fast can you get those tapes?"

"Pretty fast. We go out there all the time about truck hi-jacking and smuggling," answered Gowen.

"I'll check the fax and probably cruise the truck stops and local campgrounds."

"You return to Whiteside, I know the campgrounds," Gowen suggested.

"Better idea," acknowledge Bagnilla.

The return trip to Whiteside was productive and encouraging. Both stores at the exit ramp had surveillance equipment and store managers willing to cooperate with the FBI agent. He watched a Holland Silver Bow pull up to pump number three on the outside of the overhanging canopy. He noticed, for the first time, the model name was missing. He saw a time frame when Harley Macklin got out and inserted the fuel nozzle into the hole in the side of the truck. He watched Jackie walking across the parking lot and into the store. Once the pump cut off, Harley followed her. At the counter he watched the purchases and saw the couple paying with cash. He took note that constricting their access to cash would be helpful in slowing the couple's flight. They returned to the Silver Bow and stopped at the back. Harley pointed to the rear of the truck. They talked and entered the vehicle. He watched as the RV left the station pulling the utility trailer with the SportCraft ATV. The store managers downloaded the segments that he wanted into a USB flash drive.

Bagnilla approached the front desk clerk at motel adjacent to the gas station about the chances of obtaining a room for the weekend.

"We are full," said the clerk, "game tomorrow."

"Is there anything available in the city?"

"I'll check," said the front manager looking into his monitor. "There is a Holiday Inn in Red Bank. They have three rooms available."

"Where is that?"

"Forty five minutes north of Chattanooga, but with the evening rush hour and game traffic," he calculated. "could take an hour easily."

"Anything closer?" begged Bagnilla. "I've been on the road since Thursday night."

Wanting to cooperate with the Federal agent, the clerk looked sheepishly at him and asked, "Do you mind what it looks like, I mean outside?"

"Not as long as it's clean and has a bed," said a frustrated Bagnilla.

"Well it looks kind of… well like a New Orleans cathouse, but it is a nice clean place. I know the owner and he keeps it up well. Nothing to write home about. But I would stay there."

"Where is it?"

"Just up the road in Tiftonia, at the next exit. Turn left at the end of the ramp, then turn right at the Whiz Burger. It's on the right, you can't miss it. It will have pink and purple neon lights around the roof."

"I saw that place on my way here. I thought it was some kind of gay club. How is this Whiz Burger?"

"Nice place to eat. Dinner specials are real good and cheap. Lot of truckers eat there all the time."

Chapter 40

The sound of a car door slamming woke the couple. After brief discussion over dinner options - order in or dine out - putting the monstrous Class "A" motor coach in a public restaurant parking lot - ever decreasing cash reserves - did Harley convinced Jackie that the Wizz Burger was the closest and best option. They walked to the quirky eatery a quarter of a mile away for the evening's meal. Jackie was leery of the establishments name posted with bright orange neon that was readily seen by fast moving truckers. Harley pointed out the number of eighteen wheel tractor trailers, the number of nearly as large four wheel drive pick-up trucks pulling nearly as long open trailers, and the scattering of autos with Marion and Jackson county tags, all parked around this glowing garish beacon might indicate that this would be a memorable dining experience. She conceded this displayed a ringing endorsement of the food or ambiance or service or all three.

"A little of all, and they have great prices," he replied as he held the door open when they arrived.

Whiz Burger was indeed more than she expected. The place was brightly lit, clean and orderly, walls without dusty rusty ploughshares, plenty of uniform wearing staff, and lacked cigarette smoke they sometimes inhaled at lesser truck stops. Having seventy eight entrees on the six page menu, they ordered from the breakfast pages that often carries the cheapest items. Waitress was prompt with their order of whole wheat pancakes and two eggs over well on the side. The two orders of three flapjacks arrived with the edges spilling over the plate.

"These are huge," Jackie expressed. "We should have asked for one order."

"Why? What would you eat then," he said teasingly.

"This is more than I expected for $3.85 a plate."

"And juice is included," Harley added.

They discussed their current shortage of cash, expected expenditures, and possible source to refill the treasury. They knew from the Conner's report that Bagnilla was watching the charge account transactions. Jackie was fearful that with the up-grade status to art thieves, Bagnilla might cut off the access to their debit or credit accounts.

"If we pay for breakfast with a card, then in a few hours these people can expect Bagnilla to come charging in here," Harley said.

"Couldn't we get a cash withdrawal?" she asked

"Same thing would happen, maybe even faster."

"What about a third party?"

"What do you mean?"

"Suppose we call Elizabeth and have her send us $5,000.00 in cash by Western Union?"

"Hey!" Harley exclaimed, "That just might work. I mean they can't be watching Elizabeth's account."

"Can we call her from the room?"

"No, they could be tapping her phone. We could call using one of those cheap phones you bought."

"You can do that?"

"If you can keep the phone call down to a couple of minutes then the best they will be able to do is get a general area of where we are."

"Then we have a plan," she said.

Elizabeth had slept little the night before and had been up all day calling all of her parent's friends in Atlanta. She was comparing air fares on-line when an unfamiliar caller id popped up on the cordless phone at her desk. She thought of letting it go to voice mail, but having no word from her parents, she answered, "Hello."

"Elizabeth, I can't explain it all, but right now we don't have a lot of time to talk."

"Mom? What's wrong?" she worriedly asked. "The FBI came here yesterday asking me if I knew where you were. Is dad with you?"

"Yes, dad is with me, but we need to get you to send us some cash."

"Mom, the FBI says ya'll are art thieves, stole some antique books? What the hell is going on?"

"Elizabeth!" Jackie said in the tone of voice as if she was addressing her twelve year old child. "We don't have much time. They could be tracing this call right now."

"Mom, what is happening?"

"Hello Iizzy," Harley said over the speaker phone. "I need you to calm down and stop asking questions right now. We can explain it all later, but right now we need your help."

"Anything you need, Dad."

"We need some cash, and they maybe tracing our call," Harley said stating the problem and quickly explained their current situation with cash flow. Elizabeth did not understand but promised to wire them $5,000.00. He told his daughter to give the Western Union agent Chattanooga as the town where they would make the pick-up.

"We love you and will call again as soon as we can or when we feel it safe to do so," Jackie advised Elizabeth not to talk to anyone except with an attorney being present.

"Cooperate as best you can, you don't need to be in trouble too," her father told her.

"I'll do what I feel is best for my family," said Elizabeth, "no matter what the FBI wants."

"That's my girl. We love you." and he snapped the flip phone closed and pulled the battery.

They had walked to within 50 yards of the Cave Inn parking lot when a dusty black Crown Victoria passed them from behind. They both froze as the proverbial deer in the headlights. Being the first to react, Jackie pulled Harley behind a shrub growing by the road.

"Do you think?" she said and did not finish the question as they watched a familiar black suited man exited the automobile. He looked around and turning his back to them, walked into the office. A few minutes later he returned to his car, withdrew a briefcase from the front. He open the trunk and removed a heavy long black plastic case with metal edgings. He propped it against the back bumper. He lifted a case from the storage space and placed it on the ground. He closed the trunk and carried the three pieces to room just down from the office. He went in and closed the door.

"What now?" Jackie asked looking at Harley.

"What now?" he asked surprised at the very notion that he was expected to have a plan. "What now is, we wait and see what he is up to."

"Wait! … Here!" she stated.

"Well we don't know if he saw us … our faces, which I doubt he did with his coming from behind us."

"So why don't we get back to the room, pack up and leave?"

Just then, the office door opened and Jake, Flipper's eleven year old son, ran out and up around back of the inn.

"Let's cross the road and ease along the edge of the woods until we get behind the motel. You start packing … I want to talk to Flip." As they neared the motel they caught movement around the Silver Bow in the back corner. Jake was looking around the camper, knocking on the door.

"What is he doing?" she asked as she directed Harley's attention to Jake.

"He is looking for us."

"Why?"

"Flipper is looking out for us. Let's go," as he motioned toward the office.

"You go see what Jake wants. I am going to the room and start packing," she ordered.

Harley caught Jake returning to the office at the corner. He was just as red headed and freckled faced as his father.

"Jake, it's me Harley," he said to remind the eleven year old. "I haven't seen you since that trip to Whiteside Pit," meaning the sinkhole cave system they had helped to map.

"Mr. Harley," he spat out. "Dad said to find you and tell you that the FBI is here."

"Where?"

"Room 4."

"I saw him come in. Does your dad know what he wants?"

"He said he is looking for you … gave dad a piece of paper with your R.V. on it." he reported.

"Anything else?"

"Dad said to find you and tell you not to get caught," he said, proud of what he had done.

Harley found Jackie standing at the un-used motel bed with their belongings sitting by the door.

"Damn inconsiderate of him. Now what?" she said upon learning Bagnilla was indeed on their trail.

"Flipper said, Bagnilla asked if he had seen our Silver Bow. We are safe for the moment but I can't get over the feeling of a rabbit looking a beagle in the eye."

"What do you mean?"

"A minute more and we would have been standing face to face."

There came a sound of drops of water hitting the rain gutter hanging at the edge of the roof. They parted the curtains to see a moderate rain shower had moved in.

"Maybe it's a sign," Jackie said half-heartily.

"Maybe you are right," he agreed reaching for the phone.

"Flipper, is Bagnilla still in his room?" he asked.

"He hasn't moved since going in."

"We're going to make a run for it."

"Where, I'll come help."

"No, don't get involved. I don't want you to get in trouble too."

"Too late. I already told him I haven't seen your R.V. that's parked in my back lot."

Jackie and Harley moved the luggage into the Silver Bow. Flipper came out to see his friends off. He shook hands with Harley; Jackie gave him a big soaking hug and a thank you.

"Take care you guys and let me know what happens."

"We will," said Jackie as she closed the door with a foreboding feeling.

"Here we go again," Harley thought. The Silver Bow motor turned once and fired. He pulled the gear leaver into the drive position and nudged the motor coach out of the corner. Rain drops began to grow in size, density and tempo. Lightning flashed and a second later the frightfully close crash of it rolled up the valley. He pulled to the edge of the road and looking both ways made a right turn, pulling the trailer up the mountain.

"Why are we going this way?" Jackie asked.

"Staying in the woods I guess," and it was his only guess. His mind was not thinking clear, having been chased out of his motel room.

"I want to avoid the interstate until we figure out where we are going. I know a few more people in these woods."

It was the sound of lightning close by that forced Bagnilla's attention away from his daily report. He walked to the window and pulled the cord to open the curtains. He saw rain falling in a steady pattern. A movement in the corner of the window caught his attention in time to see a large vehicle pull onto the road to his right, pulling a utility trailer carrying an ATV behind a motor home. Although having removed his socks and shoes ahead of disrobing for a bath, he bolted from the room for the office door.

"Open up!" he yelled at the locked entrance. "Open up. FBI!"

The front was very slowly opened by Flipper.

"An R.V. pulling a trailer just left here," he said looking dead into Flipper's eyes. "Who was driving that truck?" he asked already sure of the answer.

"I don't know," Flipper flatly said. "Maybe they were just turning around."

Bagnilla, certain that was not the case, demanded to see the registration file. Flipper took too much time in retrieving his index box from under the counter. Bagnilla pulled his right hand above his shoulder and came across Flipper's head with a gun butt. Flipper dropped the box on the counter and he fell back against the wall. Then Flipper attempted to jump at Bagnilla to return the blow when he saw the black hole at the end of the Browning Automatic. He could also see a thumb pull the weapon's hammer into the firing position.

"Macklin, Harley and Jackie," Bagnilla proclaimed as he held up the incriminating card. "Were did they go?"

"How should I know?" he defiantly answered, "and better still, why should I tell you?"

"Dad!" yelled Jake as he came from the apartment joining the office. "Dad, are you alright?"

Jake moved to comfort his father. Bagnilla cut him off grabbing the young man by his neck. His right hand moved the gun against Jake's head. Flipper was too stunned at all of this to move.

"Whoa, whoa, wait a minute!" he pleaded. "Can't we just talk about this?"

"Where did the Macklin's go?" Bagnilla demanded again. "And don't think I won't do it," he said nudging the barrel against Jake's temple.

"You wouldn't?" pleaded Flipper.

"I have before and will do it again."

"You can't get away with this," Flipper said crying.

"I'll say there were two men, it was dark. I was knocked down. I had to fire," and then he shrugged.

"Now wait a minute," Flipper begged when he realized this man was nuts enough to pull the trigger. "Just wait."

"Time was up when I asked the first question. You should have been honest and fast."

"They just left."

"Where are they going?"

"I don't know!" Flipper cried out. "They didn't say. They just packed up and pulled out."

"Who do they know around here?" he demanded.

"There are cavers all over the woods."

"Who?" and he pressed the gun to Jake's head.

"I don't know! Let my boy go, please." he cried. "Harley knows every caver in the region."

Bagnilla realized every second talking would add another minute to his catching up to the slow moving motor coach. The realization came to Bagnilla that Harley was in his own briar patch. Bagnilla also knew that witnesses to his chasing the Macklins made things harder to explain. If he wanted to keep the Codex once he recovered it, then it would be easier if he did not have to explain things to any division oversight investigator.

Flipper fell dead first behind the counter. Jake would be found lying across his father's body, shot through the back of his head. There would be no defensive powder burns on his hands for the investigators to find. Bagnilla picked up the empty spent bullet casings ejected from the weapon.

"Forgive me Holy Father for I have sinned. I have done these things to protect your Son and His Bride the Holy Church," Bagnilla uttered as he searched for any hidden camera in the lobby. He left behind no forensic evidence to show that he had gunned down Flipper and Jake. There would be no fingerprints to lift from the office door handle.

The Marion County Coroner would learn from the FBI, the fingerprints taken in room eighteen, from the counter top in the Cave-Inn office, and off the handle of the back door to the office, were a match to those found in a home in Harpersville, Georgia. Elizabeth would learn from a TV reporter at the front door of her home that Harland a.k.a. Harley Randolph Macklin and his wife Jackie a.k.a. Jacqueline Philomena Macklin, M.D. would be on every television station in the five state area around Chattanooga, wanted for theft and murder.

Bagnilla took his registration card with him. He became as a whirling dervish of activity attempting to wipe away evidence of his occupancy. Once he felt secure that his identification was erased from the room, he took a face cloth and wiped the front door of the office and door knobs both inside and out. He stuffed the face cloth into the trash receptacle on his way to his waiting car.

No one saw the back end of a dark Crown Victoria dancing in the middle of the road like a mad squirrel, heading north on a rain slick Federal Highway 41, chasing after a Holland Silver Bow Motor Coach.

Chapter 41

Even with the largest engine and best towing package in its class, the Silver Bow was straining to climb the Tennessee Hills. The road could rise as high as a four story building in less than the length of a football field. U.S. Highway 41 ran to the north from The Cave Inn and Interstate 24. The Federal Highway made a wide swing to the west along the Tennessee River in a winding course through the valley between Signal Mountain to the north, Raccoon Mountain to the east and Aetna Mountain to the west. The edge of the road fell steeply after Harley passed through Cumming's Gap. In the darkness of the storm and through breaks in the tree line, Jackie could make out the lighter shape of the river. The road continued to rise and fall along the river bank as it began a wide swing around Aetna Point; first to the northwest, then to the west, then to the southwest. Jackie watched silently as the little ball compass on the dash kept spinning and bobbing in its water filled globe. Harley was hard against the front window straining to find the centerline though the driving rain.

They had passed but a few driveways leading to homes some too far off the river to be seen. Road builders occasionally allowed enough land on which someone would put a home between the asphalt and the water. Anyone passing these homes could toss rocks down the chimney as the road was that high above the roofs. The whine of the gears against the push of the motor accompanied the slapping of the windshield wipers.

"This wasn't such a great idea," he murmured under his breath.

"What?" asked Jackie arousing from her dismal trance.

"This wasn't such a great idea," he said speaking louder. "There will be no witness if Bagnilla does follow us."

"Flipper said he was still in his room," Jackie reminded him.

"I just get a funny feeling," he said.

"Is that funny like that time you started to swing across the creek on the vine that broke?"

"That was not funny," he said. "That was stupid."

"Then you are feeling stupid funny?"

"No, like something is wrong, or we are going the wrong way. I had misgivings when we said goodbye to Flipper. I didn't want to say anything at the time. I just hope he will be OK. Bagnilla could be a dangerous man."

The highway went to the southwest and descended to the riverbed between the narrow gap of Signal and Aetna Mountains. The Federal Road dropped at the same rate as it climbed on the other side of river's bend.

It was here that Interstate twenty four emerged from the gorge as well and crossed the impounded river forming Lake Nick-A-Jack. The only way anyone could cross the river for generations was to use the distinctive rusty steel truss two lane bridge. Interstate 24 now bore the brunt of the heavy traffic over the expansive lake.

The Silver Bow came to stop at the bottom of the Federal road

"We just got a break," Harley said breathing a sigh of relief. "I know where we are. And it looks good."

. "We are back where we started," Jackie said dismayed at the sight of the lake they had crossed that morning.

"And that is good," he explained. "Now we have a choice of directions. We could return to Molly and Jubal's, or go back toward Chattanooga, or continue up Highway 41."

"Where does this Highway 41 go?" Jackie asked.

"West," he said. "We'll climb over Mount Eagle, and there are several campgrounds on the way."

"I think they will be watching campgrounds, don't you?"

"Probably," Harley sadly agreed. "We need to get that money before we leave Chattanooga ... Just in case Elizabeth's phone was tapped."

"I got it," Jackie said using all the seriousness of the moment, "we could go to Andrews, North Carolina."

Why Andrews?" he asked mystified.

"That's where that guy, that bomber, Rudolph, Eric Rudolph hid out for years. Remember?"

They had camped just about everywhere in the Great Smokey Mountains. They were in The Nantahala National Forest, North Carolina in July of 1998. The FBI and local law enforcement had road blocks everywhere attempting to capture Rudolph. The retired couple had to stop for a roadblock during the manhunt. These mountain folk were the people that gave Federal Agents the nickname, Revenuers. These people spawned bootlegging and moon-shining as legitimate, if illegal, cottage industries. The Nantahala Forest is where the Cherokees went to hide from the forced march to the Western Lands; and the backwoods preachers give rattlesnakes to children to handle far from the public's eye. The irony of risking another roadblock search did not escape Harley and he chuckled. "Bagnilla would throw a fit if he found we went there."

"Took the FBI three years before Rudolph gave himself up," said Jackie.

"Why the hell not?" he said.

"Bagnilla is still at the hotel," She mistakenly pointed out. "How can we get to Andrews and still pick up the money?"

"South, down through Georgia on Interstate 54 then pick a way east. Or we could circle north then east. Up through the mountains," was the choices he offered. "Yeah," Harley said coming alive, "Yeah, we can loop around to the north and come back down into Red Bank or Soddy Daisy. We can still be in the Chattanooga area. Honey, you are great."

He pulled the Silver Bow to the right and crossed the old Highway 41 bridge over Lake Nick-A-Jack. The Federal Road, once named The Old Dixie Highway, had been the primary road from Chicago to Tallahassee. Back in the day, mountain crafters sold their own handmade quilts plus "Made in North Carolina" blankets and rugs to tourist on the route from the Keneenaw Peninsula in Michigan to the beaches of Miami, Florida. Crushed black or purple velvet blankets bearing the likeness of Elvis, Jesus, and Rebel Flags were hung out for sale. This Old Dixie Highway and hundreds of similar roads were replaced by the generic Interstate Highway system.

The Federal Highway 41 was broad and relatively flat on the other side of the river and little used now that it was void of roadside oddities, eateries, and quirky motels. Just to the east of Jasper, Tennessee, he turned north on State Route 27.

Pulling up at a four way stop, Harley asked Jackie, "Check the map. I think this is the intersection of highways 27 and 283. Do you see a sign for Powell's Crossroads?"

"Let's ask them," she instructed pointing to the light in the window of a country store. He pulled the Silver Bow as close to the front as possible. Harley, ever the gentleman would not let Jackie get out, jumped the puddle outside the camper's door to thinner water. The clerk confirmed he was indeed at Powell's Crossroads and to continue north would put him on Sergeant Alvin York Memorial Highway.

"You came up from Nick-A-Jack?" the woman at the counter asked.

"Yes," he affirmed. "Then is this Suck Creek Road," he asked waving his hand to indicate that the county road to the east was indeed Tennessee 28.

"Yes it is," said the old man sitting by the pot belly stove. Where ya'll headed?"

"Red Bank," Harley answered.

"Red Bank!" the old man responded. "You goanna' take that thing," he said as he pointed to the massive vehicle parked outside, "across Signal Mountain and down Suck Creek Road to Red Bank?"

Harley said nothing to his elder.

"You must be in a damn big hurry to drive Suck Creek to Red Bank in this weather," the old man warned.

"We have to get to her mother's," stuttered Harley with a poor excuse and nodding to the vehicle outside.

"Why not go down to the interstate and to Chattanooga?" the man advised.

"My wife's mom is in Red Bank and that would take an hour. Suck Creek would be what … twenty five minutes?" Harley guessed.

"Yea, in broad daylight with dry roads, but in that …? You must be crazy to go over Signal Mountain tonight in this storm," the old man warned again. "They don't call it Suck Creek Road for nothing." And Harley would have laughed with the man but he knew the old timer was being drastically honest.

Harley thanked them all for their help and splashed his way back to the Silver Bow.

"Well?"

"We missed the sign for the road," Harley explained as he turned to the east. He did not want to worry Jackie with the fellow's prophecy.

Jackie was relieved as the road flattened out and traveled straight. If not for the rain and low clouds, she could have seen Signal Mountain looming 1,800 feet above the road she was enjoying.

If U.S. Highway 41 was like a Water Moccasin the way it twisted up around Raccoon and Aetna Mountains, then State Road 27, Suck Creek Road was a worm.

After two miles traveling the pleasant valley road, it climbed a little then took a sharp loop to the right. The tension in Jackie found a very brief lull during a gentle left turn followed by a straight climb and gentle turn again to the right. Once over the small hill and down into a bend, she could see the road on the other side of a gully. It went up again and Harley slowed the Silver Bow to a crawl.

"My god," Jackie said, "is that sign correct?"

The yellow diamond shaped warning sign ahead showed an inverted "U" with the lines very close together. A smaller rectangle sign warned, "15 MPH".

Finding no downhill traffic coming into the hairpin shaped curve, Harley crossed all road lines with the Silver Bow. Suck Creek Road gently climbed the west side of Signal Mountain on a medium grade. After a wiggle left here and a wiggle to the right there, once on top of the mountain, Suck Creek began earning its reputation. Another warning sign showed another closed inverted "U" followed by a hard right turn. The slight wiggles in the road Harley had driven over were replaced with much tighter bends.

"Oh!" was uttered very briefly when Jackie saw the road's namesake suddenly appear out Harley's window. Suck Creek lay fifty feet below the guard rail lining the road.

Now the road gained narrower and tighter turns, totally blind turns that prevented seeing what was coming from thirty yards away. Drivers climbing the road met the hulking Silver Bow riding the yellow line dividing the lanes. Harley met the oncoming cars as he swung around bends and missed by what he feared were just inches.

At one point it was as if they were driving through a tunnel made of soaked dark brown tree branches and dark gray limestone cliffs. Jackie was frightened by the lightning. Not because of the explosive thunder, but by what the flash reviled. There was a right-of-way of four feet or less between guard rail and cliff walls. At a few points, the steel rail was fastened to the limestone mountain. The other side of the road was no better. There was a brief respite when they crossed the twisting waterway a second time. Jackie was relieved when she no longer saw the creek out Harley's window. It surprised her to see the stream out her window.

"Is that the same creek?" she timidly asked.

"Yes. The road crosses it and re-crosses … it's like that all the way down. You doing all right?"

"*e meilleur des mondes possibles*." she quoted.

"Is that from *Candied*?" Harley asked, referring to that satire where most of the characters endure as much physical torture as possible. *"The best of all possible worlds?"*

It wasn't just the heavy rain and winding road that slowed Harley's decent. Waterfalls, driven by the downpour, cascaded off the stratified limestone escarpment splashing against the picture window on the front of the Silver Bow.

"Look out!" Jackie cried.

Tree branches loaded down with sodden leaves, brushed the top of the RV.

"We can't stop!" shouted Harley over the noise of the motor and rain. "There's nowhere to pull over."

Jackie noticed the compass had stopped rotating wildly and settled down into a general south-eastern direction. The road continued to drop in front of them, but it was becoming more tame. Once she caught a quick view of the Tennessee River and the distinctive silhouette of Lookout Mountain she sighed with great relief. Another diamond shaped sign indicated River Canyon Road would be on the right. They crossed another bridge, this time wide enough for shoulders, and there before her was the Tennessee River and water front homes.

The measurement given, as the crow flies, between Powell's Crossroads and Red Bank, Tennessee, is about fourteen miles. Suck Creek Road descends one thousand eight hundred twenty three feet in elevation into the northern point of Moccasin Bend. The mileage counter in the Silver Bow recorded a total of seventeen and three tenths miles, which included the bends.

When the Silver Bow was examined on Saturday morning, they would find several small tree branches lying across the SportCraft A.T.V., and a few stuck in the Silver Bow's luggage rack.

"Thank God that was all," she muttered.

Chapter 42

Bagnilla stopped at the intersection and stared across Lake Nick-a-jack at the same interstate bridge he had crossed that morning.

"Damn!" he exclaimed.

He looked at the GPS on his dash. This time the device was working during his pursuit of the Silver Bow. Remembering Flipper's last warning, his pursuit was slowed as he scanned the driveways and houses along the way up, over, and around Aetna Mountain believing that Harley had yet another buddy that would give them refuge. There were several houses with motor-homes parked in the front yards, side yards and back yards. At each sighting, Bagnilla slowed his Crown Vic looking for the Holland Silver Bow, towing an ATV. He was frustrated at losing time when the motor-homes were of a different manufacture. He was also exhausted mentally and physically having had not slept since Wednesday night.

He had the same options as did the Macklins. Studying the GPS he saw four routes they could be on. Aggravation and frustration had set in edging on the exhaustion.

"Gowen," Gowen said when he answered the phone.

"It's me, Bagnilla," Bagnilla replied. "I just saw them."

"Where? When?" Gowen asked.

"Tiftonia, leaving the Cave Inn," he blurted out.

"Are you in pursuit?"

"I didn't realize it was them until they were over the ridge," Bagnilla lied.

"You couldn't catch up with them?"

Bagnilla was sure he caught that snide, smirking veiled reference to the Macklins using a motor home as a get-away vehicle. He said nothing in defense.

"Where are you now?" Gowen asked.

"Federal Highway 41 and Interstate 24 at some big lake."

"Nick-a-jack," Gowen told him. "You sound beat. Why don't you get a room and we'll start fresh in the morning. I mean how easy is it to hide a motor-home?"

"There it is," he thought but replied to Gowen, "everything is booked out here."

"Head for town, I'll find you something near-by."

His Crown Victoria eased onto the Interstate Highway 24 and he sped through the gap between Signal and Lookout Mountains. Gowen had reserved him a room in East Ridge. Once Bagnilla climbed the grade out of Chattanooga he found the exit and a Comfort Motel. The clerk paused in her studies of her college textbook and checked him in at 11:48 p.m. to room 107.

Saturday morning he checked out and went down the street to a crowed Waffle House for breakfast. Tennessee fans were already out clogging the restaurants looking for breakfast before the game. It was about 09:00 when he called Agent Gowen to report in and to see what intelligence had been gathered overnight.

"Cooke in Atlanta faxed in a transcription of a phone call intercepted in Flagstaff."

"Go ahead," he said as he got out his pen.

"The Macklins called their daughter Elizabeth and asked her to wire them $5,000.00 in cash," Gowen informed him.

"Good. Now we know they are planning to continue to run."

"And we know that they are running out of cash."

"What wire service are they using?" asked Bagnilla.

"Western Union."

"Can we get flyers out to all their agents?"

"I looked into that. There are over two hundred seventy five agents in what is the Chattanooga area. Grocery stores, office supply stores, banks, convenience stores and even truck stops."

"Truck stops," snapped Bagnilla. "Let's get flyers to all truck stop agencies. They might try to hide their R.V. with the trucks. How many of those are around?"

"We have eight major chain truck stops. This town has always been a transportation center."

"Anything else?"

"Yes, I almost forgot. The Tennessee State Patrol has called us. Seems there was a murder during the night at the Cave Inn. Didn't you say you saw the Macklin's leaving the place?

"I was," he paused to fabricate his lie, "I was coming out of the Wizz Burger and saw them down the street. I went through the area yesterday putting out flyers. Why?"

"Looks like it paid off. One of your flyers was found behind the front counter. The Macklins may have murdered a motel clerk and his eleven year old son. You might want to check it out. Where are you now?" Gowen asked.

"I'm still in East Ridge. Do you want to meet up?"

Yes. I'll meet you in Tiftonia. I am in Saint Elmo. I'll probably get there before you."

Bagnilla paid his tab and headed west passing the south edge of town going around Moccasin Bend. He saw hundreds of R.V.'s, travel homes, travel mansions, travel yachts, all headed toward the game in Knoxville.

"This isn't going to be easy," he thought. The Crown Vic pulled off onto the exit ramp and made a right. He passed the Highway Patrol outpost. The Cave Inn parking lot was full of law enforcement cars. Across the road in an abandoned convenience store parking lot there were two local news crews setting up satellite dishes to send in their live coverage of the late breaking news story. A crowd of onlookers gathered behind them; some the of motel guests stood in their doorways looking at the drama unfolding before them. Some stood in their doors, dressed in Tennessee Orange, pissed at being detained as possible suspects or witnesses and sure they would miss the game.

Gowen met Bagnilla at the front of the hotel and brought him up to speed on the investigation.

A guest in room number 25 walked into the office to check out around 6:40. When he opened the front door he saw Flipper and Jake in each other's arms. He closed the door and went to the room adjacent to the office. There he beat on the door until the occupant answered and he told him to call the police. The guest, a man come to only do some hang gliding, returned and stood guard until joined by the caller.

A State Trooper responded within minutes of the call being just down the street. He went in and returned visibly shaken at the sight. The Trooper immediately taped off the area with crime scene tape and waited for the investigators.

The crime scene investigator examined the flyer found behind the counter and called Gowen. There were no bloody finger prints on the flyer. The investigator reported that this was not a random robbery.

"How do you know?" Gowen asked the investigator.

"The victim, his son, and the perpetrator all were standing close. There is gunshot residue on the clothing. There are no defensive wounds on either's hands. The father was shot first. The safe in the back is un-opened."

"Really?" inquired Bagnilla.

"The father was shot in the chest. His son must have went to him and got it in the back of the head."

"You said you didn't think it was a robbery?" Gowen asked again.

"The safe is open and the money is still in there. He may have been counting the day's receipts when the shooter came in."

"So you called us because you found the flyer?" Gowen asked holding the document in his hands.

"Well there is that and I found this," said the investigator turning to the register. "Here," he said his finger pointing at the damning evidence written on a registration card. "Harley Macklin," he quoted the entry, "room eighteen."

There too was penciled in the Alabama tag number the investigator said belonged to Jubal Conner of South Pittsburg. "That's a little town west of here," said the investigator assuming Bagnilla had never heard of the city.

"Have you been in the room?" Gowen asked the man. "I just stuck my head in the door. I haven't begun processing the scene. Got too much to do here."

"May we look at it?" asked Gowen.

He hesitated at the thought of anyone entering the crime scene of what was going to be a major homicide case. He did not want the scene disturbed.

"Just a quick walk through, we won't touch anything." Gowen assured the man.

A state trooper stationed outside room eighteen opened the door for the two agents. They entered and walked to the bath room. They saw the damp towels on the floor. They found nothing out of place but the bed linen. Bagnilla looked in the trash can, saw some paper receipts and pocketed them in hopes that it would reveal the couple's next move. Gowen saw the movement and nodded approval. They left after finding nothing else.

Returning to the front office they made their goodbyes and started out.

"Keep us posted and let us know if we can help," said Bagnilla. "Here is my card. Call me directly if you find anything else."

"You might have your people interview all the witnesses and let them go. Some look so mad they have turned red orange," Gowen said with a wink at the investigator.

"Well, what next?" Gowen asked his comrade as they left the motel office to stand by his car.

"Let's go back to the office and get some bulletins out to the truck stops," answered Bagnilla.

"I'll notify the interagency network to post a lookout for these people," said Gowen.

"I want to make them suspects in this homicide. That will give us cause to put 'heavily armed and extremely dangerous' on the notice."

"We could ask the community to be on the lookout as well," Gowen suggested. "Are you thinking that maybe they will get shot?"

"Could happen. If some of these good old boys find out how old Jake was, having family themselves, you never know," he schemingly said.

"Can we put out a rumor that a reward has been offered?" Gowen mentioned.

"Rumor? I have the authority to issue a reward of ten thousand dollars to anyone with information leading to the arrest of the art thieves. Put that on the air and let's sit back and watch these poor hillbillies shoot themselves chasing after that kind of money."

"Wait here," and Gowen darted across the street to the news crews. They gathered before he could get there like a pack of starving dogs all out for one bone. He spoke with them, handed out business cards and flyers. When he returned he told Bagnilla that CNN would soon be there.

"CNN and Fox news both have crews in town. ESPN is covering the game. ABC has a crew here as well. This will go out all over the nation."

"Good. I am tired of chasing these people. Can we control the local police?"

"We have some Knights in the State Patrol as well as one member in the D.A.'s office," he said to relieve Bagnilla's fears that the Codex might find its way into an evidence locker and eventually into public court.

"We need to stress the Codex is to be returned to us for protection, as a priceless art object."

"I'll get right on it," assured Gowen.

Chapter 43

"Yeah, I guess so," Harley said to Jackie.

"Yeah, what?" she said turning her attention from the industrial complex they were passing.

"Hungry," he said clarifying his understanding of the first thing she had said since they survived the Suck Creek suicidal drive.

"Are you hungry?" she asked as well.

"I thought you asked if I were hungry?" he was puzzled.

"I haven't said a word. I was looking out the window, thinking about breakfast. But it's too early."

He started to say that he thought he heard her say the word 'hungry', but realized he heard her *think* the word hungry.

She turned again to watch idle rail cars lined up like tombstones in front of idle factories. Iron came from South Pittsburg mines to be made into the steel that help the South to rebuild after "The War" and to build the machines of the world's wars. The railroad running parallel to the Hixson Pike once moved raw materials and finished products. Foreign markets had reduced the area to one five mile long blighted industrial park. Jackie watched this rust and Kudzu covered wasteland pass by the Silver Bow window in the rain.

"Where are we going to go?" she lamented out loud to herself and to Harley.

"There is a truck stop in Soddy Daisy."

"Soddy Daisy?" the names of the southern towns never ceased to amaze her or fail to amuse.

"From an old Indian word "Tsadi," Harley said explaining." Means drinking place."

"Probably a trading post that provided whisky," she huffed.

"Probably," he agreed.

"What does Chattanooga mean?" she said asking for a translation.

"Old Indian word meaning 'See Rock City'," he said.

She laughed hard at the joke and it broke the tension web that fear had been building for hours.

He found a truck stop near the Dayton Pike intersection. It was not one of the nice clean shinny family friendly chain of truck stops travelers find along the interstate. This one had been there to see the rise and fall of the industries in this broad flat plain between the river and Signal Mountain. Black sooty dirt covered every surface, even the ceiling tiles in the restaurant were coated black. Harley inquired about a Western Union agent and was told by a plant worker headed for the mid-night shift that the Kroger would be open and had an agency in the grocery store. He added there might not be much in the cash drawer this early in the morning.

Harley realized that five thousand dollars was a lot of cash for one grocery store to have on-hand on a Saturday morning. He told Jackie of the predicament they now found themselves in.

"We can't find that much cash right now," he said in resignation.

"Can we find it later in the morning? Won't there be a bank open?"

"A bank might be the better choice."

They pulled the Silver Bow into a space between two behemoth eighteen wheel trucks, each churning diesel smoke into the already polluted air that can lie in the river valley for days at a time.

They felt comfortable enough to lower their guard and get some sleep. Harley took the front couch meaning to keep a lookout for any trouble. Jackie cleaned up with a wet sponge and laid down in the rear bedroom not removing her clothing, just in case.

About an hour later, they were both awakened when the garage mechanic started the truck engine two spaces down. Even with the massive trailers between them, the pneumatic starter on the twelve cylinder motor screamed like it was about to explode until the two thousand pound engine began to burn the foul diesel fuel.

"WHAT THE!" Jackie exclaimed running from her slumber.

"Air starter," Harley said responding to the ultra high pitched high whine of the air powered motor.

"God that scared the..." and she stopped short of emitting an obscenity beneath her position. "Excrement!"

Harley chuckled at the choice and climbed into the driver's seat. He fired up the Silver Bow's eight cylinders and let the truck idle.

"Where to?" Harley asked as if forgetting the choice they had agreed to before their brief nap.

"I thought we decided on Andrews," she provided.

"We need to get the cash, banks open in forty five minutes," he said looking at the clock on the C.D. player.

"Let's eat until then, but not here."

"I like your plan," he agreed and pulled the gears into position.

"Here you go," said the teller as she finished counting fifty, one hundred dollar bills into Harley's waiting hands. Five thousand dollars... I've never handled that much in a Western Union transaction," she happily said slipping the $5,000.00 paper band back around the wad of cash. "You going to the game?"

"Yes," he replied realizing that Knoxville could be a route to cover their movement to Andrews. "What is the best way to get there?"

"Go up to the Knoxville Pike and turn right," as she pointed in the direction. "Then you will cross the river and you will be there."

"Thanks, I'll do that." and he left the bank to find Jackie waiting in the Silver Bow. She had their satellite TV turned to CNN and saw the crowd of police cars in front of the Cave Inn.

"That was John Turner, the first man to find the bodies of Robert Franklin Wallace, known to his friends as Flipper Wallace and his eleven year old son Jake Tommy Wallace. Both shot to death in cold blood by who the police believe to be are the same people the FBI have been chasing for theft of archcological documents dating to the fourth century A.D." The reporter told his audience that the police and the FBI have issued a five state bulletin to all agencies and began to describe Harley and Jackie. The screen showed Harley's and Jackie's diver license photos.

Harley fell to one knee and softly cried "My God, oh my God no." Jackie said nothing as tears leaked through her fingers covering her face.

They continued to watch the horror of the story unfold, full of what they knew to be lies about themselves. The coverage went to a reporter standing alongside the Sequatchie Valley bridge saying that police were out in force not only for the game, but would be looking for their the Silver Bow pulling the ATV trailer. Another reporter was shown standing at the entrance to the Houseman Tunnel with a state trooper watching the traffic. "We'll be watching all bridges and tunnels for the RV," the trooper told the reporter.

"Now what?" she said through her tears. "Is there no stopping Bagnilla?"

Harley had not recovered from tragedy he had brought to his dear friend and what Flipper must have done for them to have Bagnilla to shoot them. The reporter gave no details to this, but they knew in their hearts the truth.

"We have got to turn ourselves in, stop this madness." Harley finally caved in.

"What then?" Jackie wondered. "Bagnilla will frame us for the murder. We were there. We signed in."

"I signed in. There is no reason for you to be mentioned," he said starting to offer her an alibi.

She would have none of his proposal, "We are in this together. First Eckland, now Flipper, who is next … the two of us? You heard what the reporter said 'we're to be considered armed and extremely dangerous.' Maybe Bagnilla is hoping that we will be shot on sight. That way he can get the Codex."

He stopped and considered his next move. "Well he can have it," and reached for the seat cover over the storage space.

"NO!" she said not wanting to give in to the madman. "If we do, we have no guarantee that we won't go to jail for at least stealing the Codex."

"I don't need you dead. I couldn't stand ...." and he could not finish the dreadful sentence or horrible thought.

"I do not intend to let him get that close. If we give in now he and Spruill will get the box and get away with murdering Eckland, too."

"He is offering a huge reward for our capture," he pointed out. "The hunters up here will be after the bounty and they don't care if we are alive or dead."

"Then we have got to run for it and hope that we can figure out ... out, something," she said stumped for an answer.

"We have a problem getting to Andrews."

"What?"

"We have to cross the river to get to the Smokey Mountains."

"Is there any other way than taking a bridge? Can we go around? How far is Kentucky?"

Perking up he climbed into the seat, "There are several ways across a river."

"Which are?"

"Over, under, and through," he said as the Silver Bow left the parking lot turning north.

Harley's intent was to follow the way of the pioneers and early settlers that traveled through Tennessee, crossing and re-crossing rivers and streams. These stout people used fords if shallow enough, bridges if the water was too high, and ferries when the water was too wide or deep for a bridge.

Harley knew of only one ferry still operating on the Tennessee River. At the end of Elder Ford Road, Mr. Green Berry Elder built the ferry crossing in 1853. A mule powered raft carried travelers and wagons over the river. When the water was impounded to create Watts Barr Lake, the ferry was replaced by his great-great- great grandson. Installing a gasoline powered

Barrett Ferry boat he could float two or three cars across the river. His son Marshal now ran this oddity of Americana.

It was late morning when Marshal looked up from his garden hearing the crunch of gravel under the tires of the Silver Bow.

Pleasantries and introductions were given and received. Harley thought the fee reasonable enough and asked if Marshal could accommodate them and their cargo.

Marshal had no experience moving a motor coach as large as the Class A motor-home on his ferry and asked Harley for the gross vehicle weight. Harley gave him the numbers from the owner's manual. Marshal asked for the weight of the trailer and A.T.V. This, Harley did not know exactly and ventured a guess in the neighborhood of eight hundred and fifty pounds. The ferry operator then asked for Harley's and Jackie's weight. Harley reported his at two hundred fourteen. Jackie looked shyly at him and whispered hers.

"Well, all total, I can't take you. You have to take the bridge," He said pointing down river.

"We wanted to take the ferry," Harley said. "She has never done anything like this."

"How did you find me?" Marshal asked.

"I found out about your ferry in a magazine article," Jackie lied to him.

"Which one?" for he had from time to time entertained writers wanting an interview with the last private ferry operator on the Tennessee River. "I'll bet it was Southern Comfort, or was it the Tennessee Traveler?"

She said she was not sure which one and asked if there was some way the crossing could be accomplished.

"Well," he said taking a long draw of fresh mountain air. "We can divide and conquer."

He had Harley to release the trailer and Marshal took the Silver Bow across alone and parked the lumbering truck on the road. Jackie sat on the seat of the SportCraft A.T.V. as it and the three of them crossed the river. Once hooked up again, Harley paid the fee and thanked Marshal for his service.

Marshal returned to his gardening and would not go in the house until his wife called him in to lunch. Over a meal of Tennessee style chicken fried steak and potatoes Marshal pulled up that morning, black eye peas, and sweet tea, they would watch a CNN reporter show pictures of a Holland built Silver Bow Motor Coach and that nice retired couple that had boarded his ferry that morning. He called the hotline number listed at the bottom of the $10,000.00 reward poster.

Chapter 44

Bagnilla answered Gowen's phone call as he drove the Hixson Pike.

"We have the pick-up agent for Western Union," Gowen informed him.

'Who, where, and when?" was all Bagnilla had to say to the revelation and he pulled into a truck stop near the Knoxville and Dayton Pike intersection. His notebook accepted the name of the bank, the teller, and the address where at 9:48 a.m. Harley Macklin picked up five thousand dollars in cash.

"Then he asked for the fastest way to Knoxville, to the game," the nervous young lady in the bank's conference room told the forceful FBI agent Bagnilla.

"Are you sure?" asked Bagnilla seeking confirmation, "He said he was going to the game?"

"I have never had to cash out five thousand dollars on a Western Union pick-up. Yes I remember his asking the fastest way."

"What did you tell him?"

"Knoxville Pike. It's the next intersection take a right," she said automatically.

"Thanks," he offered. "I'll be in touch."

He called Gowen as soon as he went out the door to report the conversation.

"Probably a decoy?" ventured Gowen.

"Oh yes. These people are smart," he agreed. "He knew we would be here as fast as we could trace the pickup receipt."

"What's next?"

"Have you had any leads called in?"

"None I would call creditable." Gowen gave him the short list of what well intentioned public servants thought they saw, and see-sawed over what they saw... seeing the Silver Bow, or a Rainbow, or something like that going down this or that road. We have a few reports of Holland's parked in campgrounds."

"Anyone checking them out?"

"I have called in two of my agents and sent them off to look."

"Can we trust them?" Bagnilla asked worried that the Codex might be lost.

"Yes."

"You have any campgrounds I can check. They seemed to have vanished again."

Gowen gave him several with coordinates for his GPS.

"Call me the minute you hear something" was Bagnilla's parting instructions and he went up the road.

Bagnilla found the Creeks Bend Campground. There he did find two Holland manufactured vehicles. One was the Woods Creek model and the people at the door were thirty one and thirty years old when he asked for identification. All in the campground wanted to help. They had heard of the tragedy at the Cave Inn. The second Holland was a Silver Bow. circa 1980, rusting and fading as the young Poplar and Sweet Gun trees grew around the sides of the permanently parked RV.

The Harrison Bay State Park proved to be a little more daunting an investigation. Bagnilla contacted the Park Superintendant and obtained a ranger to assist him. Several Hollands were found. One was a Silver Bow of late manufacture. The one on his flyer seemed to match the one parked in space twenty one. A call to the check-in station reveled that twenty one had been occupied by a couple from Nashville for the last two days. They approached the truck cautiously with weapons drawn.

Bagnilla pounded on the side door and waited. When no one answered he shot the lock until the door opened. Once inside they went through the cabin. The park ranger discovered the registration in the dash compartment. It belonged to a man in Tupelo, Mississippi. They found an orange ball cap with the letter V on the front. "Volunteer fan," said the ranger. "Must be at the game."

When the Vehicle Identification Number didn't match the Macklin's number, Bagnilla left the park.

He checked in with Gowen who had nothing new to report. His other agents had come up empty. The state patrol had stopped a few R.V's finding more Volunteer fans, or legitimate campers. One truck full of zealots wanted to push religious flyers off on the officers. The pair discussed Bagnilla's coming into the office. Feeling frustrated Bagnilla agreed he would after his next stop.

None of his other stops proved as interesting as Harrison Bay. He made a visit to the Redwood Fish Camp. There were motor homes there but none made by Holland. He had lunch at the Redwood Grill on the river. Bagnilla never cared much for nature and accepted the table nearest the window on the front. That side of the restaurant faced the parking lot and he could see his Crown Vic. He studied his notes until his steak dinner arrived. It was medium rare with a baked potato. The patrons on the other side of the diner enjoyed the view of Watts Bar Lake and the barges being pushed up river past Thief Neck Island.

Families in their speed boats went at breakneck speeds passing the large slower moving house boats. Their wake threaten to swamp a small ferry crossing the impounded waters. The little ferry could hardly be seen with the freeboard so low to the water. Had Bagnilla not been so focused on his notes and reimbursements, he would have seen a Holland Silver Bow, Model 3800, Class "A" motor home with the name spray painted over, that appeared to be driving across the lake.

Bagnilla asked for a receipt not only for his meal, but requested it include exactly a ten percent tip he grudgingly left. It was a very good steak dinner.

Chapter 45

The gloriously tricolored trees were thick and close to the edge of Elder Ford Road as the Silver Bow pulled the SportCraft trailer up and away from the Tennessee River. Jackie had relaxed enough to take out her digital camera and take a few pictures as they slowly climbed the bank. She stuck her head and camera out to snap a stand of brilliant hickories as they passed when there was a loud noise from inside the coach.

"God!" she exclaimed jumping at a familiar noise. It was one of the new cell phones she bought at Cumberland Mall going off to Elton John's *Crocodile Rock*.

"Careful, those things can bite," Harley said with a grin.

She made a quick face at him as she studied the display screen. She ran the numbers through her memory bank and the combination surprised her.

"It's my old phone," she said puzzled.

"Don't answer. Could be a trick," Harley cautioned as he stopped at the Cleveland Pike. Then with a moment's reflection said, "Call her back and see what is up."

"Is that safe?"

"She is the one that called you. How did she know the number?"

"She was with me when I bought these," and she reached behind her to the bag that hung on her seat. She withdrew two more pre-pay cell phones still in their plastic shells.

"Molly told me to tape the phone numbers to the packages should I lose the receipts."

"Call her back. She thought is safe enough to call you or it must be important," he instructed. "Put it on speaker."

"Molly? This is Jackie," she informed her friend. "Is something wrong?"

"My God Jackie," Molly cried. "What have you gotten yourself into?" She told them what they already knew about Flipper and Jake being murdered, they were accused, and Bagnilla was getting close.

"You believe we didn't do it?" a question she did not need to ask. "Flipper was a good friend of Harley's. He and Jake probably tried to protect us from Bagnilla."

"You cannot blame yourself," Molly counseled. "Flipper was a grown man ... he knew there might be trouble."

"Yeah, but not murder. You wouldn't think an FBI agent capable of something like that."

"But you said it. Their murder is Bagnilla's fault and we will see that he pays. Right now we have got to get you some protection. I guess you are going to continue to keep that Codex?" Molly asked confirming her suspicions.

"We are going to use it to somehow trap Bagnilla into confessing."

"You are braver than I would be. Be careful. I have something to help you."

Molly outlined how they were to drive to Neyland Stadium in Knoxville and blend in with the crowd of other motor coaches. They were to find a parking lot and try to park so that the back of the Silver Bow could not be seen from the road. This was in case the police were cruising looking for their tags. Bagnilla had the tag number of the Silver Bow Harley had left on the registration card. Molly said she and Jubal would find them.

Harley took the Cumberland Highway to the outskirts of Knoxville. He fell in behind a Fleetwood Class "A" motor coach. He chose to follow this one as the sides of the bus was painted in a Volunteer Orange theme. Big white and orange swooshes scrolled over the sides and windows of the hulking vehicle. They went down the Neyland Boulevard and the Big Orange bus turned into an alumni parking lot. Harley had to travel on until he found a lot where frat house pledges were waving orange and white flags to bring customers to their parking area.

"This looks good," he said as he pulled up to the young man holding a Corona in one hand and a hand full of currency in the other.

"That will be twenty dollars," the pledge announced.

"Twenty?" declared Harley.

"You will take up at least three spaces," the pledge said explaining his fee.

"Do you have a place where I can pull through?" and pointed toward the SportCraft trailer.

"Hey, Gene!" he yelled at a brother. "Can he pull through the alley?"

The answer came back that he could indeed pull into the alleyway between two fraternities and he would be pointed at Neyland Boulevard when he was ready to leave. The tow truck companies would see that all driveways and alleyways would be free of illegally parked cars.

"Do you think this wise? I mean what if they saw the news?" Jackie fearfully asked.

"These frat boys are probably playing The Legend of Zelda all day long."

"How do know Zelda?"

"That is all that they do these days. Wake up, drink a beer for breakfast, if they have no classes they play video games the rest of the day," Harley theorized.

They watched the parade of people and vehicles drift down Neyland Boulevard until they heard *Crocodile Rock* playing. It was Jubal calling to tell them they would be pulling up at any moment. They emerged from the Silver Bow to find their friends parking in the yard of the adjacent frat house. Jackie embraced Molly as if he had returned from the moon; Harley unashamedly did the same. In like fashion, Molly too squeezed deeply the fugitives.

Jubal was wearing a big Orange hat and Orange sweatshirt. Molly had an orange windbreaker. They looked like they were there for the game.

"How do you guys find us?"

"We are monitoring your cell phone position," Jubal answered. "You've got to take the battery out."

"I didn't think you could do it so fast," Harley said as Jubal extracted a plastic shopping bag from his car.

"You can if you have a really good IT person on staff." Jubal informed Harley. "We know they're tracking your old cell phone which Molly left at the house."

"Here are a few things that might make your adventure go a little easier," Molly said lightheartedly.

They brought them new truck and trailer tags and they would be getting new identities with new driver's licenses.

"New identities?" she asked. "What do you mean?" Jackie asked looking at the plastic card bearing her likeness.

"You are now Carolyn Diane Milton and you are married to Sheldon," Molly said nodding at Harley, "Gustav Milton."

"Sheldon?" Harley cried.

"Milton?" Jackie asked astonished.

"I thought it would be easier for you to remember since it was where you went to high school. You live at 505 Hall Street, New Orleans."

"Milton is understandable, but why are we from New Orleans?" she said astonished.

"You both love the city," said Molly, which was true their having vacationed there eight times in the past six years. "So you will be able to tell people how to get around should they ask."

"Sheldon?" Harley continued to grump, "Why Sheldon? Why not Rock or Stone? or even John. That sounds better than Sheldon."

"Shelly," Jackie teased. "Stop complaining. Sheldon was your roommate in college. Hall is my dad's name. 505 is our anniversary, in case you forget," she said stinging his memory.

"Having familiar links would help you remember these things should you get separately interrogated … like at a checkpoint," lectured Molly. "That is why I chose to name you after our daughter Carol."

"How did you get our pictures for a new driver license?" the new Carolyn asked.

Molly explained she went to the Chattanooga office Saturday morning as soon as they saw the CNN report. Once there, she pulled in all solid favors. Having over thirty years with the agency, she had many points to use. First they retrieved new Louisiana plates from the storage vault of secret identities. Second thing was to pull up their photos from the Georgia State Patrol data storage of driver's information. Molly told the Georgia State Patrol the CIA was investigating whether or not the pair were *international* art thieves. That took the staff programmer a few minutes to find a program that would give her the likeness required for the Louisiana documents.

"Jubal, does she have instructions on how to make a bomb out of kite sting and silly putty?" Harley said mockingly.

"She is scary," said Jubal, "that's what I love about her."

Harley looked at Jackie and asked, "How do you meet these people?"

"She *said* she was working as an international foreign student exchange coordinator when I met her," Jackie claimed in light of the recent discovery. "She brought some Russian students to the CDC."

"We wanted to know their capability to manufacture biological weapons," Molly added.

"And what did they learn?" Jackie asked her.

"We brought them in to see what questions they'd ask. If all they want to know is how do you make jell-o, then we can assume they don't know enough to ask how do you make VX Nerve gas."

"Like sitting in a bar and listening to a quantum physicist trying to win an argument with a drunk who saw a special on string spaghetti theory," explained Harley. "You learn the drunk *doesn't* know what he is talking about."

They discussed the plan to hide out around Andrews, North Carolina. Molly said they did not have any operatives that she knew of in the area, but, that it seemed a good idea.

"But you know Molly," Jubal said laughingly, "She probably has an operative behind every tree disguised as a black bear."

They installed the new Louisiana RV tags and tossed the old ones in the Buick. Harley shook his head over his new driver license. Jubal advised him to conceal their real ones in the truck. He showed them how to access a dead space behind the panel above the small refrigerator.

"Drug smugglers know about this," he explained to Harley as he pulled the panel from its snaps.

Jubal also brought a cover for the SportCraft. It fit as if it was custom made for the machine. The embossed name on the green cover proclaimed YAMAHA.

"What do you think?" Jubal said of his work.

Neyland Boulevard now cleared of foot traffic as other stragglers to the game continue to arrive by car. Harley eased the Silver Bow into the road and headed out to find the Alcoa Highway that would take them into and over the Great Smokey Mountains. The way in was easy enough to find by following the tourist trail into the woods. There were SUV's, some carrying kayaks, and some carrying mountain bikes on back door racks. The hikers and backpackers identify themselves with a decal of the letter "A" morphed atop the letter "T". For those in the know, this stood for the Appalachian Trail. Several vehicles, mostly Jeeps and other four wheel drive autos sported the symbol.

Photographers and urban naturalists all headed for the same natural wonders that are the Great Smokeys in the Fall. "The Season", as most business owners reverently call the first week of October until mid November. It was a time when people stampeded into the lodges, campgrounds and valleys to take in the Autumn Colors and attend mountain heritage festivals. Room rates doubled over the summer rates. Banquet halls were booked for Autumn Mountain Weddings. The old time mountain theme parks with their country and gospel music festivals packed in herds of seniors in tour busses. As the urban chic flowed into the rural wilderness, it created a traffic jam that would make the Los Angeles Freeway at rush hour look like the Berlin Autobahn. Everyone move only a few feet if and when somewhere, way, way, way up front, someone fought their way through an intersection or found a parking place.

As one long time resident who originally moved there for the peace and quiet put it, "In the fall, we get grey heads, newly-weds, and nearly deads."

Chapter 46

"We have a solid sighting on their RV," Gowen announced when Bagnilla's cell phone found a good signal.

"What happened?"

"A man called from the Elder Ferry Crossing," Gowen told him, "said he took the Macklins across Watts Bar Lake this afternoon."

"You said he took them across the lake? In a boat?"

"It's the Elder Ferry. Marshal Elder runs the old ferry that crosses Watts Bar Lake," Gowen said trying to explain this antique oddity of the American transportation system. "He will ferry a few cars from Elder Ferry Road in Marion County to Elder Ferry Road in Hamilton County. Check your GPS. Look between the towns of Eureka and Kingston."

He checked the GPS to find the roads that seemed to end at the lake's shore. There was no indication that a ferry existed. He was irritated to see that the ferry crossing was just below the Redwood Fish Camp on the lake.

"How sure is Mr. Elder that it was the Macklin's?"

"He's positive. He described estimating the weight of the RV using the owner's manual, and it said Holland Silver Bow 3800. He also noticed the name Silver Bow had been poorly spray painted over."

"Painted over?"

"That's what he said," Gowen said.

"He said he took the RV across the lake, and came back then took them. Harley had taken the SportCraft ATV off the trailer to use it to pull the trailer onto the ferry. Then once on the Hamilton county side, he had to hook it all up to the Silver Bow. Mr. Elder said it seemed to him to be a lot of trouble just to ride his ferry boat, but they kept insisting."

"Why didn't everything go across at one time?" Bagnilla asked.

"He was afraid it would over-load his ferry. He also charged for each trip and they didn't complain or bargain with him."

"Have you gone out there to interview this witness?"

"No," was Gowen's short answer. "My agents are all out canvassing the campgrounds and truck stops."

Bagnilla began to suggest that he might go over with a photo of the couple and the RV. Gowen stopped him when he said that it was on the other side of the river from his location.

"And you might reconsider when you hear this. They have some help," Gowen reported.

"You said they had some help?"

"We have the conversation on tape if you want to come in and hear it."

"I am going after the Macklins before they disappear again," he said declining the invitation.

"The call came from that location you went to in South Pittsburg ... Jubal and Molly Conner to a throw-away cell phone. I have the number and tracked it to Neyland Stadium, but they must have pulled the battery out because I lost the signal."

This was a new twist Bagnilla had never encountered in his twenty one year career. An outside party using a suspect's cell phone to call the owner.

"What kind of aid?" Bagnilla asked.

"I'm not sure. Mrs. Conner tells them to park near Neyland Stadium. Then she says is she is bringing them something they need. She never says what it is, and Mrs. Conner will find them."

"Where did you lose the signal?" Bagnilla asked.

"Near Neyland Stadium."

Gowen gave Bagnilla directions to Knoxville, Neyland Boulevard and Fraternity house row.

Five seconds passed in the conversation and Gowen ask, "Bagnilla can you hear me?"

"Yes. I am trying to think what this means. We know that these people, The Conners, gave them their truck tag. Maybe they are going to give them their drivers licenses as well?"

"They could," Gowen agreed, "but the physical descriptions of the Conner's do not match the Macklin's and there is a fifteen year age difference."

The decision was made not to backtrack to the Elder Ferry, but to send an agent out there once one was free. Gowen told Bagnilla he alone was tracking the Macklin's.

"Think they may have left the area?" Bagnilla guessed.

"Probably."

Bagnilla arrived to almost no traffic. Everyone was enjoying watching the Volunteers pouring copious amounts of fermented beverage down the Big Dog's throat and pulling that puppy inside out as Volunteer fans might say. He could hear the crowd cheering when he approached the fraternity members that waved the Silver Bow into the alley.

"Did you see this vehicle today?" he said holding the photo up for observation.

"Yes," the startled brother said. "I put them in the alley," and he pointed to the empty space.

"Did they stay long?"

"Bout an hour, maybe two hours. They left right after that other couple got here, the old people in the dusty old Buick."

"Did that other couple give them anything?"

"They did hug ... hugged each other like... they were old friends, dude," said the frat boy slurring his speech. "We see a lot of alumni here."

"Did they give them anything like a license plate?" Bagnilla asked specifically.

"I didan't see wha they had," he started and stopped for a loud and lengthy expulsion of the stomach gasses out his throat, "Oh man," he said as he fanned his mouth, "Nachos."

"What about the couple?"

"The old couple gave them ah … plastic shopping bag."

"You didn't see what was in it did you?"

"No, we get a lot of that too."

"What people passing bags back and forth?"

"Yep," he said and held up his own paper bag with a bottle of Corona concealed inside.

The young man could read the frustration on Bagnilla's face and asked the purpose of the interview. Bagnilla quickly brought the gathering crowd of frat brothers up to date. That was the first time they had heard of a murder taking place that morning in Chattanooga. Those around him were shocked when they saw the photo of Harley and Jackie.

"That's them!" proclaimed the other members gathered around their parking lot attendant who was also able to confirm it was the Macklins.

All Bagnilla could verify was that the Macklins had been there but not for long, and another older couple in a Buick was helping them. He remembered seeing a dust covered Buick at the Conner's house.

"You said the other couple drove a dusty old Buick?"

"Yeah … ya coulda grow weed … ah …. corn on the car, the dirt was so thick."

He left the intoxicated boys to their game and called Gowen to ask his opinion.

Gowen told him that it seemed that Harley was making a circle to the right. He recounted how the Macklins left their home in Atlanta, went west to Alabama, north to Tennessee, and continued north to Elder's Ferry, and now east to Knoxville. He also advised the relentless agent of the expected avalanche of tourist in the Great Smokey Mountains. Bagnilla decided to continue in the direction of Sevierville, Tennessee and started out the Alcoa Highway.

There was one more item Gowen discussed before Bagnilla signed off.

"Bagnilla" he warned him. "We are getting phone calls from other guests at the Cave Inn. They are saying someone matching your description was seen running up and down the walkway. Mrs. Conner said something about you being involved in the murder. Do you want to tell me something?"

"Nothing for you to know," he answered and flipped the phone closed.

Chapter 47

It is not too rare an occurrence for rain to fall in eastern Tennessee during October. It had held off long enough for the Volunteers to tame the Big Dogs from Georgia. The red western sky that morning was the same weather same sign understood by fourth century fishermen as well as it was to Harley Macklin. However, the clouds did not wish to share with him what they knew of the moisture they held.

That evening the fleeing couple pulled up between two titans of the road at the Sevierville Truck Stop to spend another night in their mobile home now far away from home.

Harley was awakened early again this time not to the sounds of splitting wood, but to a spitting truck driver. The owner of one the mammoth trucks was outside the Silver Bow's window checking the pressure of his trailer tires as the notion to clear his throat came upon him. He did this with the bravado of an opera singer as he attempted to dislodge from his airway, the remnants of years of smoking. This time Harley would not rush outside in his pajamas to glare his annoyance to the offender. This might result in his needing Jackie's skill as a doctor and he might not trust those skills since she had not touched a patient in years. He did pull back the curtains to see the unkempt face of an overweight truck driver wearing a "West Lumber Supply" ball cap. The driver caught the movement and stared into Harley's face before saying, "sorry" and moved on to check his tires.

Harley nudged his sleeping beauty and wished her a good morning. He made the offer to brew some hot tea. The temperature had fallen and the Sliver Bow was cooler than usual. The propane gas tank had emptied during the night and the heater did not fire. What happened to the furnace failure occurred to him when the stove failed to ignite as well. Being out of gas and low on fuel he announced that they would be filling up all tanks, and bellies at this truck stop.

Jackie had little fear of bacteria Campylobacter, Salmonella or E. Coli at this truck stop. The truck / travel plaza not only catered to the teamsters taking on thousands of gallons of diesel, but also to the incalculable number of RV, SUV, and Family Trucksters, traveling the highways and turnpikes through the mountains. The restaurant was pleasantly lit and the upholstery was in good and clean condition. Some patrons stood out as truckers, with tee shirts proclaiming belief in everything from Jesus to Bigfoot to the ending of the North American Free Trade Agreement of the Clinton Administration.

The professional truck driver also tended to display a poor bloated physique, the result of truck stop convenience foods, with their belt buckles disappearing under slabs of belly fat. All this was stuffed atop cowboy boots and they inevitability wore large leather wallets at the end of a chain in the rear pocket. These self styled free spirits of the highway stood in stark contrast to the many families waiting for a booth or table that Sunday morning. The truck drivers wanted to get back to work - the dads wanted to get to the driving range - the mothers wanted to get to the outlet stores – and the children wanted to get to the theme parks. Harley and Jackie wanted to hide, not just from the law, but from the bedlam.

The hostess said the wait for a table would be thirty minutes unless they were willing to share a large booth. They readily agreed to the novelty of dining European style. A fresh face young couple stopped their intense study of the nine page menu to smile at their breakfast guest. Introductions were simple and left to Harley to begin.

"Hi," he said, "I'm Sheldon and this is Carolyn, may we share the table with you? Otherwise we are told it will be a thirty minute wait to be seated."

"Hello!" returned the young man Joshua giving them his Christian name. "This is my wife, Hannah."

"Oh, Hannah, like in the Bible," said Harley who could not stop himself, "the second leader of the Jews and the mother of Samuel."

"That's right," Joshua replied, "From the book of Isaiah."

"Means "Favored" I think," Harley offered in friendship.

"Yes, it does," Hannah said, touched that the stranger knew this. "You must know who her husband was?"

"She was one of two wives married to Elkanah, an Ephraimite. First book of Isaiah, chapter one, if I remember it correctly," Harley proudly said.

"Why that is correct. I am impressed," she admiringly replied. "You must be a preacher? We would be pleased to have you join us, right Josh?"

"No, we are here just passing through," said Harley as they sat down. "I just have a layman's interest in the Bible. I have never been a pastor."

"Are you on your way to The Gathering?" Joshua asked with a nearly worshipful tone.

Harley stopped and looked at Jackie. She said nothing which he took as consent.

"The Gathering?"

"The Gathering," Joshua repeated nearly in prayer, "Returning God to the Nation Revival and Retreat."

"Yes, yes we are thinking about going there," Harley said hedging his intentions.

"We are going there too!" Joshua stated. "Maybe we could all go together?"

"Together?" Jackie asked alarmed.

"You mean we could follow you?" Harley said qualifying his statement.

"Yes," confirmed Joshua. "You know go at the same time. Camp next to each other."

Jackie was relieved at the explanation. "Yes maybe we could camp next to each other. So it's in a campground?"

It was Harley's turn to signal her by lightly nudging her leg with his to alert her to the *faux pas*. Revivals often are held out of doors under a canopy, a tent of some type or the old fashioned brush arbor. Harley was somewhat aware there were several church campgrounds in the Smokey Mountains.

"That might work out, only we need some supplies and I have lost the directions," Harley said pretending to be embarrassed.

"Don't worry, I have a map of where it is located," Joshua replied as he produced a folded paper from his pocket. This he spread out on the table for Harley's inspection. Jackie withdrew the small pad of paper she kept in her purse for him to copy the road names.

"Those look like Biblical names," Hannah said when she caught a glance at Jackie's pad with the names *Quintessea,* mask of *Charonion*, the *Amanic* Gates, and Antioch penciled on top of the page.

"Yes they are," Jackie confirmed trying to shield the notations from the prying eyes.

"Antioch, one of the cities Paul preached to," Hannah said, "it's in the Book of Acts."

"Now I am impressed," said Harley.

When their breakfast arrived Harley clasped Jackie's hand. She was surprised at his sudden display of emotion but he nodded toward the young couple already holding hands. He nodded that she should do the same. Being the senior male at the table, the honor of asking a blessing fell to Harley. He gave thanks as best he could being out of practice since the days of his youth. But it was for him like riding the bicycle and he ended with naming the Holy Trinity in the proper sequence.

With the morning meal consumed, Harley begged forgiveness for declining Joshua's invitation to follow them to the camp as he did need to fill the Silver Bow and propane tanks. Joshua and Hannah pulled out in their Fleetwood Class A and headed for Andrews, North Carolina and the Camp Meeting. Harley was hard pressed to understand the affection that evangelicals felt for meetings out of doors.

"What no air-conditioning?" Jackie asked.

"No heat or air but plenty of ventilation," he joked.

"I would like to have the bug repellent and ice water concession," was her observation.

"That reminds me we had better buy some repellent before we hit the road," Harley advised.

"And some sunscreen," she added.

"Not with the rain coming in," he said dryly.

As he left the store he overheard truck drivers discussing a report that a tanker truck of helicopter fuel had turned over on the Federal Highway 129, the most direct route toward Cherokee through Jacktown.

"Take Federal 441 south until you see Tellico Lake," one of the truck drivers informed him. "Then look for the state route 360 on the left. That will take you over to Jacktown. Ask anybody there and they will tell you how to get to Cherokee.

"One twenty nine is out, we need another route," Harley told his navigator when he climbed into the captain's chair. Jackie consulted the map and the GPS. She found the Route 441 and the state road 360 over the Jacks, Tellico, and Trey Mountain tops.

"There is a reason they did not put the Federal roads through there," she said with foreboding. "Too high in elevation and to twisty. This looks like a map of the small intestine."

The Federal Highway 441 was a veritable interstate compared to North Carolina's state road 360. It wasn't as bad as Suck Creek Road, but it was as close as cousins. The fog that gives the Great Smokey's it's name, did not rise like smoke but hung just over the tree tops in the valleys. Had this fog not been so bad drivers would be able to see the tops of the other motor-homes moving, as if in goose step, up the mountain passes. Again the compass went wild with direction changes every minute. In the middle of hairpin curves, the tires on the Silver Bow would spin briefly as the big rig attempted to find traction on a road wet with a drizzling rain. Harley quickly began to doubt the wisdom of this route.

He had a lucky break when he saw a sign board announcing a festival at a campground ahead and it had R.V. hook-ups. He turned in the gate pulling up next to the office. He and Jackie both froze when a uniformed sheriff deputy came toward Harley's window.

"Festival is closing," the young man announced.

"Can we stay the night?" asked Harley.

"No, sir. I'm sorry to say, the power is out right now.

"We heard Federal Road 129 is closed due to a fuel spill," Harley said, "is it still closed?"

"Yes, sir," continued the sad news," Where are you headed?"

"Cherokee," Jackie said interrupting Harley before he could spill the beans.

"Turn left going uphill to Jacktown. Then take Federal 441 to Cherokee," the deputy told them. "If you want a good R.V. camp, stop at Sandy Creek, it's along the way."

Harley thanked him for his time and help. The deputy helped Harley to turn around. He continued up the hill and rode the brakes down until he passed a sign announcing the un-incorporated Jacktown city limits.

There were two convenience stores on each side of the intersection. Each had beer signs of glowing neon in their windows. Each had a sign proclaiming that they had the coldest beer in town. "Tough choice," he wondered out loud. They took a left and just past the store found the Sandy Creek Campground.

The owner had an honor box out front of his log home and office. Harley stuffed a ten in the slot per the hand-lettered instructions on the plank above the box. He backed the Silver Bow into a space facing the road. Here, at least, was electric power available to hook up and water enough for a hot shower.

Chapter 48

The Sevierville Truck Stop parking lot was full of campers, trucks, eighteen wheel tractor trailers, and automobiles when Bagnilla stopped to post his flyers. He quickly obtained the manager's permission to aid in such a vital public service. Willing to assist in the capture of these dangerous heinous villains, the manager announced over the store's speakers that the agent was present and, "if anyone had seen a Holland Silver Bow RV pulling an ATV on a trailer please come forward." The operatic spitting truck driver, coming out of the showers, remembered having a Holland parked next to his truck all night. It stood out to him because the name "Sliver Bow" was painted over with white spray paint. He reported this to Bagnilla who asked if he saw the owners.

"Yes," he answered. "I saw that man," he said identifying Harley's picture on the poster.

"Were they pulling a SportCraft ATV?" he asked wanting to be sure these were the people to chase.

"No," the driver replied to Bagnilla's disappointment. "They were pulling a Yamaha, but it was an ATV, and it was a Holland Silver Bow," he assured him, having a brother who owned a similar model.

The hostess reported how she saw the two fugitives on Bagnilla's wanted poster, plotting with a younger couple during breakfast.

One of the pair of truck drivers approached Bagnilla with the details of the chat he and his fellow teamster had with the man in Bagnilla's picture, who was driving a Holland RV.

"We told them U.S. Highway 129 was blocked by the overturned tanker and sent them to Jacktown to get around it," said the good citizen.

"Where were they headed? Did they say?" Bagnilla excitedly asked.

"He said 'Cherokee' by way of Jacktown," the driver remembered.

Gowen called saying he would be at the truck stop shortly. Bagnilla told him to hurry he had a good lead.

"So what is the good lead?" Gowen asked him as they sat at a table.

"I have two good leads," Bagnilla stated. "Do you know the town called the Cherokee?"

"Cherokee, North Carolina ... it's an Indian Reservation," Gowen said explaining the tourist destination to Bagnilla. Gowen asked, "Is that where they are headed, Cherokee?"

Bagnilla outlined the conversations he had that morning. Their plan of action would be for Gowen to head off the Macklin's by way of going around Cheoah Lake, then, continue east to Cherokee. Once there he would introduce himself to the local sheriff and secure his help in watching the roads from the west for the Silver Bow.

"What are you going to do?" asked Gowen as he savored a real biscuit stuffed with lavender and strawberry jelly.

"I'm going to follow them to this Jacktown," Bagnilla muttered between chews of the real hickory smoked honey ham. "The last trucker I spoke to said he was sure they would go through there."

"Sounds good. What are we going to do about the Conners? Do you want me to search their place?"

"No. What I would like to know is who the hell they are?"

"What do you mean?" Gowen asked.

"Do you think these people have truck tags just lying around for people to use?" asked Bagnilla as he wiped his mouth of biscuit crumbs.

"No. I haven't given it much thought."

"Well this kind of help is more than just family members smuggling a file in a cake to their loved one on the inside. This is much more than that. Don't you think?"

"Well, yes."

"I think a lot more people are helping them."

"You mean the Greeks?" asked Gowen.

"I mean the Greeks or Russians or Turks or whatever they call themselves these days. I mean Lancard or Szalasznyj. That other church is full of heretics!" he muttered with quiet rage They're responsible for helping them out!" Bagnilla's fist came down on the table to emphasis his point. "I mean that someone with money is helping them with license plates and intelligence about our movements. Who do you know that can fund that?"

Gowen conceded the argument to Bagnilla and paused to delicately frame his next question. "What about Molly Conner's comment about you killing Robert and Jake Wallace? What was that all about?"

"Like I said, it was nothing to worry about," and Bagnilla reached for another biscuit.

"Nothing?"

"Nothing!" Bagnilla answered sharply. "She knew you were listening. Maybe she and her husband did it and are setting up the Macklin's to take the fall."

"Maybe Mr. Wallace got in your way?" Gowen angrily accused him. "Mrs. Macklin said you did it."

"Maybe he got in the way and I didn't have time to argue about it. Can you drop it?"

"Russell!" Gowen said earnestly, "You …" was all he spit out.

"What?" Bagnilla said with quite righteousness. "This isn't the first time one of us has taken a life to protect our Church . . . won't be the last."

Gowen sat in despondent disbelief for a moment. He came out of the trance to say, "But now, these times are different. It's not like we are real knights on horseback or something. When we joined the Bureau we took an oath to protect and defend the Constitution."

"You also took another oath and sealed it with your own blood, Frank. I believed you were a true believer and would be a faithful defender of our Holy Church."

"I am a defender .. it is just...an eleven year old?" and he faded.

"Just what?" Bagnilla asked attacking his comrade. "Just what? Backing out now? Well, I won't let you back out. There is no need to. We'll have all the known documents when we have that Codex," he said pausing, "Harland Macklin left his name in the register and his hand print on the back door knob. The man was shot at close range without defensive wounds. The assailant and victim knew each other. Open and shut. And even if it isn't, what can they do about it?

"Everything if they ever discover what is in that book."

"They haven't or we would have heard from them by now. They are keeping it to use as a bargaining chip once they are caught. But when they are caught, then that Codex will disappear in our evidence closet. Right?"

"OK," Gowen allowed, "OK."

"Damn right! Now pay for this, I am going to find Jacktown."

They parted at the front door, Gowen in his car and Bagnilla in his Crown Victoria. Gowen found the road twisting up to Cheoah Lake. Bagnilla found the little state route 360 Harley had used taking the monstrous Silver Bow up and into the mountains. Bagnilla came around a bend and was nearly run over by a Royal Coach class "C" motor home swinging wide out of the Music Festival parking lot. Bagnilla pulled up to the gate keeper's booth and honked his horn. The nice deputy went out to see what the obnoxious driver wanted in the drizzling rain.

"Park closed early, power's out," said the deputy assuming the man in the black suit and thin tie was a Bluegrass fan.

"I'm not here for the music," Bagnilla said holding his FBI identity card out the window for the deputy to inspect.

"Yes sir, what can I do for you?" the deputy quickly offered.

"I am looking for this RV and these people," and he handed him a flyer.

"They just left here!" he nearly shouted. "I spoke with them and told them they had to leave … we were closing."

"Are you sure? Which way did they go?" asked Bagnilla with a rising tone of excitement.

"They went up the mountain. I told them to stop at the Sandy Creek campground."

"Calm down and tell me are you sure it was them?"

"Yes, sir, I am sure it was them."

"Did you see the tag? Were they pulling a trailer?"

Deputy did his duty and reported that the tag was from out of state and not from nearby.

"Louisiana," he proclaimed. "I'm sure of it. They were prestige plates … had a pelican in the middle. I remember the first letters were FKU, but I don't remember the numbers. They were pulling an ATV. It was a big one, adult size, and it was a Yamaha." He would have no reason to have remembered the entire number and was too much for Bagnilla to hope for.

"Did you see a Yamaha ATV or did you see a Yamaha cover over an ATV?" he asked clarifying for the man.

"The cover was dark green and had white letters saying Yamaha."

"Decoy", Bagnilla thought, it was all he needed. He hit the gas pedal hard and left in a shower of pea gravel on asphalt. He would not miss them again and reached in his coat under his left arm and withdrew that same Browning automatic that days before killed Harley's friend and his son. He was traveling so fast in the gathering darkness that he missed the sharp left turn the state road makes at the fork in Ballplay, Tennessee and went half way down a county road before realizing the mistake. He turned around in a driveway and quickly made the return trip to the state road. He kicked the Crown Vic to the right and continued up and down the winding distorted excuse of a state highway.

"Jacktown Community Un-incorporated" the sign announced. He was getting excited knowing he was on their trail. He paused at the intersection and studied the two gas stations both with the coldest beer in town. He chose one on the left and went in with more fury than the storm outside.

"Do any of you!" and he pulled down the volume a notch, "Do any of you know where I can find the Sandy Creek Campground? I'm with the FBI," and he whipped out his agents badge.

None of the three men in the establishment moved. One was already out on parole and was carrying some illegal leafy substance in his jacket. The other, his companion, was a descendent of the Cherokee that hated all things Federal, and both were on their way home from work. The clerk behind the counter took one good look at the bad-tempered and unfriendly Federal agent. He assured Bagnilla the Sandy Creek Campground was to the right, about fifteen miles away. Turning and leaving without saying thanks, Bagnilla would spend the next thirty minutes in high anticipation of capturing the couple, hopefully asleep, in the Sandy Spring Campground located just to the left of the store.

The day clerk would clock out fifteen minutes later at the end of his shift. His replacement would be in an empty store to greet the returning Special Agent, enraged at being sent in the wrong direction. But each time Bagnilla left the store he would not hear the title "asshole" thrown after him.

Chapter 49

It was about time for dinner when *Crocodile Rock* began to play on Jackie's second cell phone she had just activated.

"Elton's here," Harley teased with a falsetto voice.

Jackie greeted Molly as Harley watched her face grow into a disquieting scowl.

"How long do you think we have?" she asked her friend.

"What!" whispered Harley strongly at Jackie.

"Then you don't know if he is on his way here?"

"Who?" again as he whispered his apprehension.

She held up The Hand to indicate that he needed to be quiet and she would relay all in a moment.

"Thanks Molly, thanks ever so much. We will let you know."

She relayed the warning Molly had just given her. The cell phones of Bagnilla and Gowen were both triangulated this morning. Gowen's location was the intersection of Alcoa Highway and East Jackson Street when he began a cell phone call, it terminated when he caught up to Bagnilla at the truck stop. They did not say anything in the conversation that the Macklins did not already know.

"When was this?" Harley asked running ahead of Jackie's report.

"This morning at 11:03," she said repeating Molly's precise intelligence report.

"So he is on our tail?" she asked her friend.

"Seems to be. We lost his cell phone signal as he went toward the Smokey Mountains. Cell phone towers are not allowed in the park. Did you tell anyone were you are headed?" Molly asked.

"We had breakfast with a nice young couple but we didn't say we were going to Cherokee," Jackie assured her.

"What about Harley?" Molly chided her.

When crossed examined, Harley folded and said he had asked directions of the truck drivers.

"Nice one," Molly said upon hearing the confession.

"Do you think he knows where we are?" Jackie asked.

"If you asked everyone at the truck stop how to get to Cherokee, I'd suspect he is right behind you." Molly said. "Be careful."

They continued to discuss possible escape routes as Jackie prepared water for the evening meal.

Harley was studying the map when he saw out the front window that all too familiar Crown Vic pulling up to the front of the log home. He instantly opened the circuit that would kill all lighting in the camper.

"Hey!" exclaimed Jackie.

"It's Bagnilla," he said pointing out the window.

"Do you think he saw us?" she asked fearfully.

"Put your seat in the upright position and secure all personal belongings; we're going to be in for a bumpy ride," he said dryly as he jumped into the driver's seat and reached for the ignition key.

"Open up FBI!" Bagnilla demanded pounding the front door of the log home. The owner answered at the second series of poundings to a soaking wet Special Agent H.R. Bagnilla. The man carefully examined the plastic covered photo that the agent stuck in his door. Once satisfied that the man was genuine the owner granted him entrance. Bagnilla produced his flyer and asked if the Macklin's had checked in.

"I don't know," the owner said clarifying, "we use the honor system."

Bagnilla shrugged not understanding the answer.

"You leave a ten note each night you stay," the owner said explaining his bookkeeping system.

"How do you know who has paid?" Bagnilla asked.

"I know who is new out there in the camp, and if there is a new ten dollar bill in the box, then they must have put it there."

"So who is new out there?"

He took Bagnilla to the back door and the screen porch that over looked the campground. From the position he could see the back of the camp and the front of a Holland RV.

"I see 'em," Bagnilla said and started for the front door.

"Do you want me to do anything, call the sheriff or something?"

"No! I'll handle this," he ordered as he jumped into that black car.

"That was him!" Jackie said as she poured the pot of hot water in the sink.

"Where?"

"Up on the porch," she said pointing at the empty deck.

"Hang on!" He yelled and snatched the gear lever into the first gear. Wet gravel was thrown from the rear wheels as the heavy vehicle vaulted from its hiding position in the trees, and, flying forward, separated the extension cord and water line from their respected points of attachment on the utility post.

Bagnilla too was shifting his vehicle into drive. His intent was to use the massive Crown Victoria to block Harley between two trees. The black car bolted forward as the Silver Bow closed on the escape route.

"HARLEY! LOOK OUT!" screamed Jackie as the Silver Bow was not altering its course.

The RV hit the left front fender of the Crown Vic and was last seen as a blinding white flash before Bagnilla's eyes. His car went sideways against the passing motor-coach. The ATV trailer was jumping high as Harley flew over the depressions in the gravel drive and made a high bounce when it hit the edge of the hardtop road.

They had escaped the potential trap, but Bagnilla was not to be stopped by automotive body damage. He recovered and began to pursue the Silver Bow.

Rain that was a steady drizzle, now fell in sheets as the warm air lost its battle against a strong cold front crawling over the Appalachian Mountains. Darkness and the massive vehicle would keep Harley from out running Bagnilla through the small mountain community that was Jacktown. There was little traffic on the road that Sunday night. Harley took the first left, not fully sure where it would lead but believed it to be State Route 360. He hoped the road would go up the mountain. Bagnilla would be un-able to pass at least for a while. It could give Harley time to think.

"We can't out run him," said Jackie looking nervously in the mirror outside her window.

"No, we can't," agreed Harley.

"We need something we can throw at him, maybe punch a hole in his radiator," she offered.

Harley's thoughts were broken at the suggestion of throwing something at Bagnilla's car. "We can throw something at him," he said. "Take the wheel."

Two loud snaps rang out made by Bagnilla's Browning 45 automatic pistol.

"He's shooting at us," cried Jackie.

"Take the wheel," Harley ordered her again.

"What?" We can't pull over. He'll kill us."

"Do it now, like we used to do," he said referring to those youthful antics where they would swap places behind the wheel of his 1968 Ford Fairlane as they drove down the road. "You get on top," he said as he motioned for her to sit in his lap.

"You have got to be crazy," she stammered. "We'll all be killed. We used to do that on a straight road, not in the middle of a mountain pass during a hurricane!" said she yelling at the very idea.

"You said it," he reminded her, "if we pull over - he'll kill us."

"What are you going to do?" she said moving toward the driver's chair.

"Throw something at him. Now get over here!"

She moved at his directions recalling the times that she had done this before. She would slide under his right arm and ease next to his leg. He moved over to the left as far as the car door would allow. Then they began by replacing hands on the wheel. Once she had control he eased his way under her and off the seat. She moved into the driver's position and took command of the Silver Bow. Jackie could drive the motor-home with the automatic transmission. She only allowed Harley to chauffeur her around the countryside as she took photos, read, napped, enjoyed the views and kept an eye out for estate sale signs.

It was difficult for Bagnilla to see around the Silver Bow even without the driving rain. Too often, he pulled close to that big rig trudging up the mountain. His windshield wipers were slapping buckets of raindrops as fast as they fell. He stuck his gun out the window and fired twice in the air in vain hope that they would pull over under threat of his blowing out one of their tires. He could not begin to put that brass bead at the end of his barrel on any of the wheels. Hitting the side of the truck would serve no purpose, so he continued to pursue.

"This time," he thought, "this monstrously slow moving motor-home would not get away." He lifted his cell phone from the belt holster. He dropped the phone as a car rounded the curve and passed the Silver Bow nearly hitting him head on. He slowed as his eyes darted about the wet road and the dark interior of the car searching for his phone.

Harley went to the back glass of the Silver Bow and slid the window open. He punched out the screen covering the hole. Rain, caught in the back draft behind the truck, blew in his face. He could see Bagnilla's car following, slowing in the distance. He had taken the newspaper and wadded the sheets into balls. He waited with his hands full of newsprint as Bagnilla accelerated. Harley began to toss every page of news in the swirling wet air. The balls caught the wind, some opened and some fell with the rain. Those that stayed aloft long enough landed on the windshield.

Bagnilla could see a bit through spaces left by the pages of newsprint stuck to his windshield blades. He fell back to a safe distance and reached out the driver's window to snag what he could. He tore large pieces away as the wipers fell back and forth but the smaller bits wedged under the blades and stayed there for the ride leaving blurring streaks on the glass.

Harley saw this had some effect and tossed more paper into the air. When he ran out he tossed paper towels and toilet tissue. This time Bagnilla had pulled back enough that the paper fell useless onto the damp road.

Another car went by this time blowing their horn at Jackie as she had drifted into the oncoming lane. Bagnilla kept a watchful distance. He could see Harley standing at the window. Harley could see the bright lights of the Crown Vic shining over the ATV. He went to the control panel and powered up the twin 150 watt flood lights he installed on the back of the Silver Bow. Bagnilla, temporarily blinded by these two powerful lights, slowed down to regain his night vision. The Silver Bow pulled around a bend in the road and Bagnilla's sight recovered.

He pulled down the sunshade to his eye level to block the blinding floodlights and accelerated. He had enough of the chase and wanted the Codex. He stuck his gun out the window and, pointing it at the rear window, fired a shot. Harley saw the flash of the barrel when Bagnilla stuck the gun out and ducked behind the wall. He need not bothered, in the rain, and with the bad roads, Bagnilla would need a lucky shot to have hit the window.

"He is shooting again!" screamed Jackie up front, as she tried to keep the Silver Bow in her lane. "Do something!" she pleaded.

Harley was inspired with a more foolish idea and climbed out the window. His foot found the ladder that gave him access to the top of the Silver Bow.

This time he would not be climbing up but down. He went to the lowest rung of the ladder. Before his head went below the level of the window, he yelled to Jackie. "WHEN I SAY GO," he paused drawing another breath for volume, "I WANT YOU TO KICK IT!"

"What!" she asked.

"I WANT YOU TO FLOOR IT WHEN I YELL GO – THEN TAKE YOUR FOOT OFF THE GAS!" he answered.

"What are you doing back there?" She had a mirror in the center windshield but it would not have found his body outside the window.

"I CAN TEACH OR I CAN DO!" he brusquely said, "I DON'T HAVE TIME TO DO BOTH!"

"Got it," she acknowledged.

His right hand held a wet and slippery grip on the aluminum rungs of the ladder. His left hand struggled to find that point where the ATV trailer was locked to the frame of the truck. He looked over his shoulder at the approaching Crown Victoria. He saw the flash and heard the report of another shot.

"What the hell is he trying to do?" Bagnilla wondered as he thought he saw Harley's silhouette through the wet trash on his window. He accelerated again to hide the blinding glare of the flood lights under his window shades. He was just a little astonished to see a sixty two year old grandfather, hanging on a RV ladder, in the middle of a rain storm. He searched again for his cell phone in the dark interior of the car; but trying to keep his eyes on the wet road and Harley while finding the phone, was proving to be a dangerous chore.

Harley had waited to see if Bagnilla would accelerate and close the gap between them. The road had been twisting left and right, but was also beginning to go up and down as they approached the top of the gap between the two mountains. Soon the Silver Bow would be going down the road and not up. Harley thought he saw the agent swerve and the gun barrel again. He released the trailer's safety chains attached to the Silver Bow bumper. Bagnilla had gotten a glimmer of the cell phone. He wanted to call Gowen and tell them of their approach to Andrews, North Carolina. He thought Gowen could get in front and block their path.

Harley waited until he felt the Silver Bow begin to ride up the road.

"NOW!" He yelled to Jackie.

She stomped the gas pedal to the floor as instructed and the truck lunged forward as much as it could. Taking her foot off the gas, the truck engine relaxed as did the pressure holding the trailer's lynch pin in place.

In that split second of forward and back motion, Harley withdrew that critical pin in the trailer tow hitch and watched the assembly slide free from the lock position in the frame. The nose of the trailer held in the air until the forward momentum no longer affected its travel. Free of the dragging weight, the Silver Bow jump forward. The trailer hitch buried itself in a shower of sparks on the asphalt. The eight hundred fifty pound ATV and trailer were free to slide down the mountain road. The Silver Bow rounded the curve and went over the gap and down the other side of Green Mountain.

Harley climbed back in the window and rejoined her.

"What happened?" asked a concerned Jackie having felt the jolt in the Silver Bow when the trailer was released.

"We lost him," he said watching out the rear window.

"What happened? We suddenly jumped forward like something hit us and was pushing me up the hill, and it drives different now."

"I released the ATV in front of his car," he was almost shameful in his admission.

"You what!" she demanded.

"I released the trailer as we went over the ridge."

"Did you kill him?" she asked fearfully.

"No, I don't think I did."

"We need to go back and see if he is alright."

Now Harley considered the magnitude of his rash action. It was to preserve their life, although some juries might not see it that way. The man had already killed his caving buddy and probably Uncle Willy. Bagnilla was acting alone - a rouge agent. No, Harley reasoned, he did what he deemed necessary at the time and would stand by it.

"How do you know he isn't dead?" asked the concerned doctor.

"Look if he is dead, which I really don't think he is, then we can't help him. We weren't going that fast when I released the trailer."

"Then he could be laying on the side of the road, bleeding to death!"

"Someone will find him before we can turn around," and as if it were a prophecy, they met a vehicle rounding the next curve. "There goes someone now."

"What if they don't stop? They might not be a doctor."

Harley knew he would be dead should he point out that she had not practiced in decades. "They'll find him and you can't do that much until the ambulance arrives. Right?"

The logic came unwanted to her better instincts and she grudgingly gave up her stance.

She continued to pilot the Silver Bow to the bottom of the mountain. At the stop sign she relinquished control to Harley. He turned to the right as the signpost indicated this to be the way to Andrews, North Carolina.

The town was closed down. Usually no one would have taken note of another tourist RV rolling through the square. But there were several things that did stand out - the damaged front end - the blinding flood lights on the back and what must have been a rookie driver pulling pieces of an extension cord and water hose behind the vehicle. This was noted by a couple of individuals who reported what they saw later that morning to the sheriff.

Bagnilla found his phone and had been intensely focused on searching his contact list for Gowen. He had only a feeling that his attention needed to be on his driving. It would be around midnight when he regained consciousness in the University Memorial Hospital emergency room in Ashville. He informed Gowen the Silver Bow had a new Louisiana tag with the first letters being FKU. He also told Gowen the last thing he remembered seeing was something air borne in front of his windshield with a name YAMAHA on the vinyl cover.

Chapter 50

"Good morning ladies and gentlemen, I am Agent John Loudoun for those that don't know me; I am the deputy director of the Southeastern Region of the FBI," said the man at the podium. The standing room only crowd now fell silent as all federal and state officers focused on the speaker and the silver gray screen hanging at the front of the room.

"Here are our target suspects," Loudoun said as the Power Point cast photos of Harley and Jackie behind him. He launched into the background information provided by the Atlanta office. It included Harley's career in building small office complexes and Jackie's distinguished career at the CDC No one in the crowd scoffed at the idea that these two kindly looking old retired people were international art thieves and desperate murderous felons. They focused on the details of the Codex and the murder of Flipper and Jake.

"I will now turn this meeting over to Agent H.R. Bagnilla," he said as the agent moved up to the microphone. "To illustrate how cunning and desperate these people are," Loudoun added, "they released their ATV trailer in front of his car, causing him to wreck and nearly killing him on the mountain road. They also rammed his car which makes this an attempt on a Federal Agent's life. You are authorized to use any necessary force to stop these two."

This effort to kill the agent was not quite as bad as it seemed. The SportCraft did find the front of the Crown Victoria, but did so at a low twelve miles per hour. The air bag did its job and exploded in Bagnilla's face when the bumper was hit by the trailer. They did not know or cared, it was Harley's intention to have the trailer stop in front of the car and puncture the radiator ending the pursuit. For Harley's efforts, the accident was an unfortunate bonus.

Bagnilla had hit his head and was in and out of consciousness when the ambulance arrived at the hospital. They did apply a cautionary splint to his left forearm when they found a hairline fracture in the *triquetral metacarpal* of his wrist. A CAT scan showed no internal bleeding or swelling of the brain.

Bagnilla appeared on stage wearing a narrow strip of gauze holding a bandage over his scalp wound. The bandages had the desired effect to instill in all persons in attendance that the Macklins were indeed dangerous criminals.

"Make no mistake," Bagnilla warned, "These people will stop at nothing to keep the Codex. They are the prime suspects in the murder of motel operator, Robert Franklin Wallace, and his eleven year old son, Jake Tommy Wallace."

He went on to outline the attempted murder of himself when Harley rammed his Crown Vic at the Sandy Creek Campground.

"This automatically warrants the use of deadly force when approaching these people," he said making a slight nod to his co-conspirator standing on the side of the platform.

"Agent Frank Gowen will now discuss the search plans," he said stepping aside.

Bagnilla had released himself from the hospital against the advice of the doctors and the wishes of Loudoun. He felt fine and argued that he knew these people having interviewed them in Atlanta. The emergency room was just around the corner from the Ashville Law Enforcement Center. Bagnilla, Gowen and Loudoun, along with the local sheriff, had drawn up plans to begin searching the Great Smokey Mountain area.

Sheriff Thomas Samuel Havealock or Big Tom as associates in the surrounding counties called him, grew up hunting and fishing the creeks, streams and river valleys of the Nantahala National Forest. He had been elected sheriff for the last five terms giving him a total of 20 years in the position. He called in all neighboring counties for personnel and support, including those in the adjacent states of South Carolina, Georgia, and

Tennessee. He had forty eight deputies to send out into the hills. Along with the fourteen agents of the FBI, there would be sixty two officers of the law looking for the Silver Bow.

Jackie consulted her notes from the previous morning and watched the sign posts, directing Harley until they found their way to the camp meeting early that morning.

The lights were still on at the front gate. The banner above the entrance announced it was the "Third Annual Fall Renew America Revival". It also proclaimed that it was sponsored by the "In God WE Americans Trust Committee". The Silver Bow pulled up at the gate and Harley asked for permission of the attendant to enter.

"Sir, your back up lights are on," the man said pointing to the rear of the truck.

"Thanks, I did that by mistake," he said sheepishly as he flipped the switch killing the flood lamps.

"You here for the Revival?" the man asked as he walked around the RV eyeing Harley.

"Yes, we are. Any more room?"

"What happened to the front?"

"Deer jumped out in front of me up on Tray Mountain. I went off the road to avoid hitting it."

"That's more damage than hitting a tree. What did you hit?"

"I hit the guard rail," he explained.

"You are pulling your extension cord and water hose," he said as calmly as a mechanic telling him he needed a new engine.

The man said nothing else having seen all manner of rookies making similar mistakes. He gave Harley a clipboard and asked he fill out the form it in full. "For out mailing list," was his explanation of why a campground wanted to know what church he attended on a regular basis.

Harley pulled the Silver Bow out of the driveway and Jackie sat down at the table to fill out the form. They used their new names when requested and the new address. They left out a home phone indicating they were using cell phones only. Then the personal questions began about church attendance, expectations for the week, and personal goals toward furthering the Kingdom of Christ. The form had a space asking if they were registered voters and did they have any particular prayer request on behalf of the government. Jackie grew uneasy about the questions.

"Why do they want to know if we or anyone is praying for someone in the government?" she questioned. "Is there anyone in our family that is homosexual?" she read out loud. "What kind of campground is this?" she asked Harley as she worked filling in the blanks.

"One that is going to take us in and hide us, I hope. Look around."

There were several banners and flags that they could see in the general compound. At the far end was a stage with another In God WE Americans Trust banner over the front of the canopy. Each side was flanked by flags as well. One was quite clearly an American Flag. The other looked to be the Christian banner Harley remembered from his days spent at his church's Vacation Bible School. Lining the road were RV's similar in size and shape as their own.

His confidence in their ability to hide was based on two things he had observed. The revival name indicated these people did not appreciate Washington's intrusion into their lives. The second clue was the few, small but prudently displayed, Rebel flags in front of a few RV's. This, he felt correctly, indicated these people wanted as little to do with the Federal government as possible and would resist any warrantless invasion. His hope was that if Bagnilla showed up alone, they would deny him entry.

Chapter 51

"Welcome believers to the morning devotional of the Third Annual Fall Renew America Revival and Bible Retreat. We want to begin this morning in prayer so if everybody would please bow for the blessing." The speaker on the stage passed the microphone to another man. He began by thanking the Most Highest Lord God for the attendance that morning. He then gave thanks for the pre-eminence of the expected speakers, the special guest, the special music, the special food and the special venue, the trip there and most anything else that came to mind.

Two minutes later, he ran out of special things he wanted the Lord to know he was thankful for. He then launched a new direction asking that those standing in the rain, sitting in lawn chairs, all holding golf umbrellas over their heads, to give in to the Lord's will and receive His blessings. Harley and Jackie could hear all this from the comfort of the canopy stretched away from the side of the Silver Bow. The petitioner concluded with a general benediction and returned the microphone to the emcee.

"Thank you Pastor James Jansen from the Holy to Heaven Baptist Tabernacle in Rome, Georgia. He is our representative to the "National in God WE Americans Trust Committee." Let him know how much you appreciate his being out here in the weather with a big round of applause." The meager crowd responded as best they could holding umbrellas in one hand and coffee cups in the other. Harley and Jackie went back in the warm dry truck.

"Harley, are you sure we are safe," Jackie nervously asked, "at least from Bagnilla for a few days?"

"At least a day … maybe a couple more. You need some sleep."

"I'll sleep better when I get in my own bed."

"Me too," Harley agreed.

Jackie began preparing the morning meal with a can of vegetable beef soup. She added some dry noodles and a can of chicken. She dumped in a can of carrots. To this, she spiced the mix with garlic and dried onions. Crackers would serve as the bread.

While she occupied the galley, Harley hooked up the electric wiring with a new plug on the shortened extension cord. He clamped a new connector on the water hose for the RV water system. He sat down grateful for the sanctuary and the meal. He insisted on doing the few dishes while Jackie had her rinse in the shower stall. They went right to sleep and missed the special morning classes, the special preaching of the Word, the special music, and the baptism by downpour.

They had the radio tuned into a public radio station playing the classics until the noon hour. The program went to the national public radio news and world events. The local PBS station was allotted fifteen minutes to deliver to its listeners the local news and weather. The announcer began with a disturbing story coming out of western North Carolina of a former C.D.C researcher and her husband, a builder, were the focus of a massive FBI manhunt. This headline grabbed Harley's sleepy attention. He sat up and nudged the volume up a bump to hear the report and the interview with Special Agent Loudoun in Ashville.

"Good morning," he said as he nudged Jackie. "You might want to get up."

"No I don't want to get up," she grumped back at him. "I want to sleep until noon then get up and take a long hot mineral bath."

"It is noon and you must be dreaming."

"Not anymore, and good morning. What's up?"

He repeated the news flash and what parts he could remember of the interview with Agent Loudoun. "Bagnilla survived intact," he said flatly.

"That's good to know. How is he?" she said concerned.

"The report only said he was slightly injured when I, or as they put it "the criminals" tried to get our ATV to ram his car. He has recovered at the Ashville University something hospital and is back at work."

"Ashville - University Memorial. I know Dr. Meredith Mencken there. I should give her a call later," she teased.

"Tell her to meet us here for a trout almond supper. And bring a box of the local bubbly."

"Box?" Jackie asked raising one eyebrow.

"The Dogwood City Grotto," Harley explained referring to the group of cavers in Atlanta, "was in Mentone, Alabama for a club caving trip when I went into a country store for supplies. I asked the girl behind the counter for the local vintage and she said it would be in the one gallon box," and he chuckled for a moment, then added remorsefully, "Flipper and Jake were on that trip. It was to map Johnson's Blowing Cave."

"There is someone at the gate you need to meet," Virgil Thomson told Pastor Jansen as he finished his lunch.

"Who is it?" asked the pastor wondering what merited the campground security chief bringing this to his attention.

"He is FBI," Virgil informed him.

"FBI? What does he want?"

Virgil told the man of God about the man-hunt going on since the Sunday morning news release. "He says he's here looking for the people that did it."

"He? Is he alone?"

"Yes."

"They don't usually travel solo do they?"

"Not since Wounded Knee," Virgil answered referring to a time when separated agents were murdered on that South Dakota reservation.

"Then what does he want? And why is he alone?" asked Pastor Jansen. He quickly went with Virgil to the front gate.

"Special Agent H.R. Bagnilla," he told the pastor extending the I.D. again. "I am here looking for the people that nearly killed me and we believed killed a man and his eleven year old son in Tennessee." He extended a flyer that had been copied several times over. So much so that the suspects photo was nearly faded away, and the RV picture looked like a nonspecific drawing.

Pastor Jansen considered the man, the flyer, and his whole request for a moment, then, asked, "What led you to believe that these people would be in our camp meeting?"

"I don't have any proof that they are here. I am only asking permission to look around."

Pastor Jansen and Bagnilla both were aware of the Fourth Amendment of the Constitution. The lawman would need permission to enter a private place or probable cause supported with a search warrant. The request had been made, but, Pastor Jansen's non-reply meant Bagnilla was denied entry during this brief, if veiled, exchange.

"Don't you want to cooperate with a FBI man hunt." Bagnilla insisted.

"Do you have any witness or testimony that these people are among our faithful?" Pastor Jansen asked standing his constitutional high ground.

"You do realize the people I'm looking for brutally murdered a motel keeper and his son?" Bagnilla said employing an appeal to the pastor's public service feelings.

"You claim these two are murderers, but, you haven't said who told you that they are in here," Pastor Jansen said as he continued to hold his own against the intrusion.

"You are interfering with a Federal case. These people are federal fugitives. Do you understand?" the urgency in Bagnilla's voice was apparent to all. "Everyone in here could be subjected to arrest," he said loud enough that there would be no mistaking what and who was at risk.

"And we will inspect our property and if we find anything wrong, or anyone that should not be here, we will throw them out and notify you," Preacher Jansen rebutted. "And you will respect our constitutional rights under the Fourth, Fifth and probably the Fourteenth Amendments to be secure in our homes. Or do I need to start citing Supreme Court precedent?"

Bagnilla had heard from Sheriff Havealock that this place was here, that it might be occupied by these people. The people, he had learned from Agent Loudoun, were officially the In God WE Americans Trust Committee formed to protect the Christian values they saw were missing in the country. They were associated with the religious, right wing fundamentalist, ultra conservative, almost separatist movement revivals found in the campgrounds of the Pentecostals.

Bagnilla would not gain access to the campground this day. He would return to Ashville that evening and, with Sheriff Havealock and Agent Loudoun, began a plan to invade the campground with enough force to do a proper search.

There was too much activity in the morning's schedule for Jensen and Thomson to huddle about Bagnilla. Thomson, as security chief, doubled the guard, or gatekeepers as he called them, to watch the brethren entering and leaving for suspicious activities.

"If the fugitives come in or go out let me know. But watch for the FBI and their informants trying to sneak back in," Thomson warned his post.

Pastor Jensen circulated word the committee members were to meet after the noonday meal for a quick discussion of the morning intrusion into their peaceful assembly.

"It is clear that we cannot allow the FBI or any government law enforcement agency to barge into our private meeting," one man said clearly.

They were all in agreement on the point of law, but once all other parts of the mountain had been thoroughly searched, then it would stand to reason that the Macklins either - made it through the largest roadblock in Western North Carolina driving a busted up Holland Silver Bow, three ton, white motor-coach, or, they were still in the area and needed to be found. The only area that would likely be left to search by the end of the week would be their campground. A Federal Judge would not need much to convince him to issue a search warrant. Bagnilla would lead the posse.

"Do we know if these people are here or not?" Pastor Jansen asked Virgil.

"I can look at the sign-in sheets and see who we do have," Virgil responded.

"Check the campers, see if the one they are looking for is here," another committee member offered.

"Eddy have some of your people go around looking for this Silver Bow RV. It is suppose to have front end damage," Jansen instructed Eddy Forest the Revival Director and the In God WE Trust committee chairman.

"Wait a minute," Virgil said looking up from his sheets of entry forms. "I checked in a Silver Bow early this morning around five or six. They were not pre-registered but, pulled up and asked permission to enter."

"How did they know to come here?" Jansen asked.

"Hannah and I met them in Sevierville," Joshua spoke up to say," Sheldon knows his Bible."

"What are their names?"

"Carolyn and Sheldon Milton, from New Orleans," said Virgil reading Jackie's neatly printed application.

"Good folk?" Eddy asked with the implication being are they people like us.

"Good folk," stated Joshua.

"Then I see no reason to bother these good people right now. Eddy, Joshua meet me before the evening assembly and we will meet the Milton's. Virgil keep watch for the Feds. That will be all for now, gentlemen."

Chapter 52

"Sounds like you were handed your hat," Sheriff Havealock told Bagnilla when he returned that afternoon. "I told you those holly rollers were not to be trifled with. They may look like simple good old country boys, but most of them have college degrees. They just act like they are dumber as a sack of hammers to throw you off."

"They did not hand me my hat," huffed Bagnilla. "I asked permission to enter and they denied it under the Fourth Amendment. I just obey the law I'm sworn to enforce," he said to cover his being run off.

"Then we need to obtain a search warrant, and go in to establish if the Macklin's are there or not," was Loudon's instructions.

"I don't mean to tell you Federal boys how to do your job, but didn't you just spend years up here looking for Rudolf before he gave himself up?" He had landed a sharp jab in the ribs of Loudon for he was there the entire time.

"Now all good things come to those that wait," the Sheriff went on to say. "We have both ends of the valley closed up with roadblocks. I have patrols along the Appalachian Trail and Mule Shoe Ridge on the east. They cannot hike out or drive out. We need to sit tight. The revival is over in a week. They have to get out or give up."

"We don't need to wait if we know they are in there," Bagnilla insisted.

"You do if you don't want another Waco," Havealock said reminding them of the ATF disaster in Waco, Texas. "These people probably have just as much firepower as we do. And I wouldn't be surprised if some of them didn't have some armor in the sides of those RVs.

Bagnilla left pulling Gowen with him down the hallway. They had been given the use of an office in the Law Center. Closing the door Bagnilla turned to Gowen and announced, "I can't see waiting."

"We have no choice," he said trying to stop Bagnilla. "Loudon will not sign off on us going it alone."

"What if we sent someone in undercover?"

"These people screen campers going in. You have to have someone vouch for you."

"Sounds like a damn fraternity."

"Just about is."

Gowen went on to lecture Bagnilla on The Committee forming out of past members of *The Posse Comitatus*. The Posse Movement that followed simple contorted fundamentalist beliefs about the Constitution. They rejected America's monetary system, the income tax, the judicial system, the federal reserve, civil rights for minorities, most post Civil War constitutional amendments, as well as state and federal authority over residents. The Right Righteous Reverend James Jansen was a grand nephew of Gordon Kahl martyred to the cause during a shoot out with deputies in rural Arkansas and had no love for all things Federal.

Gowen left Bagnilla sitting behind the desk. He lifted the receiver on the office phone and dialed the outside line extension.

"I would like to speak with James," Bagnilla briskly ordered Patti on the other end of the phone.

"I am sorry he is in a meeting, can I take a message?" she offered.

"Tell him H.R. Bagnilla called and to call me back," he demanded.

"Just a moment I think I hear him coming in." Pressing the intercom function on the office phone she announced Bagnilla to Spruill.

"H.R. where are you. What's going on?" Spruill said and explained that Agent Judson Harmon had came by asking about Dr. Eckland.

"Don't worry about that. I need you to meet me in Chattanooga."

"What now?" he was in the middle of the semester.

"Call in sick or something and bring Curtis with you."

Spruill could leave in family emergencies and gave such as excuse the next day.

"Do we need to bring anything?" Spruill asked before hanging up.

"Tell Curtis not to forget his gun and to bring one for you too."

"I'm not going to use a gun," Spruill flatly stated.

"You will if you need too, but you probably won't."

"Anything else?"

"Bring some rope."

"Rope? What kind?"

"The kind you use to tie a person up with," he said as he placed the hand piece in the receiver.

Chapter 53

"How'd do, brethren," Pastor Jansen said greeting Harley and Jackie when he approached their awning. They had been sitting in the shade watching the campers gathered in circles studying the Bible and other literature of the many "conferences" offered during the day. They tried to keep a low profile smiling and occasionally sending a genteel wave at worshipers. Jackie did go down to the camp comfort station for a hot shower that afternoon. Otherwise she stayed isolated and did not speak unless spoken to.

"May I come in?" Pastor Jansen begged, meaning could he come into their shade.

"Yes please do," invited Harley.

"Allow me to introduce myself, I am Pastor James Jansen and this is Virgil Thomson," he said as he extended his hand in friendship, "and you know Joshua."

"Please to meet you. This is my wife Carolyn and I am Sheldon Milton. How can we help you?"

"We had a visit from a man from the FBI," Virgil stated and watched for a reaction. "He said he was Special Agent H.R. Bagnilla," He paused to search for any effect this had on the elderly couple.

"Bagnilla? FBI?" Harley tried to look astonished but was failing.

"Yes. He was looking for a Holland model 3800 Silver Bow RV with damage to the left front."

"This is a Holland Silver Bow, but Shel hit a guard rail coming here. He said a deer jumped out in from of him, but I think he went to sleep at the wheel," Jackie said defending and aiding her poor actor. "Why would the FBI want to talk to us about that?"

"Well you know those guys," said Joshua.

"Yes," said Jansen. "We wanted to hear from you that you are not Harland and Jacqueline Macklin wanted for murder of a motel owner and his son in Tennessee." He held up the poorly copied flyer for their examination.

"I can get you our driver's license," Harley nervously said offering proof. "We're from New Orleans."

"If you don't mind," Virgil asked. "Just so we can honestly tell the FBI that you are not them."

"No problem, its right here," and Harley stepped inside the Silver Bow for the plastic bag Molly left them.

"What church do you attend?" Pastor Jansen inquired of Jackie.

Jackie, thinking only of New Orleans, came up with something she saw in a brochure. "Saint Jackson's," she answered confusing the name of Saint Louis Cathedral on Jackson Square. She also did not realize that this was one of the oldest Catholic cathedrals in America.

"Saint Jackson's?" asked a confused pastor. "I don't think I have heard of a Saint Jackson."

"Saint Jerome," Harley said to recover her mistake. "Saint Jerome Pentecostal."

"Saint Jerome?" Pastor Jansen asked still confused at a catholic saint's name on a fundamentalist church.

"Well it was the old Saint Jerome Catholic Church on Jackson Street. They kept the names so people would know where it is," Harley said as he handed the forged documents to Virgil. "There you go," he said merrily.

Virgil studied the plastic laminated forgeries Molly provided in detail. These were excellent fakes and would ring true to any un-trained eye. The detail of the print was crystal clear as was the photos. The laser cut Pelican that is on the State Seal, was on these drivers licenses. Virgil returned the cards to Harley.

"We wanted to be sure," he said. "If we are going to refuse FBI or any other law enforcement access to our church grounds we had to be sure about you."

"I understand," Harley continued, "Sanctuary."

"Why yes," said the preacher. "It is sanctuary, as long as we can honestly say that you are not the Macklins and not wanted people. Can we say that?"

"Yes. You can say that," said Harley beginning to feel un-easy about the mendacious of his identity.

"Why are you folk here?" Jansen asked. "We haven't noticed you attending any of our Bible Study Groups."

"We are just getting back into church," Harley lied. "Our daughter moved out and we discovered that we needed to return to the fold."

"Be renewed?"

"Exactly. Be renewed, restored, revived, re-born," Harley said in the rising tone of the evangelical preachers he saw on TV.

"So you haven't been baptized?" Virgil asked of Harley.

"I was speaking metaphorically. Re-make our lives into the service of the Lord," he proclaimed.

"Joshua says you really know your way around the Bible," the preacher observed.

"I have studied a little."

"Then maybe you could help teach our class on the Book of Acts?" Virgil offered. "Our group leader is down sick this week."

"Acts?" Harley asked.

"You know it?"

"Acts of the Apostles ... first book after the four Gospels? Probably written around 33 and before 90 a.d. That Book of Acts?" Harley practically beamed at his delivery.

"That Acts," said Jansen, "then you will teach it? We have some study guides."

"I have my own," said Harley and he pulled out the books he grabbed before leaving their home. He had *Strong's Exhaustive Bible Concordance* to quickly find any names that Jackie translated. He had *The Introduction to the New Testament* text book from his college studies.

It was agreed that Brother Sheldon Milton would lead the adult Bible study in the Book of Acts the next day. It would be done in one hour segments with ten or fifteen adults in each group.

"What are you doing?" Jackie asked after the committee was gone.

"What do you mean?" he said defending his actions. "I was trying to fit in."

"And, where, does that leave me?"

"Here," he said as he waved his arm around the shade. "You have the whole forest to hike ... or sit in the shade ... and continue to see what is in that box that has gotten us in this mess."

"What makes you think that I couldn't go to one of these Bible classes?"

"You won't like it. The literature is written on a fifth grade reading level," Harley said.

"So? You're teaching the kiddies' class?"

"No," he explained, "The material is written on a fifth grade reading level, to fifth graders, by fifth graders, for fifth graders. You are welcomed to sit in my classes, but don't expect much real depth in the conversation."

"These people seemed well educated. Why isn't their text material at a more advanced level?" she asked.

"Can't handle the Mysteries of the Faith, *mysterium felicitate*," Harley said and mimicked the hand gestures magician's use during illusions.

"Oh, so you think you can speak Latin? It is m*ysterium fidei*. Is that what you meant to say?"

"Why? What did I say?"

"Strangely happy."

"Well, that too," he said.

"So, you are saying the study literature is kept simple for the simple minded? Or they simply don't mind it being simple?"

"They want it kept simple. That way they don't have to think for themselves."

"Harley, You're *simplex mens*, if you want to start using Latin."

"Not fair. I don't like it when you and your father say something in Latin then point and laugh at me. What is *simplex mens*? Simple men?"

"Close ... simple minded."

He stuck the tip of his tongue at her to display his displeasure. "Most Christians don't understand the whole Aramaic, to Greek, to Latin, to German, to English translation thing, as it is," he griped.

"Why don't you explain it to them tomorrow during your Bible class?"

"Because they all think the Bible was written in the style of Shakespeare and published by Zondervan or Broadman Press in 1776 for the Founding Fathers. They don't understand editorial influences, translator mistakes, errors, and deliberate alternative meanings."

"Then educate them!" she was getting exasperated at the circling logic.

"Can't. If I start using words like the Tridentine Missal, Messianic Movement, Gnostic Antinomianism then I will be strung up faster than a Salem witch."

"That would serve you right for burning up my heater," she injected.

"I can replace the cord when we get home. Anyway, these people believe that Jesus died, Paul saw the light, they all began confessing the Nicene Creed, memorized the New Testament, and took to building churches by the end of the week."

"See there. Talk about me speaking Latin. Nicene Creed. At least here you seemed to speak with the indigenous vernacular. I would be lost talking about baptism, the Holy Spirit, and like that."

"Maybe it is better if you stay out of sight. Stick to the Latin. Work what you know. Take some pictures."

"Some wild life photos?" she asked.

"No wild life around here, but there I am sure there are some animals in the woods."

"From the way you talk and from what I see, these people might think I was a reporter or spy, or ...."

"Informant?" he finished. "Keep the camera in the bag, then, Honey"

"Good idea."

Joshua and Hannah stopped by that evening after the assembly. Harley was tinkering with the Silver Bow's electrical system and Jackie had translated another journal entry when the couple knocked at the door.

"Come in," Jackie offered inviting them to sit at the table. She put the journals in the cardboard box along with her notes.

"We didn't want to bother you," Hannah said.

"We missed you at the service tonight," Joshua noted. "Pastor Jansen delivered a good sermon on defending the faith."

"Defending from what?" asked Jackie as she slid the box against the window.

"From attacks by the liberal media, of course." Hannah said. "Those in the liberal media are out to destroy the Bible."

"You mean by burning or banning the Bible?"

"Making fun of those of us that believe in the Holy Word of God," said Joshua. "They seek to undermine our faith with facts."

"What facts?" Jackie asked wondering where this was heading.

"Like saying that God did not create the world, the whole idea of the theory of evolution."

"Maybe God works slowly? Takes time to change a dinosaur into a dog size animal, then into a horse," Jackie reasoned.

"That's another thing ... Pastor Jensen says the earth is nine thousand, eight hundred years old. Not nine billion years."

Harley came in on the end of this, "Nine thousand, eight hundred, thirty four years, six months, eight days, forty three minutes," and taking a deep breath poising as an opera singer, sang out, "and - a – partridge – in – a - pear - tree."

"Is he always like this?" Hannah asked laughing.

"Don't laugh, there will be no stopping him," Jackie said.

Harley reacted with,

> "Laugh, and the world laughs with you;
> Weep, and you weep alone;
> For the sad old earth, must borrow its mirth,
> And has trouble enough of its own."

"That was great!" Hannah said praising his poetic prowess.

"I would say thanks but that's not mine. I was quoting Ella Wilcox."

"Who?" Joshua asked puzzled at the reference.

"American poet, journalist for the Hurst newspaper chain, and free thinker. She died in 1919," Harley said. "Not the greatest poet of this country, but in her time very popular."

Harley went on to explain how he would sit in a cave five thousand feet from the entrance - with two thousand feet of solid limestone over head - he could look up find embedded in the ceiling the skeletal remains of fossilized sea creatures. "How," he asked the young couple to consider, "did this happen in eight thousand years?" The question would give Josh something to mull over the next day.

"I need to check the generator," Harley said as he went out.

"Can I help?" Joshua offered.

"Sure. Come on."

Hannah and Jackie had stayed in the camper. Jackie spoke with her about having had a successful career, marriage and a wonderful relationship with her daughter. Hannah said she had felt pressured to quit work and stay home to raise any future children. The pressure did not come from Joshua, but from the daily study groups on the family in the Christian home. They talked until Harley could no longer tolerate the cold night air. Once the men came inside the spell was broken and all agreed it was time to go.

"Nice couple, do you think?" Harley asked Jackie when they laid down for the night.

"Yes."

"What did you two girls talk about all that time?"

"Nothing," she said.

Chapter 54

"Pastor Jansen is in the last door on the left. Not many people get to see his personal office," the young woman in blue jeans and plaid shirt explained to Harley as he squeezed down the narrow aisle on the pastor's Class "A" Motor Coach. If the Silver Bow is considered to be a Lexus in the RV world, the pastor's Wheeler Peak by Tourman Motor Coach was the Rolls - Royce of motor homes. The forty two footer with four rooms that slid out, was every bit as heavy a cruiser as any charter bus on the road that day.

Harley noted the cherry paneling along the narrow passage to the back of the coach. A bright pink hue in a hidden track overhead moved with him as he went down the hall. The light before and after the pink, became pale, then more yellow before dissolving into ocean green and then dark blue. He knew the light followed him because he slowed his pace to see if the hue continued at the same speed. It did not, but stayed above Harley. Before he turned into the open doorway, he heard the voice of James Jansen welcoming him.

"How did you know I was out there?" Harley asked impressed at trick lighting.

"The light follows you down the hall. Neat is it?" Jansen asked as he left his seat to greet Harley. "I watch for the color change just ahead of your approach."

"That is a good trick. Did you have that installed or did it belong to the previous owner?" He asked on the off chance that the bus was built for a Las Vegas performer.

"I had it installed when the church bought the bus."

"So, this is a church bus ... beats the one at the First Baptist. All they have is an old school bus they spray painted white," Harley said.

"Then maybe they need to send their prayers by Federal Express. Sounds like their request are not getting to the right person fast enough," Jansen chuckled.

"Then God has blessed you better than others?"

"There you go, you got it!" Jansen said with a gloat. "God has been good to me!" he announced as he extended his arms to encompass the cherry wood paneling, deep thick carpet, concealed lighting, tinted window, rolling office and home away from home on ten wheels.

"And may God continue to help only those that can help themselves to his many blessings," Harley said.

"I have been told that you are quite good with your Bible study," Jansen said after Harley took a seat in the leather chair across from the nineteenth century style table desk. "People are saying that you have a very deep understanding of the Word of God."

"Thank you," he returned.

"May I ask where did you come by such deep understanding?

"I took religious courses through college."

"Which one?"

"Gerald – Wilcox Howell School of Divinity, just outside of New Iberia, Louisiana."

"Oh yes, I have heard of it. What I have not heard of is Saint Jerome, or Saint Jackson Pentecostal Church," said Pastor Jansen.

"Like I said, it was the Saint Jerome Catholic church bought by the Pentecostals. They just kept the name."

"I heard of G.W.H. because that is one of the colleges FOX News says the killers attended."

"Really?" Harley said, "How ironic. Maybe they are an alumni."

"Maybe he is in my campground?"

"I didn't say it was a 'he'," Harley emphasized.

"I will say 'he'," Pastor Jansen accused.

"A man is considered innocent until proven guilty, isn't he?" Harley asked.

"But even the fox is innocent until he grabs the chicken."

"Would such a man, if he were begging sanctuary in say a campground, have any chance to prove his innocence before being handed over to the authorities?"

"If, such a man were in a campground appealing for sanctuary, should he trust the leaders and let them know he is here."

"If this man asks for sanctuary, then, with his appeal, isn't he demonstrating he trusts the leaders of such a campground?

"Yes, it is implied, but, should that man give the leaders a damn good explanation why he shouldn't be turned over for the reward?"

"Oh, I totally agree, but can I ask, how could this unjustly accused man expect to remain under the protection of sanctuary?" Harley asked.

"Given the resources of the Federal Bureau of Interference and by trampling Fourth Amendment rights, I'd say about two days, tops."

Jackie was taking advantage of the nice weather that had developed that morning to work on her translations under the awning. A slight gentle warm breeze lifted the covering from time to time and she felt she were at sea under sail. The cardinal perched on the roof rack, cut loose his piercing cry and the closeness of the sound startled her.

"Good morning," Hannah said from the lane in front of the Silver Bow. "I hope I didn't startle you."

"No. It was the bird."

"I see it. It is on your roof ... it's a cardinal," Hannah said pointing at the woodland creature.

"I am just a little jumpy these days. Come on in," offered Jackie.

"Well you just looked so absorbed in your work," said Hannah shyly. "I didn't want to bother you."

"No bother, I could use the company."

Hannah stood there as Jackie put the leather journals back into the file box.

"Those look really old" Hannah said.

"They probably are. We believe they come from the fourth century."

"Really?" she said astonished to learn the age of the books. "Are you an archeologist or something? You seem so smart all the time."

"I'm a researcher," Jackie said letting it go at that. "I'm doing some translating of these journals."

"Journals, you mean like a diary?"

"Yes most of it."

"Who wrote them?"

"Sheldon and I are not sure. He is helping me to figure that out. But we think they may be the personal journals of Paul."

"You mean Saint Paul?"

"Could be."

"Really?" Hannah asked in disbelief.

"Really. Do you want to see them?" Jackie offered.

"Sure."

Jackie withdrew the volume she was working on along with the accompanying yellow pad of notes. The entry began *Dies Saturni iv Aprilis DCXCV A.U.C.*

"What is that?" asked Hannah pointing to the passage.

"Day Saturday, April 4, 695 a.u.c. which is 33 a.d. on our calendar," was Jackie's simple explanation. She showed Hannah the notes of the entry and watched the result of what she had discovered. It would be nothing like Hannah had ever seen before in her Bible studies. A firsthand account of a crucifixion, and the man named was Iesus in Latin.

"Jesus in English," said Jackie.

I have never seen the horror of a crucifixion. It would have not been possible to believe the pain and suffering that the criminal goes through until Pluto claimed their lives. Is there anything more evil that would inflict so much suffering not only on the part of the guilty, but on those that bear witness to the horror. To think that I have had a hand in this gives me no pleasure. It was a step that was necessary to take for the greater protection of all we hold dear. This had to be done to let others know their fate should they too try to bring an end to the efforts of our protector Pontius Pilate, to bring peace to the lands. Bonus constituo progrediorf maleficus A good can result from evil.

These who are frustrated with the way we run Temple services should become full participants in the activity of worship and bring their problems to us and not attack and steal from us. We Levitates have been ordained by his blessing to Aaron the brother of Moses since we have been a people. And I am of the tribe of Benjamin both entitled and ordained of El Shaddai to bring his wrath upon those that would destroy his institutions. Why cannot the people accept this? The Pharisees must be stopped from teaching and preaching revolt and uprising in the streets to the people. Now that this Iesus has been crucified with his co-conspirators maybe the others will stop the insurrection.

We were effective in his capture. Judaei of Sicarius betrayed him and let us know that the man was with the group of rebels. Gamaliel, the Elder, Joarib, Hezekiah and Japheth quickly assembled to appeal to us to release the prisoner saying that if this man was sent from El Shaddai, then we cannot prevail against him. If he be not of El Shaddai, then he will fail. I was almost swayed by his logic. Aeneas stood to speak against the man. El Shaddai would most certainly not want to see his Temple destroyed as this man did preach of doing daily in the market square. We caught several of the criminals and they await the pleasure of Pilate. We were able to keep the supporters away from his appearance before Pilate. We blocked the roads leading to the courtyard of Herod the Great. Pilate only heard from our supporters as they denounced Iesus as a criminal. Pilate appeared pleased to see that we, the police of the Sanhedrin, are rounding up the rabble. We need to conduct more raids upon rebel encampments in the other regions of Judea and to the heights Beth-Horon.

I hope I can remove these insurgents before they can stir up the wrath of Rome. I watched Pilate questioning the prisoner. He seemed not to want to condemn the man. The man did give good defense but did not acknowledge the authority of Pilate to sit in judgment. He would not accept the charges against him were true. Our supporters shouted for his death. Pilate gave his blessing to continue with the punishment and the man was taken to be flogged until he fell from the suffering. We forced each convict to carry his own means of execution through the city streets so the public could see for themselves the man who would be our king now bowing under the heavy hand of our Emperor Tiberius Nero Caesar.

We kept the multitudes away from their path for fear they may try to free them. Death came soon for that leader. The others did not die until the Sabbath was over. The coward Iesus cried out to Elijah to rescue him but in the end Morti released his soul. With the approach of the Sabbath, the Rabbi Joseph of Armetheia was allowed take his body to be placed in his burial vault until he could be prepared for funeral and taken back to Galilee. We posted our police to guard the burial crypt. The Optiones, Varius Marius, sent for a cohort of Roman's to help us secure the grave until the Sabbath is over. It has been reported that Judaei of Sicarius was robbed of the bribe and then hung by his fellow conspirators for his betrayal of their plot. It is fitting end for a turn-coat to have been hung by his own. We were hoping to make use of him in the future to find more of these plots against the Temple. Dies Solis is approaching for I have been awake all Sabbath. May El Shaddai keep and defend us from all those that would do us harm.

Hannah returned the yellow pages to the original top page and gave it a gentle push toward Jackie.

"What does this mean?" she said. "Who wrote this?"

"We think it is the man you call Saint Paul. We think this is his personal journal. Or let me explain that we think that it is a copy of his personal journal. Like today's Bible has copies of translations of his personal letters to the churches he went to. Understand?"

Hannah nodded that she did and asked about the entry that said, "we were effective in his capture? Who is we?"

"Harley thinks that Paul became a member of the Sanhedrin. He became involved with what amounted to being the Temple Police. They would go out and enforce the Laws of Moses under the direction of the Sanhedrin. They shook down merchants for the tithe and generally worked to keep the crowd of pilgrims in line."

"So you think he arrested Christ?"

"Could have. He was old enough, he was in Jerusalem at that time, if, as he writes, he studied under Gamaliel, it is possible and likely."

"And he arrested Christians like Stephen in Acts," Hannah added referring to the episode of Acts chapter 7 The Stoning of Stephen.

"Yes, of course," Jackie said unaware of the name and story in the seventh chapter.

"Have you found that yet?" Hannah excitedly asked.

"Not yet," Jackie said guardedly, "But there is one more book and several more pages to go."

Harley revealed how he purchased the box from Eudora; how they presented the two pages for the university to examine and he mentioned the offer to buy. He did not bring up their suspicions about Dr. Eckland's death, their own attempted murder, and the murder of Flipper and Jake.

"Has the book's age been verified?" Pastor Jansen asked Harley after his brief explanation of their past couple of weeks.

"We have been told by the current head of archeology at Gilbert University that the journals are definitely fifth maybe fourth century," he said referring to Spruill.

"If you have been translating these artifacts as you say, then I don't understand," Jansen said perplexed. "FOX News reports say the FBI claims a priceless collection was 'stolen' from Gilbert University."

"The FBI says many things about many people that later turn out not to be true," Harley said. "Remember that security guard at the Olympics in Atlanta. FBI said he planted the bombs. They pressured the poor man to see if he would confess. He was completely cleared of any wrong doing."

The pastor nodded consent to the validity of the statement.

"They offered to purchase the documents? I thought they were the owners?" Pastor Jansen was trying to follow Harley.

"Exactly, but then you have only my word about that offer. The college knew we had the documents when the FBI came to the house and talked to us."

Harley looked at Pastor Jansen and waited.

"How long will it take for y'all to complete the translation of this Codex?"

"Jackie has been working on the journal for weeks now, but it is slow going. My best guess is ... if Jackie continues un-interrupted is for ... all of the journal to be translated in six weeks."

"Six weeks?" Jansen said incredibly. "We can't expect the FBI to stand down that long. In fact, I wouldn't be surprised if they haven't found some judge to grant them a full and open search warrant in a couple of days."

"Couple of days?" Harley asked.

"I think we can realistically expect them by the end of the week. You are surrounded by the Great Smokey Mountain

National Park. They will be on the mountain ridges and they will be watching. They have road blocks on each end of the highway. So, if you do leave it will be on foot. I suggest that you always wear a hat pulled down low over your face so they can't take telescopic photos of you in camp. I will have to turn you over if they bring that kind of evidence to me."

"Then we need another way out."

"They may not move until they feel they have full public support for invading a church campground and, they have enough logistical support to ring the campground with agents in the woods. So rest easy right now. Why don't you skip teaching tomorrow and focus on translating the Codex. Trust me to find a way out for you."

"Sounds like a plan. And I want to thank you very much for your support."

"Keep me posted on what you find in the books, will you?"

"You bet," Harley said as he left the room with the lights trailing him down the hall.

Chapter 55

"What do you want for dinner?" Harley asked Jackie seated under the canopy at the picnic table with her notes spread out.

"What are the choices?" she answered knowing there was little in the pantry.

"There is a can of turkey chili and I could mix that with some elbow macaroni. I'll call it Thanksgiving Chili-Mac."

"What else?" she said deadpan and un-amused by his antics.

"There is some rice, and let's see, some cream of chicken soup. We have a foil package of chicken and one of tuna. There are some green peas and a can of diced tomatoes."

"Anything in the freezer?" she asked in vain hope.

"Only your mother's heart," he quipped. Hearing nothing but feeling her wrath he mournfully said, "No, we cleaned that out. Tell you what. I'll make my famous Strike Again Mung."

She thought about it for a moment and conceded to enduring his concoction of witches stew.

"That was actually pretty good," Jackie complemented Harley after the meal. "Thanks for cooking tonight. Did you do something different this time?" He was always experimenting with his mung.

"I put in a packet of dried onions, kicks up the flavor of the chicken bouillon."

She agreed this was the secret ingredient. "Any more of the Cabernet left?"

"Nope, that is the end of it. The cellar is empty." Harley served his can chicken chunks and noodles mung with a 2003 Groth Cabernet which cost them $60.00.

"I guess we won't find any more in this campground?" Jackie regretfully asked.

"You'd be surprised," Harley informed her. "The only time the Baptist speak to the Methodist is when they pass each other at the package store."

Crocodile Rock announced another phone call. Molly called to inform Jackie that one caller to her old cell phone kept insisting, in the voice mail, that Jackie get in touch with him. Jackie asked who had called. "A man identifying himself as Henry Lancard. Do you know him?"

"I know that he was a friend of Dr. Eckland. What does he want?" She was now excited and afraid of this new person.

Molly's sources informed her that Lancard was legal counsel to The Southeastern Archdiocese of the Orthodox Church in America. He mentioned an interest in the Codex Syracuse.

"The agency has little on him except to say that he is the legitimate lawyer for the council. He has a valid passport issued by the State Department," Molly informed her. "What do you want me to tell him."

"Is that all he said?" Jackie asked.

"That and he said to 'be careful,' that there might be malicious people that will first try to buy the Codex, then steal it, then hurt you for it."

A cold chill ran up Jackie's spine, an entirely auto-response to threat stimuli, but it was as if her spinal cord were suddenly laid bare to the cold damp night air.

"Give me his cell phone number."

"We think Bagnilla might be close to getting his search warrant." Molly added. "If you can make it here, Jubal and I will see to it you disappear for as long as you like."

"Molly?" Harley asked as he cleared the table.

"Yes. Henry Lancard keeps calling me," Jackie said filliping the phone closed and pulling the yellow pad closer.

"Calling you about what?"

She explained the voice mails Molly had retrieved from Mr. Lancard.

"Are you going to call him?" Harley's inquiring mind wanted to meet the man.

"Not tonight. I'll call him in the morning. Molly and Jubal think we should move."

"Why?" Harley asked surprised. "Is Bagnilla about to pounce?"

"They said they could help us disappear if we can get to them," she said.

"We can't make it in this wreck," he said acknowledging the Silver Bow's condition.

"Can we borrow someone's car?"

"I'll see, but first thing in the morning."

"Do you want to see what I have uncovered?" she asked as she flipped to the top page of her yellow pad.

*Dies Mercurii xiii Junius DCXCVII 697 A.U.C. or
Wednesday, June 13 35 a.d.*

*Is there to be no end to these people's squabbling?
I can but wonder how it is that the faith of my
mother and the faith of her father and of the faith of
Eliais ever endured this long? Even with the Laws of
El Shaddai clearly written by the scribes, the very
descendents of the brother of Moses, the lawgiver
himself, the people kick and bite and fight one
another over every little detail of their life. It is as
though they are ordained to fight one another
otherwise they would cease to exist.*

*Much has happened in the days just passed and it
is now that I am able to write again. It is a great
responsibility with which I am charged. I am to keep
the peace for all of the northern parts of the city and
among our people of the Lord. Pilate has grown
weary of those that preach the destruction of Herod's
Temple. Those Greek apostolate living among us, are
now discontent with the protection provided by our
governor. The Greeks have come to believe these
leaders of this new rabble from Galilee, that theirs
is the one true path to El Shaddai and will return of
their Messiah. This vain claim has come to us before,
and has failed before, and will fail again.*

*I am frustrated at every turn in my efforts to
enforce the laws of our people. I have not the
wisdom, understanding and words to bring these
people back into the ways of our Temple. These
fishmongers and common laborers from the north
argue and quarrel amongst themselves over the care*

of the widows of their sect. The rebels lead the masses against our Temple.

They did appoint seven of the Greeks to distribute their funds so as to care for the widows. I have reported the names of these seven to Aeneas, Summas and Datam. One of the seven is already dead and in the Bosom of Abraham. May El Shaddai be merciful with him.

I was most cunning in my plan. We, twenty four in number, did follow these bandits as they went about the northern city. Sephanos from the city of Macedonia, was again calling for the destruction of the Temple. With the aid of Elionaeus I led my fellow police, and with Varius Marius hidden with a cohort of solders, we arrested this man.

We took him swiftly to defend himself before the high priest and the elders. He did not find any friends in the high court. We charged him with leading the people against our protectors to destroy our traditions. No one came forth to give him counsel or to defend his cause. He sought to lecture the Elders of the Temple on the history of our people: and he not a child of Father Abraham but a pretender to the Faith. May El Shaddai protect and defend us from such madmen.

He preached and recited to the Elders from the Torah from the Prophet Isaiah that The El Shaddai did not need a Temple. That we should all gather in a tent like common goat herders. The others like him are meeting in templum sedes. He did proclaim that he and his people would destroy this House of The Lord God and build a new Temple of the People. At this the Elders began to rend their clothing and grind their teeth against him. He stood and with his fingers pointed to the heavens, declared that he was the one that was ordained by The Lord God and that he could see the dead prophets come to aid him in his task.

The Elders had their fill of this man's blasphemy and with accord and with one rush did seize him and take him into the outer courtyard. There did Summas and Datam begin to throw stones at the man in vain effort to quit his cries of iniquity. This did not stop him. Then with Varius watching from around the corner, I cried to stone him. I was burning like a torch tipped with sulfur. In order to gain the full force of their efforts, the Elders gave charge to me to keep watch over their outer cloaks as they threw stones at the madman.

It is fortunate that Aurelia lives in the southern portion of the city and does not have to bear witness to these terrible events. I am indebted to Datam for she has began to work in his household teaching his children to read and to write. I am so happy for her and for her son Thaddeus. I would that one day I will be granted a meeting with Afranius that I may address the grievance done to her by his leaving my sister with child. I am fond of my old friend but he should bear the responsibility raising his son. May El Shaddai keep us all and watch over us.

Harley pointed to her one unaltered entry, *templum sedes?* he asked.

"Temple house was my best guess," Jackie proposed. "Our understanding of it might be church. Their homes were their churches, right?"

"My God," whispered Harley in a hushed reverent tone. "Acts, Chapter seven, verse fifty eight. 'They laid their coats before a young man named Saul'."

"I take it you recognize this?" Jackie asked.

"It is all here… It all makes sense. Saul in Greek and Paul in Latin, went about arresting the followers of Christ. This is the Stoning of Stephen, it's got to be!" Harley said quietly excited at her find.

Chapter 56

We got em'!" proclaimed Agent Jones exiting the darkroom where he had just developed film taken via long range camera. Shooting from Mule Shoe Ridge above the In God WE Americans Trust Campground, agents in the Reconnaissance and Surveillance Operations had been taking pictures of all the motor-homes in the camp. Although Harley had pulled the Silver Bow's broken front bumper towards the forest, the rear and its tag could be seen. Agent Jones had been enlarging the images when he saw the same partial tag letters, FKU, Bagnilla saw just before the SportCraft with is Yamaha cover, hit his windshield. That would be enough for a probable hearing to establish just evidence and cause for issuing a search warrant.

"Its 4:00," said Big Tom Havealock. "Judge Elliott will probably be gone by now."

"Gone?" questioned Bagnilla, "Gone where?"

"Golf. He has a permanent date every Wednesday afternoon at the Ashville Dog and Pony Club, has had for twenty years now."

"We will just have to interrupt him then," proclaimed Bagnilla.

"Do that and you better stress the flight risk these two pose. Otherwise, he may examine it with a fine tooth legal comb for errors and send you back with it."

Bagnilla gathered up the list of warrants he wanted issued along with the photos, and, with Big Tom driving, headed for the golf club.

They announced themselves to the manager. The man got on a public address system that ringed the course to warn players of changing weather (just in case the game became so intense they lost track of gathering storm clouds) to announce Bagnilla's arrival and was seeking the judge. Judge Elliott did not carry a cell phone and had little regard for those who couldn't be in his court without one stuck to their head. He really hated hearing an announcement to report to the front desk immediately. Though ready to throw Big Tom under the jail and pump daylight to him, the judge studied the surveillance photos of the get-away truck. He immediately signed the warrant papers and Big Tom radioed word back to the office to get the posse ready.

Invasion plans went into motion. Photos and physical descriptions of the Macklins' were distributed to all officers. Bagnilla gave verbal warning that the box of documents was to be brought directly to him for special protection and processing. Once all were briefed and issued necessary papers, the convoy proceeded down the highway.

"No one in or out, unless I see them first," Bagnilla ordered.

"Good Morning," Harley cheerfully announced himself at the young couple's motor-home door.

"And to you as well," returned Joshua. "Come on in. Would you like some breakfast. We are having bacon and eggs."

Harley had not seen fresh eggs in days and would have devoured any placed before him.

He politely refused, excusing himself as having already eaten. He and Jackie shared the one remaining bag of whole-wheat muffins and jar of blackberry jam.

"We are going to make a run for it," Harley said.

"Where?" asked Joshua.

"Where isn't good for you to know," Harley advised them.

"Your RV isn't going to make it," Joshua pointed out. "And with the damage, will stand out like a sore thumb."

"We'll need to borrow a car from someone in camp," Harley said. "Know anyone willing to risk my driving?"

"We can let you use our Saturn," referring to the ION they pulled behind their R.V. "Everyone knows we keep the keys in the ignition where anyone could drive it away," he said with a grin.

"I can't, you guys need that car," Harley politely refused.

"We have two more cars back home," said Joshua, "and a F-350 for our horse trailer."

Harley was a bit astounded this couple had amassed such wealth, but asked to confirm their offer.

"Giving us the car knowing we are making a run for it makes you an accessory. If I tell you where we are going, then it is all the worst for you."

Hannah looked at Joshua biting her lower lip. She nodded consent to him.

"If they catch us, it'll go to the impound yard," Harley added.

"And if they don't catch you, then it'll come back and go to the junk yard, the way you drive," Joshua teased. "Take it with our blessings. We can stand up to the FBI. I'm a junior partner with the Lord and Griffin Law firm."

"I've heard of them," Harley said incredulously. "I'm damn impressed."

"Well you can pick it up, ah … steal it," Joshua said correcting himself, "anytime."

"That would be great," Harley said. "Could we 'steal' it in about an hour?"

"You can get it now," Joshua said tossing the keys to Harley.

He drove the car to the Silver Bow. Jackie had been packing that damnable white file box with her notes and the journals. Their plans were to make the run to Chattanooga and meet Henry Lancard who was driving up from the archdioceses in Atlanta. Once he was in the area, they would arrange a meeting in a public place by cell phone. Lancard was a bit puzzled at getting called and hearing a woman's voice that was not Molly Conner. Once Jackie explained the circumstances they were in he understood.

"CNN reports that the FBI claims you have the Codex. Is that right?" he asked.

She admitted that she had knowledge of its whereabouts and could get it when the time comes. But, she insisted, would not bring it to the meeting.

"Bagnilla with the FBI says you killed Wallace and his son. I'll not ask if that is true for I have my doubts about it."

She took a quick short breath of fear at the mention of their nemesis. She only wanted a face to face to discuss what was happening. Given that he was a legal counsel, although not necessarily their lawyer, he could promise confidentiality.

They took few possessions least they looked like they were trying to run. The box containing the Codex was left on the back seat with a coat tossed over it. They tried to look as casual as possible. Jackie packed a cooler with Cokes so they would not have to stop for something to drink. Harley did say good bye to Pastor Jenson thanking him for his sanctuary.

He turned the Saturn south on State Highway 360 and entered the flow of tourist out to take in the fall color. He drove to the road block just over the hill. Six police cars were parked there with their drivers standing in the middle of the road questioning everybody that passed. One would motion him to stop, while the other walked to the back of the car to check the tag.

"Nice morning, isn't it?" Harley said handing the young man the forged driver's license.

Officer Trammel according to his name tag, held the plastic license at an angle to bring out the laser cut security sticker. It flashed a silver pelican in his eyes and he found it acceptable. "Yes sir, you can go now."

Leading the pack, Bagnilla pulled up to the front gate at the campground. Virgil came out to meet him and examine the freshly signed search warrant. Regrettably, he allowed the posse to pass thankful that they did not use a forced entry. Pastor Jenson anticipating the raid, rose from his seat on the stage to announce the FBI agents were there and seeking cooperation of all in the camp. He also warned them to stay with their campers. Soon as Bagnilla was in the gate, he was off to secure the Silver Bow. The door was locked. Big Tom pulled the lug wrench from the trunk and stuck it in the crack where door meets frame. He pulled the bar and the latch gave up its hold. Once inside Bagnilla tore open all drawers. Searched everywhere, and came up empty. The deputies outside knew the layout of motor homes enough to pull all the sewer hoses out.

"God damn it!" Bagnilla exclaimed.

Crocodile Rock chimed once again as Lancard called Jackie. He was afraid they had been captured he said in a hurried conversation. It was all over the radio once the wire services found out that the FBI had raided the camp.

"When?" asked Jackie astonished at the news.

"Right now. According to the satellite radio news service," Lancard said.

"We haven't heard a thing."

She told him that they were on the road and would meet somewhere around the Cumberland Mall area.

Once she ended the call, Harley glanced at her and asked if she thought it odd that Molly or Jubal had not called to alert them the raid was occurring. "I would think they would be able to watch for that kind of movement."

"That does worry me," she said worriedly. "I hope everything is alright. They have been our eyes and ears so far."

"Maybe they are not where anyone can reach them," said Harley darkly.

The trepidation was interrupted by the cell phone singing. The caller id was Molly's.

Jackie answered and Harley saw from the corner of his eye Jackie stiffen and her stomach jumped as if she had a strong hiccup.

"What?" she asked into the device. "Where are you?" She looked at Harley with worried surprise. "Listen to this," and she punched the speaker button.

"Meet Bagnilla, he will call later today."

"Jubal?" Harley asked not quite believing it was their savior, "what is going on?"

"Mr. Macklin," said a man's voice. "We have kidnapped your friends. Say hello," the voice said to someone nearby.

Harley could barely make out the sound of Jubal's words, but his accent confirmed he was the speaker.

"You will go to Tiftonia and wait until Bagnilla calls you. Do understand?" said the stranger.

"Yes," answered Harley worried about why the caller was directing them back towards The Cave Inn.

"Where in Tiftonia?"

"There is an empty strip mall shopping center at the corner of Brown's Ferry and the Cummings Highway. Do you know it?"

"Yes," acknowledged Harley. "It has a barbeque place in it."

"Wait at the parking lot for our call and we will make a swap."

"Swap for what."

"The Codex."

"What Codex?" Harley asked as Jackie listened.

"The Codex Syracuse. We know you have it and you have it in your possession right now. Bagnilla has searched your camper and didn't find it. If you don't show up with the Codex when we call, then we won't show up with your friends. Are you getting the picture?"

"Are you with Lancard?"

"No," assured the voice, "has he contacted you?"

"Yes we were meeting him at Cumberland Mall today," Harley informed the voice.

"Then he is too late to stop us."

Harley and Jackie gave each other a surprised, questioning, look.

"Who are you?" demanded Jackie.

"We who have protected the secrets of the Codex," came a cryptic response.

"Who are you? What secretes?"

There was a pause and a noise as if someone was covering the phone. The instrument picked up a lot of background noise.

"Mr. Macklin, I have said enough. Be in the parking lot, and I suggest that you get there now," and the call ended.

Harley and Jackie agreed it had been the voice of James Spruill talking to them.

The couple drove past the exit for Cumberland Mall, Lancard would have to wait. Nothing he could say would stop them from rescuing Molly and Jubal. It was an impulsive move on their part for they had no idea how many this "we" the caller referred to were there. Who were the protectors of the secrets left them blank for an answer. They begin to play their fears off one another suggesting all manner of evil plots and conspiracies until Jackie realize that this was running in circles and demanded they stop the guessing. They topped Cemetery Ridge and descended into the valley of Chattanooga. They could see the entire downtown area for a moment as Interstate 24 went over the ridge clinging to the mountain side.

"I have an idea," said Jackie and she began to punch up a phone number on the last of her unused cell phones.

Chapter 57

The crocodile began to croon again. Jackie answered immediately, "Hello."

"Where are you?" It was Bagnilla calling.

"We are at the Tennessee Aquarium," answered Jackie with some confidence.

There was a pause as Bagnilla asked someone about instructing the Macklins to meet in Tiftonia, as they were ten miles apart.

"Gowen told you to meet us here, in Tiftonia."

"Then what," asked Jackie. "Are you going to kill us like you did Flipper and Jake?"

"I don't know what you are talking about," Bagnilla lied. "They were alive when I left chasing you two art thieves. Now get to Tiftonia in eight minutes or we drop your friends in one of these sinkholes around here."

"No," Jackie responded.

"No what," asked Bagnilla.

"No to us showing up in an empty parking lot where you can kidnap us and drop all of us in a sinkhole. Soon as you get your hands on the Codex, you have no reason to keep any of us alive to testify against you. We will meet you in a public place."

There was another pause as Bagnilla again consulted with Spruill. "You have somewhere else in mind?"

"Yes, the Tennessee Aquarium parking lot," said Jackie as she bargained for all their lives. "It's public but it is closing time and the parking lot is emptying."

Spruill had been listening in and urged Bagnilla to accept the offer.

"We will be there in fifteen minutes," Bagnilla confirmed.

"We'll be at the corner of Broad and Second, right in front of the building where you get your tickets."

Ten minutes later two vehicles, one a Ford Taurus the other a white van, pulled into the specified parking lot containing few other cars scattered around the area.

Her new phone began to chirp, announcing the incoming call.

"I don't see you. Get out of your car and put the box on top of it, then walk away," ordered Bagnilla.

"Then what?" Jackie asked.

"Then we will release your friends."

"What happens to the Codex?" she wanted to know.

"It goes to a place where it will be cared for."

"To be studied and published?"

"Never," Bagnilla warned.

"And what happens to us?"

"You will be cleared and charges dropped. Trust me."

"That is just it. I don't trust you. How do I know that Molly is still alive?"

"Can you see the van in front of the ice cream store, the one on the corner of the ticket building?"

"Yes."

On an unseen queue, the side door opened and Spruill displayed the captives, Molly and Jubal hands bound and mouths covered with bright orange duct tape.

"I see them," Jackie lied.

"Get out of the car."

"I am out," she said.

"Where, I don't see you."

"I'll blow the horn."

Bagnilla heard the sound of a car horn blow three times in succession and began to walk quickly toward the noise.

He still held the cell phone and told her to blow again. At this command she did so and he changed course slightly.

"Again, I still don't see you."

The horn in the Saturn ION across the lot sounded but there was no one inside. Jackie was using the remote access fob and the locate function to blow the horn drawing Bagnilla in the direction she wanted.

"Now," she said to him before he could respond to an obvious ruse. "I'll tell you where I am and you come to me."

He was so close he could feel the weight of the box and smell the molded parchment. He quickly asked, "Where?"

"See the hospital sign?" she instructed, "to your right?"

"Yes," he spotted the sign, Edwards – Southern Regional Hospital, at entrance to the parking deck. He could also see her waving behind the sign. Once she had his attention she ran for the emergency entrance. Bagnilla went after her. He raced inside and to his surprise found that she was sitting calmly in the lobby of the emergency department's waiting area. He sat down, fuming, across from her.

"What is this?" he said curtly. "You saw your friends. We can still take them down to the river and drown them."

"I'd expect you to do something like that. Then how will you find the Codex?"

"Where is it and where is Harley?"

"He has the box in a safe place," she said sitting as calmly as she could muster under the circumstances. Her arms were folded across her chest and her left hand held her cell phone.

"Where is it?" Bagnilla demanded as his emotions were getting shorter at the delay.

"On the roof," she informed him.

"Roof?"

"Take the elevator to the top floor. Get off and take the stair well on the south end. It will take you to the roof. He'll make the swap there."

"You're crazy lady," he said getting up, "any funny business and I'll kill you all as I would a terrorist."

She thought she would be safe if he went to the roof, but Bagnilla wasn't giving up his security either.

"You are going with me." And at that he slid his coat past the butt of the Browning automatic.

She stood up without a word and they calmly entered the elevator. Bagnilla press the top floor button. It stopped only once to pick up passengers going two floors up. They did not speak or look at one another.

The doors opened and Bagnilla grabbed her by the upper arm and pushed her down the hall in the direction of the stairwell. He had his gun out as she hit the panic bar on the stairwell door.

The shaft was dimly lit under a single florescent fixture over the landing of each floor. His shoes echoed as he climbed the concrete steps. The door at the top had a small window set in it. Bagnilla looked out before opening the door. He could see Harley with a white legal size box at the edge of the roof.

"All right," Bagnilla shouted as he opened the door. He pointed his gun at Harley. "Step away from the box."

"Let Jackie go!" he yelled back.

"I'll shoot if you don't step away," he answered.

"Are you going to shoot me like you did Flipper Howard and his son?"

"No, I shot them because he lied to me. I'll do you two for the fun of it!"

"Shoot and the box falls to the parking lot below and in front of the hospital entrance," Harley said holding the box at the edge of the roof's low retaining wall.

Distant sirens were getting louder with each passing second.

"Better hurry, the police are on the way."

"I have the police under control," Bagnilla bragged. "I won't tell you again, step away from the box." Harley pushed the box closer to the edge and held on daring the man to shoot. He was gambling that he might survive if he were shot on top of a major trauma center with a doctor at his side.

"The police know we are here," Jackie said. "The Chattanooga Police have been listening in to my cell phone. They've traced the phone here." She held up the electronic communication gadget with the screen projecting 911 in large numerals.

The sirens were closing on the hospital. The first of many blue flashing lights were reflecting off store windows as the vehicles approached. His position would be untenable in a few minutes as there was only the air conditioning equipment to hide behind. He knew SWAT teams would be on the roof shortly. He fired a shot into the air.

"Drop the box or I shoot her," he instructed as he put the gun against Jackie's head. "I'll say the two of you jumped me, it'll be self defense."

Harley released the box and it was seen no more as gravity now possessed it.

Bagnilla jumped as if to chase the box off the roof. Harley stopped his advance toward the edge with the announcement, "It landed in the shrubs next to the exit door. If you hurry you can get to it first."

The sirens were being turned off as the police cars were parked and officers went racing to all the entrances.

Bagnilla released Jackie and darted into the stairwell.

Harley ran to Jackie and they hugged tightly.

"Let's go get the box," he said.

They went down the same stairwell and exited at the first door. Just before it closed they heard a single gunshot. It startled them and they paused in their flight, looking with fear that they might be the cause of someone else being killed for the secrets of the Codex. Once in the hallway Harley led her into a patient's room. The room was a single patient room with large patio doors opening to a view of Lookout Mountain. There, on the patio deck, was a white file box with the corner split and clean sheets of paper spilling out.

"Now," said Harley, "let's see what happens." Looking over the side they could see police cars ringing the building. People were gathering on the sidewalks to study the action. But one figure in a dark suit was running in the opposite direction. It was Bagnilla fleeing the scene. They could see police cars in front of the ice cream shop escorting Spruill and his accomplice, Curtis, away in handcuffs.

Bagnilla ducked behind Joshua's ION. She again squeezed the locate button on her remote but the horn did not sound. She pressed the trigger once more with both thumbs to no avail. She pointed the devise at the car as a sorceress might her magic wand, but the car sat as a silent witness to Bagnilla's escape.

"DAMN IT!" Jackie exclaimed. "Too far away."

They could see Bagnilla as he disappeared around the corner building. Harley was on the phone to the 911 operator but they could not relay the information fast enough to throw up road blocks around the area.

Jackie had kept her arms crossed while with Bagnilla. In her hand, close to her chest, the cell phone was connected to the Chattanooga 911 operations headquarters. A captain in the department along with Special Agent Jay Cooke, called up from Atlanta to replace Gowen, had been monitoring the conversation, the threats and the confession, while tracking the phone's location.

Chapter 58

The Macklin's were interrogated for two hours and with Loudoun's consent, released on bond with the stipulation that, until this was all over, they were not to leave the country. The State of Tennessee did not want them to return to Georgia but respected the judge's order.

Flipper's sole employee, a maid at The Cave Inn, mentioned missing towels in room number four. Flipper's registration index was also missing a card for room four. A preliminary examination of a print left on that plastic box of receipts showed Bagnilla had been there. The motel clerk came forward to say he sent Bagnilla to the Cave Inn an hour before the reported shooting. Two witness at the Whiz Burger remembered seeing the man in the tatty suit. "No one tips exactly ten percent," said the waitress. The restaurant's and motel's videos backed up the stories.

Frank Gowen stepped up to share the conversation he had as Bagnilla saw the Silver Bow leaving the motel. All the reported sightings led the State's investigator to find fingerprints on the shower curtain and exclusive footprints on the bathroom floor proving Bagnilla was at the motel. Unmistakable scratches on the forty five caliber bullets extracted from the two heroes, matched a registered Browning 45 Automatic last known to be in the possession of H.R. Bagnilla. Agent Loudoun had no choice but to issue the arrest warrant for his missing employee.

The Codex was secreted by Jackie within the hospital as the sheriff deputies ran into the building searching for the Macklin's. The judge called upon her to deliver the documents as they were considered evidence in a murder case. However, in her defense, their lawyer, Tony Benicar pointed out that the documents were only a link to a motive, not actual evidence of Bagnilla's guilt in the crime. The judge conceded and allowed the Macklin's to maintain ownership of the Codex until such time as it might be required by prosecution.

"Mr. and Mrs. Macklin," inquired a dark Middle Eastern European looking man.

"Henry Lancard I presume?" Harley said as he extended his hand toward him. He was large, smiling and friendly in his distinguish manner.

"Yes, and you must be the most notorious couple since Bonnie and Clyde … Jackie and Harley," he said.

Lancard begged a vacant interview room from the sheriff that he might talk with the infamous couple. He introduced himself as the counsel for the Archdioceses of the Eastern Orthodox Church, and a scholar in search of the Codex Syracuse.

When the Macklin's asked for an explanation, he began to deliver his tale. Lancard paused and drew deeply from the air in the room before beginning his lessons.

"It has long been believed that the Codex Syracuse existed by evidence of scribes, priest, monks, scholars of antiquity mentioning it in their personal journals. Some had seen and remembered portions of verses and passages. There are scraps of pages matching the Codex in various museums around the world. Some have been confirmed as being from the same hand, from the same person. That person lived at the end of the second century. He translated the original Greek journal into Latin." Lancard paused to let this soak in and asked if they understood. Harley and Jackie indicated that this was the easy part to digest so Lancard continued his tale.

"We in the Eastern Church believe that Paul took control of the early church from the Holy Apostles and with it began what you call the Catholic Church," he again paused in his lecture.

Harley spoke up to ask, "How could this have happened?"

"Are you familiar with the New Testament?" Lancard asked to establish Harley's understanding of the Holy Scriptures.

"I have a little more understanding of the New Testament than most laymen," he said to answer the challenge.

"Please accept my deepest apologies ... I did not mean to insult your intelligence, I only wanted to establish a base line of understanding."

"Tell you what," said Harley welcoming the test. You lay your best trail through the woods and if I fall behind I'll give a shout."

Lancard took a moment to interpret Harley's intention and began another short lecture.

"The Holy Apostles, Peter and James the brother of Jesus, had charge of the church at Jerusalem after the resurrection, would you agree?" Lancard asked the couple much as he does in cross examinations before court.

"Yes, Jesus gave Peter the Keys to the Kingdom of Heaven, Mathew, chapter 6, around the middle of the chapter if I remember it right," Harley answered.

"Verse 19," said Lancard, "it is the basis of the authority of the pope ... that his authority comes from Saint Peter, himself."

"That's the word from the Vatican," said a smirking Harley.

"Then by what authority did Saint Paul move the center of the church from Jerusalem to Rome?" asked Lancard.

"His divinely inspired ordination from his vision on the Damascus Road," answered Harley.

"You do not read Latin do you?" Lancard asked of Harley changing the topic, "You haven't read the journals have you?"

"I read Latin quite well," Jackie injected as she had been sitting by in silent observation. "We have made a good headway in our own translation."

Lancard did not respond quickly but took a pause looking at her in wonderment.

"What have you discovered? How early does the journal begin, how far does it go back in history?" Lancard had loads of questions but the Macklin's were not encouraged to deliver the answers.

"If we correctly interpreted the dates our author uses, then to the First Century," answered Jackie, "but I have a question."

"Go ahead, ask what you will," offered Lancard.

"What makes this document worth the lives of three people?"

"First century?" repeated an astonished Lancard. "How did you determine the dating? I thought they were fourth century, third at best."

"Harley worked out the calendar dates," Jackie acknowledged. "What makes this worth the lives of three people?

Lancard then remembered the tragic human cost to keep the documents from the true thieves.

"The Codex Syracuse has long been thought to be a direct translation from St. Paul's own personal journal into Greek," Lancard explained. "With the proof from Paul's own hand, we in the Orthodox Church can prove that we are the true and ordained church established by Jesus Christ through Saint Peter, and not the bastard church established by Paul. If we can find within the documents, the actual confession of Paul acknowledging he manipulated the Followers of Christ and the disciples, we can show how he was intent on using fraud to further his own agenda."

"And what was that agenda?" asked Harley.

"To control of the Followers of Christ with *his* false conversion and ordination, that the faithful would follow *his* erroneous lessons of the resurrection, surrendering the tithe to *his* pockets and give all allegiance to the church he quietly established in Rome. These were simple fishermen given to believing what educated men such as Paul told them. He supplanted the Disciples of Christ in Jerusalem."

Harley rested his chin in his hand and his elbow on the table. Two fingers spread across his lips and rested on his mustache. "I can see this," he acknowledged. "I often wondered why Paul had three Damascus Road conversions."

"Each more elaborate than the first," Lancard agreed.

"To enhance his claim of ordination by the very Hand of God," said Harley.

"That's been our belief for centuries," Lancard said.

"He made it up. He went to Damascus maybe to infiltrate the following there to find the leaders," Harley advanced his theory. "But once he was inside he saw how easily he could manipulate the illiterate followers."

"Exactly our opinion," Lancard agreed. "What are your plans for the Codex? Are you going to donate it to the university or some institution where it can be studied and made available to the public for examination?"

Jackie said she would finish the translation shortly and would reveal all in one public press conference. This was favorable to Lancard, however, Jackie would not be moved to discuss any of her work. With that Harley opened the door and the couple left.

The celebrated couple went with Jubal and Molly to the farm for peace and quiet. The media tried to follow, but Jubal took the mountain roads so fast he left the media vans as lost as Bagnilla was last Friday morning and choking on the dust.

Jackie went to work on the Codex with Harley standing by her side, guiding her to find the key words he needed to understand what made these parchments worth men's lives.

They found the name of the city of Damascus. Paul wrote he had been given charge to go and attempt to talk the governor of the city to turn over his citizens for the Church in Jerusalem to judge. With him were *Summas, Datam,* and *Varius.* On the way, Paul was overcome by exhaustion trying to chase down every one that spoke against the temple in Jerusalem. He wrote before he started his journey, of how tiring and troubling it was to find these people.

"Maybe he and his friends hatched the plot for him to go undercover on the way to Damascus?" Jackie theorized.

"The Damascus Road vision is troubling," Harley said.

"His entry into the journal said he had not written for three days," Jackie said. "He feels that he had been blind to what was happening. Then he writes of his admiration of the dedication of the followers of Jesus. On one hand he wrote in the letter to the Romans, the High Priest and Council of Elders ... they knew he was going on some kind of raid," said Jackie of the passages.

"Yes, he did, chapter 22," Harley explained. "In the book of Acts, the Damascus Road experience happened three times, more progressive than the last."

"You keep repeating there are three different versions," Jackie confirmed.

"There are three reports of the Damascus Road vision," he said, "Acts chapter 9 he said he heard a voice."

"So, plenty of people hear voices. What did this one tell him to do?" Jackie asked.

"He heard a voice and said the rest of his posse heard it too," Harley explained. "The voice, told him to go to the city and wait. 'Word will come to you'," he added with a mocking thundering voice.

"The voice could have been generated by anxiety disorder ... post traumatic stress having been the person that turned in Jesus for crucifixion ... then there is the ever popular schizophrenia, which would began in someone at what we guess was his age," was Jackie's diagnosis.

"But then he was supposed to have been struck blind."

"Blinded by the light?" she had to ask.

"Well," said Harley, "The first version did mention it."

"Which version did not?" she wanted to know.

"The second one in Acts 22. It went from a flash of light to a light that 'shone around me'," Harley quoted.

"Is that the Aureole, the luminous clouds or that circle of light thing in religious pictures?" she asked.

"That is the idea," Harley agreed, "First, he states that everybody with him sees a light and hears the voice. In chapter 22, it is only he that sees the light and no one else hears a voice. Then in Acts 9, it took Ananias three days to heal him, in 22 it seemed only an hour," Harley paused before continuing the lecture. "At the third telling, in Acts 26, he says all the boys with him, saw the light, all fell to the ground and they all heard a voice ordaining him to preach to the Gentiles. And he was not blinded by the light in this version, but walked on to Damascus."

"You have to question his validity," Jackie observed. "Tell me," she asked, "the third time, was he facing some kind of judgment?"

"Why, yes," Harley explained, "it all comes from the same incident, in Jerusalem." He paused to put the events into proper order as best he could. "Paul, went to Jerusalem and spoke in the temple. The Jews there did not like what they heard and wanted him arrested. A centurion came to scourge or give him a lashing. Paul protested saying he was a Roman citizen by birth. This caused the centurion to hand Paul over to the Tribune, who heard the same defense. Funniest thing is," Harley paused to say, "Paul constantly claimed he was a member of the Sanhedrin, a Pharisee, and born into Roman citizenship."

"He could have been sporting the Legion tattoo as evidence of his citizenship," Jackie said.

"If he did, he would be the first Roman Pharisee member of the High Jewish Court, the Sanhedrin," Harley injected. "That would have been impossible back then. It would be kind of like having a member of El Qaeda in the White House."

"Then he was released?" Jackie asked. "During interviews with suspected criminals, they will often embellish their story to establish the authenticity and accuracy of their case of innocence," she went on to explain.

"His sister Aurelia 's son, Thaddeus. You remember?" Harley inserted. "You found a name of the 'young man'?"

"Yes," she answered. "What has he to do with the case?"

"Thaddeus tells the Tribune about a plot to kidnap and murder Paul. The Tribune takes him to the Governor Felix. Felix then examines him, finding him guilty only of preaching a new religion, leaves him in jail for two years. A new governor, Festus lets him out," Harley explained. "But the Jews urge Festus to lock Paul up again, which he did and turned Paul over to King Agrippa, who did have the authority to execute him, but didn't."

"What happened then?" asked Jackie.

"Paul was sent to Rome to face Caesar."

"Which means either he was a natural born citizen of Rome," said Jackie. "Or he was a Jew that had the funds to pay bribes, or won citizenship with military service. But in the journal he says he was born a Jew in Tarsus."

"Exactly," said Harley, "he is living in two worlds at the same time."

"I ran across the name Felix and a mention of what he called a *beneficium*. It went something like, 'I have sent *beneficium* to Felix to secure my release.'"

Harley was surprised and asked her thoughts on the translation.

"To pay a benefit," she said. "To give someone something that would benefit them ... a bribe."

"So you have an entry for Felix?" asked Harley. "What other names did you see?"

"There was Peter, James, and Silas, then several cities and provinces such as Pamphylia, Cilicia, Myra, Lycia and Malta."

"Malta?" asked Harley raising an eyebrow.

"That's an island, isn't it?" she responded.

"Yes. It's an island off the coast of Italy. Acts chapter 27 says Paul was shipwrecked while being sent to Rome for trial. He was placed in house arrest once he arrived and made his case,"

Harley said to explain. "Paul would have been before Nero ... Tiberius Nero Caesar in whole. I doubt Nero would have allowed any trouble maker to have house arrest."

"He didn't," said Jackie to his surprise. "It was Afranius Burrus."

"Burrus?" Harley asked. "Nero's tutor and advisor? Burrus who was married to Paul's sister? I read that journal entry myself," Harley said proudly.

"Burrus left Aurelia with Thaddeus in Jerusalem then went to Rome," Jackie reminded him. "Paul said in an entry near the end of the Codex that he basically blackmailed Burrus into exiling him to Malta. He described it as a nice place. So how did he blackmail Burrus?"

"He threatened to reveal Burrus had plotted to put his own son, Thaddeus, on Nero's throne. Fearing Nero would have him poisoned, he did as Paul asked," explained Harley.

"It seems as if the Codex is not quite legitimately yours," Lancard told Jackie during a phone call. "Cardinal Arkadios gave the Codex to Professor Eckland for safe keeping. He feared the Knights Of Malta were about to steal the journal and either destroy it or hide it in the Vatican Archives. He wanted the renowned Dr. Eckland to study and validate the documents. It would establish beyond question our claims of legitimacy."

"I have been expecting this," Jackie said for Molly had alerted her that the Cardinal had contacted the State Department about the return of artifacts important to Sicily.

Harley held up his hand rubbing his fingers together in the sign of "What about my money?" Jackie waved him off.

"I would ask you to allow us to continue the original wish of the Cardinal and return the Codex to Gilbert University for study for two years and publication," she answered, "We want to honor the memory of Dr. Eckland."

"I will have to get approval from the Cardinal and get back to you," Lancard promised.

"Good day, we will be in touch. But right now we need to run."

They hurried to the chapel where funeral services were being held for Flipper and Jake. The medical examiner had kept the bodies in evidence for a week. Several of Flipper's family members had explored caves with Harley and knew that he was not the murderer. The community of cavers surrounded Harley and Jackie with affection and condolences.

They readily welcomed having the famed couple attend the service. They offered Harley the honor of delivering the eulogy. He declined in face of the pressure from the media circus. The heroic couple did not use the front entrance, but rode in the funeral home's flower van to the back door of the lovely stone chapel in McLemore Cove. There was a brief ceremony delivered by the pastor before several of Flipper's and Jake's fellow cavers stood and related their favorite stories about the two. There was not a dry eye in the house.

As the pastor rose to the podium to conclude the service, a car horn just outside the windows, began to blare over and over and over. The congregation stirred as hands immediately went into pockets and purses seeking the remote key fob to silence the alarm. Key rings were in the air as buttons were being pressed. Finally, the signal was received and the noise stopped. There was a moment's pause … then the giggling began when some saw the noisy intrusion into the solemn moment as just the kind of stunt Flipper would pull. Harley's eyes flooded with fond tears.

The congregation stood as the final hymn was sung and that sad pair of coffins were rolled out the front door. The media, gathered on the other side of the road, jockeyed for a position to film the procession. Most wanted to see if the Macklins would make an appearance. But they were denied their shot of the day as Jackie and Harley left the way they came.

"You are going to the cemetery," announced the driver as they returned to their seats.

"No, don't, we didn't want the media to follow us," Harley instructed.

"The media is not going to follow, watch this," and the driver nodded out the front window.

The caving community is a tight knit group of individuals. If one falls in a cave, then one hundred show up for the rescue, arriving before being called for by the authorities.

The first hearse pulled away from the church and waited in the narrow lane until the second was ready. A sundry of beat to hell, rust and mud crusted vehicles, pickup trucks, Jeeps, and automobiles all bearing a little yellow tag identifying them as cave explorers, lined up behind the two long shiny black carriers of the caskets. Then, with one accord, they pulled away from the church.

The media trucks had been waiting across the road in the cow pasture as instructed by the church members and local officials. This field dropped down, away from the paved roadbed, and was covered with a thick carpet of grass. It looked like a perfect place to park. Spelunkers had cut the field the day before. The rain fell all night long. The wet loose grass, on top of Tennessee mud rich in bat guano and cow pies, made for very difficult maneuvering.

Most of the trucks could not climb the slippery slope to the road. Those that did make it up the incline found the road blocked by empty cars and trucks bearing the same little yellow tag as those following the hearse. The absent owners car pooled to the grave side as they often do when going to distant caves. Flipper and Jake were interred without a single news photographer in sight.

As the mourners surrounded Harley and Jackie to offer condolences, a man with his ball cap low over his forehead, wearing the dirty grounds keeper coveralls appeared. He carried a rusty shovel and inched ever closer to the grieving group. None saw Bagnilla as he pulled his Browning 45 from his pocket, intent on extracting some deranged vengeance upon the couple.

"Hold it!" shouted one of the mourners as others pointed a variety of handguns at the central figure.

Jackie and Harley turned to see the cause of the commotion. Upon seeing the face of Bagnilla behind the weapon, Harley put his arms about Jackie and turned her to be between the revengeful Bagnilla and his most cherished love.

The state attorney general had the Tennessee Bureau of Investigation put some of their agents, known for their caving exploits, in the funeral procession on the chance that Bagnilla would show up seeking revenge for this old retired couple ruining his life. He was reluctant to quit, but realized the game was over and submitted meekly to being handcuffed.

"We were bait!" Jackie exclaimed at the agents.

"Very attractive bait," said an understanding Harley. Then he added;

> There was an attractive bait fish,
> For whom Bagnilla had an evil wish.
> But the agents did find,
> Bagnilla in time,
> And now his career is finished.

THE END